THE TROUBLE WITH LOVE AND HATE

CAT SCHIELD

HER BEST FRIEND'S BROTHER

YAHRAH ST. JOHN

MILLS & BOON

First Published in Great Britain 2022
by Mills & Boon, an imprint of HarperCollins*Publishers* Ltd
1 London Bridge Street, London, SE1 9GF

www.harpercollins.co.uk

HarperCollins*Publishers*
Macken House, 39/40 Mayor Street Upper,
Dublin 1, D01 C9W8

The Trouble with Love and Hate © 2022 Catherine Schield
Her Best Friend's Brother © 2022 Yahrah Yisrael

ISBN: 978-0-263-30393-3

THE TROUBLE WITH LOVE AND HATE

CAT SCHIELD

For Robin Selvig.

One

Chase Love sat on the couch in his office, his two-year-old niece asleep on his lap. Her older sister lay on the floor near his feet, her forehead puckered in concentration as she plied bright crayons to her favorite coloring book.

At the conference table across the room, real estate agent Sawyer Thurston was on her cell phone, trying once again to negotiate a deal with Chase's irascible third cousin. A decade earlier Rufus Calloway had inherited a tumbledown Charleston house that had sentimental value to Chase's mother. Since then, Maybelle Love had been trying to convince her estranged cousin to sell the abandoned property.

"I don't care how much they're offering!" Rufus's enraged voice came through the cell phone's speaker loud and clear. "That family is never going to get their hands on my property."

After the declaration, Rufus must've put an end to the conversation because Sawyer lowered the phone and blew out a weary breath. "Well, that's a hard no."

"Yeah."

Sensing business was done for the moment, four-year-old Annabelle was a blond streak as she sprang off the floor and skipped toward Sawyer. "Look what I colored."

"Wow!" Chase's longtime friend crouched to admire the drawing. "That's really beautiful. When you're done with it, may I put it up in my office?"

"Oh, yes." Always pleased to have her artwork praised, Annabelle carried the coloring book back to the box of crayons on the floor.

While his niece returned to her art, Sawyer made her way toward him. To accommodate the muggy July temperatures, the slender brunette wore a sleeveless white blouse and bright floral skirt.

"What's our next step?" Chase asked, indicating the empty cushion beside him.

Sawyer settled onto the sofa, glanced at the sleeping child and shot him a look of grim determination. "Rufus is not going to sell the property to anyone in your family."

"I'm not ready to give up."

"I know. It's just that rumor has it his financial situation has gotten worse. He's going to sell the property to someone and it's not going to be anyone in your family. That being said, I might have a buyer who would satisfy both Rufus and your mom."

Chase hated the idea that the Calloway property would slip through his family's fingers, but Rufus was holding all the cards. "My mom wants the house restored to its former glory. If we can't buy the property, it's important that the buyer understands the home's historic significance. It will destroy her if the home is torn down and a modern monstrosity gets built in its place."

"I know." Sawyer shot him an exasperated look. They'd had this conversation so many times over the years. "This person is keen to renovate a historic property. As soon as

I found out Rufus was going to sell, I got in touch with her and told her all about it." Sawyer's real estate focus was primarily on historical properties and she frequently brought clients to East Bay Construction, the renovation and construction company owned by Chase and his partner Knox Poole. "I explained that you've done all the preliminary work getting the architectural plans ready and figuring out what structural work needs to happen to bring the buildings up to code. She's really excited to work with you."

"You already talked to someone?" Chase wasn't happy with this development, but he appreciated Sawyer's pragmatism. Their mother was dead set on owning the property and stubbornly refused to consider any options. "Who is it?"

"Someone new to the area," Sawyer said, and seeing Chase's frown, rushed to add, "but with strong ties to one of Charleston's oldest families."

Something about Sawyer's caginess sparked concern. "Who is it?" He repeated the question with soft menace.

"Teagan Burns." Sawyer actively avoided meeting his gaze as she spoke.

"Ethan's cousin?" Chase was stunned by the suggestion. Ever since showing up in Charleston last month, the New York socialite had been making trouble for Chase's best friend, Ethan Watts. "Absolutely not."

"Oh, come on. She's the exact sort of client you love to work with. Passionate about restoration." Dimples flashed in Sawyer's cheeks as she added in a coaxing tone, "Unlimited funds."

Chase ignored Sawyer's teasing, unwilling to even consider her suggestion. "You neglected to add drama-free," he prompted.

"I found her to be sensible, smart and quite likable. And I've already pitched her you as her partner on the project."

Unconvinced, Chase shook his head. "That will never work."

"Come on." The enthusiasm in Sawyer's blue-gray eyes took on greater fervor. "She's smart, ambitious and knows exactly what she wants."

"You sound like you feel sorry for her."

"She made a mistake. I don't think she's a terrible person. You know why she's interested in the Calloway property, right?"

"Because she wants to renovate a historic house."

"And provide transition homes for women leaving domestic abuse situations."

Leave it to Sawyer to hit him where he was most vulnerable. For many years, his older sister had been in an abusive relationship. She'd done an excellent job hiding the situation from her family and Chase had never forgiven himself for missing the signs. When at last Nola had managed to escape her situation, she'd had her family to turn to. Not all women were as lucky.

"It's why she's been looking for multi-family properties," Sawyer continued. "I've shown her several buildings and homes around downtown Charleston, but the Calloway house was the first one that fired her imagination."

"So she's seen it?" The poor condition of the turn-of-the-century Victorian had been scaring off buyers for a decade.

"Just the listing photos. I'm showing her the property in a bit." Sawyer leaned forward. "I know you and your mom are dying to have a say in how the main house is restored and Teagan wants to do some good in the community. It's a win-win for everyone."

"All I see is a scheming troublemaker who intends to manipulate things to make herself look better." Chase couldn't imagine accepting Teagan as a client. "And I don't trust her not to cause my mother more distress."

"I am convinced she recognizes how badly she screwed up and will be honest and straightforward from now on."

Chase shook his head. "I'm not sure she can help herself. Look how she schemed to muscle in on Ethan's position at Watts Shipping and tried to involve her sister in the scheme."

"She admitted that was a huge miscalculation. I'm convinced that she came to Charleston determined to fit in with her biological family and misjudged how close the Wattses are and how they rally around each other. She's devastated that everyone is so mad at her."

Ethan's family had been looking for the missing Watts heiress for years and had finally found her after a genetic testing service had connected the biological relatives. Her arrival in Charleston had been greatly anticipated; however, she hadn't turned out to be all they'd hoped.

From what Chase had heard from his best friend, Teagan wasn't interested in developing a relationship with her Charleston family. Instead, she'd set her sights on being named the next CEO of the family's company, Watts Shipping, a position Ethan had expected would be his one day. In order to do this, she'd had to distract her cousin from figuring out what she was up to. Teagan had encouraged the attraction between Ethan and her adoptive sister, never imagining the pair would actually fall in love, or that Sienna would choose to take Ethan's side.

"You should at least hear her out before rejecting the idea," Sawyer said.

Chase wasn't convinced. "How did you two meet?"

"Through Poppy not long after Teagan arrived in town. Way before everything with Ethan blew up." Poppy Shaw was Ethan's cousin. It spoke to how badly Teagan had mucked up with her Charleston relations that Poppy, a free spirit with a forgiving nature, refused to stick up for her. "I've shown her a bunch of houses that need restoration, but none of them were quite right for her needs. I think the Calloway property would be perfect."

Despite the crushing disappointment at not being able to secure the house for his mother, Chase could see the potential in finding a buyer eager to bring the historic home back to its former glory. But not Teagan Burns. The partnership would aggravate his best friend and Chase couldn't trust her altruistic motives.

"No."

Sawyer narrowed her eyes. "Why?"

"Because she's from New York City."

The real estate agent released an exasperated breath. "What does that have to do with anything?"

"This is my family's house we're talking about. She won't be able to appreciate the history—"

"There are plenty of historic buildings in New York."

"Buildings they're tearing down to make way for modern skyscrapers."

"You haven't even met the woman. Why not at least hear her out?" When he didn't immediately refuse, Sawyer's expression grew calculated. "I'm meeting her in fifteen minutes at the house."

It was looking like whether or not he was on board, Teagan Burns might become the owner of the Calloway property. Grinding his teeth, Chase pondered the sleeping child draped across his legs and the one with the tip of her tongue stuck out as she colored a cartoon alligator. What was he supposed to do with his nieces? Nola wouldn't be back to pick up her daughters for at least another hour.

"Bring them along," Sawyer said, reading his mind.

Chase grunted. "To a business meeting?"

"So, now it's a business meeting?" Sawyer looked pleased. "That means you're actually considering working with Teagan on the project."

Was he? More likely, she would take one look at the

ramshackle Victorian and reject it out of hand. The condition of the house and scope of the project would intimidate even the most experienced developer. He doubted the transplanted socialite would have the gumption to tackle a full restoration. Which meant the house's future was in jeopardy.

"It means," Chase grumbled, "I'm committed to saving my mother's ancestral home."

A bold statement, but his disquiet about Teagan persisted as he eased to the curb fifteen minutes later before the house owned by Rufus Calloway. Its position, directly across John Street from Chase's home, offered a constant reminder of the bad blood between the two branches of his family. Five years prior, Chase had purchased his historic "single house" fixer-upper and begun its transformation, hoping that Rufus would see the fine work being done and sell Chase his rundown Victorian. Unfortunately, his third cousin wasn't about to give up on the grudge that had twisted his family for a hundred years.

A white metallic Mercedes SUV sat before the property. On the sidewalk side of the vehicle stood a willowy blonde woman with her back to him.

Teagan Burns.

Although she'd been in Charleston for many weeks, Chase hadn't had time to meet her. Too many renovation projects needed completion to be entered into the city's annual Carolopolis Awards. And considering how poorly the socialite had treated his best friend, Chase was glad he hadn't wasted his time on her.

Now, if he wanted to do right by his mother's ancestral home, it looked like he wasn't going to have a choice.

With his jaw locked, Chase took her in. A sleeveless cream-colored dress skimmed her slender curves while a large designer bag, handles nestled in the crook of her left elbow, drew attention to her toned arms. Beachy waves of golden locks cascaded to her waist. Polished and sophisticated, she looked out of place in front of the weathered, gray structure.

Four-year-old Annabelle had fallen asleep during the ten-minute drive and grumbled as Chase lifted her out of her car seat and set her on her feet. In contrast, Hazel had been revived by her earlier nap and was raring to go.

Sawyer had not yet arrived as Chase made his way across the street—flanked by his nieces—and approached the New Yorker. "Ms. Burns?"

Teagan turned at the sound of her name and her eyes widened as she took Chase in. Something primal and alluring flared in her eyes, and for a moment his awareness of the street and his nieces fell away.

"I'm Chase Love."

"Well, hello." Her breathless greeting and dazzling smile left him momentarily blindsided.

Although Ethan had shown him pictures of Teagan Burns when it first came to light that she was the long-lost daughter of his aunt Ava, those images didn't have the impact of seeing Teagan's beauty in person.

"Sawyer Thurston is a business associate of mine. When she mentioned that you were interested in the Calloway property, she thought it would be good if I was here for the walk-through since I know it so well."

Since his name triggered no recognition, he'd left out his connection to Ethan. If they ended up working together in the future, he would have to deal with that problem then.

"Of course. Your company has a wonderful reputation when it comes to historic renovations. I look forward to hearing your evaluation." She cocked her head and glanced at his nieces. "And who are these two?"

"I'm Annabelle and this is my sister, Hazel."

Both girls favored their mother in personality and could chat up a storm. Toddler Hazel wasn't quite mastering full sentences, but she'd picked up several amusing phrases from her older sister.

"I'm Teagan." Green eyes dancing with delight, she bent from the waist and extended her hand to Annabelle. "Nice to meet you both."

The indulgent smile she bestowed on his nieces annoyed Chase. So did the way his gut contracted at the sucker punch of her flawless beauty and disruptive charm. He'd expected her to be high-strung and bossy, a showy woman who relied on her looks and superior attitude to take charge. Instead, Teagan was a disconcerting blend of sensuality and elegance.

Although Hazel was usually wary of strangers, she bloomed beneath Teagan's captivating smile and even reached out for a handshake. Before he realized what was happening, Chase caught himself appreciating the social-ite's ease with the children. A second later, her eyes snagged his and their palms came together. The unrelenting sun and muggy air made her skin a bit sweaty and awakened the citrus notes in her perfume, making his head swim. Captivated by her beauty and charm, his body flared with sudden sexual awareness. Panic followed. How could he possibly find her attractive? Doing so was a keen betrayal of Ethan's friendship.

"Sawyer should be along any second." Hating the husky note in his voice, Chase loosened his grip, setting her free. He cast a desperate glance toward the street, willing Sawyer to appear and rescue him. "In the meantime I can fill you in on some of the house's background."

"You said we could have ice cream," Annabelle pro-tested, tugging on his hand, the heat and her aborted nap making her cranky. "When are we going to get ice cream?"

"Ice cream," Hazel echoed, jumping up and down on his left.

"Soon," he soothed, glancing from the reproach in Annabelle's blue eyes to Hazel's flushed cheeks. He hit both girls with a winning smile, wondering if he could successfully tour the property before they melted down. "We just need to show Ms. Burns around this house."

"Why?"

The answer left a bitter taste in his mouth. "Because she might want to buy it."

Annabelle shot a dubious look at the place, taking in the weed-choked front yard and broken picket fence. "Why would she want to do that?" Her gaze shifted to Teagan. After taking her in, Annabelle leaned against Chase's leg and stage-whispered, "Is she crazy?"

Chase mustered all his willpower and just managed to keep from glancing Teagan's way. In somber tones, he declared, "It will be fixed up before she moves in."

"I don't know." Annabelle made no secret of her skepticism. "It's pretty ugly."

"Making ugly houses into pretty ones is what I do," he reminded her, flicking a look toward Teagan and finding her watching their exchange with interest.

"But this is really ugly."

"That's exactly why I want to buy it," Teagan put in, her gaze taking on a fervent glow as her attention shifted from Annabelle to the derelict house. "I'm excited to restore this house so that it looks beautiful like all the other homes on the block."

"We live in an old house," Annabelle announced, shaking her head. "My mom always complains that stuff doesn't work."

Teagan's lips curved in a wry smile. "Well, since your daddy is so good at fixing up old homes, maybe he could repair some of those things."

"My dad's a doctor." Annabelle beamed. "He fixes people."

"Oh." A line appeared between Teagan's perfect eyebrows. She shot a quizzical glance Chase's way. "I'm sorry. I thought…"

"He's not my daddy." This amused Annabelle to no end.

"I'm their uncle," Chase supplied as both his nieces dissolved into fits of giggles.

"I see…"

Teagan measured him with fresh perception, making Chase's temperature spike. Apparently, she approved of the view because a half smile appeared and invisible threads of enticement radiated from her, reaching for him. His heart thumped in hard, erratic pulses, flooding his system with adrenaline. This woman was even more trouble than Ethan had made her out to be.

"Yes…well…"

He was never at a loss for words, but his acute reaction to Teagan caught him off guard. Worse, somehow, he'd misplaced his integrity. Finding himself attracted to the woman who'd injured his best friend went against everything Chase stood for. Ethan had always counted on Chase to have his back, which wouldn't be the case as long as Chase perceived Teagan as anything other than a shallow, manipulative interloper out to harm anyone who got in her way. Time to dash icy water on this sizzling connection between them.

His phone pinged with a text. Glancing down, he scanned the message and ground his teeth. "Looks like Sawyer is delayed. She suggested we begin without her."

Teagan must've picked up on his irritation because she gave a crisp nod and reined in her sex appeal, becoming all business. "Of course. Let's get to it."

Teagan took refuge in business, needing a moment to catch her breath and let her swooning senses recover their equilibrium. Although Sawyer had talked up the talented renovation specialist, the single promotional shot of him on his company's website hadn't prepared her for the impact of meeting the handsome, powerfully masculine architect in the flesh.

And then they'd shaken hands.

As if the heavy Charleston air wasn't enough to raise her temperature, the sudden flash of heat when they'd touched had made a weird combination of goose bumps and perspiration erupt over her entire body. She was ridiculously glad that Chase Love was neither married nor the father of these adorable girls. While she'd met several charming men since coming to Charleston, not one had awakened a mad impulse to bat her eyelashes and swoon. The rugged renovation specialist inspired a giddy, breathless delight that made her want to melt against his sturdy, muscular frame.

Unfortunately, there was the little matter of the steely set of his jaw and flinty hazel eyes that took her in and found her wanting. Teagan would be blind not to see that the man didn't like her. Still, his broad shoulders and stern demeanor sparked a mischievous impulse to flirt with him. Not a great idea when Teagan wanted to be taken seriously as a real estate investor. Runaway hormones would be a major problem if she'd be working in close contact with Chase for the foreseeable future. *If* being the operative word.

She was in the midst of wondering how to convince him she was an earnest businesswoman with definitive goals when the younger of the two girls said something that inspired his lips to curve into a fond smile. Her heart did a somersault.

Holy…wow! From forbidding to dishy in the blink of an eye. Teagan found herself swooning all over again.

"Shall we start with the three smaller residences?" Chase asked, blessedly oblivious to her inner turmoil. "My sister should be along in fifteen minutes to pick up these two. It'll be better to see the main house without them as a distraction."

"Sure," she murmured, hoping he'd put down the heat in her cheeks to the unrelenting sunshine.

Chase gestured for her to precede him along the cracked concrete walk that led toward the lopsided front porch. Giving the main house a dubious glance, she headed past the crumbling Victorian and set her sights on the three buildings beyond. With Chase out of view, it was easier to re-orient her thoughts and refocus on the reason she was here.

In addition to the main house, the large lot accommodated three guesthouses with individual addresses that she intended to fix up so they could become transition housing for women at risk. Teagan had been inspired to attempt the project after meeting Zoe Daily, owner of a boutique in downtown Charleston called Second Chance Treasures. The store specialized in arts and crafts items made by survivors of domestic abuse. Although she'd been looking for a historic home in need of renovation since coming to Charleston a month ago, Teagan was inspired to look for a property that could also serve women in need after hearing Zoe's story of living in the back room of the boutique after leaving her abusive husband while she financed her dream of helping other women in similar circumstances.

"Sawyer mentioned they were in better shape than the main house."

"They are. These houses have had tenants in them until recently," Chase said, keeping an eye on his nieces as they explored the overgrown backyard. "They were built in the mid-fifties."

A lockbox attached to the middle of the trio held the keys to all three. While Chase opened the front door, Teagan pursed her lips and pictured what she'd like to do to the exterior of each cottage. First of all, she intended to paint them bright colors to make each home feel special. White shutters and trim would tie them together.

Chase left to unlock the other two houses, leaving Teagan to peruse the middle one. A cozy living room, tiny kitchen, two decent sized bedrooms and a bathroom badly in need of updates. Lay down some durable flooring and add some modest but stylish furnishings and the place would be a sanctuary for women and children who badly needed a safe place to restart their lives.

"What do you think?" Chase asked as she exited the house.

"It's not as bad as I expected. Barring any hidden problems in the walls, I imagine I could have them fixed up and ready in a month." As Teagan checked out the other two houses, her enthusiasm for the project swelled.

"Ready to see the main house?" he asked, his expression less forbidding as he corralled his nieces and gestured toward the two-story Victorian.

"Sure."

The original paint color had long ago faded from the nineteenth-century siding. The decades of neglect left Teagan wondering how much of the home's original features remained intact. She was giddy with the idea of taking a historic home from disastrous to glorious. It would be so much better if the decorative moldings, heart pine floors and fireplaces were all there.

"Excuse me," Chase said before heading away from her down the front walk.

Teagan had been so absorbed in the house, imagining it painted a buttery-yellow with turquoise and soft coral accents, that she hadn't noticed a white SUV idling at the curb. A lovely blonde woman circled the vehicle to embrace the little girls. A sudden lump formed in Teagan's throat as mother and daughters reconnected. Not once growing up had she or Sienna been that joyful to see Anna Burns. Their mother had never been a warm, affectionate woman. Her demonstrations of love took the form of shopping sprees and elegant lunches where the girls were expected to behave like civilized adults.

A stab of resentment caught Teagan off guard. She didn't recall wanting her childhood to be different. Her adoptive parents Anna and Samuel Burns had given her everything money could buy and Teagan had no complaints about her private school education, designer everything or the incredible vacations in Europe. Sure, they didn't hug, nurture or read bedtime stories. That's what the nannies were for.

It wasn't until Teagan arrived in Charleston and was welcomed into the arms of her biological family that she discovered the joy of being loved. A year earlier she'd submitted her DNA to a genetic testing service in the hopes of finding her father or connecting with her mother's family. Never had she imagined that her search would lead her to Charleston.

Because her adoptive parents had raised her to be ambitious and prone to suspicion, Teagan had been on guard when her Southern family—her cousin Ethan excluded—had snatched her into their lives and showered her with gregarious affection. The lack of trust had led her to make a whole host of mistakes.

An overachiever from her crown to her toes, Teagan knew she couldn't leave Manhattan behind without having something to make relocating to Charleston worth her while. Running her biological family's company seemed like the perfect answer. That her cousin Ethan was already poised to become the next CEO of Watts Shipping was merely a hurdle to be cleared.

Unfortunately, her single-mindedness had led her to hurt the one person she'd always been able to rely on, her older sister Sienna. Adopted into the Burns family as an infant, Teagan's experiences growing up on the Upper East Side of New York City had taught her to battle fiercely to achieve her goals. The cutthroat world often favored circuitous methods instead of straightforward action. And she'd brought those tactics to Charleston with disastrous results.

Teagan hadn't taken into consideration that acting duplicitous wasn't in Sienna's nature when she'd badgered her sister into spying on Ethan for her. Nor had she predicted that her sister would fall in love with Ethan. It was Teagan's fault that the couple had gone through a disastrous breakup before reconciling. If Teagan hadn't been so focused on herself, she might've seen that something real and lasting had developed between the pair and backed off. Instead, she'd let stubborn determination blind her to what was best for Sienna.

Swept by uncomfortable emotion, Teagan turned her back on Chase and his family and concentrated on the house. The Victorian's flaws were something tangible she could repair and restore. So much easier than fixing the broken relationships with her sister and Charleston relatives. Those couldn't be improved by her design aesthetic or a bunch of money.

Since her biological family wasn't speaking to her at the moment, Teagan decided she'd demonstrate she wasn't a selfish, unfeeling shrew. She intended to behave. No more schemes or plots. She would display her philanthropic side by saving a historic home in downtown Charleston and offering three dwellings as a safe haven for victims of domestic abuse. In time, she hoped, someone would give her another chance.

"As you can see, the house is in rough shape," Chase stated as he joined Teagan in the home's gloomy twenty-foot-long foyer.

A zing of pleasure traveled along her nerve endings as his clean, masculine scent surrounded her like an enthusiastic hug. Her strong reaction to him was unexpected since he wasn't her type. Teagan liked her men charming and flirtatious. Chase Love was serious and principled.

Nor had she come to Charleston to find romance.

But that body. His beautiful face. And those piercing green eyes.

He was a tantalizing enigma and she couldn't bring herself to dismiss how he made her feel.

Tearing her gaze from his forbidding profile, Teagan glanced around her. Undaunted by the boarded-up windows, peeling wallpaper, water-stained ceiling and filthy pine floors, she surveyed the original fireplace details, nine-foot pocket door that separated the living and dining rooms and intact plaster details.

"I've looked at a lot of options around the downtown area," she said. "Some worse. Some in better shape. At least this one has a roof. And all the extra houses fit perfectly with my vision for the property."

"It's a lot to take on," Chase continued, shooting her a sideways glance.

"I don't know how much you know about my background in New York…" She strolled down the wide hallway leading toward the kitchen at the back of the house.

"Sawyer mentioned you've bought and rehabilitated several historic properties in Manhattan."

"I have. It's important to save architectural gems for future generations to appreciate."

Chase studied her for a moment before asking, "So, why not stay there and do that?"

Startled by his cool tone, Teagan's chin rose defensively. "Because I was hoping for a new start with my Charleston family."

Silence fell between them as room by room they moved through the house. Tiny tracks in the dirt indicated a whole slew of critters had invaded when the humans had moved out. Teagan's attention kept shifting between her surroundings and her heightened awareness of her muscular tour guide. His keen gaze missed none of the house's flaws and he took special care to point out every problem she'd encounter during the restoration.

"I feel as if you're trying to talk me out of buying the house," Teagan said as they stepped onto the sketchy front porch.

From their brief interaction, she'd gathered that he was a straight shooter, someone who wouldn't sugarcoat the situation or cheat her. Given the sketchy business practices she'd encountered in New York City and the incessant machinations of her social group, Teagan found Chase's candid approach refreshing.

"I just want to be clear." Chase grappled with the stubborn lock on the front door, before saying, "It needs a lot of work."

"I already knew that from the photos." Teagan couldn't stop smiling. Everything inside her was screaming that this was the property she was meant to have. "But most of the work will happen on the main house. It's really just cosmetic fixes for the three homes in the back."

"It's going to be expensive. And with a property this neglected, the potential for hidden problems is enormous."

"Regardless, I think this is the perfect project for me." Unwilling to be deterred, Teagan stepped gingerly to the loose railing and surveyed the neighborhood. "I know I'm going to love it here when it's done."

Snorting at her enthusiastic proclamation, Chase deftly avoided the rotten boards as he descended to the safer footing of the front walk. While he waited for her to join him, Chase pulled out his phone and scanned the screen. During the tour, the smartphone had buzzed numerous times, but he'd never checked any of the messages. She was accustomed to managing multiple tasks at the same time, giving none of them her complete attention, but this man brought purpose and drive to whatever he set his mind to. Teagan found it both thrilling and daunting.

"I'm going to call Sawyer right now and put in an offer," Teagan said, pulling out her own device. She was in the process of scrolling through her contacts when Chase spoke.

"Before you do," he began in clipped, harsh tones, "you should know that I have reservations about taking you on as a client."

This was not at all what she wanted to hear. Still, she had sharp wits and charismatic charm in her bag of tricks.

"I see." Teagan set aside her frustration. She couldn't tackle a problem unless she knew what was wrong. "Anything you care to share with me?"

Chase pondered her question in silence, his features set into disgruntled lines. "Not yet."

As much as Chase's reluctance disappointed her, Teagan sensed it would do her no good to push him. "Thanks for meeting with me today. I'll let you know when I hear back from Sawyer that the buyer has accepted my offer."

They parted and headed to their cars. Before she got in, Teagan gave the weathered Victorian one long last look. In order to realize her vision for the property, Chase must accept her as a client. His passion for restoring historic homes matched her zeal for preservation. They would make a fantastic team and she intended to make him realize that. Because once she set her sights on something, she usually got it.

And right now, she wanted Chase Love.

Two

Without committing to any sort of follow-up meeting with Teagan Burns, Chase beat a hasty retreat. Earlier he'd scheduled a walk-through of a restoration project his company was handling. Now, as he met with the general contractor at the work site, he struggled to focus on the checklist of items he was concerned about. Instead, he found his thoughts returning over and over to the New York socialite. A glint of brass fixtures recalled how the sun turned her hair to liquid gold. The verdant garden behind the house summoned the mischievous sparkle in her eyes that had caused his chest to tighten.

Chase ground his teeth and cursed.

Banishing his acute reaction to her might've been possible if he'd encountered any problems at the construction site, but for once, the work was progressing smoothly. So, instead of chasing down missing materials or scrambling to reschedule trades, he had time and headspace to contemplate how he could've possibly been attracted to the woman.

Granted, she was gorgeous, the sort of elegant beauty that most men would appreciate and desire. But Charleston was filled with leggy blondes sporting come-hither smiles and none of them could compete with his passion for restoration—a fact that frustrated Ethan every time he tried to set Chase up.

Before meeting Sienna, Ethan had been one of the city's most sought after bachelors. He'd doggedly inflicted his packed social calendar on Chase, dragging him out to this function or that casual meetup. But Chase had little patience for small talk or meaningless flirting. The women he did make a connection with were ones in the market to remodel a home or redesign a space.

Yet when it came to Teagan, he'd struggled to keep his mind on the house tour. The distracting floral scent of her and the soft sounds of interest or approval she'd made had set fire to his libido. He knew a hundred details about the house, but he'd struggled to summon even the most basic of information. Thankfully, she'd been so wrapped up in taking the home in that she hadn't noticed his less than stellar performance.

Deciding he'd inflicted his ill humor on the crew long enough, Chase got back in his car and headed toward his office. He'd scarcely driven a few blocks when his phone lit up with a call from Sawyer. Based on his meeting with Teagan, he suspected Sawyer's news was about to complicate his life.

"I received a call from Teagan," she began after a quick greeting.

"And she wants to make an offer on the Calloway property," he declared, the lump of dread in his gut offset by an unsettling flutter in his chest.

Despite the New York socialite's commitment to bring the Calloway house back to its former splendor, the location of the home meant that she'd be his neighbor. Was that worth achieving his vision for the neighborhood?

"She thinks it's perfect," Sawyer continued, oblivious to his distress. "And she wants you to handle the renovations."

"I don't know that I have time," he hedged, even as the need to be involved bore down on him.

Sawyer huffed. "That excuse might work with other people," she said, "but not with me. I know exactly how important that house is to your family and how determined you are to see it restored properly."

"Yes…well…"

The situation surrounding this entire project was complicated for so many reasons. First was his mother's desire to purchase the property and their cousin's unwillingness to let her have it. Second, if Teagan bought the house and outbuildings, Chase's desire to manage the renovation would require him to work with her and that would surely rub Ethan the wrong way. Rock meet hard place.

"My mom's going to be disappointed that the house is going to an outsider."

"Maybe…"

Something in Sawyer's tone triggered his suspicion. "What are you not saying?"

"She might've already called me."

If Chase hadn't been driving, he would've squeezed his eyes shut in dismay. Instead, he hit his left turn signal and angled away from the office and headed toward his mother's house.

"What did you tell her about the house?"

"She already knew that Rufus put it on the market and asked me if you'd made an offer." Sawyer hesitated. "I told her about the call."

"Was she upset?"

"I'd say she's more determined than anything."

That sounded exactly like his mom. Chase wished for

the thousandth time that Maybelle's personality had a little less steel and a touch more willow in it. Once her mind was set on something, she was hard to dissuade.

"I'd better go see her." And hopefully talk her into a more reasonable stance regarding the house.

"Good luck."

Chase headed south toward the 1843 home his mother had "downsized" into after her husband's death. At nearly five thousand square feet, with four bedrooms and five bathrooms, the house had been added on to several times over the years so that its original architectural style was hard to determine.

"Hello, Mother," Chase said as he entered the comfortable living room and spied Maybelle Love seated at her great-grandmother's writing desk. Crossing to her, he leaned down to kiss her cheek.

"What a nice surprise," she said, getting to her feet. Looping her hand around his left arm, she drew him toward the gold damask sofa near the big windows that overlooked the lush side yard. She sat down and patted the seat beside her.

He wasted no time. "Sawyer said you called her about the Calloway house."

Maybelle nodded. "I heard from my cousin Lemon that Rufus has put the house on the market again." Her blue-green eyes grew reproachful as she stared at her son. "How come you didn't call me about it?"

He steeled himself against his mother's disappointment. "I only just found out a few hours ago."

"And you couldn't take a minute to pick up the phone and keep me apprised of the situation?"

"I should have." Chase braced himself to explain to his mother that negotiations were dead in the water. Rufus had refused to even entertain their offer. "It's just that I wanted to have good news for you."

Relations had been strained between the two branches of Maybelle's family since the reading of her great-grandfather's will.

"Sawyer told me what happened," Maybelle explained. "I think we should definitely offer him more than what the house is worth."

"I'm not convinced there's a number high enough to overcome the bad blood between our families."

Maybelle waved her hand, dismissing Chase's concern. "Apparently, he's in dire need of an influx of cash…"

"That entire family is always in dire need," Chase grumbled, barely able to contain his exasperation with the whole messy situation. "He just won't sell it to us."

"Nevertheless, we should keep trying. You know how important that house is to me." The desperation in Maybelle's gaze tore at Chase's heart. "I couldn't bear it if someone ruined it."

"I won't let that happen," Chase assured her, determined to keep that promise.

His mother inhaled a ragged breath and stared out the window at the greenery beyond. She blinked rapidly several times, and then gave a pragmatic nod. "Then we'll have to figure out another way to save the house."

"Such as?" he questioned warily.

"Sawyer mentioned she has a client who is very interested in the property." Maybelle fixed her son with a sharp stare. "I understand you met with her earlier today."

Chase wasn't prepared to talk to his mother about Teagan's interest in the Calloway property when he hadn't yet decided if he should work with her. "She's an investor from New York."

He used the descriptor deliberately, knowing his mother wouldn't want the house to go to someone from "off," an outsider who couldn't fully appreciate the home's place in Charleston history.

"It's my understanding that she's quite passionate about restoration and intends to bring our historic property back to its former beauty."

His skin prickled as his mother's words sank in. Maybelle's enthusiasm struck him as odd. For decades he'd listened to his mother complain that her ancestral home was suffering from neglect and how she longed to purchase the property and save it for her grandchildren. Why all of a sudden was she so eager to let it go to a stranger?

"So she says." He kept his tone cautious.

His mother gave him a sharp look. "Do you have a reason to think she's not being up front with you about the house?"

The question caught Chase off guard. Maybelle should've heard that Teagan was on the outs with her Charleston family and the reason why.

"Nothing concrete," he admitted.

"What's she like?" Maybelle asked, her eyes bright with hopeful interest.

Chase pondered the myriad impressions Teagan had made on him, but decided against sharing those with his mother. The last thing he wanted to do was encourage her romantic notions. Ethan wasn't the only one frustrated with Chase's lackluster love life. Maybelle wanted both her children happily settled and disliked that each of them lacked a romantic partner.

Nor did he want to bring up Ethan's troubles with his long-lost cousin. So, that left Chase with sharing her professional background.

"She has some restoration experience," Chase said. "I understand she's done several projects in Manhattan."

"You know, if we can't buy the house ourselves, this might be a good solution. Sawyer said Teagan was quite impressed with the work you've done and would like you to head up the restoration." Maybelle beamed with maternal pride. "I know I would sleep better knowing the house was in your talented hands."

"Are you really at peace with having someone you don't know own your family's home?"

Maybelle clenched her hands together and turned somber eyes on her son. "If acquiring the property for us is impossible, we should make sure it falls into the right hands."

The Watts and Love families had enjoyed close social connections for decades. In fact, Maybelle and Ethan's mother had been in the same debutante class; they'd married weeks apart and given birth within months of each other. Both families had hoped that Ethan's older brother Paul and Chase's older sister might be destined for each other. While that pairing didn't work out, Ethan and Chase had become fast friends while still in diapers.

"I understand what you're saying." The trouble was Chase didn't trust Teagan. "I'd really like to make Rufus another offer. Something he really can't refuse."

His mother emitted a delicate snort. "And what if he keeps us dangling and the house gets snapped up by someone else in the meantime?"

"The property has been empty and neglected for years. That's why thus far no one has been willing to pay what Rufus has been asking for it." Chase just needed a little time. "Let me try to find someone besides Teagan Burns to buy the property."

"Someone you can guarantee will want you to handle the restoration?"

Of course there were no guarantees. Waiting was a risk. For all any of them knew, a different buyer could demolish the house and build something brand-new. True, the value was in the land and the home's history, but not everyone shared Maybelle's passion for the latter.

"What exactly do you have against Teagan Burns buying the house?" Maybelle's gaze sharpened on her son.

"Sawyer said she's passionate about historical restoration. Plus, she has the resources to do things right. It seems to me that she'd be your ideal client."

Hearing his mother echo Sawyer's earlier argument, Chase found himself stuck for an answer that would satisfy her without getting into the drama between her and Ethan.

"She's from New York and runs several businesses there. Eventually, she's going to have to head back. I'm concerned that once she's gone her interest in Charleston will wane. In all likelihood that will happen before the renovation is complete and who knows what will become of the property then?"

"Simple," his mother stated. "We'll buy it from her. In fact, this whole situation might be to our advantage. Rufus will never sell us the property, but we could cultivate an excellent relationship with Teagan Burns in the hopes that someday we can buy the house from her."

Unable to defend his persistent reluctance to have anything to do with Teagan or to refute his mother's clever strategy, Chase resigned himself to a long-term association with the New Yorker.

"That might work," he grumbled, anticipating a tense phone call with Ethan in the coming days.

"It will work." Maybelle looked satisfied for the first time since Chase had arrived. "And I think we should start getting to know Teagan right away. I want you to bring her by for lunch. You'll do that for me, won't you?"

"Of course." Chase recognized the futility of arguing with his mother, and could only hope that Teagan made a less than stellar impression. Because only then would Maybelle move heaven and earth to block the socialite from getting her family's ancestral home.

Immediately after touring the Calloway property, Teagan had called Sawyer Thurston and arranged to meet the real estate agent at Eli's Table in two hours for a cocktail. When she arrived, Teagan noticed the restaurant was next door to the Gibbes Museum of Art and wondered how many hours Sienna had spent pursuing the extensive collection.

Thinking of her adoptive sister cast a shadow over what had been a stellar day. Their estrangement nagged at Teagan, especially when she hadn't had any success persuading Sienna to respond to any of her calls or texts.

Apologizing didn't come easily to Teagan. From an early age she'd watched her parents navigate New York society. If people got in their way, sometimes they got hurt. The same lessons that taught Teagan to be ruthless aroused Sienna's sympathy. Teagan didn't enjoy the havoc she sometimes wrought, but she couldn't bring herself to let down her guard and show weakness either. Still, she'd been wrong to use Sienna the way she had. And admitting that out loud to her sister was the first step toward repairing their relationship.

If only Sienna would let her try.

While Teagan waited for Sawyer to arrive, she took several selfies and posted the best one on Instagram. Charleston provided her with an abundance of excellent photo opportunities to populate her social media account and by tagging all the various restaurants and shops in the area, she'd picked up a substantial number of new followers. The extra attention was nice, but she'd also noticed a drop in likes and comments from her New York friends.

It was a different world down here. Charleston was more like a weekend getaway for her Manhattan associates than somewhere they'd consider for a long-term move. And while they'd been enchanted by her early posts, as one week had stretched into several, they'd lost interest, preferring to gossip about weekend parties in the Hamptons, fashion and whatever flavor of the week struck their fancy.

Her phone rang. Although she didn't recognize the number, the area code was local. "Teagan Burns."

"This is Chase Love."

Her toes curled as his smoky voice filled her ear. "Chase." She almost purred his name. "Did you have a change of heart?"

"You might say that." He didn't sound particularly happy about it. "I have some architectural plans for the Calloway house at my office. You should come by and take a look at them. Then we can see if we're on the same page."

"I'd love that. But tell me…" His unexpected about-face had rendered her giddy. "Is this Charleston's version of inviting me up to look at your etchings?" In the silence that followed her words, she could imagine his dismay at her flirting.

"The plans are at my office." Once again, he'd met her banter with gruff practicality. "I don't know what your schedule looks like, but I have an hour at ten tomorrow morning if you are free."

Teagan rushed to accept the time, afraid he might change his mind about working with her. "Ten sounds perfect."

"Then I'll see you tomorrow."

Before she could say goodbye, he'd ended the call. Delighted by the turn in her fortune, Teagan began adding Chase into her contacts. She'd just finished capturing a screenshot of his profile picture from his website when a shadow blocked the afternoon sunshine. Assuming it was Sawyer, Teagan glanced up. The positive energy that had buoyed her since Chase's phone call died when she spotted the arrival.

"Declan."

She cursed herself for sounding like a breathless debutante but couldn't blame herself for the panic that flared. She'd never imagined her nemesis would still be in Charleston instead of eight hundred miles north in his corner office overlooking the Hudson River in Manhattan's financial district.

"Hello, Teagan."

Without asking for her permission, he settled on the chair beside her and crossed his long legs, his arm resting casually on the table to show off his Piaget Altiplano watch. Today's choice of exquisitely tailored suit was dove gray with a white shirt that he left open at the neck to reveal a triangle of masculine skin. Unable to recall the last time she'd seen him so casually turned out, Teagan applauded Charleston's heat and humidity for forcing him to surrender his usual sartorial elegance in favor of comfort. It was nearly impossible to get the better of Declan Scott.

Designer sunglasses hid his striking amber eyes, enhancing the air of mystery he loved to cultivate. While his opponents speculated about his next move, they weren't noticing that he was already five steps ahead of them. Heaven knew she'd learned that the hard way, too many times to count.

"You look as gorgeous as ever."

She wasn't fooled by his buttery tones. The man was a rattlesnake, poised to strike.

As a teenager, she'd been less immune to his swagger and the searing keenness of his soul-crushing gaze. That was before she understood the soul of an evil genius lurked behind all his dreamy masculine beauty. If he'd been in a movie, he would've been the villain intent on world domination. In the real world, Declan was a cagey businessman, determined to control the biggest share of Manhattan real estate and working toward that goal one ruthless negotiation at a time. The Brookfield Building stood in the way of his multi-billion-dollar development plans.

"Why are you still here?" she demanded, eager to get to the point of his visit.

"You are in possession of something I want."

"The Brookfield Building." The slim gold rings on Teagan's fingers glinted as she waved away his intentions. "I might sell it someday, but only to someone who will appreciate the beauty of its facade and the character it adds to NoMAD."

NoMAD, short for North of Madison Square Park, was an up-and-coming neighborhood once known for its cluster of wholesale stores along Broadway. Now, the area was anchored by a series of posh hotels and luxury condos. A high concentration of trendy bars and restaurants made it a popular spot for weekday after-work crowds.

The Brookfield Building had occupied the corner of 5th and 29th in Midtown Manhattan since 1895, withstanding the relentless march of developers determined to replace New York landmarks with sparkling glass monuments to their ambition and egos. Declan Scott was one of those developers. For the last five years he'd been busy buying up buildings that stood in the way of Scott Tower.

He'd battled preservationists anxious that Midtown could soon reach the tipping point between the architectural mix of old and new and watched in satisfaction as his opponents' applications to save historic buildings were rejected by the Landmark Preservation Commission.

Only the Brookfield Building remained as the last holdout. Until six months ago, the property had belonged to Edward Quinn. Despite pressure from Declan, he'd staunchly refused to release the architectural gem from his portfolio. The building held a special place in Edward's heart. It had been his first purchase, the foundation on which he'd built his empire.

Now Teagan owned it. "You're wasting your time. I'm not going to sell to you."

Unfortunately, no matter how many times she'd refused to sell it to him, Declan wouldn't take no for an answer.

Declan's vexation showed in the twitch of one eyebrow. "My latest offer will change your mind."

Teagan shook her head. It would not do to let him glimpse any weak spots in her defenses. "If Edward wanted you to have the building, he would've sold it to you before he died."

Or left it to his son, who didn't share his father's passion for historic buildings and would've agreed to sell the property to Declan before his father was even buried.

Instead, Edward had bequeathed the late nineteenth century ten-story building to Teagan.

She'd known Edward since childhood. The Burns and Quinn families had been neighbors in the Hamptons and it only made sense that when she wanted to know the ins and outs of Manhattan real estate, she'd interned at Quinn Real Estate.

Although he'd been both a mentor and a great friend, taking her under his wing and fueling her passion for preservation, Edward's decision to give her the Brookfield Building had been an enormous shock. To her. To Edward's family. And most definitely to Declan.

He'd been furious, even going so far as to accuse her of—how had he put it?—seducing the old man into leaving the building to her. The charge had proved that Declan Scott wasn't omniscient, but that didn't make him any less dangerous, as his latest stunt had demonstrated. He'd sent several anonymous texts to Ethan. By mixing inflammatory insinuations with a dash of truth, Declan had turned her cousin against her and almost destroyed Sienna's chance at a happily-ever-after with Ethan.

Declan inclined his head. "Why don't I buy you dinner and we can discuss it?"

"There's nothing to discuss," she pointed out in crisp dismissal.

She'd first locked horns with Declan in high school.

She'd marched into Bennington-Hill Academy, a sophisticated freshman with her own jewelry line, confident in her ability to set trends and rule her classmates the same way she'd done at her former school. And of course, she had, but in the process, she'd challenged the status quo. Declan Scott had been very much at the top of the school's social hierarchy. He hadn't been interested in a tit-for-tat exchange; he'd nearly crushed her. Since then, they'd had numerous trifling skirmishes, but interfering in her attempt to establish herself in Charleston went beyond anything either of them had ever done in the past fifteen years.

"Have you ever known me to give up without getting what I want?" Declan asked.

"I'll give you that. You are persistent." The increase in each successive offer demonstrated his determination to secure the land on which the Brookfield Building stood. "And you play dirty. Such as the anonymous texts you've been sending to Ethan. That was low. Even for you."

"You didn't give me much choice." A muscle jumped in his jaw. "If you'd just sold me the Brookfield Building, you would've never heard from me again."

"So, instead of accepting my decision, you decided to get personal."

"It's business," he shot back. "And I do whatever it takes to win."

"This isn't a seat on a charity board that will benefit me or a penthouse apartment I want to buy and renovate." She pointed a perfectly manicured finger at him. "It's my family. You and your tactics have caused irrevocable harm."

"That should give you a sense of just how important the property is to me." Declan leaned forward. "And you obviously needed to be reminded that I'm not the only one with something to lose."

Teagan kept her expression from revealing the deep anxiety she felt at this reminder. Already his interference had caused rifts with her family. She dreaded how much more he could do if she didn't give in. Ruthlessly she hardened her will and resolved to fight him no matter what.

Declan set a large white envelope emblazoned with Scott Development's logo on the table. While she would never accept one of Declan's increasingly lucrative offers, wondering how much he intended to offer this time made her pulse accelerate. It wasn't that she needed the money or reveled in having something to hold over him—although watching him gnash his teeth at her series of refusals had caused several brief flutters of glee.

"The price is the same as before." He nudged the envelope in her direction.

She wasn't surprised that he hadn't increased his offer—he'd already bid double what the building was worth—but his confidence chilled her.

"I might not be able to match your experience negotiating deals," she said, "but I'm pretty sure you need to sweeten the offer once it's been turned down."

"You didn't let me finish." The left corner of his lips twitched as if he held all aces. "Sell me the property and I'll leave you alone."

Tired of his machinations, Teagan let her bitterness show. "I don't think there's anything left for you to ruin."

"There's always something more."

Her heart gave a big bump at the threat. "Edward didn't want you to tear down the Brookfield Building and entrusted me with it to make sure that didn't happen."

"Which only goes to show how his faculties had slipped in the last few years."

"Maybe." She shrugged off the double-edged insult. "But in the end, he still managed to beat you."

Although her comeback had surely drawn blood, Declan was too skilled a negotiator to let that show. "I'm not beaten."

No. And she could see from the way a muscle jumped in his jaw that he intended to fight on until the bitter, bloody end. She just hoped she was still standing when the dust settled.

Three

"Let me see if I understand what's going on." Ethan's scowling face filled Chase's computer screen.

Chase's best friend was calling from Savannah where he was currently spending time working at his biological mother's company, trying to decide if he wanted to succeed her as CEO or continue to work for Watts Shipping and eventually end up running his adoptive family's company.

Like Teagan, Ethan had also utilized a genetic testing service to search for his biological relatives. Around the same time as she'd been discovering her Charleston roots, Ethan had connected with his birth mother, Carolina Gates. Chase knew that as happy as this had made his friend, the discovery had produced a complicated mix of emotions in those around him.

"Teagan wants to buy that rundown relic your mother has been trying to get her hands on for years," Ethan continued, "and you are considering helping her renovate it?"

"Rufus won't sell the property to us," Chase pointed

out, splitting his attention between his friend's tirade and the budget figures for an extensive renovation project that was close to completion. Thanks to several unexpected issues, he had to figure out a couple places to cut expenses and then convince his client they couldn't afford to spend a hundred and twenty-five dollars a square foot for tile. "If Teagan gets it, she's committed to doing a historic restoration rather than tearing it down or turning it into a modernized nightmare."

"What makes you think she'd be willing to let you take charge of the restoration?"

"We spoke." Chase's thoughts shot back to that meeting and his unwelcome attraction. "She's coming by in an hour to view the drawings I did for the house and look at the old photos of the place."

Given how much of the house's plasterwork had been lost to neglect, he was fortunate to have so much original reference material to work from. Since his mother had been trying to buy the house for years, Chase had a file filled with copies of original blueprints, historic photos and his own architectural renderings of how they could bring the house up-to-date while preserving its authentic charm. This wasn't the first time Rufus had entertained selling the house he'd let fall into neglect since his grandmother Francis had died ten years earlier. Chase was quite convinced that his third cousin enjoyed tormenting Maybelle by opening up the possibility that he would let her have the house only to snatch the hope away.

"Have you lost your mind?" Ethan demanded. "Why would you even consider letting her get her hands on your family's property?"

Bristling at his friend's unfair charge, Chase shifted his full attention to the computer screen. From the moment Sawyer had put Teagan together with the Calloway property, Chase had known he would be torn between his loyalty to his mother and his best friend. Their diverging goals and opinions meant he couldn't please both.

"This house is important to my mom," Chase stated, his tone crisp and determined. "I will do whatever it takes to save it. And Teagan says she's committed to a restoration."

Ethan must've noticed he'd pushed his friend too far because his tone became more reasonable. "You can't trust her to do the right thing."

"I understand your skepticism." Chase sighed. "But Teagan could be our only shot at influencing what becomes of it."

"Okay. Let me think about this." Ethan's eyes narrowed in a way that Chase recognized and had learned to dread. "Maybe this can work to our advantage."

Chase dug his fingertips into the tense muscles at the nape of his neck and braced himself. "How so?"

Oblivious to his best friend's disquiet, Ethan laid out his plan. "By handling this restoration, you are in the perfect position to keep an eye on her while I'm away in Savannah."

Ethan's proposal was the exact sort of thing Chase had been dreading.

"There's no one else I can count on to do this."

"What about Poppy or Dallas?" Chase suggested, listing Ethan's twin cousins. "I'm sure they'd be happy to keep an eye on her."

"Although they're mad at her now, she's likely to get them back on her side."

After meeting the delectable New Yorker, Chase couldn't argue. Even though Teagan's scheming to usurp Ethan's presumptive role as future CEO had led to the alienation of her sister, as well as all her cousins and two sets of aunts and uncles, she wouldn't rest until she'd redeemed herself in their eyes. Plus, she had her grandfather in her corner. Grady Watts was so thrilled to have his long-lost granddaughter back in the family bosom that he'd turned a blind eye to her underhanded ways.

"You, on the other hand," Ethan continued, "are the one person she won't be able to charm into getting her way."

Normally, Chase preferred substance over style, but the way his meeting with the enticing Teagan Burns had gone, he might not be as invulnerable as Ethan believed. Still, he kept that bit of disturbing data to himself and offered up an alternative excuse.

"Look," he said, "this isn't a good time. I've got a dozen projects in various stages of completion and the nominations for the Carolopolis Awards are due by the end of next month. I don't have any free time to spend with your cousin."

"She's dangerous," Ethan argued. "I don't want anyone else to get hurt. Hey, you know I wouldn't ask if it wasn't absolutely necessary for me to spend time in Savannah with my mom and figure out what I'm going to do about her job offer."

Biting back a curse, Chase nodded. "I get it. I'm just not sure what you expect me to do with Teagan. It's not like I can follow her around Watts Shipping or anything."

"I'm not really worried about Watts Shipping," Ethan said. "I clued Dad into what Teagan's been up to on that front and it's not like he's going to hand over the reins to someone with no experience. I'm more concerned about what might happen with the rest of my family. If Teagan was willing to use her own sister to get what she wanted, imagine what she would do to the relatives she barely knows."

"I don't know why you're worried." Chase pictured the three women Ethan had mentioned. "Those three can take care of themselves."

"Humor me."

Chase should point out that Ethan could turn to his

adoptive brother for help, but the cybersecurity expert was newly engaged to Lia Marsh and determined to avoid any of Ethan's future machinations.

Many months earlier when their grandfather Grady had grown ill and lost his will to live, Ethan had come up with an insane ruse to introduce a stranger as Grady's long-lost granddaughter so he could meet his beloved daughter's child before he died. The ploy had unexpected results. Connecting with his granddaughter caused Grady to rally. He stepped back from death's door and regained his strength. Unfortunately, this left Ethan, his brother Paul and the counterfeit granddaughter, Lia Marsh, embroiled in a complicated mess.

By the time the truth came out, Lia and Paul had fallen in love and not long afterward the genetic testing service had connected the family with Teagan.

"So?" Ethan prompted. "Will you help me out?"

Despite his distaste for the task, he and Ethan were as close as brothers and Chase would do everything in his power to keep Ethan's family safe. "Fine."

"I knew you would." Ethan beamed at him. "Thanks."

After grumbling something in response to his friend's warm appreciation, the call ended and Chase turned his attention back to the overstretched budget. Half an hour later he had the numbers back under control and had emailed the client his notes on the changes they would have to make. Which left him with five minutes to prepare for Teagan's arrival. Not enough time for him to collect his wits and decide on a plan for how to balance Ethan's request against his own moral compass.

Chase unrolled the architectural plans for the Calloway property and weighed down the four corners with glass paperweights featuring photos of his two nieces. As his gaze traced the exterior lines of the main house, he pondered what it would mean to his mother to see the property restored to its former glory.

Promptly at ten, Teagan appeared in his office wearing a long floral skirt and a white sleeveless crop top. For several erratic heartbeats he stared at her in tongue-tied appreciation while she crossed the room with her hand extended. A standard business handshake sent ripples of awareness across his skin and he was beset by the urge to yank her closer so he could slide his lips along her neck.

Chase wasn't given to poetic imagery, but caught himself comparing the scent of her to sun-kissed magnolias and succulent peaches. It wasn't that she smelled like either of those things, but both evoked pleasant memories and reminded him of a time when he'd been happy.

"Wow, when did you have time to pull all this together?" Teagan's verdant gaze took in the table covered in drawings, giving Chase a much-needed moment to recover.

He cleared his throat, struggling to shake her effect on him. "I've worked on architectural drawings for the Calloway property for a long time."

"And all these photos of the inside?" She picked up one of the family photos and studied it. "Did you get these from the former owners?"

"Some of them. I've been collecting reference images for a while."

She circled the table, taking everything in while he strove to keep his attention off the expanse of bare midriff between the hem of her top and her skirt's waistband. This proved impossible. One glimpse of her toned abs left him adrift in the desire to coast his fingertips over her pale skin.

"Do you do this much extensive research with every home you restore?"

"Not every one." Chase ground his teeth and wrenched his complete focus back to the blueprints. "This house in particular is one I am quite familiar with."

"Because?" She raised her eyebrows and waited for his answer. When he took too long to respond to her prompt, she prodded, "Oh, come on. You opened the door."

"It doesn't matter."

"Now I'm intrigued." She sidled closer. "But I think you knew that I would be, didn't you?"

Her bare forearm brushed his, short-circuiting his judgment. "The house belongs—" Chase stopped himself just in time and resolved to keep quiet about his personal connection to the job until he decided if he should accept the project. "—to an old and prominent family."

"That's all fascinating. With all the historic homes you restore, I'll bet you've heard dozens of stories about Charleston's oldest families. I'd love to hear more."

Seeing the avid interest on her beautiful face, Chase pumped the brakes on his storytelling. With his promise to Ethan hanging over him, Chase opted for self-preservation. "I don't think that's a good idea."

"You have to eat, don't you?" From the look of Teagan's winning smile, she wasn't going to give up easily.

"I'm very busy and…" It wasn't like him to beat around the bush. He had many reasons to keep things between them strictly professional, but top of the list was his acute attraction to her. "Before we agree to work together on this project, I need to set you straight on something."

Taking in his grim expression, Teagan inclined her chin with slow deliberation. "Such as?"

While he recognized that what he had to say next might just cost him the chance to restore his mother's ancestral home, Ethan's favor chafed Chase's conscience like forty-grit sandpaper.

"Ethan is my best friend."

Although her brows knit and her lips tightened, Teagan's voice reflected curiosity rather than irritation as she asked, "And that's important because?"

"When he found out you were interested in buying the Calloway property, he asked me to keep an eye on you." Chase paused to gauge her reaction to his announcement. "In case you planned to make more trouble for his family."

Well...hell.

As Teagan absorbed Chase's words, her guard automatically went up at this revelation. Disappointment, humiliation and annoyance tumbled through her. Well, at least she now understood his grim, unfriendly vibes. How disappointing that the first man she'd found attractive in a long, long time was predestined to dislike her.

"I'm not sure what Ethan told you—"

A lifetime of self-preservation had given her strong defenses. No matter how badly she was hurt, she'd never let anyone know that she gave a damn one way or another. Yet, for some reason she did care how this man perceived her.

"You used your sister as a pawn in a bid to become the next CEO of Watts Shipping."

While her first impulse was always to defend her tactics as sound strategy, in this case, the scheme had hurt Sienna and damaged their relationship. She'd behaved badly and intended to fix what she'd broken.

"And I regret it."

"Do you? Or are you just telling me what you think I want to hear?"

A thrilling little shiver stole up her spine at Chase's merciless stare. Teagan sucked in a long, slow breath to calm her madly erratic pulse. When had it ever excited her to be scolded after being caught red-handed in one of her schemes? Never. She far preferred when everyone feared her. Among her fellow socialites, she'd never cared if people disliked her and took it for granted that everyone gossiped behind her back.

She appreciated the way Chase put his opinion of her on

the table and wasn't daunted by his obvious dislike. Knowing exactly where she stood with him was a refreshing change. And her sense that no amount of flirting or charm would change his attitude provided an intriguing challenge.

"How about I tell you my side so you have a better understanding of me?"

He crossed his massive arms over his broad chest and nodded. "I'm listening."

Since coming to Charleston and meeting her birth relatives for the first time, she'd discovered that family could be warm and loving rather than distant and critical. Yet she hadn't fully appreciated the way they'd enthusiastically embraced her, and had continued to employ the sort of maneuvering that was second nature to her in New York. Her win-at-any-cost attitude had caused her to bully her sister Sienna into a scheme aimed at beating out her cousin Ethan for the top spot at their family's company. Her tactics might have been devious, but her motivation was straightforward.

"My adoptive family owns a property development company in New York City," she began, wondering if her story would encourage Chase to sympathize with her motivation. "And I'd always hoped that one day my father would decide to put me in charge instead of my older brother."

Chase stood silent and still beside her, a powerful presence that gave her the support she needed to keep going. It wasn't that she believed he would accept any explanation she might make. Chase was Ethan's friend, and as such, he was on her cousin's side. But she longed to tell her side of the story, bare the whole ugly truth, and maybe by owning up to it, she might be forgiven.

"But you see my father is…old-fashioned." Hearing the stress in her voice, Teagan paused and closed her eyes briefly to suppress her anxiety. "He intended my brother Aiden to take over Burns Properties."

"You think you should've been in charge?"

"Father made it very clear that I wasn't in the running. No matter my qualifications, ambition or strong work ethic, I was not his biological child."

Teagan hesitated to explain further. Exposing her vulnerabilities only ever led to her getting hurt. She'd gone as far as she could outside her comfort zone.

"Is that why you started looking for your biological family?"

"In part."

How could she begin to explain all the years she'd hungered to be with a family who truly wanted her? How she'd ached for the mother that had died when she was less than a year old? Wondered if her biological father knew she existed. Growing up she'd hated how being adopted made her an easy target for her classmates and the way her adoptive mother showed her off like a custom-made gown.

Meeting her Charleston relatives had filled the gaping hole in Teagan's identity. She was the granddaughter of Grady and Delilah Watts and the niece of firstborn Miles—currently at the helm of Watts Shipping—and eldest daughter Lenora, who had married well and produced twin daughters Poppy and Dallas with husband Wiley Shaw. And she was the daughter of Ava, youngest of the three siblings. Headstrong and free-spirited, Ava had fled the family fold, running away to New York at the age of eighteen with the intention of becoming a world-famous model and instead ending up pregnant.

Before coming to Charleston, Teagan hadn't known that when Ava had left South Carolina, she'd cut all ties, so her family hadn't known about Teagan or the fact that she'd been barely a year old when Ava had died in a tragic accident.

"Look," she continued, "everything I told you, it's not an excuse for my motivation or how I handled things. Just because Ethan was adopted and I was biologically a Watts didn't mean I should get to run the company."

His clear hazel eyes bore into her. "If you wanted the CEO position, you should've worked hard and beaten Ethan fair and square."

Teagan acknowledged his point with a nod. "Let's just say that in my experience, working hard isn't always enough for me to get what I want."

"So you manipulate situations to get what you want."

"When I have to." She didn't like his disappointed expression and vowed to change his mind about her. "It's always served me in the past, but things haven't worked out for me here. In less than a month I've manage to alienate my entire Charleston family. Poppy and Dallas barely speak to me. My aunts and uncles are coolly polite. The only person who doesn't seem at all bothered is Grandpa Grady and I think that's because he has no idea that I was the reason Ethan and Sienna broke up."

"So, why don't you go back to New York? Sawyer mentioned that you own several profitable businesses there."

Teagan's heart melted. Chase would have no idea how gratifying it was to have her successes recognized as opposed to her failures.

"I'm stubborn," she replied. "When I want something, I make sure I get it."

"And you want to be the future CEO of Watts Shipping."

Teagan shook her head. "I don't belong there. It was just my ego that made me go after the job in the first place."

"Then what's here for you?"

"My family." A tight ball of misery formed in her gut as she contemplated all the missteps she'd made since coming to Charleston. Initially, she'd been too arrogant to recognize that she was an outsider here and behaved like an entitled brat. She was determined to repair all that she'd damaged, but wasn't sure if any of them would forgive her. "And the opportunity to make my mark on Charleston."

"By renovating a historic property."

"And contributing to the community by providing transitional housing for women in need," Teagan put in, reminding him of her altruistic leanings.

"You're still maneuvering so things work out in your favor," he pointed out with relentless disapproval.

"Clearly my scheming ways are a part of who I am and difficult to shake," Teagan began, shifting her attention to the drawings of the three houses on the back of the property. "But I'm not the horrible person everybody believes me to be. I really do want to help people."

To her relief, a flicker of uncertainty clouded Chase's features. Maybe she was finally getting through to him. Good.

"Given what happened between Ethan and me, I can see why you hesitated to be involved in this project at all. What changed your mind?"

"What makes you think I have?"

His aggressive tone caught Teagan off guard. She'd touched a nerve and this wasn't a man to toy with. Still, her curiosity couldn't be contained.

"Given all the time and energy you put into planning this renovation, I can't imagine that you'd be happy to see someone else taking over the project." Impulsively, Teagan let her earlier attraction shine bright as she grinned at him. "And I think once you get to know me, you'll discover I'll be a fantastic partner."

From the moment she'd turned around the day they met and had spied him approaching her, she'd been bowled over by his masculine energy and vigorous good looks. But what had slipped past her defenses had been his sweetness with the little girls.

Her initial assumption that he was their father had compelled her to tamp down the fierce and overwhelming rush of attraction. The fever that had seized her in those first moments was unlike anything she'd ever known. Struck by a hunger to give herself to him and drown in his pale green eyes, her entire body had been consumed by a sizzling energy.

Even now, knowing that he'd been set on her by Ethan, Teagan couldn't set aside her baser instincts and behave sensibly. This man lit a fire in her blood and she wanted to revel in the heat.

"Would you be free for lunch?" With her family giving her the cold shoulder and Sienna not speaking to her, Teagan was feeling isolated and more than a little lonely. "To discuss the project further," she elaborated, finding herself oddly breathless. "I'm sure you'll see I'm one-hundred-percent committed to doing the best, most accurate historical restoration of this property. We'll be a great team. Just wait and see."

While that was true, she also craved more time in his company. The fond way he'd smiled at his nieces told her that a warm heart lingered beneath his gruff exterior. Add to that her physical attraction to him. How every time their gazes collided, butterflies exploded in her stomach. Still waters ran deep and she couldn't wait to discover what else lay beneath his impenetrable exterior.

"I'm afraid I don't have time today."

That wasn't a definite no and Teagan decided to capitalize on it. "How about tomorrow then?" she coaxed, eager to spend more time with this perplexing man. "My treat."

"It's really not necessary."

She cocked her head and regarded him. "Are you playing hard to get?"

"No, not at all," he retorted, sounding shocked. "It's just that this is our busiest time of the year with the nomination deadline for the Carolopolis Awards fast approaching."

"Well, you have to eat sometime. How about dinner?"

"Dinner?" The way he echoed her invitation with a dumbfounded expression did little to bolster her ego.

"You're supposed to be keeping an eye on me, right?" She had no idea what impish compulsion had prompted her to hurl that revelation back at him. "What better way than to join me for dinner?"

"You won't let up until I accept, will you?"

"See, you get me." Feeling as if she'd won an important skirmish and not wishing to rub it in, she regarded him solemnly. "We're going to work well together."

He snorted. "If by 'well' you mean you'll badger me until you get your way."

His observation delighted her. "You're not like Ethan, are you?"

"How so?"

"He's a better schemer than you."

"That's never been up for debate. Be it business or personal, I have always found that situations are less complicated if I'm up-front."

"Maybe I should give that a try."

"Based on how things have been going for you with your family, it might be a good idea."

Teagan couldn't help herself; she laughed. "You don't pull any punches, do you?"

"Not when I think someone can handle it."

To her dismay, she found her cheeks heating beneath the frank directness of his gaze. "And you think I can?" She wasn't sure if he'd offered her a compliment or criticism.

"I'm certain there's little you can't handle."

Again, based on his matter-of-fact tone, she wasn't sure whether to take his remark as praise or reproach. He was Ethan's best friend and destined to take her cousin's side. Yet, she warmed to his words as if he liked her strong personality.

"Mostly that's true, but I get the feeling you're more than a match for me."

This seemed to catch him off guard. "Why do you say that?"

"Because I'm not accustomed to people who call me out and it's rather refreshing."

"Really? I would think you'd hate to get caught scheming."

"Not really. Where I come from, if you're not the one manipulating the situation, you're the one being outmaneuvered."

"It won't do you any good to try to control me."

"No," she mused, curiously excited by his challenge. "I don't imagine it will."

Chase scrutinized her for several seconds before nodding. "I'll pick you at seven o'clock tomorrow night."

Teagan beamed. "I'll be counting the hours."

Four

"You told her I asked you to keep an eye on her?" Ethan's voice blasted through the phone speaker.

As soon as his meeting with Teagan had ended, Chase had called Ethan to share how things had gone. "Yes."

"Why would you do that? Now she knows we're on to her."

"She already knew that." Chase employed the overly patient voice he used when his nieces were particularly tired and irritable. "And you know I'm not one to play games. Plus, it should deter her from acting out if she thinks I'm keeping an eye on her."

"You don't know Teagan. She's relentless." Ethan's exasperation gave way to a huge, resigned sigh. "Well, since we don't really have a choice, let's try it your way."

Chase refrained from pointing out that they were already doing it his way. "Good."

"Between you and Paul, I have too many straight shooters in my life."

"You're welcome," Chase said, familiar with his best friend's grumbling.

Ethan's older brother was a former police officer who currently owned a cybersecurity business and shared Chase's tendency to see the world in shades of black and white, good and bad, right and wrong. Both Paul and Chase had pursued martial arts as kids and Chase's hero worship of Ethan's older brother had always bugged him, especially during a phase in high school where Chase had considered pursuing a career in law enforcement. But in the end, it was construction that captured his imagination and heart. After college he took over East Bay Construction, the company his family began twenty years ago, and partnered with Knox to double the size of the business.

"So, what's your plan for keeping an eye on Teagan now that she's on to you?"

"We're having dinner tomorrow night."

"Dinner?" Ethan sounded dumbfounded. "You asked her out to dinner?"

"No. She asked me. She wants to discuss my ideas for the Calloway property."

"Be careful."

"It's dinner." Hearing his friend's doubtful grunt, Chase added, "Strictly professional."

"Since when do you date your clients?"

"Since my best friend asked me to keep an eye on his cousin. How exactly did you think I was going to go about that?"

"I thought maybe you'd be more discreet."

"Like maybe I'd skulk around Charleston, peering at her from behind bushes?"

"Sure. That works."

"You know, if you're unhappy with my methods, you can always find someone else to do your dirty work."

"There's no one I trust."

That wasn't completely the case, but Chase decided against mentioning Ethan's brother Paul in this particular moment. "You don't sound as if you trust me."

"It's not you I'm worried about."

Chase was reflecting on his last conversation with Ethan as he stopped his SUV outside the Birch-Watts Estate. Picking up Teagan at her grandfather's house came uncomfortably close to this being a date. Part of him was tempted to sit in the car and honk the horn to let her know he'd arrived, but his mother would skin him alive if she heard he'd done something like that. Instead, heaving a gigantic sigh, he exited the vehicle and trudged up the curving stairs to the front door.

Chase had spent a considerable amount of time here growing up. The extensive grounds included a pool and had been a frequent gathering spot for friends and family. The Federal-style house had been built in 1804 and remodeled several times, but always with an eye toward preserving and enhancing its original architecture. Although he'd never been involved in any of the updates to the main house, Chase had remodeled the carriage house several years earlier and turned it into a cozy living space.

Grady's housekeeper ushered Chase into the spacious foyer and indicated the formal living room. Chase had arrived a few minutes early and hadn't expected Teagan would be ready. In fact, he expected that she'd keep him waiting. To Chase's delight, the living room wasn't empty. Grady sat near one of the windows, his cane beside him, a recently released biography in his hands.

Knowing how concerned the family had been by their eighty-five-year-old patriarch's failing health, it was good to see Grady looking so robust. The return of his long-lost granddaughter had given him a reason to live. Chase just hoped Teagan didn't disappoint him.

"Good evening, Grady," Chase said as he settled into a nearby chair.

Grady looked up from his book and smiled. "Chase. Good to see you. What brings you by?"

"I'm here to pick up Teagan. We're having dinner."

The old man's eyebrows rose and his eyes danced with pleasure. "You don't say. Well, you have good taste. My granddaughter is both beautiful and accomplished. I think you two will make a fine couple."

Before Chase could correct Grady's misinterpretation of the situation, a feminine voice spoke from the doorway.

"Oh, Grandpa don't scare him away." Teagan shot Chase a saucy wink as she went past him and settled beside her grandfather. She slipped her arm through his and dropped a quick kiss on Grady's cheek. "If Chase thinks I have designs on him, he'll play hard to get."

"Why would he do that?" Grady asked, taking Teagan's hand and giving it a quick squeeze. "He'd be lucky to have you."

"That's sweet of you to say." Her voice quavered slightly as if Teagan was gripped by some overpowering emotion.

The affection between Teagan and her grandfather looked real, but Chase recalled her saying that Grady was the only member of her family who was speaking to her at the moment. Perhaps she was playing at being a doting granddaughter to preserve this final relationship.

"You be good to my girl." Grady fixed Chase with a stern glare. "She's having a rough time at the moment."

Chase opened his mouth to point out she'd been the one who'd caused the trouble to begin with but ended up nodding instead. "Of course. She's in good hands." Why he'd added the second part, Chase had no idea.

Grady looked satisfied. Teagan glowed with smug delight.

"We'd better get going." Teagan deposited another kiss

on his wrinkled cheek and then stood. "I'll see you tomorrow morning for breakfast."

"Have fun, you two."

After bidding Grady goodbye, Chase followed Teagan to the front door. Once they were outside and out of earshot, he shot her a dark look.

"What was that all about?"

"Whatever do you mean?" she asked, all innocence and sweetness.

"You gave Grady the impression that we're dating."

"I thought it sounded better than explaining that Ethan asked you to keep an eye on me in case I feel like getting up to more mischief."

Before meeting up with Teagan tonight, he'd been perfectly comfortable in his lightweight blazer. Now, as he watched her glide down the steps ahead of him, each stride flawless in her impossibly high heels, Chase found his temperature rising. Another woman exhibiting her outrageous behavior would've left him cold. But every scorching glance, the tantalizing body language that beckoned to him, her provocative quips all made his temperature spike.

Tonight she wore a shimmering gold minidress that screamed sophisticated New Yorker. With her long blond hair braided and pinned in a loose updo with face-framing wisps, she was glamorous, ultra-feminine and brimming with confidence. Conflicting emotions consumed him. For all she drove him crazy, his desire for her remained constant and compelling.

"You could've explained that it was a business dinner," he pointed out, opening the passenger door for her.

She slipped into the vehicle. The move caused her hem to rise and Chase was helpless to resist stealing an appreciative glance at her long, toned legs.

"I could've. But then I wouldn't have had the chance to watch you stew."

Before he could take the bait, Chase closed the door and circled to the driver's side. As he slid behind the wheel, he asked, "Have you told him you made an offer on the Calloway house?"

"I did and I explained that you and I are going to work together to restore it." She paused while he started the engine and put the car into gear. "Grady told me your mother's cousin refused to sell her the property after he inherited it."

While this wasn't common knowledge in the community, the Love and Watts families had a long history of friendship. Grady would think nothing of sharing the information with Teagan. Chase had opened the door by mentioning that the property was important to his mother and then refused to elaborate. For a schemer like Teagan, ferreting out these sorts of secrets would be second nature.

"Why is that?" Her avid gaze acted like a truth spell on him.

"There's bad blood between our families going back for generations."

Might as well tell her the whole story and deny her the satisfaction of dragging it out of him. Not that denying her gave him any pleasure. The ludicrous notion ricocheted around his brain, making his head hurt. How had this woman gotten under his skin so fast, compelling him to consider what she would and wouldn't enjoy?

"It must've been something terrible for your families to still not be getting along."

He'd told her more than he intended to—might as well spill all of his family's ugly past. "My great-great-grandfather split his fortune between his two children. The daughter inherited money while the son inherited the business and the house. She invested well in her husband's business and her family thrived. He lacked her sound judgment and ran the family business deep into debt." When he paused to consider how much more to share, Teagan's rapt expression prodded him to continue. "Rufus has the same terrible business sense as his father, grandfather and great-grandfather and resents how well my mother's side of the family has done for themselves. I don't think there's any amount we could offer him to overcome his bitterness."

"This must be terribly hard on your mother."

Chase steeled himself against Teagan's sympathy. If the woman wasn't twisting his hormones into knots with her flirting, she was tricking his emotions with her clever insight.

"She's very sentimental."

"And you're very protective of her."

Even though his mother had a backbone of Southern steel, he'd always done his best to cushion the blow each time Rufus turned down their purchase offers.

"She's my mother."

The restaurant he'd chosen was a five-minute drive from Grady's house and he was lucky to score a nearby parking spot.

"You know," Teagan began, as he shut off the car and jumped out before she could finish her thought.

Chase opened the passenger door for her and Teagan shot him a warm smile as she exited the vehicle. "The restaurant is this way."

As they strode side by side toward the restaurant, she finished her earlier thought as if no time had elapsed. "It's really sweet the way you worry about your family. And it's not just them, is it? I'll bet you safeguard anyone who's important to you."

She spoke as if this was something exceptional. Wasn't protecting loved ones just the right thing to do?

"Can we please just focus on the Calloway restoration tonight?"

"Oh, we'll get to that." An intriguing smile bloomed on

her pale pink lips, stirring his discomfort. "But first, I want to learn everything there is to know about you."

So she could figure out how better to manipulate him? Chase growled in irritation. "There's not much to tell."

"You underestimate my interest." Teagan raised an eyebrow while her eyes danced with beguiling amusement.

Rumbling with displeasure, Chase opened the restaurant's front door and ushered Teagan into Fig. The establishment's clean, simple decor was the perfect backdrop for its excellent culinary offerings. Since they sourced locally, the menu changed with the seasons and Chase visited frequently.

The hostess led them to a linen-clad table against the wall. While Teagan settled onto the booth seat that would give her a view of the restaurant, Chase settled opposite her, facing the blank white wall which provided nothing to distract him from her beautiful face.

A waiter appeared to welcome them and get their drink order started. Teagan pursed her lips as she studied the menu.

"I feel like something bubbly to celebrate our first date," she said. "How about a bottle of the Ruppert-Leroy champagne?"

While the waiter nodded his approval, Chase sighed. Would it do any good to protest that they weren't on a date? Teagan was a force of nature when she set her mind on something. And while Chase was not a pushover, he decided to save his energy for the important battles ahead.

Once the champagne had been served, Teagan lifted her glass and toasted, "To the beginning of a successful partnership."

Chase echoed her salute, deciding this was a pledge he could get behind. Despite being polar opposites in temperament and behavior, Chase believed they were of like minds when it came to the restoration of the Calloway house.

It was because of this, and to ensure his mother's peace of mind, that Chase was willing to put up with Teagan's provocations.

"So," Teagan began, her eyes dancing with mischief. "What is it you do when you're not making Charleston beautiful?"

"Eat and sleep." It wasn't far off, but he didn't want to bare his personal life to Teagan. Seeing her determined expression, he added, "Since I have a tendency to take on too many projects, I work all the time."

"How did you get into renovation?"

"My mother is passionate about Charleston," he explained. "Its history, architecture, culture. She's active in the Preservation Society and sits on the boards of several local museums."

"That tells me a lot about your mother, but little about you. When did you know you wanted to be an architect?"

"After my dad died. I was a sophomore in high school at the time." Refusing to be drawn into a moment of connection, Chase glanced away from the sympathy reflected in Teagan's expression. "My mom took over running East Bay Construction and I started helping out with the renovations after school and during my summer breaks. I think both Mom and I felt close to him doing the work he loved."

"I'm sorry for your loss. That had to be a tough age to lose your dad." She made a little face. "I don't know why I said that. There's no easy age to lose a parent."

As he nodded in agreement, it occurred to Chase that Teagan had never had time with either of her birth parents growing up. She'd come to Charleston in search of her mother's family. He wondered if she'd had luck locating her father.

"My mom died before I turned one," Teagan continued, her mood contemplative. "I'm sure it was devastating to lose her, but I don't remember that time or her at all."

"What about your dad? Did you have any luck finding him through the genetic testing service?"

"No." A flicker of something caught his attention before she veiled her gaze with her long lashes. "But I did learn who he was. Unfortunately, it wasn't until after he died. He sent me a letter through his lawyer."

The vagueness of her explanation roused Chase's curiosity, but he was reluctant to probe. He'd never seen her this subdued, and this deeply contemplative side of her engaged his protective instincts. Beneath her sassy, confident exterior lay a tender spirit that had seen its share of sorrow. The urge to throw his arm around her and nestle her into the shelter of his body thrummed in him.

"So, he knew who you were."

She gave a rough little laugh. "All along, apparently. He was more than twice my mom's age, with a family." Her lips tightened as if she was fighting emotion. When she spoke again, her voice shook. "I don't know if it was one night or a torrid affair. The one clear fact is that I was a big mistake."

"Did he say that in the letter?"

"No." She shook her head and her melancholy scattered like droplets of water. "But he wasn't in a position to divorce his wife and abandon his kids so I'm sure my mother's pregnancy wasn't exactly welcome news."

"So you have half brothers and sisters?"

"One of each."

Chase wondered if she'd reached out to them. "Are they in New York?"

"Yes."

"Did you contact them?"

"He asked me not to."

This struck Chase as unfair.

"At first it bothered me." A pregnant pause hinted at how

much. "But in the end, it's what motivated me to contact the genetic testing service and here I am."

And to Chase's surprise, he was glad of it. Despite the troubling drama she'd brought to all their lives, her keen interest in saving the Calloway house made her the perfect partner for him.

"Wait." Her eyes narrowed. "How come I asked you a question and ended up being the one baring my soul?"

"Obviously, you needed to get it off your chest and share it with someone."

"I did." She sipped her wine and stared contemplatively at the candle on the table between them. "No one else knows about my real dad."

"Not even your sister?"

Teagan gave an awkward half shrug. "I was crushed that he wanted me to keep our association a secret. It made me feel unwanted and you've probably figured out that I'm not accustomed to letting down my guard. Sharing something that painful…" She trailed off with a grimace.

Then why are you telling me?

Even as the question popped into his head, Chase was hammered by a startling development. He'd become her confidant. The role made him uncomfortable. It implied an intimacy that went beyond client/contractor. He wanted a professional relationship with her. She was a complicated, vexing woman who somehow managed to stir his protective nature as well as his libido.

Keeping his distance was imperative. But every time he tried to resist, she drew him in. How else could he explain why he'd agreed to have dinner with her? Or why he noticed the nuances of her body language and expressions?

"Okay," she gusted out on a breathy laugh. "Enough about me. I know you don't work 24/7 so what is it you do for fun?"

"Martial arts." When Teagan's eyes widened, he added, "I'm a black belt."

"You don't seem the type." She cocked her head and scrutinized him. "I mean, you're built like someone who could kick ass, but you don't strike me as…aggressive."

Chase heaved a resigned sigh and gave her his standard answer. "Consistent training not only conditions the mind and body to have strength and stamina, but also helps the body fight disease, stay flexible and strong. It also provides stress relief and releases pent-up energy."

Her lips rounded into a surprised *oh*. "Sounds like I should give it a try."

This was not what he'd expected her to say, but since she'd given him an opening, Chase had a suggestion. "I teach a beginner's class on Wednesday afternoons. You're welcome to come."

Teagan nodded enthusiastically at his invitation. "Just tell me where and when and I'll be there."

He'd thrown the suggestion out there never imagining she'd agree so readily. Should he warn her what to expect? That would be the right thing to do. But Teagan enjoyed teasing him too much and he deserved a little payback.

"We can have dinner afterwards." His offer erupted before he had a chance to consider what he was thinking.

Teagan blinked in surprise, and then grinned in delight. "I'd like that."

At the studio where Chase trained and taught, Teagan stepped out of the locker room wearing borrowed martial arts gear, the long white belt tied in a tasteful bow at her waist. Initially at a loss for what she was supposed to do with the thick material, she was feeling pretty smug at her artful styling. While she knew her New York friends would ridicule her for wearing the shapeless pants and jacket, something about donning the required ensemble made her feel physically powerful.

Flipping her long blond hair over her shoulder, Teagan strode toward the studio where the classes were being held. Before she reached the end of the hall, however, Chase stepped out of an office and caught sight of her. To her dismay, a shiver raced across her skin as she took in his solid frame dressed in all black. He pivoted in her direction, his pale green eyes taking in her appearance. A disgruntled scowl pinched his brow.

"That's not how you wear the belt."

"No?" Uncharacteristically giddy beneath his raking regard, she peered up at him from beneath her lashes, all too aware that any attempt at flirtation would fail, but compelled to try anyway. "You'll have to show me. I've never done this before."

With a grunt of acknowledgment, he snagged one end of the bow and tugged it loose. The abrupt move pulled her toward him. Pulse racing, she held still as he unceremoniously gathered the belt into his hands, and then wrapped it around her waist twice. He had to put his arms around her to complete the move and with mere inches separating them, she inhaled the rain-kissed scent of his shampoo. No overpowering aftershave or cologne for this man, just the fresh scent of soap and the invigorating mint of toothpaste.

Damn.

Her mouth watered. She wanted to devour him, to slide her lips over his smooth, tan skin and nibble her way along his throat. Her hands were clutching his sleeves before the impulse registered. Still in the process of tying the belt, he started to step back and noticed her grip. One eyebrow arched.

"Sorry." With effort, she straightened her fingers and released him. "I…" Unable to summon an excuse, she shook her head.

With brisk, efficient movements, Chase stuck his fingers between the belt fabric and her stomach, pulling one of the loose ends through the space he made. Teagan clenched her teeth and bit back a groan at the contact. There was nothing personal in his touch, but that didn't prevent her nerve endings from going on full alert. It was growing clear that her physical attraction to this man would be her downfall.

"There."

Lost in her body's agitation, she'd missed that he'd completed his task. Glancing down at the perfect knot, she murmured, "Thanks."

"Let's go."

He might not like her, but Chase was a Southern gentleman through and through. Turning aside, he gestured for her to precede him into the studio. Teagan took an unsteady step forward and then another, the fog clearing from her brain as she erased the proximity between them. She was almost breathing normally as the studio occupants came into view.

Teagan stopped dead as her gaze landed on her fellow classmates. After surveying the five-and six-year-olds dressed in their all-white *dobok* uniforms, she glanced over her shoulder at Chase.

"You neglected to mention that it's a beginner's class for *children*."

"Did I?"

She could swear a hint of amusement crept into his flat response, but his expression remained bland. Still, she was convinced that he'd deliberately set out to throw her off-balance. Well, he'd succeeded.

Before she'd come to Charleston, a stunt like this would've provoked her swift and vicious counterattack. Her keen defenses, honed through growing up as an adopted child to movers and shakers on Manhattan's Upper East Side, never permitted her to look foolish or anything other than in complete and seamless control. New York's exclusive social scene was a dangerous place for the gullible and inattentive. The sweet and kind were ripe for ridicule and destruction. Strike the first blow or die an excruciating public demise. Being on top was the only place to be, but the battle to stay there was never-ending. Someone was always trying to cut her legs out from under her. Like a spy behind enemy lines, she was constantly watching her back.

Unfortunately, she'd brought this edgy, paranoid energy with her to Charleston. Too late to avoid damaging her reputation with them, she'd recognized that her biological relatives were genuinely delighted to receive her into their family. She didn't need to scheme or manipulate anyone to gain position or acceptance. If she'd only trusted their warm welcome and explored joining the family's shipping company instead of acting like an entitled jerk and deciding it was her right to run the company, maybe she wouldn't be on the outs with everyone now.

She'd never loved being viewed as the villain, but appreciated the power it accorded. Her enemies, acquaintances and even some of her friends in New York were afraid to cross her. But since coming to Charleston and being wholeheartedly embraced by her true family, Teagan had noted a change in her attitude. At first the shift had been subtle and too weak to combat a lifetime of conditioning, but after her huge blowout with Sienna had sent shockwaves rippling through her Charleston family, Teagan had recognized that she'd messed up all her relationships.

A lifetime of conditioning left her struggling to break through her guards. It tore at her to have failed so badly with the family that meant so much to her. How did she make it right when everyone turned their back on her?

Calling upon the breathing techniques she utilized in yoga class, Teagan strode to the back of the group and offered a tight smile to the little girls on either side of her.

They seemed to find their adult classmate acceptable because after casting welcoming grins her way, they sobered and focused on the tall man at the head of the class.

Without saying a word Chase captured the attention of every student. His commanding presence radiated authority and the rambunctious group settled, awaiting instruction.

Chase began by snapping his feet together, slapping his palms on the outside of his thighs and bending sharply at the waist. All the children imitated him.

"Today we're going to be working on three things." He paused briefly. "Repeat after me. Yes, I can."

The whole group chorused the three-word declaration. In an instant the energy in the room went from zero to ten, but Teagan found herself a beat behind. Determined to do better, she was focused and on the ball when the children showed off their biceps and repeated, "Do my best!"

"And finally," Chase said. "Discipline."

Teagan didn't think she was feeling paranoid when Chase's gaze touched on her as he spoke the word. No doubt he thought she could use some.

Teagan found herself captivated as well, but for a slightly different reason than the children around her. Her social group was filled with powerful men: billionaire businessmen, trust fund darlings with the world at their feet, European royalty and even a few professional athletes. Yet for all their money, success and charm, none of them awakened the hunger that filled her as she watched Chase guide his young charges.

By five minutes in, Teagan's heart rate was elevated, not only by the sight of Chase but by the physical exercise, and she wondered if she could keep up. She was feeling a little less overwhelmed when Chase sat them all down for stretching. Thanks to yoga, her flexibility was stellar.

After class, Teagan made a beeline toward the bathroom to freshen up and change back into the white lace cropped pants and matching off-the-shoulder top. She slipped her feet into hot-pink sandals, returned the borrowed *dobok* before making her way to the lobby. Since Chase had not yet arrived, she fluffed her hair and quickly uploaded the selfie she'd taken in the *dobok*. She'd picked up a bunch of new followers in recent days who were gobbling up everything she posted about her Charleston visit. No doubt they would be intrigued that she'd taken up martial arts.

"Are you ready?"

Chase had appeared while she was checking on the latest posts from the clothing line she ran with her mother. Since coming to Charleston, she'd turned over the social media for the company to her assistant and was pleased to see how well Angela was handling the account.

Teagan slipped her phone into her clutch and smiled at him. "Of course."

Chase pushed open the studio door and gestured for her to precede him. "The restaurant is nearby." He frowned as he regarded her four-inch heels. "Are you okay to walk there?"

"I live in New York City."

"So, is that a yes?"

"I regularly walk several miles a day in shoes just like these," Teagan explained with a wry smile. "So, that's a yes."

His response was a terse nod. "We're going this way."

"You're really good with the kids," Teagan remarked as they walked side by side down King Street. Her heart fluttered and thumped with each casual brush of his arm against hers. She couldn't remember the last time she'd felt this giddy in a man's company. It didn't help that Chase Love was tall, virile and adorably stern. "They hung on your every word and move."

"You sound surprised."

"I guess I am." How could she phrase this without stepping wrong? "You're so…big and…intimidating."

Yet everyone seemed to see straight past his unsmiling demeanor to the devoted heart that motivated him.

"I only intimidate the people that cross me."

His words made her shiver. Goose bumps sprang from a keen yearning to never get on his bad side. She didn't fear him physically. Despite his size and martial arts training he would never do harm. She knew that. No, the real danger lay in his negative opinion. Given that he'd heard nothing but terrible things about her, what chance did she have to win him over?

Their destination turned out to be The Darling Oyster Bar. Tucked into a historic hundred-year-old storefront, the airy restaurant's predominantly white decor was broken up by brick accents and pops of color in the form of mint green booths.

"I should've asked if you like seafood," Chase said as they waited for the hostess to return.

"I love it," Teagan answered, surveying the cozy space.

It was then that she realized every female in the vicinity had noticed him. The reason was clear. The man truly was a work of art. His face was all classic masculine angles with chiseled cheekbones and a jawline that could slice open a girl's heart. The perfection of his muscular form combined with his absolute confidence ensured that Chase was sucking up all the oxygen in the room.

Teagan stepped a little closer to him to assert her claim and scowled at the smiling hostess who'd greeted Chase by name.

"It'll be an hour for a table," she said.

"Popular spot," Teagan murmured, delighted the delay would enable her to spend more time in Chase's company.

"How long for the raw bar?" Chase asked.

The hostess glanced toward the horseshoe-shaped bar beside the front windows where customers sampled from the restaurant's wide selection. "We have two seats open now."

Chase turned to Teagan. "Are you ready to taste some of the best oysters around?" His eyebrows rose as if challenging her to refuse. "Or we can wait for a table."

Teagan had never backed down from a dare. "Bring them on."

Approval flashed in his eyes, warming Teagan to her toes. Her hunger for him to like her was off the charts. The realization caught her off guard. She'd stopped looking to others to validate her around grade school. What was it about Chase that made her crave his admiration and respect? The man had done nothing but cast skeptical glances her way and display no sign of recognizing her abundant appeal.

What she wouldn't give to have him overcome by desire. To back her against a wall and seize her mouth with his. She'd clutch his powerful shoulders and encourage him to glide his long-fingered hands over her every curve. Teagan grew a little short of breath just imagining their tongues coming together in the perfect mating dance.

"Are you okay?" Chase's matter-of-fact tone banished her erotic daydreams.

Teagan blinked and found him peering down at her. Somehow, while she'd been caught up in her thoughts of him, they'd been seated at the raw bar. Off-balance and sizzling with unsettling cravings, Teagan let herself go along with the flow. She was usually too guarded to act impulsively. But something about Chase encouraged her to set aside her need to control the outcome and let her emotions lead her.

A lock of his dark blond hair had fallen over his forehead and obscured his eyes. Before she could second-guess the wisdom of reaching out to him, she'd brushed the thick strands to one side.

"You need a haircut."

He reared back as if she'd struck him and Teagan felt her cheeks heat. Blushing? Impossible. Losing her cool wasn't something she did.

"I'll make an appointment with Poppy," he murmured, avoiding her gaze.

At the mention of her hairstylist cousin, Teagan took herself in hand. This wasn't a date. He was spending time with her to keep her from doing damage to her family. The reality of the situation struck her like a lash.

"She's really talented." Embarrassment poked at Teagan. Why couldn't she stop herself from acting like an idiot around Chase? What had happened to her slick New York sophistication? "In fact," she continued, sliding her hand beneath the heavy curtain of her waist-length hair. "I was thinking about turning her loose on my hair. The heat down here makes me want to get rid of this length. Maybe I'll try a lob."

"Lob?" Chase echoed.

"Long bob. About here." Palms down, Teagan rested her fingertips on her shoulder to demonstrate the length.

To her immense shock, Chase reached out and pinched a strand between his fingers, testing the texture. "Your hair is nice as it is."

Electricity raced from her scalp to her toes, but it was his compliment that rocked her. So, of course, instead of graciously accepting the praise, she blurted out the first glib thing that came to her mind.

"Wow," she croaked. "I think that's the first nice thing you've said to me."

"That's not true," he countered, releasing her hair and turning his attention to the menu. "I remarked on your form during class."

Struggling to recapture her wits, she murmured, "You did approve of my stances."

She had no idea why teasing the serious man entertained her. Maybe it was his immunity to her lighthearted flirting. To her surprise, bright color appeared high on his cheekbones. Was he blushing? Maybe he wasn't made of stone. His nieces had certainly brought out his softer side. The fond smiles he'd sent their way had sure aroused a disconcerting flutter in her heart.

"You caught on quickly." Chase ordered a neat Monkey Shoulder scotch and Teagan echoed his choice. "I wish all my students paid such good attention to my instruction."

"Well, your students are five-year-olds, so I think the bar is pretty low."

He shot her a searching look that Teagan leaned into. Tingling awareness zinged through her. His muscular shoulder was mere inches away, Teagan's heart bucked. A myriad of sensations besieged her senses, all of them deliriously fun and intriguingly dangerous. She couldn't stop her gaze from running along the imperfect line of his nose that looked like it might've been broken a time or two. Nor could she steady the erratic pace of her heart as she let her senses open to him. She wanted to burrow her fingers into his thick hair and absorb the heat of his skin.

"Shall we start with Single Ladies?" Chase asked, yanking her focus back to the restaurant.

"Single ladies?" she repeated dumbly, convinced she'd missed the context of his question.

"Would you rather try something else?"

"Um…" Rarely did she get caught completely flat-footed. "No, I mean, I guess that's fine."

"They're my favorite. I think you'll enjoy them as well."

"Huh." She sipped at the whiskey the waitress had set before her and regarded him over the rim of the glass.

"What?"

"I didn't get the idea that you were such a ladies' man." Chase frowned at her. "I'm not."

"Then what's with all the talk about single ladies?"

He pointed to a line on the menu. "We are here to eat oysters, right?"

"Oh." Teagan focused on the writing and mused. "So, *those* are the single ladies you like to eat."

"You really are a troublemaker, aren't you?"

Teagan offered up a cheeky smirk. "It's all part of my charm."

Five

He absolutely, positively could not, should not, find Teagan Burns attractive. She played games, manipulated people for her own gain and thrived on making him uncomfortable. If another woman exhibited any of these behaviors, he'd have walked away. However, because of these exact stunts, he'd committed to keeping an eye on Teagan, which meant he was also around for those brief unguarded moments that revealed other facets of her personality. The wry humor. Self-doubt. And the most tantalizing and hardest for him to resist, her passion for historic buildings.

Rather than notice the cool floral notes of her perfume or the delicate bones where her upper arms and shoulder came together, Chase focused his attention on the crisp Chablis he'd ordered to pair with the delicious raw oysters the server placed before them.

"Is there anything else you need?" she asked, her attentive gaze darting between Chase and Teagan.

Teagan surveyed the platter containing a dozen locally

sourced oysters and shook her head. "This looks perfect." She picked up her wine glass and held it toward him. "To my first Charleston oysters. I'm glad to be sharing them with you."

Too steeped in Southern manners to leave her hanging, Chase lifted his glass and tapped it to hers. The delicate chime was nearly lost amidst the chatter of voices in the high-ceilinged space, but somehow the tiny sound resonated like a crash of thunder in Chase's chest.

"I hope you find them to your liking."

"Oh, I'm sure I will. After all, good company often elevates one's enjoyment of a meal, wouldn't you agree?"

Had she heard the husky undertones that roughened his voice? Her teeth flashed in a quick smile as he sipped his wine and watched her over the rim. Convinced her dancing green eyes were casting a spell on him, he resolved to work harder to keep his guard up in her presence.

"Flirting with me will do you no good," he declared, gesturing for her to choose the first oyster.

"That's where you're wrong." Teagan selected an oyster and dotted it with cocktail sauce. She brought the shell to her mouth, but instead of slurping it straight down, she inhaled the scent of the oyster. "You've underestimated the amount of pleasure I get from seeing you fight to keep from enjoying yourself when I do."

"You couldn't be more wrong about me."

"Really?"

Teagan loosened the oyster with the tiny fork and placed the shell's edge against her lips. Chase sat mesmerized as the oyster disappeared. He watched her jaw work as she chewed and caught himself leaning forward in anticipation of her next words.

"Then I guess your reactions are all part of my imagination," she purred, settling the oyster shell face down on the bed of ice. "And you're not the least bit intrigued by me."

The sudden, warm pressure of her fingers against his thigh made Chase jump. All too aware that his involuntary reaction had proved her point, he sucked in a frustrated breath between his teeth.

Chase placed his hand over hers, determined to pull her fingers away, but found himself unable to do so. "Oh, I'm intrigued."

"Good."

She sounded far too smug for his liking. Acting in a way that was completely foreign to him, Chase cupped the side of her face with his free hand and leaned over to plant a strong kiss on her smiling lips. Her body froze as he grazed his teeth over her lower lip and flicked his tongue forward to taste her. The sweet tang of cocktail sauce blended with the fruity Chablis, and he groaned softly as she leaned into the kiss.

A chorus in four-part harmony blasted joyously through his brain as he savored the contact with her soft mouth. Fierce pleasure shook him to his core. Chase was a heartbeat away from losing himself in the white-hot joy when he remembered where they were. Setting her free took all his willpower. With his equilibrium battered by his loss of control, Chase returned to his former position.

"What was that for?" Teagan asked, a raw note of confusion in her voice.

"You weren't angling for a kiss?"

"Maybe." Hot color bloomed in her cheeks. "I don't know."

Chase let a raised eyebrow do the talking for him.

"Fine, yes!" Her half smile took the sting out of her aggrieved tone. "Since when does a proper Southern gentleman kiss a lady in a crowded restaurant?" She raised her hand. "And don't tell me I'm not a lady. Or claim you're not a proper Southern gentleman. You know what I mean."

"I guess you bring out the worst in me," he said.

"Funny," she mused, her eyes softening to rain-drenched willow. "I think you could bring out the best in me."

Chase had no idea how to respond so he turned his attention to the platter of oysters between them. "What did you think of your first Single Lady?" he asked, selecting an oyster. He loosened it with his fork before tipping the shell and letting the oyster slide into his mouth.

Teagan watched him with rapt interest. "You don't use any of the horseradish or cocktail sauce."

"The better to taste the oyster."

She followed his example on her second one and made a delicious sound, half moan, half murmur of agreement. Chase caught himself wishing they were somewhere private so he could take their earlier kiss further. He resisted the urge to dig the heels of his hands into his eyes and wipe away the image of them naked and writhing against each other.

What was wrong with him? Was he really thinking about sleeping with Teagan? The ache in his body was impossible to ignore. He wanted her more than he remembered wanting any other woman. The shock of it frustrated him. He needed to keep his head in this game. He owed it to Ethan and his mother to make sure his interaction with Teagan didn't blow up in their faces.

Even though he had no idea what exactly could go wrong, he knew becoming physically involved with her would put stress on their working relationship. And how could he explain to Ethan that he'd fallen under her spell?

"Thank you for bringing me here," Teagan said.

"There are a lot of restaurants in Charleston that serve outstanding seafood dishes."

"I'd love to visit a few of your favorites with you." She slid him a hopeful look.

A warning bell sounded, but as Chase spent more and

more time in her company, he found the alarm easier to mute. "I think we can make that happen."

Her eyes flared as if she hadn't expected him to agree. A second later, she seemed to give the matter more thought. "This is lovely and you're being an exceptional escort, but I do have to ask if the only reason you invited me is because of the favor you're doing for Ethan."

He knew what she was getting at. With the chemistry between them taking on a life of its own over the last week, she'd shared a lot about her background and life in New York. Bottom line, she was far more complex and sensitive than she showed the world. As to whether this would lead him to trust her, Chase had yet to figure out.

"I did make a promise," he said, ducking the answer she wanted.

"And that's all there is to it?" Teagan's intent gaze probed his expression, digging for reassurance.

"No."

His grudging answer prompted relief to flicker across her expression. The momentary vulnerability disappeared so fast he wondered if he'd imagined it.

"I'm very attracted to you," she murmured, "and I want us to get to know each other better, but I wouldn't want to make the mistake of getting between you and Ethan."

The idea that he would have to choose between her and Ethan hadn't occurred to him until this moment. Nor did he think the decision would be all cut-and-dried. The more time he spent with Teagan, the more fascinated he became. Who knew what would happen after a long renovation?

"If you behave yourself," he reminded her, "there won't be any problems."

At his words a wicked smile curved her luscious lips. "What fun is it to behave myself?"

Chase breathed a sigh of relief at her quicksilver return to flirting. She was bossy and sure-footed when it came to manipulating the people around her. Serious, reflective Teagan was dangerous to his self-preservation. "Maybe if you avoid meddling with your family, we could avoid future disagreements."

"But then you wouldn't be tasked to keep an eye on me." Her palm made contact with his thigh once more. "And I think you like what's happening between us."

Her touch was just as unsettling this time around. In fact, he was finding it difficult to concentrate on anything except his thundering pulse. With the urge to kiss her growing too sharp to ignore, he set his fingers beneath her chin and coaxed her upper body closer.

"It pains me to say this." He brushed her lips with his. Excitement sparked at the glancing touch and he savored the sweet pain. "But you might be right."

Dressed in pastel workout gear, Teagan stood on the screened second-floor back terrace of her grandfather's mansion and listened to the sounds of feminine voices coming from the pool behind the house. Several times a week her cousins joined Ethan's future sister-in-law Lia in the morning for an hour of paddleboard yoga. Prior to falling out with her cousins, she'd often joined the trio and basked in the easy camaraderie. But once her relationship with her biological family cooled, Teagan had felt unwelcome and stopped going.

It wasn't like her to retreat after a setback, but she'd had such optimism about becoming part of the Watts family. Unfortunately, her New York style of getting what she wanted didn't work in Charleston. Instead of fitting in, she'd become a pariah.

And it wasn't just her Charleston family she'd upset. The one person she'd always believed she could rely on had cut ties. Sienna hadn't deserved to become Teagan's unwilling pawn. Reflecting on every decision she'd made since coming to Charleston, Teagan recognized that a lifetime of never quite feeling as if she fit in had driven her to act badly.

She'd never allowed any of her New York friends to glimpse the insecurity that fueled her behavior. All too aware that her adoptive mother only valued her beauty and that she had no worth to her adoptive father at all, she grew up determined the world would recognize her intelligence and ambition.

Squaring her shoulders, Teagan made her way down the outside stairs to the path that led through the dense foliage of the estate's lush garden. Anxiety made her stomach churn. Teagan had made mistakes before and suffered the consequences, but she'd always brushed criticism aside. This time it was different. These people were her blood relations and she couldn't treat the rift lightly.

She shouldn't have been surprised when upon spying her coming toward them both Poppy and Dallas abandoned their yoga positions and paddled toward the pool's edge.

"Good morning," Teagan said, failing to keep the disappointment out of her tone as the twins exited the pool. "I guess I'm too late for morning yoga."

"I have to get to the salon." Poppy tossed her sister a speaking glance while wrapping a colorful sarong around her slim form. "Catch you later." She directed the remark to no one in particular, but Teagan was sure it didn't include her.

"And I have menus to finish up for tomorrow's dinner party at the Harrisons'." Dallas picked up her board and followed her sister toward the two-bedroom carriage house they shared on the estate.

During the flurry of the Shaw twins' exit, Lia had sat cross-legged on her board, a tranquil lotus floating on the turquoise pool. Now, she shot Teagan a searching look.

"I guess they still hate me," Teagan remarked, sitting on a chair by the side of the pool.

"They don't hate you," Lia corrected, getting to her feet and assuming the warrior pose. "It's just that this family is tight and very protective of each other."

Once again Teagan faced a painful truth. For all that she was a Watts by blood, she remained an outsider. "I get that and I don't really blame them for keeping their distance. I screwed up trying to mess with Ethan's future at Watts Shipping."

"Unlike most everyone else, I don't think you're solely to blame for what happened. When Ethan started getting those anonymous texts warning him about what you and Sienna might be up to, he could've discussed them with you instead of letting the whole thing become one big pointless game."

Preoccupied with her own mistakes, Teagan had never considered that Ethan had played a part in the whole debacle. "Why didn't he ask me about the texts?"

"Because he thrives on intrigue in much the same way you do."

Teagan winced. "I wouldn't say I thrive on intrigue. More like it's how I learned to cope with difficult situations. All too often I found that talent and hard work wouldn't get me what I want. So, I found alternative ways to achieve my goals."

Her social circle didn't include intimate friends. Her adoptive parents and brother weren't the emotional sort and their approval came after she'd succeeded at something. Growing up she'd equated acceptance with achievement. Receiving positive reinforcement for doing whatever it took to win had given her a skewed notion of best practices.

Her Charleston family was different. They'd welcomed her with open arms and no expectations. She hadn't had to prove her worth to them. They'd accepted her as she was.

Unfortunately, rather than embracing the supportive environment, Teagan had fallen on old habits.

"So, I've been thinking of a way to fix things with the family and to prove that I'm more than what they've seen so far. Before I came to Charleston, I'd decided to make a positive contribution to the city. I'm hoping to create transitional housing shelters for victims of domestic abuse as well as fund programs that will offer these women career training."

"That all sounds amazing. And since Dallas is getting closer to opening her restaurant, she would benefit from your business expertise."

"I'd really love to help her with that." Teagan grew more optimistic. "Any idea how to reach Poppy?"

"I think what would go furthest with her is if you reunited with your sister."

"Sure. Of course." But even as Teagan agreed, she wondered how to repair the breach in her and Sienna's relationship. "I've already reached out to her many times, but she's not quite ready to talk."

"Sounds like you two just need to get into the same room."

"With her and Ethan living in Savannah at the moment, that's even less likely to happen."

"Maybe you need some help."

"What kind of help?"

"Rumor has it you've been out with Chase Love a few times. Why don't you ask him to reach out to Ethan for you?"

"I don't know," Teagan said, cringing as she imagined proposing Lia's idea to him. "Chase is pretty anti-scheming."

"Even for a good cause?"

"Even so."

Lia looked thoughtful for a moment and then nodded.

"Well, I'm sure something else will occur to you. In the meantime, just keep coming down for morning yoga and making an effort. I'm sure they'll see that you're trying."

Following Lia's advice, Teagan reached out to her sister once more as she walked back to her bedroom. She wasn't optimistic that Sienna would answer, and wasn't surprised when she'd received no response in the time it took her to shower, dress and head to her favorite coffee shop.

Since it was Saturday and she had no plans for the day, Teagan took a detour on her way back to Grady's house. It had been not quite a week since she'd put in an offer on the Calloway house and she grew more anxious to hear back from the seller with each hour that passed.

She didn't need to get into the house; the memory of the tall ceilings and beautiful original fixtures were embedded in her mind. Instead, she wandered past the main house and into the back courtyard where an old wrought iron bench had been left to rust. She sat and gazed around the overgrown landscaping, imagining the azaleas trimmed, flower beds bursting with vibrant plants and the brick walkways restored. With a fountain offering trickling music, the space would become a soothing sanctuary for women who had not known much peace, and a playground for their young children.

Her thoughts turned to the man who would bring her vision to life.

Chase Love continued to confound her. And damn, if that didn't make him more fascinating. His kiss—kisses—had done thrilling things to her insides. And when he'd admitted to wanting her, she'd nearly dragged him from the restaurant and around the corner to the nearest boutique hotel. Not that she could've manhandled him if he didn't want to go. Her nerves were still on fire wondering if he would have agreed had she asked.

Probably not. His loyalty to Ethan outweighed any desire for her. It would take time for Chase to trust her and he wouldn't advance things to the next level unless he was convinced she wouldn't burn him.

As she was rounding her car, a familiar form appeared across the street. She grinned in delight and waved.

"What are you doing here?" Chase asked, heading in her direction.

"I might ask you the same question," she countered with a mischievous smile. "I know Ethan wants you to keep an eye on me, but does it include stalking me all over Charleston?"

His gaze shifted to the Calloway house. "That's not why I'm here."

"No?" She arched a skeptical eyebrow.

For a long moment, Chase looked as if he was grappling with something. Then he gestured with his thumb toward the house directly across the street. "I live there."

Teagan couldn't believe her luck. "Seriously? Are you saying that we're going to be neighbors?" She beamed at him. "Does that mean I can pop over whenever I need to borrow a cup of sugar?"

Chase gave the matter some thought. "I'm not sure I have any sugar."

"What? Are you trying to tell me you're already sweet enough?"

"Honestly, Teagan," he exclaimed, but his exasperation seemed forced.

"Honestly, Chase." She took a step into his space and watched his nostrils flare. "You might look all tough and act all intimidating, but deep inside you're a cream puff." She set her finger against his unyielding chest and nudged. "A sweet, gooey cream puff."

He growled. "Cream puffs are not gooey."

"Maybe not, but they're sweet and my favorite dessert." She splayed her fingers over his heart and basked in the heat radiating off his sun-warmed skin. All of a sudden, she desperately wanted to be alone with him. "So, since we're about to be neighbors, don't you think you should be all neighborly and give me a tour of your house?"

His lashes flickered. "I was on my way out."

"I don't need to see the whole house." She leaned forward and whispered, "You can save your bedroom for another time."

He gave her such a stern look that she couldn't resist a giggle. The girlish sound coming out of her was a strange and marvelous thing. When it came to Chase, she never calculated what she said or how she behaved around him. Instead, she just went with her feelings of the moment and it was liberating to be herself, unshackled from others' expectations.

"Fine. A quick tour. It'll give you an idea of the quality of work I do."

They crossed the street and approached his house. The structure was long and narrow with a set of steps leading to a broad side porch and the front door. Teagan had only seconds to take in the neat boxwood planters flanking the entrance and the romantic porch swing before Chase ushered her through the double doors and into a cozy foyer.

Gleaming wide-plank heart pine floors led the way to a tranquil living room painted the palest sage green and decorated with a white sofa flanked by sapphire velvet armchairs. A dramatic seascape featuring various shades of blue and turquoise hung above the fireplace, but it was the beautiful molding details and fireplace surround that snagged her attention.

"The house was built in 1852," Chase narrated as he led the way across the hall to the large dining room and, without pausing, swept her into an enormous chef's kitchen. "At the time I bought it, this was the second-worst house on the block."

"That's certainly not the case anymore."

Although Teagan rarely fixed elaborate meals, she could see herself puttering around the big island, chopping fruit for her smoothies and assembling appetizers for happy hour on the back patio.

"I'm really in love with this kitchen. Having panels on the fridge and dishwasher gives the cabinets a seamless look. And this is…?" She smoothed her hand across the white countertop veined with gray.

"I chose quartz for its durability, but many of my clients have gone with marble."

"I can see we're going to have a lot to talk about," she told him, smiling wistfully. Design was her favorite part of the process and she couldn't wait to get going on the house across the street.

All too soon the tour was over.

For over a week now she'd been flirting madly with Chase in an effort to find out if he was attracted to her. Yet, despite how many times she'd rehearsed these words in her mind, having the opportunity to speak them caught her flat-footed.

"There's something that's been on my mind," she told him as they stood in the foyer prior to exiting the house. Her breath hitched at the risk she was about to take.

One eyebrow rose but he gave her the space to speak her mind. This was another thing she appreciated about him. He actually listened to her. She was tired of men who either monopolized the conversation with stories about themselves or bombarded her with opinions about her favorite subjects.

Still, she'd be a fool not to recognize that the two of them couldn't be more different. Yet as drawn as she was to Chase's stoic strength, she wondered if anything about her appealed to him. Sure, he'd kissed her—a couple times in fact—but never once had he taken things a step further.

Maybe she was imagining the chemistry between them and he wasn't attracted to her.

Although she was dying to touch him, she kept her hands clenched at her sides. Her hunger for Chase had built to a point where she could no longer flirt and tease in the hopes that he'd take a hint and kiss her again. The man's preferred way of communicating was blunt and direct, so maybe she needed to take the bull by the horns and speak plainly.

"I know you don't like me. Nor do you have any reason to be nice to me. But this thing between us…" Teagan was so short of breath she could barely get the words out. "The chemistry or attraction—whatever it is—I can't stop thinking about you. About *being* with you."

The confession was a wild wind that swept away Teagan's pride, leaving her bare beneath Chase's stony stare. Shivering with both terror and excitement, she scoured his implacable expression.

Boom. Boom. Boom. Please. Please. Please.

Each thunderous beat of her heart was a wordless plea for him to act. But the seconds ticked by and he remained rooted in place, fueling her anxiety. "Oh for heaven's sake," she snapped, sounding strangled and desperate. "Say something!"

"That's not a good idea."

Hysterical laughter vibrated in her throat. "You think I don't know that?"

"Ethan…wouldn't understand."

Would his loyalty to Ethan prove stronger than the heat between them? And if it did, would her longing for him fade or strengthen? Did she want Chase because she couldn't have him or did his passion for restoring historic homes make him her perfect match?

"It's between us." Teagan's heart fluttered as his eyebrows drew together. "You don't need to tell him."

"And how long do you expect me to keep it quiet?"

His question caught her off guard. "I'm sorry...?"

"What do you see happening between us?" he elaborated, his green eyes boring into her.

Unsure of his thoughts, Teagan scrambled for the answer that would satisfy him. "I thought I made that clear. You and me together in bed...or out of it. I'm not opposed to taking a few risks if that's what you're into." When her cheeky retort landed with a dull thud, Teagan pushed out a sigh. "I don't know how much clearer I can be. I want to have sex with you."

"And then what?"

"I don't know..." Teagan exhaled. Why did the man have to be so difficult? "Dinner might be nice."

Now it was Chase's turn to sigh. "I mean, where do you see this going?"

"Does it have to go anywhere?"

His scowl deepened. "So, all you're looking for is a distraction while you're in Charleston?"

Teagan's mouth dropped open. How had that been the conclusion he'd derived from her bold admission? Did he think she was some sort of mattress-hopping hedonist who used men and cast them aside?

"Why are you making this so complicated?" she grumbled. "I'm attracted to you and I think you're attracted to me. All I want is to spend some time exploring that." The way he'd forced her to explain herself was infuriating. Yet, she'd come too far to back down now. "We don't need to bring Ethan—or any other member of my family—into it." She flung up her hands in an uncharacteristically flamboyant gesture. "Look, if you're not interested, just say so and I'll never mention it again."

He was silent so long that she nearly fled in abject humiliation. What stopped her was a hot, fierce glow in his eyes that disabled her muscles and hampered her ability to move. Teagan's chest was too tight to draw a full breath so she stood before him, sipping air into her stalled lungs and growing dizzier by the moment.

"Chase—" His name on her lips was a husky plea.

Needing something solid to hold on to while her head spun, she reached out and set her fingertips on his muscular forearm.

"Fine. You want to know if I'm interested." His voice was husky, tortured even. "I'm interested."

Six

"Really?" She gasped as a quiver traveled down her lean length.

"Really."

Sparks exploded in her eyes, setting off an electrical overload of desire that sizzled and popped its way along his nerve endings. With his confession on the table between them, Chase expected her expression to reflect smug satisfaction at his agreement, but she looked more relieved than triumphant. Relieved that he hadn't rebuffed her? Was that even possible? Surely the confident Teagan Burns realized he'd been losing the battle with his libido from the moment they'd met.

When he considered the type of woman he usually dated, they were nothing like Teagan. If asked for a list of preferences, uncomplicated and sweet-natured would top his list. Teagan was multi-faceted, too clever for her own good, and provoking his discomfort energized her. Yet since their first encounter, she'd also defied his preconceived notion of her and surprised him over and over.

Chase lifted his hand and threaded his fingers through her long hair. He'd kissed her twice before, but not the way he wanted to. Not the way his body demanded. He was hungry for her. Starving. She, and only she, could put an end to this aching, empty feeling inside him.

"Then let's do this," she murmured, the intensity of her will hammering at him. "Now. Here."

Strong in her vulnerability. Determined in her desperation. She was powerful and yielding, complex and straightforward. Giving into this pull between them would end badly. Their opposite natures would eventually put them at odds. But Chase hadn't become a black belt without getting his ass kicked from time to time.

"You don't want me to take you to dinner first?" His amused tone belied the frantic need clawing at him.

She cocked her head and arched her eyebrows. "*This* is the moment you pick to show me you have a sense of humor?"

"I'm not trying to be funny."

Why was he still talking? He should just take her the way she'd asked him to. Here and now. Hard and fast against his front door and purge her from his system without making anything more of it. Instead, he was having visions of a romantic dinner at Husk, followed by a drive through the historic district. And after the anticipation had built to the shattering point, he would enjoy a long night of exploring exactly how hot she could burn.

"It's probably the genteel thing to do." She gave a husky laugh. "But there's no way I can wait that long."

As if to demonstrate just how needy she was, Teagan drove her slim body into his solid frame. Sucking in a lungful of her scent, his senses went on full alert. As he wrapped her in his arms, she lifted up on tiptoe and tunneled her fingers into his hair.

"Make love to me, Chase."

An intoxicating euphoria surged through his veins. His lips descended, claiming her mouth in a feverish kiss. A moan rose from deep inside his chest. Her slender form trembled as he pulled her close. Chase found his own body quaking as her lips parted and her tongue danced against his. The ache in his loins flared, but it was the spasm in his chest that spelled trouble.

Rational thought grew hazy as he kissed her deep and deeper still. She was a flickering flame in his arms, all heat and need. Catching fistfuls of his hair, she matched his hard kisses with fervent eagerness. Bit by bit the passion consuming him muted his doubts until there was only his blinding desire to possess her.

But not like this. Not here in his foyer. He wanted her in the middle of his bed where he'd imagined her so many times. Despite her height, she was light as a downy feather when he picked her up. Or maybe the need rampaging through him added additional fuel to his muscles. Chase took the stairs two at a time, arriving on the second-floor landing barely winded.

She wore a loose-fitting dress that he whisked over her head a second after her feet landed on his bedroom floor. Despite his heart's urgent drumming, Chase paused to look at her. Disheveled golden hair framed flushed cheeks and dancing green eyes. She smoothed her palm across his chest, no doubt to savor the frantic pounding of his heart. A slow, feline smile curved her lips.

"You look like you've never seen a woman before," she teased, reaching behind her to unfasten her bra.

"Never one like you," he breathed, his mouth going dry as she cast aside her lingerie and stood naked before him. "You're not just beautiful." He cupped her cheek, determined to soothe away the uncertainty that caused her to gnaw at her lower lip. "You're challenging and exciting one minute, and then funny and vulnerable the next. Sparring with you keeps me on my toes. I imagine the same will be said for making love with you."

She'd grown serious as he spoke, but her words remained playful. "I wouldn't want to disappoint."

He heard the plaintive call for reassurance and shook his head. "Impossible."

Her fingers traveled down the front of his shirt, plucking one button after another. Chase got to work on his belt and zipper. Soon, his clothes had joined hers on his floor. Before they came together, they stood, breathing hard, staring at each other.

"You are even more impressive without your clothes on." She smoothed the pads of her fingers across his chest while shaking her head in appreciative amazement. "I never imagined... Your chest. Your arms. Those abs." Her gaze drifted lower and one eyebrow shot up as she took in his jutting erection. "Wow." She expelled the last word in a breathless rush. "Just wow."

"You're staring at me like you've never seen a naked man before."

"I like funny Chase," she purred, taking his hand as she began easing backward. She stopped when her thighs hit the mattress and met his gaze. "He makes me feel at ease."

He cupped her breast, running his thumb across her tight nipple, and smiled when she gasped. Leaning down, he nuzzled her neck and murmured, "Want to hear the knock-knock joke Annabelle told me yesterday?"

"Later," she growled, her hand coming between them.

He'd barely recovered from the incendiary brush of her knuckles against his belly when she wrapped her long fingers around his hard length, ripping a muffled oath from him. He managed to suck in a single breath before his lungs stopped working. Closing his eyes, Chase covered her hand with his, savoring several seconds of excruciating bliss even as the wildness threatened to consume him. Gently pulling her fingers away, he pressed a lingering kiss into her palm, and then scooped her up and deposited her on the bed. He was upon her a second later, his lips riding the delicate column of her throat, nostrils drawing in her unique scent.

Her hands were busy on him, trailing fire across his shoulders, riding the terrain of his back muscles, driving her fingers into his hair. Pushing aside the siren call of her perfect breasts for the moment, Chase licked across her collarbone and nipped the strong cord in her neck.

When his lips reached her ear, he murmured, "I need you to come for me."

"I'm down for that."

Smiling at her eager response, Chase drew circles around her breast with his lips. Her body writhed in restless eagerness long before he settled his mouth over her nipple. At the same time he dusted caresses along her thigh. With each advancing inch of his fingertips, her quaking grew.

"Chase…"

Her breath came in shallow pants as he reached the place where her thighs came together. Moving with great care, he parted her feminine folds, seeking her wetness. Her lashes floated down as he slid his finger into her slippery heat, and he imagined how she would feel when he drove into her. Her hips bucked as he grazed her clit and circled it, paying attention to what made her moan, the hitches in her breath. She ground herself against his hand, swiveling and rocking as she chased her pleasure. As much as he wanted to join her so they could come together, it was equally wonderful to watch her shatter as an orgasm tore through her.

"I'm sorry," she said, her apology shocking him. "That was really fast." Closing her thighs, she pressed his palm tight against her as the last few waves of her climax pounded her. "It's been a while…a long while and I've been thinking about you—about this—ever since we met."

No words had ever sounded so perfect. "Ah, Teagan." Reluctant delight tinged his voice. "The things you do to me."

Chase kissed her hard then, feeling her skin melt into his. Electricity crackled between them, a powerful current of energy that created an endless, glorious connection. He nibbled his way down her neck, while his fingers coasted across the glorious swell of her breasts. She moaned when he circled her nipple with his tongue, and her back bowed as she thrust herself against his mouth, silently begging him for more.

"You are perfect." His voice was a raspy murmur against her quivering abdomen as his tongue dipped into her navel before drifting across her hip bones.

"No. You are." She gasped the last word as his tongue followed the path his fingers had traveled earlier, trailing into her heat and causing her to shut her eyes and cry out. "I've already come once," she protested even as her fingers tunneled into his hair and pressed his mouth tight against her.

He liked the ravenous sounds she made. The way she offered herself to his pleasure. Her breaths came in desperate pants as he plied her with lips and tongue toward another orgasm.

"Chase," she keened his name and came hard against his mouth, growing hotter and wetter with each shattered cry. And still he kept on, settling into a rhythm she liked until her thighs spasmed and she launched into yet another climax.

Only when she lay panting and limp, her flushed face hidden behind long fingers, did he pluck a condom from the nightstand and tear it open. She lifted onto her elbows, her gaze hot and greedy as he slid it on. Noting the way she watched him, he grasped himself and gave several long, slow pumps, loving the way her eyes flared and her tongue slipped across her passion-bruised lower lip.

"Get over here, you gorgeous man," she commanded huskily, reaching for him. "I need you inside me now."

"I love a woman who knows what she wants," he said and then he was moving between her thighs, her softness yielding to his hard demand.

Her hand came between them, fingertips guiding his hard length to her soft heat. He rubbed the head of his erection against her and groaned. She set the soles of her feet on the mattress and pressed up so that he slipped a little way inside her.

"Teagan…" He kissed her and grappled with the lust raging inside him.

She skimmed her fingers over his abs and around to his back, murmuring a distracted, "Yes, Chase?"

"It's been a while for me, too."

"So take me quick and hard," she commanded in an urgent whisper. "We can take our time later."

Her fingernails sank into his naked butt, the sharp pain driving him into her. Intense pleasure shot up his spine. He hadn't realized he'd closed his eyes until a meteor shower blazed across his mind. A curse exploded from his lips as she laughed with pleasure. The joyful sound was almost as amazing as being inside her. She wriggled beneath him, tipping her hips to take him deeper.

He held himself suspended in her heat for several seconds until the raging in his blood reduced to a manageable simmer. Despite her urging to make this first time hot and fast, he wanted to make it perfect for her. With her lips against his ear, murmuring wicked phrases, he began to move inside her. Despite the need clawing at his body, Chase refused to yield his control. He wasn't going to take anything from her when all he wanted to do was to give.

So, he harnessed the discipline he'd learned through years of martial arts training and thrust into her with smooth, even strokes while remaining focused on the cues her body offered. The sounds she made, her moans, the staccato exhalations and the encouraging words spilling from her lips that told him to speed up, slow down or drive harder.

He wasn't surprised that she knew what she liked and how to get it. She'd always been direct. In bed it was no different. The way she wrapped her legs around his waist and held herself tight against him drove him toward his own explosive orgasm. He loved how she rocked and ground against him while sexy, helpless noises erupted from her lips.

With his own pleasure building into a smoking volcano, he could no longer tell if his lungs were working properly. They surged together, finding a frantic pace that stripped them down to male and female. There was no more Teagan and Chase. Only hands and skin, heat and friction.

Sweat broke out on his skin as lust began to short-circuit his brain. He had to hold on. She was so close. But he was closer.

Chase ground his teeth and growled, "Come for me."

"You first."

Damn the stubborn woman.

"Come now, Teagan." He slid his hand beneath her butt and held her as he slammed into her.

She emitted a startled moan as the first ripple of her climax took hold of her. With his last thread of willpower, he held off his release for a few frantic heartbeats so he could watch her come. He wanted to imprint the memory of her eyes glazing over and the transformation of her face as her expression shifted from focused concentration to euphoria. He'd never seen a woman surrender to pleasure like that and it was only then, amidst this moment of profound intimacy, that he allowed himself to be swept off the cliff into his own concussive orgasm.

In the aftermath, Chase lay on his back, staring at the ceiling while Teagan's breath puffed against his chest. The contentment spreading through his body left him grappling with the consequences of letting Teagan in. He knew better than to trust her and recognized that any relationship with her wouldn't be easy.

But this woman shared his passion for restoration and in bed she'd proved both bold and enthusiastic. He recognized that his appetite for her was a deep well that might never run dry.

The stark, terrifying reality was that Teagan Burns was his match in every way, the partner he never knew he needed and the dream girl he'd never seen coming.

During the days following his first night with Teagan, Chase noticed himself falling deeper beneath her spell. Thoughts of her consumed him during the day when he was supposed to be working, and at night he spent endless hours with her in his bed, learning every inch of her skin, what drove her wild and the limitless power of their passion for each other.

He should've been glad that she'd headed off to New York to deal with some issues that had arisen in her absence. Time apart was the ideal solution to his bewitchment. Distance would allow his head to clear and reason to reassert itself.

Instead, he'd been plagued by a raging ache for her kisses and a gut-churning loneliness that only her intoxicating presence eased. The lingering scent of her on his sheets and his discovery of a pair of her black lace panties beneath his bed kept memories of her fresh in his mind. As did the rapid-fire exchange of text messages that began when he woke and continued long into the night. She'd invaded his life so seamlessly that it seemed impossible that they'd known each other less than two weeks.

On the morning of the third day without Teagan, Chase was on a job site when his phone rang. Excusing himself from the general contractor, he answered the call.

"Where are you?" Sawyer asked, sounding tense and unhappy.

"The Carlson job."

"Is that the one on Montague?"

"Yes."

"I'm five minutes away."

She hung up on him before Chase had a chance to ask her what was wrong. At least he didn't have to wait long for the explanation. He had just enough time to wrap up the final punch list items before her car arrived at the curb.

Sawyer exited her car and waited for him on the sidewalk. As he approached, he noticed the way her appreciative gaze trailed over the updated facade. "Wow, that looks amazing."

"Thank you. So, what's up?"

"We might have a problem."

"You've just described my average day," he quipped, realizing Teagan's habitual bantering was rubbing off on him. "What's happened?"

"There's another offer on the Calloway property."

"Damn!" Chase's gut tightened at this unwelcome news.

"I know. Crazy, right?"

"Crazy," Chase echoed, thinking of all the months it had sat on the market when Rufus had tried to sell it before. "And unexpected. It's never stirred anyone's interest before and now there are two people vying for it."

"It is surprising," Sawyer agreed.

Rufus had a knack for ruining perfectly sound businesses by throwing money at inventive opportunities that never worked out, which was why he was once again keen to sell the Calloway house. It was also why a lucrative offer might override his determination to do right by a house that had once been in his family.

Chase visualized a worst-case scenario. If Teagan didn't get the house, there was a real possibility that his mother's ancestral home might go to someone who only saw the value in the large lot in the heart of downtown Charleston. Maybelle would be devastated if the home was destroyed.

"Have you told Teagan?" Chase asked, imagining her disappointment.

"I called, but she didn't pick up, so I left a message." Sawyer looked worried. "She put in a solid offer—above asking—so I think she should be okay, but I thought if she also wrote a letter explaining how she wants to offer the three houses on the property to at-risk women that he might be swayed to let her have the house."

"Do you think it will work?" Chase didn't want to come off as pessimistic, but his cousin had never been particularly altruistic. If the other offer was stronger than Teagan's, they ran the risk of losing the property.

Teagan's passion for the project had intensified Chase's already keen enthusiasm. Two years ago, Rufus had put the house on the market and Chase had envisioned securing the property and undertaking an extensive renovation. When Rufus realized Chase and his family were the only interested parties, he'd cancelled the listing. Since then, Chase felt as if he had a vested interest in seeing that the renovation was done to his exacting standards. In addition, because the house was across the street from his own home, he'd be constantly aggravated if the construction was subpar.

"Time will tell," Sawyer said. "Rufus might be swayed by a generous offer, but I can't imagine anyone paying more than what Teagan offered." She held her hands palm up in a helpless gesture.

"Does he know she intends to work with me?"

"Not that I know of. It might help if you avoided her until we're under contract, but given what Ethan wants you to do that seems impossible."

"I'm really between a rock and a hard place on this whole affair," Chase grumbled, wondering how his life had gotten so complicated when all he'd thought to do this summer was be left in peace to complete his current projects and prepare for the Carolopolis Awards. "Do you think you could find out who the other buyer is?"

Although offers were usually anonymous, sometimes an agent dropped a little tidbit about their client. Chase was alive with curiosity and concern.

"Funny you should ask…" Sawyer gave him a sly smile. "Rufus listed the property with a guy who works out of the same brokerage as Emmett." Emmett Morris was Sawyer's second cousin and if anyone could persuade him to reveal juicy tidbits it was her. "I thought you might be interested in listening in as I give him a call."

Chase leaned against the hood of Sawyer's car and crossed his arms. "Let's do it."

"I was hoping you'd say that." Sawyer must've been just as worked up about the competitive offer as Chase because her body hummed with a jittery energy as she cued up a number and put the phone on speaker.

"Hey, cuz." Emmett's nasally tenor sounded genuinely happy to hear from Sawyer. "How are things with you?"

"On the whole, pretty good. How about you?"

"We're in real estate, darlin'. It's a mad mad world. But you know that."

"I do." Both cousins chuckled. "Hey, look, I was wondering if you could help me out. I have a client who put in an offer on Rufus Calloway's old place."

"I heard. Although I can't imagine why anyone, much less two anyones, would be interested in that eyesore."

Sawyer shot an apologetic glance Chase's way, but he merely waved off her concern.

"I can't speak for the other interested party, but my buyer has been looking for a historic home in need of work. She's dying to restore the property and turn the cottages out back into transitional housing for domestic abuse victims."

"Phil-an-thro-py," Emmett declared and Chase could imagine him nodding enthusiastically. "I can get behind that."

"So, you can see why she's freaked out that someone else is interested in the property. Is there anything you know about the other buyer?"

"Not much. I did hear that the guy's from New York, though."

This news gave Chase a jolt. He would've preferred someone local who could appreciate the home's value was not just in the location, but also its history. What were the chances that someone else from New York would be as passionate about restoration as Teagan?

"Wow! New York. That's where my buyer's from, too." Sawyer turned a confused look on Chase. "Who would've guessed that the Calloway property would entice buyers from so far away?"

"I don't know why you're surprised," Emmett said. "Seems like there's more and more outside money moving into Charleston every month."

And to Chase's mind, not always for the better. He worried that in their determination to occupy one of the prestigious historic homes in and around downtown Charleston that outsiders would fail to appreciate the artisan details as well as the dings and flaws that represented the home's long history. How many heart pine floors had been torn up to make way for manufactured hardwood or original fixtures tossed out as contemporary bathrooms were added?

"As I mentioned, my client is interested in restoring the

property," Sawyer continued. "I don't suppose you have any sense what the other party intends to do."

"I didn't hear, but I can dig into it a bit if you want."

Sawyer raised her eyebrows at Chase and he nodded.

"It would be great if you could."

"I do know one thing. The other offer was really good."

Higher than what Teagan had offered? This didn't bode well. If Rufus was seeing dollar signs, he might be blind to what would become of his great-aunt Maybelle's childhood home.

"Over asking?" Sawyer prompted.

"Definitely."

Chase recalled Teagan's hungry gaze as she'd toured the property. He'd recognized that look. It reflected his own eagerness every time he took a project from disastrous to dynamic. In his career he'd taken a lot of risks. Not all of them had paid off financially, but the satisfaction in a job well done had outweighed the hit to his bottom line.

He eyed Sawyer as she ended the call. "What do you think?"

"I don't want to be pessimistic," she replied, her blue-grey eyes clouded with worry. "But this could be a problem."

Seven

On the third day of her New York visit, Teagan met her mother in their fashion line's design studio.

"Well, it's about time you came home," her mother said, not attempting to sugar-coat her displeasure.

Was New York home? Teagan wasn't sure anymore. More and more and despite the mess she'd made, she envisioned her future in Charleston. It's where her birth mother had grown up and the city was steeped in her family's history.

And then there was Chase. She'd never known anyone like him. After only two days in New York, she missed him terribly. He'd surprised her as a lover, demonstrating that fierce passion simmered beneath his flinty demeanor. Given how he'd resisted her in the beginning and made it clear that he wasn't keen on being attracted to her, once he'd decided to surrender to the incandescent chemistry between them, he'd given her everything.

Her skin tingled as she recalled his impassioned groans

and delighted sighs as his powerful body had driven her to the stars. Each time he'd been so tuned into her every need. His consideration had only increased her desire and made her appreciate him all the more.

Never before Chase had Teagan been with a man who cherished her. Feeling safe had allowed her to be vulnerable with him and their deep intimacy transformed her.

"We need to talk about the designs for our Spring line," her mother said, referring to the clothing company they'd started the year Teagan turned thirteen.

While the line bore Teagan's name and the designs were shaped by her creativity, Anna Burns was the driving force behind the company—especially in the early years when Teagan just wanted to be photographed and admired wearing pretty clothes.

"Of course," Teagan agreed. "And while we're discussing it, I wanted to let you know that I plan on opening a boutique in Charleston."

Her mother made a derisive sound. "Why?"

"My roots are in Charleston and I intend to establish myself there." The fervent declaration surprised her until Teagan realized that she spoke with her whole heart.

"Your mother left Charleston," Anna reminded her. "She came to New York to establish herself here. Why would you want to go backwards?"

Teagan didn't consider embracing her Charleston roots to be a step backwards. "I have family there."

"I thought we were your family."

"You are." Uttering those two words didn't reverse the way Teagan had been feeling since learning her father had no intention of turning the family business over to a girl he'd adopted. "But they are, too. And I want to get to know them better."

Anna Burns sniffed. "You have a life here. Businesses. Responsibilities. Friends. Why are you wasting your time in Charleston?"

"I don't feel like I'm wasting my time." But she hadn't exactly been successful thus far. Still, running back to Manhattan with her tail between her legs wasn't the answer either. She'd learn from her failures and avoid making the same mistakes.

In her heart of hearts she knew that she had gone down to Charleston in the hope of winning everyone to her side. She wanted to be embraced as one of them, and though she'd made a mess of things, she just needed a little more time to fix what she'd broken.

The Calloway house was a symbol of this next step. She would take something broken and bring it back to life. And in the process, she would prove she belonged in Charleston. A year from now she would be hosting friends and family and aiding women who needed help. Her vision left her feeling satisfied and at peace, a very different sensation than she'd known until now.

In New York she was constantly vying for the limelight. Even her most charitable moments were captured and posted for the world to see. It left Teagan wondering if she was actually doing good or just looking as if she was doing good for the cameras. She wanted more substance in her life.

The urge to pick up her phone and call Chase seized her while Anna was showing her swatches of the fabric under consideration. Everything about him appealed to her. Despite their rocky start, was she thinking the way she was because of how he challenged her? Or was he influencing her by just being who he was?

Swept by the need to connect with him, she composed and sent a text.

How are the revised plans for the house coming?

She'd taken a business tone with him because what she really wanted to ask him terrified her. Did he miss her?

Because her body ached for him. She was now seeing her future through fresh eyes, and that future included more days and nights with Chase. Her blood sang its need to feel his breath warming her skin, for his hands to grip and guide her body to the most acute pleasure she'd ever experienced.

To her astonishment, he replied almost immediately.

I spent last night making the changes you requested.

This filled her with a significant amount of delight.

So you were thinking about me last night. That sounds nice.

This was the exact sort of flirtation that annoyed him, but she was starting to think that despite his grumbling, he might like it a little. In any case, the flirtation was a terrific way to mask her fear of his rejection.

I think I've included everything we talked about.

Always the professional. Suddenly, she wanted to rattle his calm and get past his walled exterior. His kisses told her that he wasn't as unaffected as he acted most of the time. That her touch drove him wild. That their sexual chemistry was mutual. Just the thought excited her because her insides fluttered with delight whenever he was near. She was good at reading people and couldn't reconcile how he could seem so unaffected and then kiss her with such exquisite fervor.

I've been missing you.

Sending such a revealing declaration was a risk, but as she'd learned long ago, no risk, no reward. Still, she felt like her heart had shrunk to the size of a pea before he responded.

You've been on my mind a lot. When are you coming back to Charleston?

It wasn't a declaration of undying affection, but for someone like Chase, admitting even this much must've been difficult. And that he wanted a return date made her eager to complete her business and rush back to him.

Since it's obvious we can't stand to be apart, I'm going to cut my trip short. I'll be back the day after tomorrow.

Another lengthy pause followed her text. Was he regretting giving her a glimpse into his psyche? Her hammering heart left her breathless as she awaited his reply.

Send me your flight information and I'll pick you up.

This response leveled Teagan. She never imagined he would put himself out for her. Part of her knew that it was probably his Southern manners taking over, but another more hopeful part of her wanted to trust that he had feelings for her.

Thank you. I'll let you know when I have the information.

She wondered if this was too cool a response, but then he replied with a thumbs-up emoji and she was enchanted all over again. Damn the man for surprising her at every turn. She might've been able to keep her wits about her if he hadn't demonstrated such adorable gallantry.

"Teagan!"

Her mother's impatient call snapped Teagan out of her

reverie. She quickly scanned the designs and fabrics before making her selections. In five minutes she'd determined the spring line and aimed a smile at her mother.

"There," she said. "That should be a wonderful collection. Don't you think?"

Without waiting for Anna to agree, Teagan picked up her purse and headed for the door. She had two more stops to make and several appointments to cancel since she'd decided to cut her trip short.

As she pushed through the building's main entrance and made her way across the sidewalk to hail a cab, a limo glided to a stop before her. A darkened window lowered in dramatic fashion, revealing the sculpted lines of Declan Scott's smug face.

"Are you stalking me?" she demanded, hiding her disquiet behind sarcasm.

Why could she never seem to anticipate Declan's moves? Each time he caught her off guard was a skirmish he won and she was so weary of losing to him all the time.

"Let's just say you make it very easy to bump into you."

Teagan knew at once what he meant. Her Instagram account. She tried to tag the local restaurants and shops as much as possible to give the businesses she visited some social media exposure. As she'd arrived at the design studio, she'd paused in the foyer to take a selfie beside the Teagan Burns fashion logo in order to stimulate interest in their upcoming fall collection.

"If I'd known you were using it to track me, I would've stopped broadcasting my location." She leveled an unfriendly glower at him. "Don't you have things to do? Why are you here hassling me?"

"I signed some paperwork for a new property I intend to acquire and thought you might be interested in having a drink with me to celebrate."

"Let me guess, you found another historic gem in Midtown that you can't wait to tear down."

"It is historic, but I wouldn't exactly call it a gem." Declan paused for a beat. "And it's quite a bit farther south than Midtown."

Teagan noted Declan's smug satisfaction and braced herself for the blow. They'd engaged in enough skirmishes over the years for her to recognize that he was holding a winning hand.

"Good luck with it."

With those parting words, she pivoted and headed off to hail a taxi. She hadn't taken more than two steps before she heard the sound of a car door slamming behind her. A moment later, Declan caught her arm and spun her to face him.

"I don't have time for this," she ground out, shaking off his hand. "I'm late for an appointment." A lie, but he wasn't listening to her anyway.

"Come have a drink with me." The predatory glee in his eyes made Teagan grind her teeth. "Aren't you at all curious about the property I'm so eager to buy?"

"Not in the least."

"You should be."

His dark warning made her shiver. "I'm no longer interested in New York real estate. I'm shifting my focus to Charleston."

"So am I."

The malice on Declan's face sent her anxiety spiking through the roof. She stared at him with rising dread.

"What do you mean?" But she was pretty sure she'd already figured it out.

"Turns out that you are not the only buyer interested in the Calloway property."

Ruthless, arrogant bastard.

"You…" Any further words were strangled by a massive lump forming in her throat.

"Rufus Calloway was very excited about my offer." He paused to let that sink in before twisting the knife. "It's double the asking price."

"I can match that," she told him. "And I'll let him know that I plan to offer the three cottages on the property as transitional housing for domestic abuse victims."

"I'm sure you'll write a charming letter detailing all the good you plan to do for Charleston, but I'm guessing Calloway won't give a damn about your sentimental blathering."

Teagan's heart gave a desperate lurch. "You don't know that."

"Also," Declan added, acting as if he hadn't heard her, "I considered the possibility that you might try to outbid me so I let him know that you are colluding with Chase Love and intend to turn around and sell the house to him and his mother."

"That's not true." The urge to scream tore at her throat.

"Isn't it? From what I've heard you two have gotten quite close. Why wouldn't you sell your boyfriend the property his mother has been after for years?"

The thought that Declan had been spying on her and Chase made Teagan sick, but she couldn't let Declan know that he'd upset her.

Pushing down all her anxiety, Teagan summoned her best nonchalant shrug and met his gaze. "While I will admit I was quite taken with the Calloway property, it isn't the only property in Charleston that will work. I'll find another. And if you go after that one, I'll seek out another. You're going to spend a lot of time and money beating me out of every single house I look at."

"But I don't need to beat you out of every property. I just need to beat you out of this one. Because it's rather significant to your new lover, isn't it?"

Of course. Declan had done his research. No doubt he knew exactly how important the house was to Chase. Once again Declan had struck at someone Teagan cared about in order to get at her.

"Just sell me the Brookfield Building, Teagan. And prevent your boyfriend's family home from being razed to the ground."

"You can't do that," she cried, panic getting the best of her as she imagined what a waste that would be.

"I can and I will." Declan gave a merciless laugh. "I told you what it will take for me to leave you alone."

"Edward never sold you the Brookfield Building and I won't either." Brave words, but could she really afford to keep the promise she'd made to her dead father?

"Edward," Declan scoffed. "You don't seriously think he gave a damn about you, do you?"

For a panicked moment, Teagan wondered if Declan knew the true nature of her connection to Edward Quinn. He could do a lot of damage with that information.

"Edward left you the building because he filled your head with ridiculous notions of saving Manhattan's architectural gems. And he knew you were one of the few people brave enough to take me on."

Even through her relief, Declan's words lashed at her, exacerbating the insecurity she'd grappled with since learning Edward was her father. Of course he hadn't cared for her. If he had, he would have claimed her. Instead, she suspected he'd been the one who'd arranged for her to be adopted by the Burns family. Had he known about Ava's family in Charleston? If he had, would he have returned her to the Watts family? What would her life have been like if she had grown up surrounded by her Charleston relatives, loved and appreciated? Teagan couldn't help but think she would've been a completely different person. Someone worthy of love.

"Well, you're right on one account," Teagan said, all too aware that if Declan didn't get his way, he would hound her all the rest of her days. "I am more than happy to take you on."

"Maybe for the moment." Declan looked utterly unruffled by her challenge. "But will you still feel the same after I've taken everything away from you?"

The disquiet that had plagued Chase during Teagan's absence was replaced by rumbling pleasure as she strolled through the sliding glass Arrivals door and headed straight to where he stood beside his SUV. The unbridled pleasure of her smile the instant she spotted him awakened a familiar hunger in him.

As soon as she drew within arm's reach, he stepped forward, wrapped his arm around her and claimed her lips in a sizzling kiss that betrayed just how much he'd missed her. She kissed him back with equal enthusiasm, proclaiming her own delight at their reunion. They were both breathing raggedly by the time he broke off the kiss. He surveyed her flushed cheeks with satisfaction as he escorted her into the passenger seat before stowing her carry-on.

He'd barely merged onto the interstate, heading south toward downtown, when he asked, "Are you available to have lunch with my mother?"

"But we've only been dating a couple of weeks." Teagan widened her eyes in a dramatic fashion while a sassy half smile teased at the corner of her lips. "Isn't it a little soon to bring me home?"

Despite knowing she was playing with him, Chase's gut tightened. He reminded himself that they weren't dating. A couple of dinners and the fact that he couldn't keep his hands or his lips to himself didn't mean anything romantic was happening between them. He was simply doing his best friend a favor by taking her out. As for all the fantastic sex... That was a little harder to justify. After all, Teagan was a beautiful, seductive woman who flirted with him at every opportunity. And he was a red-blooded male with little immunity. In fact, the only thing that cooled his libido was when he questioned whether her scheming ways were a thing of the past.

So what explanation could he rally for how he'd missed talking to her this past week while she was in New York? With her absent from Charleston, he should've been able to focus completely on work. Instead, he'd caught his attention straying too often to his phone, as if he could manifest a call or text from Teagan.

"She wants to talk to you about the Calloway house," Chase said, his chaotic thoughts making his tone brusque. "And your plans for the property."

"Did you tell her about the other offer?" Teagan asked, her voice suddenly low and tight.

"I mentioned that someone else has shown interest in the property." Chase tried to keep tension out of his voice as he added, "The other buyer is from New York."

"Sawyer mentioned that." Teagan stiffened a bit, then huffed out a laugh. "I guess I'm not the only one who thinks Charleston is a great investment."

"Of course. We get a lot of people from out of town interested in obtaining property in the downtown area," he said. "It's just that the renovation on the Calloway property is a major undertaking. You'd think they'd want something that carried less risk."

Though her expression was tight, Teagan gave a single-shoulder shrug. "It's an amazing property in a wonderful neighborhood."

Something about her demeanor was off. Chase couldn't quite put his finger on it. He suspected she was worried that she might lose the Calloway property, yet she was covering it up with false bravado. She might just be trying to ease his concerns or convince herself to remain optimistic.

"So, lunch with your mom," she declared in overly bright tones. "When did you have in mind?"

"Does tomorrow work for you?"

"I'm free. But will it work for you?"

Her question confused him. "What do you mean?"

"I'm only asking because you refused to have lunch with me when we first met," she said. "Claiming that you were too busy."

"Why are you assuming I'd be there?"

He often used work as an excuse to avoid social situations, but Teagan was the first person to call him out on it.

"You couldn't possibly allow me to meet your mother alone." She knew him too well.

"It's lunch with my mother," he said, giving in. "I always make time for her."

"Seems like you make time for all the women in your life. Your sister. Your nieces. Your mother."

She hummed with approval, but it was her knowing smile as she deliberately didn't include herself in the list that caused his heartbeat to skip. Because he was making time for her in his life. A great deal of time.

"It's the way I was raised."

"And one of the things I find most attractive about you." Her gaze did a slow, heated tour of his body, leaving little doubt what else she liked about him.

Usually when women flirted with him, Chase found the frivolous banter tiresome. He preferred his conversations straightforward. Having a meaningful dialog that exchanged opinions or shared facts or stories was more up his alley.

In Teagan's case, he suspected that she recognized his disdain for small talk and was pushing his buttons. The more he dug in and refused to answer in kind, the brighter her smiles and more provocative her words. She was a vexing woman, yet he couldn't shed his craving to be with her.

"So, lunch?" he growled at her.

"Tell your mother I'd love to," Teagan said, abruptly serious. "What time will you pick me up?"

Chase frowned at her. Why was she interpreting lunch with his mother to discuss the Calloway house as anything other than a business meeting? "I thought maybe we could meet there."

"Come now," she teased. "What happened to your Southern manners? Your mother invited me to lunch. Obviously, she's curious about the woman you've been seeing. Don't you think you should pick me up?"

"I might be coming from a job site and..." Chase knew if he overreacted, she would've won. "Fine," he grumbled. "I'll pick you up at twelve fifteen."

"I'll be waiting."

And she was. He arrived promptly at the time they'd arranged and before he'd shifted his SUV into park outside the front door of her grandfather's mansion, she was descending the curved front steps. With his gaze riveted on her, Chase exited the vehicle and raced to open the passenger door. She seemed to enjoy his chivalry as much as he enjoyed treating her like his special lady.

"How do I look?" Her green eyes sparkled demurely up at him from beneath her long lashes.

Today she wore a fluttery floral dress in peach tones with a purse and strappy heels to match. It was the perfect outfit to dine with his mother. Maybelle was going to love her. Curse it all.

"My mother will be enchanted," he declared in matter-of-fact tones as he gestured her into the passenger seat.

"And you?" Teagan stepped into his space, bringing with her the scent of jasmine. Her fingertips rested lightly on his forearm and the warmth of her seared through his fine cotton shirt. "Have I enchanted you as well?"

A slight catch in her soft voice tickled his nerve endings. It was all Chase could do not to wrap his arm around her waist and demonstrate her powerful effect on him. This was just another version of the same game. He couldn't be bamboozled by her change in tactics.

"Does it matter?" he countered, drowning in the need to cup her flushed cheek and revisit the delicious texture of her lips, the soft moans she made when he took her lower lip between his teeth. "It's my mother you need to impress."

"But it's you that I dressed for." Her fingers clutched at his sleeve. There was no flirtation in her manner, just openness and honesty. "I want you to find me attractive."

"You already know I do," he said slowly as if he could somehow avoid the trap she'd laid for him. "You are the most beautiful woman I've ever seen."

She sighed and looked disappointed. "I think if I was an original marble fireplace, you'd be more enthusiastic."

He almost smiled at that. She knew him too well.

"You know you're beautiful," he said. "Why does my describing you that way disagree with you?"

"Because beauty isn't enough." Abruptly, she let her hand fall away from his arm. "When I said I want you to find me attractive, I mean that you find *me* attractive. Not just the exterior but what's in here and here." She pointed to her head and her heart. "I can't take credit for being beautiful. My drive, intelligence and ability to make things happen has always played second to my pretty face and blonde hair."

Her passionate declaration enabled Chase to better understand what drove her. "If you want me to value what's inside you, then why don't you stop toying with me?"

Teagan's eyes went wide and Chase wondered if he'd been too blunt. A second later, she burst out laughing. "So, what I'm hearing from you is that you'd like me to be more direct?"

Why did he feel as if he'd stepped from the frying pan into the fire? "It would help if I knew what was going on in that beautiful head of yours."

"I'll think about that," Teagan said, actually sounding as if she meant it. "In the meantime, why don't we head to your mother's house for lunch. I don't want to make a bad impression by being late."

Minutes later, as they walked hand in hand up the steps that led to his mother's broad front porch, Teagan grew more somber. In fact, she looked positively grim.

"Relax." He gave her hand a gentle squeeze. My mother said she's been looking forward to seeing you for a while now. She approves of what you want to do with the Calloway property."

"She won't mind that I want to use it to help women in need?"

"That's part of why she's so delighted to have you developing the property."

"I'm glad to hear it. I imagine she's very disappointed that she can't buy the house herself."

"My mother is equal parts determined and practical. She was willing to do whatever we could to buy the house from Rufus. But she's not taking things to unreasonable extremes. She'd rather the home be purchased by someone who can appreciate it."

Teagan's gaze suddenly averted, but not before Chase spotted a flicker of something that triggered his uneasiness. He knew that she was accustomed to going it alone and that in times of stress, she regressed into familiar patterns. He could only hope that she wasn't concocting some mad plan that might blow up in their faces.

"What if I don't get it?" Teagan's voice was so soft it was almost a whisper. Her eyes held a haunted anxiety when she finally looked at him. "Will your mother hate me?"

It was a sign of her strength and her willingness to be vulnerable with him that she was able to voice her fears.

Moved, Chase reached out a hand to cup her cheek. "She could never hate you for something out of your control. Real estate is a tough business. Especially in a market like this one. And dealing with Rufus is tricky. My mother understands that."

Seeing that his reassuring words hadn't had their desired effect, he wrapped his other arm around her waist and pulled her close. Dipping his head, he captured her lips in a searing kiss that made the world fall away. Her hands dug into his back as she returned the kiss with blazing heat. They stood that way on the shady porch until someone cleared their throat.

Chase was breathing hard as he broke off the kiss. Glancing toward his mother's housekeeper, he noted her fond grin and offered her a cheeky wink.

"Your mother's been asking after you," she said, her voice dripping with amusement. "Shall I tell her you need a few more minutes so you can...wrap this up?"

"Oh, no," Teagan exclaimed, breaking free from Chase and running her hands along her skirt. "I mean we can certainly finish...our conversation later."

"Of course. Come in."

Chase was grinning broadly as he set his hand into the small of Teagan's back and escorted her across the threshold. Seeing the always-in-control Teagan Burns flustered was something he relished.

The housekeeper escorted them into the living room where his mother was busily typing on her smartphone. As he crossed the room with Teagan, Maybelle set the phone down and rose to greet them. His mother wore a linen suit in pale rose with a silk floral scarf around her neck. She ran an appraising look over the new arrivals before giving an approving nod.

"You must be Teagan," his mother said, holding out both hands in welcome. "My son is quite taken with you."

Although Chase wished his mother hadn't led with that, he had to agree that was the case.

"I don't know if he's taken with me." Teagan took his mother's hands in hers, looking pleased. "But I do believe I've convinced him to like me a little."

Maybelle shot her son a sharp glance. "Oh, I think he likes you more than a little. Especially given the clinch I saw on my front porch."

Chase sensed that if Teagan's hands had been free they would've been clapped over her burning cheeks. His own skin had grown uncomfortably warm. Well, what did he expect when he'd kissed Teagan like that at his mother's front door? And of course Maybelle would be avidly curious about the woman who'd captured his interest, since his mother had given up on seeing her workaholic son fall in love.

"You have a beautiful home," Teagan said as Maybelle led the way into the dining room. "I understand helping to restore it is what triggered Chase's love of architecture."

"It certainly did. Until then I thought he was going to open a martial arts studio. He earned his black belt at age fifteen and it was all he talked about. That changed after my husband died. Even though he was only seventeen, Chase stepped up and became the man of the family."

"At such a young age." Teagan gave her head a slow, sorrowful shake.

"Yes, Chase has always been so strong. He took such good care of us during those hard times." His mother glanced his way. "He still does."

Normally Chase would be put out listening to a pair of women discussing him as if he wasn't sitting at the same table. Instead, he was oddly charmed by the way his mother and Teagan had taken to each other.

"I've seen firsthand how good he is with children," Teagan said. "Makes me wonder why he never got married and started a family of his own."

"My guess is he's been too busy working," Maybelle replied. "I think all he needs is someone who shares his passion for restoring historic homes and can jolt him out of his routines."

Maybelle's summary left Teagan looking less delighted and more like a trapped animal. Her smile didn't quite reach her eyes as she declared, "Seems like I meet both of those requirements."

"I hope so." Maybelle reached over and patted her son's hand. "I'd like to see him with someone who makes him happy."

"Especially now that Ethan's getting married," Maybelle continued. "The two of them were thick as thieves since they were young."

"It's really wonderful that my sister and Ethan found each other." Teagan's expression had grown pensive. "He makes her so happy."

"Sounds like it's just as fortunate that my great-great-grandfather's house brought you and Chase together."

"I hope so," Teagan said, glancing his way, her serious eyes assessing his thoughts on the matter. When he gave her a reassuring nod, she exhaled and offered him a tremulous smile. "I know I'm really glad it did."

Eight

"That went well," Chase remarked, his tone neutral as he drove them back to his place.

Was he worried it had gone too well?

Not since he'd first brought it up had they discussed his promise to keep an eye on her for Ethan. Was Chase anticipating their growing closeness might cause a problem between him and his best friend? A painful knot formed in her chest. Would his loyalty to Ethan wrench him away from her?

Or would her own actions be to blame?

Teagan had been vacillating between guilt and giddy euphoria at his mother's warm welcome. She knew she should tell Chase that Declan had put in the competing bid for the Calloway property, but she feared once Chase found out, he wouldn't want to have anything to do with her anymore. The thought of losing him tore at her.

Except for her quick trip to New York City, they'd spent every night together. She'd never fallen for anyone this fast.

She was consumed with Chase. His powerful body had become her playground, all those delicious muscles a never-ending source of blissful delights. She melted every time he held her face with his tender fingers and kissed her. And she relished how they spent hours necking on his couch, their hands sliding over clothes, letting anticipation build as they learned what each other liked. They were slowly forging a connection that went beyond lust or physical need, and with every day that ticked by, Teagan fell harder.

Which made her dread the looming storm on the horizon all that much more. Meeting his mother today had brought all her fears to the surface. Past experience told her to bury her agitation. She would just have to fix what was going on with Declan and keep Chase and his family from discovering the danger to their ancestral home. Would she be able to figure out how to best Declan before the truth came out and her tranquil little world became a hurricane of accusation and blame?

There was only one answer. She had to.

"I really like your mother," she said, forcing her thoughts back to Declan's comment.

"She likes you, too."

His opinion made her jubilant. "You can tell?"

"I can."

The approval radiating off him made her want to tear off his clothes and devour him. Fortunately there wasn't a lot of traffic and the distance between the houses owned by mother and son wasn't more than a few miles. They were already holding hands so all she had to do was raise his knuckles to her lips and nibble suggestively. He glanced at her, his hazel eyes kindling.

"I want you," she told him.

"I want you, too," he answered with a wolfish smile.

Loosening his grip on her hand, without releasing her entirely, he trailed the tips of his fingers beneath her dress and up her bare thigh. Teagan swallowed hard, her thighs falling apart to give him the access they both craved. He brushed the pads of his fingers across the crotch of her panties and sucked in his breath.

"You're wet," he remarked smoothly, his deep voice stroking her nerve endings, making her shudder.

"I'm hot for you" she answered, her voice not as steady as his. She'd never hidden her susceptibility to him. Why bother when her responsiveness aroused him? And she liked turning him on. "At home, I intend to encourage you to do all sorts of sexy things to me."

"I like the sound of that." Once again, his finger glided over her most sensitive area.

A low moan escaped her throat as she pressed his hand against her. When had she become so raw and needy?

"Aren't we there yet?" she whined, making the corners of his lips twitch.

He was so beautiful when he smiled. As much as she loved his smolder, the sheer joy in his laughter fired a longing to make him happy. Too bad it wasn't her destiny to live an uncomplicated life. This time she'd been with Chase was just a momentary lull before the next skirmish began.

Declan had fired a warning shot across her bow. He wanted the Brookfield Building and intended to complicate her life until he got it. And right now he had his sights set on destroying her relationship with Chase.

Which was why she intended to take full advantage of what time she had left with Chase, before he discovered what destruction she'd brought into his life.

Teagan launched herself at him as soon as he'd parked and opened the passenger door for her. Spinning, stumbling, kissing and tearing each other's clothes off, they made their way through his kitchen and upstairs to his bedroom. Naked and smiling, she fell onto the bed and watched with heady anticipation as he slid on a condom before coming for her.

He pounced on her, rolling them both across the mattress until he lay on his back and she straddled him. They came together in a practiced surge, Chase filling her in a powerful stroke that ripped a whimper from her. She bit down hard on her lower lip and rocked against him, loving the feeling of him inside her. His strong hands kneaded her breasts, driving her wild, while the friction of his plunging thrusts pulled at her clit. Teagan twisted her hips, grinding hard against him and climaxed fast.

With each wave of pleasure rolling into the next, she had no chance to catch her breath as Chase flipped her over, lifted her onto all fours and pushed inside her once more. With her first orgasm still rumbling through her, she dropped her head and savored the way his smooth, powerful thrusts started to build her hunger all over again.

When his teeth sank into her shoulder, claiming her in a wild, primal way, she came again and came hard. Yet, he still didn't follow her. Instead, he pulled her close, stilling all movement as he plied her buzzing ears with endearments and coaxing words. While her breathing slowed, he repositioned them on their sides. With his clever fingers, he drew soothing circles on her belly, making her tremble. His nose drifted into her hair where he hummed in delight. She smiled as his lips deposited tender kisses along her neck and at last, he began to move again inside her once more. This time his strokes were languid and tender, as if she was the most precious thing in his life.

Her last orgasm snatched her up in a different sort of wonder. Deeper and longer than the first two, rolling thunder rather than a blinding lightning flash. She savored the exhilaration of Chase's hoarse shout and the buck of his body as he came moments later. She clenched her inner muscles, determined to hold on to him as long as possible, as if by staying intimately linked she could keep the rest of the world at bay.

As her pulse slowed and her breathing became regular once more, Teagan floated in Chase's arms, all too aware that she was falling for this man. In moments like these she could pretend that they could become something that would last. It wasn't just great sexual chemistry. It was caring and camaraderie. She didn't just hunger for Chase's glorious form—she wanted to know everything that made him tick.

Turning and burying her face into the crook of his neck, Teagan savored the lethargic contentment that filled her. Yet it was hard to ignore the buzzing anxiety that tightened her chest and shortened her breath.

"It was fun listening to your mother tell stories about you and Nola growing up," she murmured, determined to focus on this precious moment and not dwell on potential future disasters. "You obviously had a happy childhood." Wistfulness tinted her tone. "No wonder you get along with her so well."

"I imagine it was different for you?"

"I can't remember a time when any of us were allowed to play as children. My parents always pitted us against each other. They lavished on my brother Aiden all the praise and attention the firstborn and male heir could possibly ever want or need. It made him entitled and lazy. Meanwhile, Sienna was mostly ignored. That may be what enabled her to turn out so nice."

"And you?" Chase prompted.

"I've always had issues surrounding being adopted." She continued to be astonished by how easily she shared her vulnerabilities with Chase. All the fears she kept hidden from family and friends seemed to roll off her tongue beneath his somber attentiveness. Despite knowing that he'd agreed to keep an eye on her for Ethan, she never worried that whatever she told him would come back to harm her. Trusting someone with her darkest secrets was novel for her, and yet because it was Chase, it wasn't at all scary.

"What sort of issues?"

"Always feeling like an outsider in my own family. It was as if a part of me was missing. My mother died shortly after I was born. My father wasn't in the picture. There was always this feeling that I wasn't wanted."

"The fact that you were adopted by the Burns family indicates that's not true."

"I was a beautiful child." She shrugged at the flare of amusement in his eyes. "It's not vanity. It's a fact. I know that because my mother often pointed out it was why she chose me to adopt. Sienna's a year older and when it became apparent that she wasn't the prettiest of children, my mother decided to get herself a toy she could dress up and show off to all her society friends."

Chase slipped his fingers through hers, the soothing gesture giving her the courage she needed to go on. "I imagine that hurt."

"Until I was nine, I didn't know any better. And then came the day when I overheard two women laughing about how much it embarrassed my mother to have produced such a plain daughter and how she'd only adopted me because I was pretty."

"Ethan mentioned your sister isn't close to your parents. Did she know how your mother felt?"

"Until I'd overheard those women, I never paid much attention to how Sienna looked. She was just my older sister who entertained me by drawing pictures and telling me stories. She's a really talented artist. Not that she would acknowledge it. I'm pretty sure she hasn't picked up a sketch pad or a brush since graduating college."

"Why not?"

"Our mother badgered the confidence right out of her. In our family, if you can't do something perfectly, then you shouldn't bother to do it at all."

"All of this sounds really harsh."

"By most people's standards it is, but the Burns family is like nothing you've ever seen. The smallest misstep can haunt you for a long time."

"So you developed a tough skin."

"I imagine that's not particularly attractive to you." She took his hand and guided his fingertips to her shoulder, smiling as he grazed her soft skin with his gentle touch.

"If you think I'm not attracted to you," Chase said, dipping his head to kiss his way from her lips to her ear, "then you've not been paying attention."

"Oh, there's a big difference between this—" she gestured to her body and face "—and all that's ugly and broken inside."

"Have you forgotten what I do for a living?" His eyes glowed as he captured her gaze and held it. "Ugly and broken don't scare me."

Far from making her feel better, Teagan felt panic rising at his words. "You make ugly and broken things beautiful. Is that what you intend to do to me? To take everything that's wrong with me and fix it?"

Chase frowned. "That's not what I meant. The unique combination of perfection and flaws makes you special. I don't want to change you or fix you."

His earnest expression sent a ripple of pure pleasure dancing along her spine. It would be so easy to fall in love with this man. He seemed to know exactly what she needed to hear. Giving in to the strong feelings he evoked could place her on a tight rope without a safety net to save her if she fell.

"Not even a little?" she teased, cradling his face in her palms, her entire body surging with blinding joy at the way he was looking at her. "Admit it, you'd like it if I wasn't so selfish or prone to scheming."

"Maybe you're selfish and scheming because you've never had anyone taking care of you before."

"Damn," she muttered, unsure she deserved to be this happy. "You really are perfect."

After scrutinizing her expression for a long moment, no doubt trying to decide if she was bantering with him in an effort to dodge strong feelings, Chase rolled her beneath him and seized her lips in a hard kiss. Her heartbreak vanished in a furious explosion of desire. Teagan clung to him, worshipping the strong arms that held her and the gentle hands that caressed her skin. But before she went up in flames, Chase ended the kiss.

"No one who knows me would say I'm perfect," he told her, his lips moving across her eyelids and down her nose.

A sob caught in her throat at his tenderness. Rather than argue with him, Teagan decided to proceed a little farther along the treacherous path she'd set herself on.

"Okay, so I'll amend what I said." She summoned a deep breath and let it out on a shaky exhale. "You are perfect for me."

"Where are we going for dinner?" Teagan asked, taking in their surroundings as Chase left the downtown area and drove them fifteen minutes north to the "Neck" of the Charleston Peninsula.

"Bennett's Pub."

She glanced over her shoulder at the road behind them. "Isn't that downtown?"

"It is."

As the SUV passed through the white columns with their stately wrought iron gates, Teagan's attention sharpened.

"You brought me to a cemetery?" Her gaze moved across the numerous tombstones, both elaborate slabs of granite or carved sculptures and the more modest headstones that marked the passing of loved ones.

He nodded. "Magnolia Cemetery, where some of Charleston's most notable have been buried since 1850. It was created on the site of Magnolia Plantation after health concerns prohibited burials in the lower city." He paused and glanced at her, seeing the tension building in her. "I thought you might be interested in seeing where some of your family are buried."

One golden eyebrow rose. "If this is supposed to get me hot, you need to rethink your seduction technique."

Although her words and tone were meant to be flippant, Chase heard a quiet echo of distress. Teagan's walls might be a mile thick, but they were pitted with holes. Between what she'd told him and what he'd gleaned from Ethan about Teagan's adoptive parents, a clear picture had formed in his mind of what her childhood had been like. Samuel and Anna Burns appeared incapable of bolstering the self-esteem of either daughter even as they lavished praise on their eldest son.

Both Burns sisters had grown into wary adults with significant trust issues. In the case of Sienna, she'd been swept off her feet by the magic of Charleston and Ethan's determined pursuit. Although the couple had gone through a rough patch thanks to Teagan's meddling, it hadn't taken Ethan long to realize he'd made a huge mistake letting her go back to New York without the air cleared between them. Chase had seen his charming best friend date all sorts of women, but not one of them had captured his heart like the down-to-earth art curator.

"I mean, sure, some women are turned on by graveyards." Teagan kept up her banter when Chase didn't immediately respond. "I'm not one of them."

He knew she was trying to bait him into playing her games, but he'd been around her long enough to recognize that her flippant, one-sided conversation masked confusion and anxiety. Interesting. What was worrying Teagan? He couldn't imagine her being afraid. Although the cemetery was a favorite spot for nightly ghost tours, in the afternoon, with sunlight filtering through the live oaks, the mood was tranquil and sacred.

"Over there is the special section reserved for Confederate soldiers killed during the Civil War," Chase declared, pointing to the neat rows of headstones.

Teagan sat in silence as he parked the car and shut off the engine. He took a moment to admire her beautiful profile as her gaze swept the final resting place of so many of Charleston's old families.

"Are you okay?" he asked, suddenly concerned by her fixed expression.

"Of course." She stopped picking at the fabric of her wide-leg pants and fluffed her long hair. "When am I not okay?"

"Never," he lied, reluctant to shatter her illusion of strength.

"Damned straight."

While Teagan was getting better at showing vulnerability, she preferred to pick her moments rather than have them thrust upon her. He was fast learning that while she enjoyed delivering surprises, she wasn't keen to be on the receiving end of them.

"Ready to meet your grandmother?" Chase asked, opening his car door. Without waiting for her reply, he circled the vehicle and opened her door. One glance at her face told him she was a million miles away. He held out his left hand to her while gesturing with his right. "She and the rest of your family are over there."

For several heartbeats Teagan stared at his hand while birds chattered in the tree branches above them. "What if she doesn't like me?"

His chest tightened at both the question and her lost-child voice. "Impossible."

"I can't believe I'm saying this," Teagan responded in aggrieved tones, "but you're right."

Tossing her golden mane, she set her palm against his and shifted her weight until one expensively clad foot reached the ground. Chase's pulse jumped at the warm glide of her fingers against his skin. Every time his body came into contact with hers, no matter how fleeting or inadvertent, it was like touching a live wire.

The strength of her effect on him should worry Chase more than it did. Ethan trusted him to keep his head around this woman. Disappointing those closest to him went against everything he believed in. Letting his hormones get the better of him was risky. Chase had made Ethan a promise and falling for Teagan jeopardized that.

And then there was the low hum of agitation that had gripped him since she'd returned from New York. Something was off. He would just have to work harder to keep his emotions in check while he figured out what was going on with Teagan.

"I think you'll find out I'm right about most things," Chase responded, knowing it would annoy Teagan. Focusing on her irritation would strengthen her.

"That's something we have in common," she said.

"It's like two immovable objects meeting. One of us will have to give."

Teagan shot him a sly grin. "Or we might just come to rest against each other, forever locked in a give-and-take."

Chase's gut tightened the way it did during a match when he realized he faced a more skilled opponent. When it came to flirting, Teagan would always have the upper hand. He shifted his grip on her hand and wove their fingers together. She drew closer to his side and settled her head against his shoulder.

The wind whispered through the ancient live oaks as they strolled across the neatly trimmed grass. The hushed peacefulness of the cemetery wove a spell around both of them. At last, they reached the cluster of graves where the most of the Watts family had been laid to rest during the last century and a half.

"This is my family," she murmured, her gaze scanning the names and dates of her ancestors. Her grip on his hand tightened. "There are so many of them."

"George Watts came to South Carolina in 1792 and bought a plantation an hour north of the city. Shortly before the Civil War, the family moved to Charleston and founded Watts Shipping."

"You know so much more about my family than I do."

"Aside from the fact that our families have been friends for years, I'm in the restoration business. I know a lot about the history of Charleston."

Teagan let go of his hand and moved toward a headstone. "This is my grandmother." Her hushed voice barely carried the short distance between them. "Delilah Ann Bennett Watts."

"Descended from one of Charleston's older families."

"She died so young."

"The same year Ava left," Chase confirmed. "Your aunt Lenora insists her mom died of a broken heart, but it was really the cancer that took her."

"And Grady never remarried."

Chase shook his head. "He adored her. No other woman could compare. As many found out."

"It must've been hard for him to lose her so young."

"From what I've heard he was never quite the same after losing his wife and daughter in such a short span of time." Chase couldn't imagine the strength it must have taken for Grady to survive a double blow like that. "I think what kept him going was his determination to bring Ava home." He nodded toward one of the newer grave markers.

Teagan crossed to it and gasped. "It's my mom."

"I told you Grady was determined to bring her home.

They found your mom buried on Hart Island in New York and brought her body back here."

"All these years she was here and I never knew." Teagan shook her head. "Wow."

Chase noticed the quiver in the hand he held. He glanced over and saw the sheen of tears in her eyes and the wobble of her lower lip before she caught it between even white teeth.

"You must think I'm ridiculous," Teagan declared with a weak chuckle, dashing the back of her free hand across her cheek. "I mean why should I get all upset? All my life I've known my mother was dead."

Chase's heart gave a sympathetic lurch. "I imagine it's a relief to know she's here."

"I wonder why no one told me she was here."

"You haven't been in Charleston that long. I'm sure someone would've gotten around to it."

"They might have if I hadn't screwed up my relationship with them." Self-reproach consumed her voice.

"Hey." Chase turned her to face him. "Nothing has happened that can't be fixed."

For a second, he thought his words might've penetrated the protective shell she'd built around herself.

"I've been trying, but no one wants to give me a chance to make things better." Brittle and dismissive, she spoke from a deep well of pain and frustration. "Oh, what am I even doing? I don't fix things. I break them. Isn't that why Ethan told you to keep an eye on me? To make sure I don't damage anyone else?"

"In the beginning, sure—"

"And now? You're with me because you think I've changed? Well, I haven't. I'm still the untrustworthy schemer I've always been. So, you'd better watch out or you'll get hurt, too." Teagan turned her back on her family's graves.

Her vehemence drove a spike of ice into his chest. Was she still scheming? Since returning from New York, she'd seemed troubled, but he'd brushed aside his worries with excuses about things going on with her businesses. But just now what she'd said left him thinking of a wounded animal snapping at anyone who reached out to help. Had something happened in New York that left her feeling desperate? Or was this just another facet of Teagan's personality that he'd not yet glimpsed?

Before Chase could settle on a reason for her outburst, Teagan was striding toward his SUV. He rubbed the back of his shoulder, digging his fingertips into the knots in his muscles, convinced the persistent tension hadn't been there before Teagan had entered his life.

Why was she so damned determined to present the ugliest version of herself? Did she really believe that if she actively made people dislike her, she wouldn't get hurt? As defense mechanisms went, it made no sense. Didn't she realize the tactic's long-term disadvantages? If she never let anyone believe in her, how would she ever be truly happy?

Nine

Silence filled Chase's SUV as he drove them back to downtown Charleston. Although she was ashamed of her outburst and wanted to apologize, she hadn't yet come up with a reasonable explanation for her agitation. She really should tell him about her run-ins with Declan and the certainty that the Calloway house was on the verge of slipping through their hands. But every time she opened her mouth to explain how Declan was using Calloway to pressure her into selling the Brookfield Building, she imagined Chase's disgust and chickened out.

Once he heard the story, Chase was sure to hate her and she couldn't bear that. Nor would telling him stop the inevitable. She could only stay silent, hope Rufus Calloway believed in her vision for the property, and in the meantime, savor whatever time she had left with Chase. And that started with dinner tonight.

Bennett's Pub was a popular place because of its awesome patio. At night, strings of lights crisscrossed overhead, lighting the space and providing a festive ambience. Teagan had enjoyed several wonderful visits with her cousins and experienced a rush of melancholy as she and Chase made their way through the crowd.

With his ability to see over the heads of most of the patrons, he must've spied an open table, because he nudged her left. After another ten feet, Teagan came to an abrupt stop as she spied the couple in front of her.

Her throat closed up as she scanned her sister's stiff expression and Ethan's warning glare, before shooting a bewildered glance over her shoulder at Chase. His expression seemed to say, *You aren't the only one who can manipulate a situation.* Her heart pounded with joy and terror. What if Sienna refused to talk to her?

"This isn't an ambush," Teagan rushed to tell her sister. "I had no idea you'd be here."

"I know."

Old Sienna would've lowered her head, dropped her gaze and looked miserable. New Sienna had the benefit of a solid masculine presence at her side, a man who adored her and would cut down anyone who considered harming a single hair on her head.

"So, what do you want to do?" Teagan asked her sister. "Shall we parlay or retreat?"

Sienna sighed before saying, "Let's grab a glass of wine and talk." She indicated two empty stools at the bar. "Just us two," she added as Ethan stood to accompany them.

"Are you sure that's okay?" Ethan asked, shooting Teagan a suspicious glare.

"Sure." Sienna offered him a look brimming with affection and appreciation. "Why don't you and Chase grab a drink? I'll be okay."

"Text if you need me."

The sisters made their way through the busy bar and snagged the barstools. After ordering two glasses of white wine, Teagan said, "I would've thought he'd know by now you can handle me."

"He does." A private smile curved on Sienna's lips as the bartender set the drinks before them. "He just wanted you to know that he has my back."

"I'm glad."

Sienna looked surprised at her sister's admission. "Really? Since when?"

"Since the day you went back to New York and left me alone in Charleston." Teagan snagged her sister's left hand and pulled it close so she could admire the diamond on her ring finger. "Nice. I'll say this much, the man has good taste. Congratulations."

"You don't think it's too fast?" The couple had known each other for less than two months and Sienna wasn't one to make major life decisions without weighing everything carefully. Yet, the pair had enjoyed an instant attraction and despite Teagan's scheming, they'd grown close during Ethan's journey to find his birth mother.

"Do you?" Teagan countered.

"No." A wide grin bloomed. "I can't wait to marry him."

"Have you set a date?"

"October, I think."

"That soon?"

"We don't want a huge wedding so there won't be a lot to prepare."

While Teagan wondered if Sienna would invite her, silence stretched, filling the space between the sisters while enthusiastic conversations buzzed around them.

"Look," Teagan began, hoping she was coming across as sincere. "I'm sorry about what I did to you and Ethan."

When Sienna spoke, her voice held remembered anguish. "I almost lost him because of it."

"I didn't know how serious it had gotten between you, and even if I had, I might not have stopped." Teagan dug deep to find the courage she needed to keep going. "I know it's not a good excuse, but some things that happened in New York this past year combined with my anxiety about being accepted by my Charleston family and made me unreasonable and irresponsible."

"What happened in New York?"

"I didn't tell you what Dad said to me when I told him I wanted to run Burns Properties. He said I had three strikes against me. I was not the oldest, I was a woman and I was not his biological child."

"Oh, Teagan."

"Being adopted has always bothered me, but that was a hit I didn't see coming." Teagan's throat tightened. "I guess when it comes down to it, Aiden was the only one of us both our parents wanted."

"Well, they're welcome to him," Sienna retorted in a rare show of bitterness. "Dad was crazy not to let you take over the business. Our brother will mismanage the portfolio into bankruptcy."

This was the most connected Teagan had felt with Sienna since they were teenagers. She regretted getting caught up in New York's cutthroat society and losing her sister in the process.

"So, you and Chase," Sienna murmured, doing a poor job of muffling her keen curiosity.

Teagan shook her head. "It's not like that." She refrained from adding that Ethan had asked Chase to keep an eye on her. It might sound as if she resented her cousin, when in fact, he'd done her a huge favor.

"Really? That's not the impression Chase gave Ethan."

Sienna's words jolted Teagan to her toes. "What did Chase say?"

"It's not so much what he said, but the fact that Chase talks about you constantly."

"We're collaborating on a house I want to restore." Teagan refused to give in to disappointment.

"So all those dinners together haven't led to anything more?"

A flush broke out on Teagan's skin, but she just shook her head.

"Oh, that's too bad." Sienna actually looked disappointed, as if she was wishing for all the best things to come to Teagan. As if the sisters hadn't exchanged painful verbal spears the last time they'd been together.

"Whatever." Teagan waved her hand. "He's made it perfectly clear that I'm not his type. And he wants to keep things professional between us." While that was no longer true, Teagan wasn't sure what Chase was looking for from her.

"You know," Sienna said, smiling warmly at Teagan, "I think coming to Charleston has been good for both of us."

"Maybe for you. You fell in love with the man of your dreams. Meanwhile, I've alienated my long-lost family and pretty much everyone wishes I'd go back to New York."

"That's not true. You just need to be patient and it will all work out." That Sienna continued to support Teagan, despite the harm she'd done, demonstrated what a wonderful person her sister was. "But what I meant about you coming to Charleston is that you seem different now. In New York you had all this frenetic energy that needed an outlet. Your friends were always trying to outdo each other and nothing you achieved satisfied you." Sienna paused and scrutinized Teagan. "From what I hear you seem at peace these days."

Teagan's stomach muscles clenched at the idea that her family was discussing her. But what did she expect?

"What might've worked in New York backfired brilliantly here. I didn't understand how a tight-knit family would rally and support each other. I could've been part of the exact sort of family dynamic I've longed for, but I didn't trust that they'd accept me." Teagan clenched her teeth as misery swelled. "And now everyone hates me."

"They don't hate you."

"Distrust, then." Teagan took a big gulp of wine. "It was stupid of me to think I deserved to run Watts Shipping someday because I was a blood relative and Ethan was adopted. Stupid and callous considering how much it hurt when that was Father's rationale for giving Burns Properties to Aiden."

"Oh, Teagan, it'll all work out. You'll see."

"I don't think I'll be sticking around that long."

Sienna studied her. "You're leaving?"

"As people keep pointing out, my entire life is in New York. I have three successful businesses there that I've been neglecting while chasing an impossible dream down here."

"Is it really impossible?"

"I came down here hoping to become part of a family," Teagan choked out, hating the way her throat tightened as anguish filled her. "Instead, I feel like an outsider."

"That's because you haven't let them in. All they've seen of you is the face you present to the world." Sienna reached out and covered her sister's hand with her own.

A gentle squeeze nearly shattered Teagan's heart. Lately, her emotional stability was as robust as a soap bubble. She was constantly on the verge of being torn apart from within.

"Are you two doing okay?" Chase's deep masculine voice spoke from behind her.

"We're fine," Sienna answered while Teagan sucked in a steadying breath.

His clean scent enveloped her like a warm blanket on a chilly morning, but she resisted the comfort of it and kept her spine ramrod-straight. The temptation to lean back against his solid strength was almost more than she could withstand, but she shouldn't get accustomed to relying on him that way. His sleeve brushed against her bare arm as he signaled to the bartender and her pulse stuttered at the glancing contact.

"Should we grab a table and have dinner?" Ethan asked, the offer indicating he'd put aside his earlier hostility—at least for the moment.

"Thanks, but I think I need to pass," Teagan said, desperate for the space to contend with her rioting emotions. "I'm suddenly not feeling well."

All three of them stared at her in concern, but it was Chase's keen gaze that pierced her.

His palm settled, warm and reassuring, into the small of her back. "I'll take you home."

"No," she insisted, the tightness in her throat making her voice hoarse. "You should stay and catch up. You and Sienna should get to know each other. I'll order a ride." Teagan glanced from Chase's unwavering care to her sister's confusion. "I'll be okay. I'm really glad we had a chance to clear the air a bit."

Sienna wore a slight frown as she nodded. "Of course."

"Maybe now you'll stop ignoring my texts?"

"I'm sorry. Of course, I will. I just needed some time."

"I understand." Teagan turned to Ethan. "I'm really happy for you two."

"Thanks."

If she thought Chase would let her walk out on her own, Teagan was doomed to be disappointed. As she made her way through the bar area toward the front entrance, he trailed after her. Once they stood outside, Teagan turned to him.

"You should go back inside. I'm okay." Desperate to escape before she dissolved into tears, Teagan keyed the rideshare app on her phone.

"Are you upset that I didn't tell you we were meeting up with your sister?"

Teagan desperately looked for the nearest available car.

It was a few minutes away. She booked it and turned her attention to Chase.

"I'm actually glad that I didn't have a chance to prepare anything to say. I think it went better because I spoke from the heart." She tipped her head back and stared up into his face. "Things are better between us, so thank you."

"Then why are you leaving?"

Seeing Sienna and Ethan together had awakened Teagan to the emotional intimacy she longed to build with Chase. Despite the fantastic sex, mutual passion for historic buildings and his support as she'd laid bare her painful past, complete trust remained elusive.

He'd noticed that she'd been jittery since meeting Declan in New York. She longed to share her problems with him and work together to find a solution, but feared he'd turn on her once she warned him that at any second the Calloway house could be yanked away. Once she told him why Declan had gone after the house and how he planned to demolish it as punishment, Chase would regret ever meeting her. Nor could she stay silent and hope that Declan wouldn't contact Chase to explain exactly who was responsible for his family's loss.

"I'm really not feeling well." It was true, although her symptoms were emotional rather than physical. "And you should get to know my sister. Given how close you and Ethan are, she's going to be a big part of your life going forward."

"I guess that means by extension you will, too." He cupped her cheek in his large palm and held her mesmerized with no effort at all.

"It's hard for me to say what the future will bring." The lie was acid, eating away at their connection. She saw quite clearly what was in store for her and the anticipation of pain wrenched at her.

"What does that mean?"

"It's just that ever since I went to New York, I've realized how hard it's going to be to extricate myself from my life there. I have businesses to run and my friends..."

"I thought you were planning on staying in Charleston." He looked confused, hurt, unsettled. "What happened to making your mark on the city and reconciling with your family?"

"As I said, I'll have to see how the situation plays out. I came here originally to connect with them and made a mess of things. Apologizing isn't getting me anywhere and I'm at a loss for what to do next." No matter what she did, what she'd done to hurt Ethan had kept her cousins from trusting her again. Teagan was beyond feeling lost and alone. "I'm no longer sure if staying makes sense."

"What about your plans to renovate a historic house?"

Chase was the only one anchoring her to Charleston at the moment and she needed some reassurance from him that he was the solid ground that would let her fight on.

"I really fell in love with the Calloway house and I don't know that I can move on to another property if I don't get it."

"Did you hear from Sawyer? Was your offer turned down?"

"Not yet." Teagan's heart contracted. She longed for Chase to sweep her into his arms and proclaim that he couldn't imagine his future without her, but that wasn't how he felt apparently. "I'm just bracing myself for a worst-case scenario."

Chase's eyes widened. "It sounds like you're giving up."

"I'm being sensible."

Luckily, Teagan's ride stopped at the curb before he could bombard her with more arguments. She pulled his hand away from her face and offered him a wan smile. Stepping toward the car, she jerked open the rear door and settled into the back seat.

"I'll call you tomorrow." Before he could reply, she shut the car door.

Her last glimpse of Chase tore at her heart. His stunned expression left her drowning in misery. He didn't know it yet, but she'd ruined everything for him. And when he found out that she'd chosen to hold on to her Manhattan building and put the Calloway house at risk, he'd never be able to forgive her.

Chase wound his way back through bar patrons and saw that Ethan and Sienna had secured a high-top table. His brain felt foggy as he angled toward them. What had happened to cause Teagan to bolt like that? He and Ethan had kept an eye on both women as they talked. The conversation had seemed to be progressing smoothly until the very end when Teagan had grown more and more agitated.

"Is she okay?" Sienna asked as Chase slid onto a stool at the table.

"I don't know." His instincts told him to protect Teagan, and he hated the way she'd withdrawn from him, taking whatever was bothering her onto her slim shoulders. "What were you two talking about there at the end?"

Ethan bristled as if Chase was accusing his fiancée of doing something wrong, but Chase ignored him. He wasn't interested in picking a fight, just gaining insight.

"She's really upset by how everyone continues to give her the cold shoulder." Sienna shot a sideways look at Ethan. "I've seen her face a lot of setbacks but this is the first time she's ever seemed…helpless."

The description of Teagan's mental state kicked Chase in the gut. He glanced at his best friend. "Is there anything you can do to smooth things over? She's talking about heading back to New York. Possibly for good."

"She really got to you, didn't she?" Ethan's level tone wasn't quite flat enough to keep his opinion from showing.

"Yes." Chase wasn't going to make excuses or deny how he felt about her. "I've gotten to know her really well these last few weeks and she's more complicated than she seems."

Sienna's agreement reflected in her nod, easing some of Chase's angst. "She hides a lot of hurt behind her attention-seeking ways." Sienna grew pensive. "Usually, she lashes out when she feels threatened. This is the first time I've ever seen her run."

Run.

In his gut, Chase recognized that's exactly what Teagan was doing. Running. From Charleston. From her family. From him.

Chase's phone rang while they were ordering dinner. His pulse kicked up, hoping it was Teagan, and then slowed to a sluggish thump as Sawyer's name appeared on his screen. Disappointed, he shook his head at Sienna's hopeful expression and answered the call.

"Is Teagan with you?" Sawyer asked. "I've been trying to get ahold of her."

Hearing the tension in her voice, Chase didn't need to be a mind reader to know that Teagan hadn't gotten the house.

"Rufus went with the other offer, didn't he?"

"Yes." Sawyer sounded as gutted as Chase felt. "Chase, I'm so sorry."

"Was it the guy from New York or did another offer come in?" As he asked, Chase noticed Ethan and Sienna exchanging worried glances.

"It was him. I gave Emmett a quick call and he said no other offers came in." Sawyer paused for a second and then said, "Chase, his offer was double the asking price. Why would anyone pay that much for that property?"

"I don't know." He closed his eyes and thought of what this was going to do to Teagan, to his mother. "I'll give Teagan a call and break the news."

"Thanks. Let her know I'll pull new listings for her when she's ready."

Chase hung up, thinking that there was no way Teagan was going to be ready to find a new property. He thought about how she'd spoken when they parted earlier. It was as if she'd had a premonition that bad news was coming and had been bracing herself to face it.

"What's going on?" Ethan asked.

"It's the Calloway house." Chase couldn't believe that after decades of waiting, the property had slipped away from them. "Teagan didn't get it."

"Oh, man." Ethan reached for Sienna's hand, a clear indication that these two were stronger as a couple than as individuals. "I'm really sorry. I know how important that house was to your mom."

"And to Teagan," Chase put in, swamped by the need to go to her and share in her disappointment.

"Did you say something about the other offer coming from someone in New York?" Sienna put in softly, her forehead puckered with a frown.

Chase nodded. "The guy paid double." He glanced at Ethan. "You know what the place looks like. Why would he do that?"

Again the couple across from him exchanged concerned looks. They obviously had something on their minds and Chase was in no mood to drag it out of them by degrees.

"Spill it. What do you two think is going on?"

"Declan Scott," Sienna said.

"The guy who messed with you two by sending all those anonymous texts?" Chase was dumbfounded. "That can't be right."

Sienna's pretty face tightened in anger. "This sounds exactly like something Declan would do to get back at Teagan."

"He wants something from her," Ethan murmured, his gaze turned inward.

Chase regarded him in annoyance, wondering why no one had thought to inform him of this threat until now. "Did he say what?"

Before Ethan could answer, Sienna inserted her own question. "When did you run into him?"

Ethan focused on Sienna. "Around the time you went back to New York. I found out he was staying down here and went to confront him. He said that…" Ethan swore viciously and looked pained. "Teagan refused to give him something he wanted and he intended to show her how that felt."

Sienna hissed through her teeth. "That sounds like Declan. I'm sure he wasn't happy that we found our way back to each other, and while I'm sure it amused him that her whole family turned their backs on her, he wouldn't let up until she came crawling."

The picture Sienna painted didn't sit well with Chase. The urge to fly to New York and punch the arrogant bastard in the face made him see red.

"What does she have that he wants?" Ethan asked, sighing in frustration as Sienna shook her head.

"When it comes to Declan, it could be any number of things."

Chase barely registered the exchange between Sienna and Ethan. Only two people knew the answer to why Declan had gone out of his way to hurt Teagan, and one of them was less than two miles away. His stool scraped against the concrete flooring as Chase pushed back from the table.

"I need to go talk to Teagan," he announced. "She needs to know what happened."

"Tell her to call me if she wants to talk," Sienna said.

With an abrupt nod, Chase headed for the exit. On

the way to his vehicle, he tried Teagan's cell, but it rolled straight to voice mail. Either she was talking to Sawyer or her phone was turned off. His gut twisted as he replayed how he'd caught glimpses of anxiety and sadness in her since she'd returned from New York. Their limited time together hadn't enabled him to learn all her moods. In hindsight, he imagined a scenario where she'd run into Declan and their confrontation had rattled her.

Disappointment sat heavy on Chase's shoulders. Why hadn't she shared with him any of what was going on? It was possible she'd been utterly blindsided, but given the way Declan had taunted Ethan, the man enjoyed tormenting his foes. Teagan was accustomed to fighting her own battles and probably hadn't considered dragging him into the fray. He'd been under the impression that they had formed a partnership to restore the Calloway house, but obviously they weren't of like minds. What did that mean for what was happening between them romantically?

Earlier she'd made it sound as if she was ready to give up on making Charleston her home. Where did that leave him? Was their brief fling at an end? Despair flickered at the edge of his awareness. He wasn't prepared for her to go. There was so much more to explore between them.

Answers, he told himself as he pulled up to the Watts home. He needed answers.

At the door, when he asked after Teagan, Grady's housekeeper directed Chase to the back terrace overlooking the gardens. She looked startled when he stepped through the door and rose from the wicker sofa as he drew closer.

"What are you doing here?"

"Sawyer called me. She's been trying to get ahold of you."

"I lost the house." Calm. Matter-of-fact. Resigned.

"I'm sorry." He curved his fingers over her shoulders in

an effort to comfort her, but she remained tense beneath his touch.

"Me, too." Teagan gave her shoulders a little shake and stepped back, dislodging his hands. "I know how much you want to restore the property for your mom."

"I was with Ethan and Sienna when Sawyer called. They thought that it might be Declan Scott who bought the house."

Teagan seemed to withdraw into herself at the news and wouldn't meet his gaze. Her voice was low and hoarse as she said, "It would be something he'd do."

Chase's gut twisted at her demeanor. He'd never seen Teagan look so completely miserable. Or…guilty?

"When Ethan spoke with him last month Declan indicated he was messing with you because you had something he wanted." He watched her closely as he relayed this. Again he sensed she wasn't surprised. "Is that true?"

"Yes."

So, did that mean the Calloway house had been lost because of some ridiculous war she was waging with Declan Scott? He held back his anger, determined to get the whole story before reacting.

"And you believe he's the one who put in the winning bid?"

"I know so."

Chase asked his next question with as much patience as he could muster. "How can you be so sure?"

"Because he told me. Threw it in my face actually. Damn him."

Her answer caught him on the temple, blindsiding him. "When?"

"While I was in New York."

She'd been acting different since returning to Charleston. At least now he understood why.

"Declan Scott bought the Calloway house." Chase

couldn't wrap his head around any of it. "Why would he do that?"

"Because he knew I wanted it."

Ethan's words came back to him then. "Because you refuse to give him something he wants and he intends to show you how that feels?" Chase watched her reaction, growing ever more disturbed at the way her face hardened into a grim mask of resolve. "What does he want?"

"It's always something with him." Teagan waved her hand dismissively.

"What sort of something?"

"Suffice it to say that he and I have been engaged in an ongoing feud for a decade, and when things don't go his way, he plays dirty."

Chase recognized that Teagan hadn't actually answered his question and suspicion flared. The way she held her cards close was a clear warning. He wasn't hearing the entire story.

"So, the Calloway house has become a casualty of some sort of war you two are engaged in?"

"Yes."

"Is keeping the house away from you punishment enough?" Chase asked, wondering what sort of messed-up world she lived in where people hurt each other for sport. "Or does he have plans for it?"

"He won't sell it if that's what you're wondering." She grimaced, her gaze avoiding his. "It's only value to him is that he can use it as leverage against me."

"What sort of pressure can he put on you?" Chase took her by the upper arms and turned her to face him. Dread made his next words rougher than he intended. "Doesn't he realize that you can just go find a different property? Is he planning on buying up half of Charleston in his vendetta against you?"

Her body language indicated she was spoiling for a fight.

This woman knew one way to handle setbacks—dig in and get dirty.

"He threatened to level it." As soon as the words were out, she looked stricken.

Chase's heart sank. What was wrong with Declan Scott that he would destroy a two-hundred-year-old treasure to get back at Teagan? And what had she done to deserve such treatment?

"He's going to tear down the house. My great-great-grandfather's home." Pain reverberated through his hushed voice.

No doubt seeing Chase's expression caused her temper to falter. "Oh, Chase," she said on a shaky breath. "I'm sorry. This is all my fault."

And it was. All of it. Despite all appearances, she'd learned nothing from the rift between her and her family. Now, another of her stupid games was on the verge of having real consequences.

Realizing he was still holding her, Chase whipped his hands away. Staring down at her beautiful face, he was consumed by self-loathing.

"On that, we both agree."

Ten

"How do we fix this?" Chase demanded, his gaze cold and merciless.

We. How do we fix this?

Had he used the plural pronoun deliberately? Did he still see her as a partner in their quest for the Calloway house? Or was he just a warrior going to battle to fight for something he loved and viewed her as a fellow soldier?

Whichever he meant, Teagan was dizzy with relief that he hadn't just stormed out of her life, abandoning her to the desolate void that had been her inner landscape before he'd shown her how magical life could be.

"I'm not sure we can." She breathed the last two words, scanning his granite expression, looking for some chink in his defenses she could cling to. "Declan has probably already wired the money to your cousin. There's no interrupting the sale at this point."

She wasn't going to sugarcoat the situation. He'd never believe her anyway.

Chase's eyes narrowed. "What about the thing you have that he wants?"

Teagan stopped breathing at the implication of what he was asking. Was she willing to give up something important to her to secure a different outcome? That was a damn fine question. She stood with one foot planted on two different destinies. She could keep the New York property and walk away from Charleston, her family and Chase, or she could surrender the Brookfield Building to Declan and start a new life in Charleston.

Having both was not an option.

If she screwed up in Charleston a second time, her family would ice her out forever and whatever she and Chase had begun to explore would be cut off. Even if she fixed the situation with the Calloway house, Chase might discover something else about her he couldn't live with and her biological family might always treat her as an outsider.

And if she kept the Midtown building away from Declan? She could return to New York, her pledge to her father intact, and resume her life as if these weeks in Charleston had never happened.

Only they had. And in meeting her blood relatives, and embarking on her relationship with Chase, she'd been altered. The process had been painful—a breaking of the defenses that had kept her safe from heartbreak. A resculpting of the protectiveness that enabled her to fight for her life.

Her old tricks no longer worked. Neither manipulation nor schemes brought her closer to what she truly wanted. Instead, she'd lost precious ground. Her future in Charleston had suffered a mortal wound. Yet, with the changes in her, returning to her old life in New York no longer seemed feasible.

Chase's grim stare succeeded in drawing an explanation out of her. "He wants a historic property."

He nodded, able to appreciate this much of what motivated her. "Why is it so important to him?"

"Declan is developing a block in Midtown, a tower that will bear his name and dominate the skyline." Teagan pondered the renderings she'd seen of the glass skyscraper and contemplated all the architectural gems that had once stood in its way. "The Brookfield Building occupies a tiny corner that he needs to complete the project."

To Teagan's surprise, sharing her story with Chase released some of her anxiety. Maybe she'd been wrong to keep her worries bottled up. The other things she'd shared with him had seemed to deepen their connection. Maybe going all in wouldn't end with rejection.

"If he was hoping to convince you to sell the building to him, it seems like a bad move to antagonize you."

"It's always like that between us." Teagan huffed a bitter laugh. "Declan doesn't charm when he can bully."

"So, Declan can't begin his project without you."

"It's not as if this is fun for me," she snapped, not liking the way Chase phrased his conclusion. He made it sound like she was deliberately blocking the property developer, as if messing with Declan was her agenda.

Chase didn't react to her vehemence, just kept marching forward with unrelenting wariness. "Is there a reason you don't want to sell him the property?"

"It's a historical building, built in 1895 in a Romanesque Revival style. The facade is ornamental red and white brick with a limestone colonnade base and cornice with spires. Not only is it striking, the building has a who's who of famous tenants."

Teagan couldn't help herself; she found the photos of the building on her phone. Like a proud mother showing off the child she adored, she extended the screen so Chase could see it. His gaze flicked from the building to her face and back down.

"I understand why you would hate to see it demolished."

Of course he'd understand. He'd devoted his life to preserving Charleston's history in its buildings and landmarks.

"Have you applied for landmark status?"

As if she hadn't thought of that. Stuffing down her indignation, Teagan said, "Back when Declan began buying up the buildings in the neighborhood. The Landmark Preservation Commission has eleven commissioners. Six are required to designate a landmark and Declan has a lot of *influence*." She put a particular emphasis on the last word and Chase nodded as he caught her inference.

"What about putting something in the contract that stipulates he has to incorporate the facade into the development?"

"He'd never go for it. The modern monstrosity he's erecting is Scott Tower, a tribute to his greatness. He's not going to want some old turn-of-the-century eyesore as its cornerstone."

"It sounds like you're in a bad spot."

She offered up a bland smile. "It's not the first one I've been in."

"What I don't understand is given how desperate he is to get the property, why did you buy it? He must've been in process with this project for years. Did you mean to get in his way?"

"I didn't purchase the property." Explaining how it had come to her would prompt more questions that she wasn't ready to answer.

"I don't understand."

"Someone gave it to me."

His eyebrows rose. "Why would they do that?"

"Because they weren't in a position to keep the property safe any longer and knew I was the best person to keep fighting Declan." That at least was the truth.

"Someone *gave* you a multi-million-dollar property."

Chase shook his head in disgust. "What aren't you telling me?"

Not wanting to disappoint him, but unaccustomed to giving away any advantages in the midst of a skirmish, Teagan debated how much to tell Chase. It wasn't that she didn't trust him, but the reality was she'd only been sleeping with Chase for two weeks and she owed a lot to Edward Quinn, who'd not only mentored her, but had given her the encouragement lacking from the man who'd adopted and raised her. At the time she might not have known Edward was her father, but she'd loved him like a daughter.

Were she and Chase close enough that she could risk explaining their connection and trust that it would go no further? Because if Declan ever got wind that Edward was her biological father, he would use the information to hurt more people than just her.

"Obviously, it's something you aren't willing to share," Chase said when her silence stretched too long.

He stepped back from her, his body suddenly ramrod-straight, his face devoid of emotion. His remoteness was unlike anything she'd seen from him before and it recalled every time she needed someone's support and they turned on her instead.

"You don't understand what Declan's like," Teagan said, her heart shrinking away from Chase's cold stare. "The lengths he'll go to win. He delights in playing dirty. In fact, I think he prefers it that way."

"So, what's your plan? How many more people are you going to let get hurt while you play his games?"

"That's not fair." Teagan dug her nails into her palms as her voice cracked. Helpless despair rolled over her. "Do you really think I'm doing this because I want to?"

"I really don't know." He surveyed her for several interminable seconds. "I guess there's nothing more to say. Obviously, you've made your decision."

"You make it sound like it's all cut-and-dried."

"Isn't it?" he countered. "You admit that you've known about his involvement since your trip to New York and didn't bother to warn me. Seems to me you've just chalked this up to a loss."

"You can't seriously think this is easy for me. You don't understand what the Brookfield Building means to me."

"How could I possibly when you won't tell me?" His voice cracked like a whip, but there was underlying pain beneath the frustration. "Did seven generations of your family live there? Do you have some sort of personal connection that would explain your stubborn need to hold on to it?" He paused, breathing hard while his cold gaze swept her. His next words came out on a lethal growl. "Or are you just determined to win?"

She felt as if he'd tried to run her over with his car. "Do you think I'm anything other than devastated by what Declan's been doing?" She paused for a brief moment, giving him space to answer. When he didn't, she rushed on. "I've been at war with him since we were in high school."

"Something about that must be working for you."

Teagan recognized that Chase was angry. With her. With the situation. But his criticism was a devastating wake-up call. The closeness she'd imagined between them was little more than the postcoital bliss of fantastic sex. Physical attraction wasn't trust and support.

"Did you ever believe that I gave up my scheming ways?" She scanned his expression and the last of her hope shattered at what she saw. "Why did you even bother to be with me if I was so abhorrent to you?"

"You didn't seem that way when we were together."

"Really?" Unshed tears burned her eyes. "Then how did I seem?"

"Warm and loving." His description shredded her heart.

"I guess I fooled you." She forced a bitter laugh, hating

the shock that lashed across his face. "I mean, that's what you're thinking, isn't it?"

"I don't know what I'm thinking, really. I know what happened between you and Ethan. I know what you're willing to do to the people you love to get what you want. Am I supposed to believe that isn't who you are? That the woman I've held in my arms these past two weeks is the real you?"

Teagan sucked in a shaky breath. "So, you don't believe people can change." She threw herself into the fray already knowing her desperate campaign to change his mind had come too late. "That love can change people for the better?"

Even though he flinched at her use of the word *love*, she recognized that she'd been infatuated with him from the start. They'd had a lot of fun together. The sex had stirred her body and soul.

But Teagan had never known a deep, intimate bond or experienced a craving to make her partner happy. She was so accustomed to taking or receiving, believed she deserved to possess anything she fancied. Having never sacrificed for another's happiness, did she even know how?

"What are you saying?" He was a freight train of indignation. "That you've changed because of love?" His voice was harsh with dismay. "That you love me?"

"I'm not sure I know how." Avoiding any repeat of the word *love*, Teagan continued, "All I know is that since being with you I've been able to let my guard down and stop having to be invincible." She expelled her breath on a ragged little sigh. "It's exhausting trying to keep up the appearance of confidence while waiting for those around you to spot your weakness. I mean, look what happened with Declan and the Calloway property. He knew I wanted the house and how important it was to you and your family. That by snatching it away he harmed not only me, but your family. Destroying our relationship in the process made it almost too perfect."

Chase's eyes went wide as she brought the pieces together. "The instant you showed an interest in my family's home was the moment I lost everything."

"Not everything," she whispered, thinking of all the people who loved and supported him.

"No? How am I supposed to explain this to my mother? She liked you. Trusted you. Now, I have to inform her that the house she's been waiting all her life to save is on the brink of total destruction."

Teagan flinched away from his accusations, but what could she say to defend herself? She'd been so excited about the potential in the Calloway property, so thrilled to be working with a talented, passionate architect who got her vision. That her attraction for him had grown into a passionate connection with the potential for a truly deep and meaningful relationship had seemed so utterly perfect that she'd let her guard down.

This never would've happened if she'd been in New York. In familiar surroundings, where watching her back was as necessary as breathing, Declan never would've outmaneuvered her again. But becoming part of her Charleston family had distracted her. The Calloway house had excited her. And being with Chase had opened her heart.

One by one, Declan had ripped away what she loved.

If anyone had lost everything, it was her.

After Chase finished throwing blame in her face, Teagan left him on the back terrace and fled inside. Abandoned to his anger and misery, he stood frozen, cursing himself for ever getting involved with Teagan Burns.

It wasn't like him to engage in problematic relationships either in business or his personal life. Consciously or subconsciously, he'd been holding out for the deep, committed love his parents had enjoyed. Which was why it made no sense how willing he'd been to tangle his future with

Teagan, not knowing if she was looking for something that would last. The instant he'd agreed to show her the Calloway house, he'd started down a path to heartbreak. Instead of being drawn in by her excitement to team up for the restoration, he should've maintained his distance.

But he'd been caught off guard by the way she'd risked rejection when she'd opened up about her feelings for him—feelings she'd implied had grown into something powerful and transformative. *So you don't believe people can change? That love can change people for the better?* Chase shook his head to rid himself of the memory of her words even as he stared at the door through which Teagan had disappeared. Swept by a forceful yearning, he wanted to race after her and ask questions that had nothing to do with the trouble Declan Scott had stirred up.

Instead, Chase went in the opposite direction, down the circular iron staircase that led to the garden and along a crushed gravel path back to the front of the house. He spent the short drive to his mother's house wrestling with his churning emotions, but found no peace. As he pulled into his mother's driveway and shut off the SUV, Chase recognized that he was in no state to handle her grief. But how could he delay telling her? As it was, during his brief detour to talk to Teagan, someone might've called Maybelle and broken the news. Chase hoped that wasn't the case. His mother would need his support.

He'd forgotten it was her housekeeper's night off and stared at his mother in disconcerted silence when she answered the door. She wore a bright caftan and no makeup, but decades of a vigorous beauty routine left her looking far younger than her sixty-six years.

"Chase, what a surprise." She stepped back and ushered him inside. When he didn't move, she took a closer look at his face and frowned. "What's happened?"

Shaking free of his momentary paralysis, he stepped into

the house and wrapped his arms around her. She made a startled noise and patted him on the back.

"You're scaring me."

"Sorry." He pushed her to arm's length. "I have something I need to tell you."

"It sounds serious."

She led the way to a cozy den at the back of the house where she retreated in the evenings to watch her favorite shows and work on her needle felting projects. The bookshelves were crammed with the figurine sets she'd completed throughout the years, including a collection of Disney figures her granddaughters adored.

Settling into her favorite chair, Maybelle clicked off the TV and gave him her full attention. "Go ahead."

Since his mother had always been a proponent of ripping off the Band-Aid, Chase wasted no time getting to it. "Teagan didn't get the Calloway house."

Maybelle sighed in disappointment. "I'm so sorry."

Her response confused him. "No, I'm the one who's sorry. This is all my fault."

Now it was his mother's turn to look puzzled. "How is it your fault?"

"If I'd discouraged Teagan instead of showing her all the plans I'd done that got her so excited about the house, she would've moved on to something different and maybe Sawyer could've found another buyer who would be interested in restoring the house."

From Maybelle's frown, his explanation hadn't made things any clearer. Chase explained to his mother all that he'd learned from Sienna, Ethan and Teagan that evening. She listened to him intently, saying nothing until he wound down and lapsed into silence.

"That poor girl."

Chase couldn't believe it. His mother was sympathizing with Teagan? She was the one who'd caused the entire mess.

"How can you say that?" he said, storming. "We lost the house because of her."

"Earlier, you said this was all your fault." His mother cocked her head and studied him. "Now, you're blaming Teagan. It seems to me that the true villain is the man who bought the house in order to force Teagan's hand."

"But it's Teagan who won't sell him the building he wants."

His mother's eyes narrowed. "And you think she should?"

"I…"

He knew exactly what he'd wanted to say. She should give up the building in New York and get the Calloway house back from Declan.

"I don't know if she wants to save this historic building or to beat Declan Scott. They have a long, antagonistic past." Chase could see his mother wasn't coming around to his way of thinking. "Look at the way she used her sister in a scheme to beat out Ethan as the future CEO of Watts Shipping. And three weeks ago Ethan asked me to keep an eye on her and make sure she didn't cause any more trouble."

Maybelle drummed her fingertips against the arm of her chair. "Do you consider me a good judge of character?"

"Of course," he growled, suspecting where she was going.

"And Sawyer, what about her?"

"I get it. You both like Teagan and I'm being too critical." Chase struggled for a way to make his mother understand. "But it's because of her that Declan Scott is poised to demolish the house that's been in your family for over a hundred years."

"Chase, it's just a house." His mother's soft words were probably the biggest shock he'd received on a day filled with bombshell revelations.

"A house you've wanted to save for decades."

She shook her head sadly. "Not at the cost of hurting anyone."

And that's when it hit him how badly he'd handled the situation with Teagan. Had he really prioritized a run-down house over the woman he'd made love to? Would she have shared her troubles if his doubts hadn't made him insensitive to her disappointment and fears? Maybe if he hadn't limited his emotional response to her and given her a glimpse into how he felt, she might've trusted him enough to explain why Declan Scott had been terrorizing her.

The vastness of his failure shocked Chase. "I really screwed up."

His mother picked up an oblong lump of pink wool and her felting needle. "I'm sorry to hear that."

Her disappointment made him feel worse than if she'd scolded him for a solid hour.

"I think after what happened she's going back to New York."

"You can change her mind."

His stupid, rebellious heart leaped with hope. Chase wrenched it under control. "I don't know if I should."

Maybelle stopped what she was doing and stared at her son. "Why ever not?"

Because it would require not just an apology, but a plea for her to stay. And she would want to know why—to know what was in his heart.

"All her friends are in New York," he said instead, the excuse sounding lame even to his ears. "She runs three businesses there. Do you really think she's going to give all that up?"

His mother's look seemed to say, *She would for you.* But her answer was much more practical. "Teagan has family here. She intends to do good things in Charleston."

"Her family won't speak to her."

"She has you."

"That's a big leap," he said, the words tasting like ash. "I've only known her a few weeks."

"I learned long ago not to believe a man's words, but to pay attention to his actions. No matter what you say, you've been behaving like a man who's falling in love."

Her words were a tornado axe kick straight at his jaw. Mind reeling, Chase automatically defended his position, forgetting that facing an opponent with his emotions engaged would only lead to defeat.

"We're so different," he argued. "She's not at all who I imagined spending the rest of my life with."

"Hmm," his mother muttered noncommittally, picking up a long strand of pale gold wool.

"Life with her would be a roller coaster ride."

Was he up for that? And what convinced him that she would remain interested in him long-term? But the thought of losing her filled him with dread. How could he survive not seeing her every day and making love to her every night? She was the first woman who'd ever annihilated his guard and warped his common sense. No wonder he had gone a little crazy.

Like it or not, he'd fallen in love with Teagan Burns. And he suspected it had happened the day she'd gamely joined his beginner martial arts class and learned how to stand, fall and strike alongside a group of five-year-olds.

"I have to fix this," Chase murmured.

"Yes, you do," Maybelle agreed without looking up, but as she focused all her attention on the blonde princess coming to life in her hands, his mother was smiling.

Eleven

After she left Chase on the back terrace, Teagan went straight to her room and locked herself in. Dry-eyed and miserable, she threw herself on the bed and stared at the ceiling while regret and self-loathing pummeled her spirit.

Was this the pain Sienna had experienced when Teagan's scheming had come to light and her sister had ended things with Ethan? Teagan pressed her palm against her aching chest and beat down the urge to cry. It wasn't in her nature to surrender to emotional distress. Usually, she swallowed the difficult feelings, came up with a new strategy and enacted some plan that would ensure she came out victorious.

But how could she win when the only man who'd ever truly made her happy was disgusted by the person she was? She had no one to blame but herself. It was one thing to control the narrative. She'd owned up to behaving in a way that had alienated her sister and her Charleston family. Maybe she hadn't demonstrated the proper amount of regret, but that didn't mean their hostility didn't hurt.

She hated exposing any sign of weakness. Letting anyone glimpse the anxiety and self-doubt beneath her sophisticated exterior meant dropping the armor that kept
her safe. This meant no one really knew her. Not even the
sister Teagan loved.

Sienna had witnessed how their mother's selfishness and
their father's dismissal had affected Teagan, but she had her
own issues with their parents. Maybe if Teagan had asked
her sister for help, the two of them could've stood against
their parents and become happier for the mutual support.
Instead, Teagan had studied social strategies from her aloof,
ambitious parents and sculpted herself into a titanium socialite with a Teflon coating.

After a mostly sleepless night, Teagan pulled out her
phone and dialed Sienna's number. To her surprise and delight, her sister answered.

"I'm just calling to say I'm sorry for bailing last night,"
Teagan began. "And for what I did to you and Ethan. I know
I already apologized and I meant it, but I didn't understand
how much pain you were in when you left Charleston. As
always, I was selfish and insensitive."

"It's okay." Sienna's voice was soothing and kind.
"Chase told us what happened with the house. Why won't
Declan stop messing with you?" Sienna's furious outburst
nearly made Teagan smile. "What is wrong with him? Can't
he just leave you alone?"

"He wants the Brookfield Building. It's the only property left standing in the way of his tower."

"What does that have to do with you?"

"I own it and he's been badgering me to sell it. If I don't,
he's threatening to destroy everything and everyone I love
in order to get it."

"So sell him the damned thing and be done with it."

"I can't." Teagan sucked in a deep breath. She was so
accustomed to keeping things to herself that sharing her

secrets was like having a tooth ripped out without Novocain. "Edward Quinn left the building to me."

"He left it to you?" Sienna sounded both surprised and puzzled. "Why?"

"Because it was the first property he ever owned and it's an architectural gem. He trusted me to do the right thing with it."

"I get that, but Edward is gone and Brookfield is only a building."

Teagan hadn't told her sister about discovering her biological dad. Only Chase knew that much, and yet she hadn't been brave enough to share his identity. Nor had she explained to Chase her father's connection to the Brookfield Building and why Teagan was clinging to it. Suddenly Teagan was tired of keeping everything to herself. It was time to let someone all the way in. And who better than her sister?

"Edward was my father."

From the silence that followed the announcement, Sienna was having a hard time absorbing the news. "Your father?" she finally said. "Oh, Teagan…" Empathy filled her sister's strangled exclamation. "How long have you known?"

"Not until after he died. When he left me the building, he included a letter with the deed, telling me about the affair with my mother and asking me to keep our true relationship secret."

"Is that why he mentored you?"

"I think so. It would've been nice to know back then, but in the end, it didn't change my love for him. He was the one person who believed in me without reservation."

"That's not true. I've always been in your corner. Just because I don't approve of your tactics doesn't mean I'm not cheering you on to victory."

Gratitude flooded Teagan. "I appreciate that. Although

I'm not sure I deserve it. I haven't always been the best sister to you."

"Not true. You were the only one who encouraged me to go to art school."

Teagan was surprised that her sister had appreciated such a small thing. On the other hand, given the way they'd been raised, even the tiniest bit of encouragement could go a long way.

"You're incredibly talented. It was the perfect place for you." And the experience had given Sienna the confidence she needed to become an art curator, a career she not only loved, but was also spectacularly good at.

"Have you explained to Chase about Declan and the Brookfield Building?" Sienna asked, getting back to the heart of Teagan's problem.

"Yes."

"And about the fact that you inherited it from your biological father?" Sienna blew out an impatient breath at Teagan's lack of a response. "You have to tell him."

"It won't change anything. Declan is still going to tear down the Calloway house and Chase will never forgive me for putting his family in the line of fire."

"You can apologize to him," Sienna pointed out. "I'm sure he'll forgive you."

"I've already apologized." Teagan blew out a hopeless sigh. "He's too angry with me to listen to any of my excuses."

"Saving a building your father spent his life protecting is not an excuse. It's what Chase has been doing with the house that belonged to his mother's family. He'll understand your decision." Sienna paused to let her sister speak, but the lump in Teagan's throat prevented any words from breaking free. With a sigh, Sienna added, "You can't keep shutting everyone out and trying to handle things by yourself when you feel threatened."

"Not everyone." But even as the denial left her lips, Teagan recognized the truth in Sienna's statement. "Okay, so I suck at letting people in."

"You started by trusting me. Now, trust Chase."

"I think it's gone too far for that," Teagan said.

"I don't know Chase all that well, but from everything Ethan has said about him, family comes first. He'll understand you're honoring your father's final wishes."

"And what about his mother's wishes?" Teagan prompted, thinking back to Chase's comment about his mother's heartbreak. "It's been her lifelong dream to restore her family's house. Thanks to me it's going to be gone forever."

"That's Declan's fault. Not yours."

"It's two sides of the same coin."

"So, what do you plan to do?" Sienna asked. "I'm sure you realize that as important as that building is to Declan, he's never going to stop until he gets it from you."

"I know." And her future looked lonely and bleak because of it. "I think I have to go back to New York. If I'm not here, hopefully Declan will stop messing with you all."

"But you and Chase…"

"That's over."

"I don't think so."

Teagan's heart fluttered. "What makes you say that?"

"Because I saw you two together and I recognize love when I see it."

As tempting as it was to accept her sister's opinion as gold, Teagan leaned toward skepticism. Sienna was newly in love, so of course she was optimistic that her sister had made her own romantic connection.

"He's not in love with me," Teagan murmured. "And he never will be. I'm just the woman who he's been sleeping with for a few weeks." She laughed bitterly to cover her anguish. "The one he agreed to keep an eye on for his best friend in case she caused more trouble." Teagan paused to let Sienna absorb that. "I'm pretty sure he's kicking himself for getting blindsided."

A sob mangled the last word. The tears she'd been struggling to hold back rushed up and spilled down her cheeks. For several seconds she couldn't breathe, couldn't talk and couldn't stop the panic spreading through her.

"I don't think you're giving him enough credit. He looks at you like you're the most amazing woman on the planet."

"That was before we found out about Declan buying the Calloway house."

Sienna was quiet for a long moment and then she said, "Ethan is going back to Savannah tomorrow. How about I stay in Charleston through the weekend? We can hang out and talk."

"I'd love that," Teagan declared gratefully, her voice a shaky mess. "You're always there for me. I hope you know how much I appreciate you."

"I do."

"I'm going to book us a suite at Hotel Bennett," Teagan said, overwhelmed with love for her sister. "They have an amazing spa there so we can pamper ourselves, eat room service, raid the minibar and talk. How does that sound?"

"Like the perfect weekend with my sister."

Teagan had never been so grateful to hear Sienna call her that. "I love you," she said, her spirit noticeably lighter since the phone call began. "I can't wait to hug you."

"I love you, too. Hang in there."

As much as she'd enjoyed reconnecting with her sister over the weekend, Teagan couldn't shake her misery over what had happened between her and Chase. It didn't help that Sienna was blissfully preoccupied with Ethan, planning a fairytale wedding and busy expanding her art curating business in the area. The sisters had grown closer than ever over the last two days and Teagan was determined to nurture their connection.

Teagan had spent her time away mulling her future plans and arrived at no clear direction. Although her heart longed to stay in Charleston, Teagan recognized that Grady was the only other person besides her sister that would encourage her to remain. As soon as she entered her grandfather's house, Teagan located Grady in his favorite spot in the living room and settled beside him. His fond smile made her throat contract. As excited as she'd been to meet all her Charleston relatives, Grady had touched her heart the most.

"Chase took me to Magnolia Cemetery," she told him. "I saw where both my grandmother and my mom are buried. Thank you for bringing her home. It makes me happy to know she's back where she belonged."

"She was never happy here." Grady sighed deeply. "But I couldn't leave her all alone in that New York graveyard."

"Everyone who knew her says she was a wild child. I guess the excitement of New York was a lure she couldn't resist."

"My daughter was headstrong and wouldn't listen to anyone. I worried about her in that big city all by herself. And it turns out I was right."

"I thought you might like to see this."

Teagan pulled out the other item her father had left her, an old photo of Edward and Ava taken in Central Park. They sat side by side on a blanket, beaming at the camera. From the date on the back of the photo, Teagan figured her mother had been about three months pregnant at the time. Whether Edward knew was unclear, but Teagan wanted to believe that when he'd found out, he'd been happy.

"This was my dad." She handed Grady the photo. "His name was Edward Quinn. He was an amazing mentor and taught me everything I know about New York real estate. I didn't know he was my dad until after he died when I received a letter from him and this picture." Teagan sucked in a shaky breath as her grandfather smoothed his fingertips across his daughter's beautiful smile. "He also left me a historic building. It's that particular property that's been causing a great deal of trouble for me and everyone around me."

While Grady listened intently, Teagan went on to explain about Declan and the anonymous texts he'd sent to Ethan about her, and how she'd created problems between Ethan and her sister in her quest to be accepted by the family. She explained about Chase and how Declan had bought his family's house and was planning to destroy it if Teagan didn't sell him the Brookfield Building.

"What should I do?" she asked as her tale wound to an end.

"I guess the question you first need to ask is what do you want?"

"I want to keep all of you safe and that means getting Declan off your backs."

Grady waved his hand, dismissing her words. "Don't worry about us. We Wattses have endured tougher opponents than Declan Scott. What will make you happy?"

"Getting back the Calloway house for Chase. I was so happy when I thought he and I were going to be able to restore his family's home together. Plus, I want to create a safe place for victims of domestic violence."

"But to do that you need to give up the legacy your father left you."

Teagan nodded. "How can I choose between them?"

"I guess it's the difference between holding on to the past or sacrificing for your future." Grady took her hand between both of his. "Tell me, if your father was here today, what would he tell you to do?"

Teagan laughed. "He'd tell me to get the Calloway house back and stick it to Declan in the process."

"Then, that's what you should do."

Seeing the mischief in her grandfather's eyes, Teagan's heart clenched. This was the acceptance she'd longed for—the support of someone willing to take her side even when she screwed up.

"Then, that's what I'll do." Teagan swallowed hard. "And when I come back to Charleston, I promise I'm going to find a way to make amends with everyone. I know I've made mistakes, but I'm not the same person I was when I came to Charleston. I hope I can show everyone that I've changed."

"I'm glad to hear you talking like that," came a deep masculine voice from the doorway leading to the hall.

Teagan turned to face Paul Watts and blinked as hot tears filled her eyes. "You are? I wish the rest of your family felt the same. After everything I did to Ethan, they're having a hard time forgiving me."

"I'll talk to them." Paul's somber green gaze flicked towards Grady. He studied his grandfather's expression for a long moment before returning his attention to her. "We spent too many years looking for you to give up on the relationship."

Paul's words filled Teagan with hope. As the eldest of the cousins, his opinion counted for a lot.

Clutching her grandfather's hand, Teagan swallowed the lump in her throat and whispered, "I'm really happy you feel that way. Thank you."

Twelve

A few days later Teagan strolled into Declan's office with the contract he'd presented to her some weeks earlier. The satisfaction in his smug smile made her blood boil. Although she and Ethan had spent the last few days brainstorming possible ways to outsmart Declan, nothing they'd come up with could save both historic buildings from being torn down.

In the end, Teagan accepted she could save either the Brookfield Building or the Calloway house. The choice stopped being complicated when she realized that choosing Chase's happiness took the sting out of failing her father. She'd ruined any hope of a future with Chase the instant she endangered his family's home, but she would delight in knowing that he would look out his window every morning and revel in the Calloway house being restored to its former glory. And maybe he'd think fondly of her and not regret their time together.

"I'm glad you've come to your senses," Declan said, watching her with predatory glee.

"You didn't give me much choice."

"What are you talking about? It's your choice to sell me the Brookfield Building in exchange for the Charleston property you want."

"Don't forget the other part of our deal. You promise to never contact me again."

Declan's grin grew positively vile. "You'll be bored without me around to challenge you."

"Challenge me?" Teagan scoffed. "Is that what you think you're doing? More like you've made it your life's work to ruin anything that makes me happy."

"I suppose you're talking about that derelict shack you want so badly to own?" The sarcastic twist to Declan's question broadcast just how little he thought of Teagan's version of happiness.

Teagan defensiveness flared. "It's going to be beautiful when I'm done restoring it."

"I imagine your boyfriend was pretty upset with you for losing it to me. Are you even together anymore?"

"No," she admitted, bitter defeat in her tone.

Declan snorted. "But you're hoping this grand gesture will win him back? Why are you bothering? Why waste your time on some small-town architect? I guarantee you'll be bored with him inside six months. New York is where it's at. With what I've offered you for the Brookfield, think of the empire you could start with that."

"I don't want an empire," Teagan replied, thinking about Chase and her dream of being accepted by her family and making a positive impact on Charleston. "I just want a place where I belong."

"You don't belong in that backwater town."

Teagan bristled at his scathing remark. "Charleston is a historical gem and it's where my roots are."

Declan arched his eyebrows, looking entirely bored, but there was avarice in the gaze he slid toward the envelope in her hand. "Did you sign the contract?"

"Yes."

Adrenaline surged, goading her pulse to greater speed as Teagan nodded. To an outsider it must've looked as if she was trading a diamond tiara for a necklace made of macaroni. But for her, the value of each wasn't in its market price, but its sentimental worth. To her. To Chase and his family.

As Declan reached out his hand for the envelope, raised voices came from outside in the hall. Declan paid the disruption no heed; his gaze remained fixed on the envelope. Teagan turned as the office door opened and Chase strode in.

She gaped at him. "What are you doing here?"

With her full attention riveted on the determined set of Chase's sculpted lips and the flash of concern in his eyes, she barely noticed Declan step forward and seize the envelope in her hand.

"Stopping you." Chase executed a swift martial-arts move that forced Declan to release the envelope with a grunt.

Teagan clutched the envelope to her chest. Her heart expanded at his rescue. Never before had anyone tried to save her—from herself or any of the battles she'd waged. She'd always fought unaided, schemed to balance the power inequity.

"Don't do this." Chase's expression was earnest as he stood before her, his hands clamping on to her forearms. "We can figure out another way."

"There's no need." With trembling fingers, Teagan reached out and cupped his cheek. She smiled into his blazing eyes and whispered, "Let me do this for you."

Chase turned his lips into her palm. The kiss shot a lightning flash of joy through her.

"You've already given me so much," he murmured. "I'm sorry I didn't believe in you before."

"It's okay." And it was. She could see that he believed in her now and that was all that mattered.

"But I *know* what the property means to you."

Despite his special emphasis on the word *know*, Teagan was certain he had no idea of her true attachment. She'd only shared the truth with Sienna and Grady. Both had promised to keep it secret, which meant that Chase had chosen to sacrifice something important to him and his family so she could be happy. Teagan never imagined her love for Chase could grow more powerful, but obviously she had a lot to learn. She smiled, imagining the infinite joy the future held for them.

"Not as much as you do," Teagan told him, before glancing toward Declan, who watched their exchange with disinterest. "We have a deal. I sell you the Brookfield Building in exchange for the Calloway property."

Declan's handsome face lit with triumph as he reached out for the envelope.

Teagan held it out of reach. Did Declan think that love had turned her into a fool? Before she gave him everything he wanted, Teagan intended to extract an important promise.

With Chase's muscular body offering her his strength, his hands cupping her shoulders in a show of unity, she said, "And you agree to leave me—and everyone close to me—alone forever?"

Declan took in the towering sentinel behind her and sneered. "Out of sight. Out of mind."

"Good." She dropped the contract on his desk, then, reaching into her purse, she extracted her cell phone and sent a text. "I've wired what you paid for the Charleston house."

She leveled a stony stare at Declan until he summoned

his assistant and arranged to pay her the amount agreed to in the contract they'd both signed. A few minutes later, another text appeared on her phone, confirming the transaction.

"You'll probably want these." Declan tossed a courier envelope her way. The metallic clink of keys sounded as the projectile came straight at her head.

Teagan was too stunned to duck and only Chase's sharp reflexes, honed by years of martial arts training, kept the sharp corner of the package from striking her cheek. She didn't need to hear Chase's incensed growl to recognize that his restraint was on its last thread.

"Let's get out of here." Teagan caught Chase's free hand and tugged him toward the exit. "We have a whole lot of celebrating to do."

In his eagerness to put distance between Teagan and Declan Scott, Chase set a blistering pace on the way to the elevator bank. Teagan's heels clicked a staccato rhythm as she kept up with Chase's stride. Despite his best efforts to convince her to not let Declan have the Brookfield Building, he'd failed her. Chase said nothing until they entered the empty car and the doors slid shut.

"Why did you do that?" he demanded. "Why did you sell Declan the building your father trusted you to keep safe?"

Teagan gazed at him in shock. "How did you know about my father?"

"Sienna told Ethan. He told me."

A disappointed sigh slipped past her tight lips. "She promised me she'd keep it a secret." But there were no secrets between Sienna and the man she adored, unlike those that had separated her and Chase.

"Why?" Chase arched an eyebrow. "Because you had this noble sacrifice planned and didn't want me to interfere?"

"It was all I had to bargain with," Teagan insisted. "And I

didn't want you to think I was manipulating you into owing me something in return."

"But I don't understand. Why would you give it up?"

"To save the Calloway house."

Chase kicked himself for guilting her into the rash act. "You shouldn't have done that."

"Why not? It's important to your family and I would do anything in my power to see it saved."

"I'm sorry." The apology rumbled out of him, but Chase knew it wasn't enough. He owed her not just his gratitude, but his trust and admiration. "I said all the wrong things to you that night on the terrace."

"You were angry and disappointed."

"That's no excuse. I had no business taking it out on you. Especially not after I failed to create a safe space for you to confide what Declan was up to."

"I'm not good at asking for help."

"Because you've faced too much rejection when you have."

He'd listened to her stories but hadn't comprehended the impact on her behavior until he'd witnessed her actions firsthand. With the love and support his family and friends provided, he couldn't imagine her coping with difficulties alone.

"Are you going to be okay? Declan has the only thing your father ever gave you."

"It might seem that way, but while it's the only tangible thing I ever received from him, what matters to me is what I gained all those years he mentored me. Edward believed in me when my parents didn't. He taught me how to appreciate historic architecture and awakened my passion for preservation and restoration." Teagan smiled. "From him I learned how to fight for what I believed in and that it's okay not to get what you want if the people you love are happy."

Any response he might've made was halted as the elevator stopped, the doors opened and two men stepped into the car.

"Thank you for having my back today," she began softly, staring at the descending numbers. "How did you know where I'd be?"

"Paul tracked your phone."

Eyes flashing, Teagan stared at Chase. "He tracked—"

"I didn't want you facing him alone."

Before he could add anything more, the elevator doors opened, depositing them in the lobby. As they headed toward the exit, Chase tucked her hand into the crook of his arm, noting the icy chill in her fingers.

A black town car awaited them at the curb. Teagan drew Chase toward it. The driver opened the rear door and Teagan settled in with Chase beside her. While they waited for the driver to get behind the wheel, Chase handed her the shipping envelope Declan had tossed at her.

"Declan didn't seem too happy about letting you have this. Do you think he'll leave you alone going forward?"

Teagan withdrew the keys. "He might be a ruthless businessman, but he's never been one to go back on his word."

"Not even to take revenge?"

"Against me?" She cocked her head and studied him with raised eyebrows. "Whatever for? He got what he wanted."

Chase almost smiled as he pondered the surprise that awaited Declan.

"We're in your debt," he told her. "I'm in your debt."

Her lighthearted mood dimmed. "That's not why I did it. I don't want you to feel like you owe me. It was the right thing to do." She gave a self-deprecating laugh. "No one's ever accused me of doing the right thing before."

"That's not true." He thought about his long conversation with Sienna. Teagan might downplay the good she'd done, but a long list of people who'd once needed help owed her a lot. "We all misjudged you."

"No, I think you all judged me perfectly." Her expression tensed. "I am a self-absorbed know-it-all that runs roughshod over people."

"But you're more than that. You're quick to help people who need it. And you don't expect anything in return."

"So you'll be thinking fondly of me from here on out?" Beneath her radiant grin lurked candid vulnerability.

Chase put his arm around her and drew her close. He cupped her cheek and grazed his lips over hers. "I've been thinking fondly of you for a long time."

"Stop." She sagged against him, her breath puffing against his cheek. "Your Southern charm is showing and you know I'm quite susceptible to it." When he slanted his mouth along her jawline and down her neck, she groaned. "Keep that up and…"

"And what?" He nipped at the sensitive spot where her neck joined her shoulder.

Her fingers tunneled into his hair, drawing him closer. "I have a private plane waiting to take me back to Charleston," she purred. "Let's get on it and I'll show you."

"I like the sound of that, but before we do, let's take a little detour." He gave the driver the address for the Brookfield Building and noted Teagan's jolt of surprise.

A shadow passed over her expression. "Why are we going there?" She sounded both mystified and sad.

"I thought you'd like to get one more look at it."

"Before Declan tears it down?" A vigorous shake of her head betrayed how hard giving up the building had been. "No thanks."

"But I've never seen it in person and I'd like to, very much," Chase insisted. "It's important for me to appreciate what you gave up so that the Calloway property could live on."

"It wasn't the sacrifice you think," she said. "It wasn't just for you. I did it for us. I really want you and me to collaborate on restoring your family's home. I'd like for us to create a charitable foundation for the property so that it will be safe forever." She offered him a tremulous smile. "I think your mother would like that, don't you?"

"I can't let you do that," he told her, thinking of the hefty purchase price. "It's too much."

"Are you worried that I might ask for something in return?"

Her mischievous expression told him she was teasing, but it was hard to ignore the way his stomach muscles clenched. "Whatever you ask for, I would willingly give."

"That's a dangerous offer you've just made. I could ask you for all sorts of things you'd hate."

"I'll take that chance," he told her. "What's your fondest wish?"

"The chance for a fresh start." Her smile was like a sunrise. "With you."

Her words kicked him in the gut. "Teagan…"

"Being with you helps me be the best version of myself and I'm a little afraid to leave your shadow for fear that I'll regress and become someone you won't want to be with."

"I don't think that could ever be possible."

"Then why did you push me away?"

"Because the way you make me feel is so strong. I was afraid of it. Until you came along, my only passion was for historic restoration. And then you blew into my life with your sassy New York vibe and your knack for turning my world upside down and opened my heart to what I've been missing." He ran his knuckles across her flushed cheek. "I love you."

Her eyes shimmered with unshed tears. "I love you, too."

"I don't want to live another second of my life without you."

The town car came to a stop beside the building that had mattered so much to Teagan and her father. Excitement sped through Chase as he drew Teagan from the car and stood beside her on the sidewalk, staring up at the building. The architect in him appreciated the ornamented red-and-white brickwork and limestone cornice bookended by twin spires at the corners, echoing the church spires across the street.

"It really is amazing," he murmured.

"Too bad Declan is going to tear it down." Despite the brave face she'd been wearing, Teagan's voice throbbed with despair.

"He will find that hard to do."

Chase reached into his inner coat pocket and drew out a rolled-up piece of paper. It was fastened with a bit of red silk ribbon for drama. Something sparkled in the middle of the bow and Teagan gazed in confusion from the scroll to Chase.

"What's this?"

With a smile, he unfastened the bow and held the paper in one hand, the glistening diamond ring in the other. "Which would you like to talk about first?"

"Why is it only during the big moments that your sense of humor appears?" She exhaled in a rush and pointed at the diamond ring.

Nodding in approval, Chase dropped to one knee before her. "Teagan Burns, my love, I want to restore properties and raise children with you for the rest of our lives. Will you marry me?"

"Oh, yes." Teagan bent down and cupped his face, kissing him urgently.

Chase surged to his feet and wrapped his arms around her, lifting her and swinging her in a full circle. Oblivious to any nearby pedestrians, he kissed her long and deep, claiming her now and forever as his.

"Are you sure about this?" Teagan cried when they at last needed to come up for air. She looked half terrified that he'd change his mind, even as her voice dipped into its familiar flirtatious tones. "I can't promise that I'll settle down and be a proper Charleston wife."

He dusted a kiss across her forehead. "Do you even know what that entails?"

"Supporting my handsome, accomplished husband and everything he does." Her imitation of his mother was spot-on.

"That goes both ways, you know. I fully intend to support my ambitious, clever wife in all her endeavors."

"Oh, please don't do that. I need you to keep me on the straight and narrow."

"Don't sell yourself short. I think you've lost your taste for scheming."

"Maybe. But I'm worried that you can take the girl out of New York but you can't take the schemes out of the girl."

"As long as the girl stays in Charleston, I can handle a little scheming."

"But never with you. I might not have told you about Declan, but I've always been honest when it comes to how I feel about you. That at least I can promise will never change."

"Shall we make that part of our vows?"

"I don't see why not. I, Teagan Burns-Watts, solemnly swear to be honest and transparent with you for the rest of my life."

"And I, Chase Love, promise that I will never doubt you again."

Her green eyes sparkled with unshed tears as she said, "That's a pretty big leap of faith."

"It's one I owe you. For too long I ignored my instincts about you and let others fill my head with their opinions. I should've trusted you."

"To be fair, I made a mess of things before you and I met."

"You hadn't yet learned how to trust me," he told her. "I know that's different now."

"That's because of you. You gave me a safe place to land."

"And then I failed you."

"Not failed. You opened my eyes and gave me the motivation to fix all that I'd broken."

He brought the rolled-up paper into her line of view. "I hope this makes your decision to sell the Brookfield Building a little less painful."

Looking utterly mystified, Teagan unrolled the paper and scanned the page. "I don't understand. This is a report from the Landmark Preservation Commission about the Brookfield Building."

Chase's lips curved into a self-satisfied grin. "It's been designated a landmark."

"How?"

"I called Knox and Paul," he explained. "No one knows more about securing landmark designations in Charleston than my business partner. After you mentioned Declan's influence over certain members of New York's Landmark Preservation Commission, Knox connected with a schoolmate of his that is active in New York real estate."

Chase had recognized that he couldn't go to war with Declan unless he knew the playing field, and from everything he'd learned about the property developer, having a half-assed plan in the works would only end in defeat.

"Once we knew the players, I contacted Paul to do some research on them."

A month earlier the cybersecurity specialist had been integral in figuring out who'd been sending the anonymous texts warning Ethan about Teagan's scheming. In addition to preventing cyber threats, Paul was also quite adept at digging up all sorts of information on people. He had a network of private investigators and law enforcement he worked with all across the country.

"He used his connections to figure out what sort of dirty

tactics Declan was using to pressure six commissioners to stall the vote on the Brookfield's landmark status." Chase grinned at her. "Once we applied a little pressure of our own, they agreed that the application should be approved. And voilà."

"You saved it," Teagan murmured in delight. "For me."

His heart skipped a beat as her expression grew radiant. She was the only woman for him and he would've done so much more to prove that to her.

"I knew what it meant to you."

"It meant so much." Teagan winced. "I hope you know that I'm eternally grateful for what you did for me and I'm thrilled that it won't be torn down, but the Brookfield Building is my past." She paused and the fierce light in her eyes held him captive. "You and the Calloway house are my future."

Her fervent pledge demonstrated why he adored her.

"I love you." Chase cupped her face in his hands. "I promise you'll never regret your choice."

Bringing his lips to hers, he sealed his vow with an earnest kiss.

When he lifted his head, Teagan whispered, "I am yours, Chase Love, now and forever. Never doubt how much I love you." Then she took his hand and drew him toward the waiting town car. "Now, take me home to Charleston where I belong."

* * * * *

HER BEST FRIEND'S BROTHER

YAHRAH ST. JOHN

To my best friends: Therolyn Rodgers, Tiffany Griffin, Tonya Conway and Mattie Alexander.

One

"Hello?" Wynter Barrington called out as she used her key to enter her family's estate in Terrell Hills, located northeast of downtown San Antonio. She plopped her large duffel bag and suitcase on the floor, tossed her keys in the antique bowl on the table and shook off her jean jacket. It was early January, and she'd forgotten how cold it could get in Texas. Today it was forty degrees. When she'd made it to baggage claim, Wynter had hoped a family member would be there to pick her up, maybe with a thicker coat? Instead, there had been no one.

Was she surprised?

Her father, Gregory Barrington, was always caught up with work and building his wealth, as if there weren't enough zeros in his bank account. Her mother, Melinda, flitted about from one charity or social meeting to another. And her older brother, Corey? Ever since they were kids, he'd seemed intent on antagonizing her. He would push her down in the mud and dirty her school uniform or dunk her in the pool. It was no wonder she had decided to forgo Christmas with the family in favor of another month in Bali.

Wynter took in the freshly polished black-and-white marble floors, the gorgeous spiral chandelier, the long, sweeping staircase to the second floor and the stone-covered arches to the main rooms. An enormous bouquet of calla lilies stood center stage on the foyer table. Everything looked the same, but it didn't feel the same.

She couldn't believe she was here for her aunt Helaine Smith's funeral. Helaine had passed away in her sleep a few days ago from a brain aneurysm. Her aunt had been the one person in the family who stood by Wynter's side, even if she didn't agree with Wynter's actions. A year ago, Wynter was so unhappy that she chucked her job at the family's investment empire, where she'd been working in the marketing department, and escaped her ho-hum life. Why? Because she wanted to be like her aunt, who'd led a bohemian lifestyle and traveled the globe.

Her family thought Wynter was off her rocker, but Helaine had always been supportive. Wynter was determined to make her travel and leisure blog, *Wynter's Corner*, a success. It didn't just focus on travel content, but instead was about immersing oneself in another culture and trying new foods or activities off the beaten path. She gave tips and tricks on finding cheap flights and accommodations and creating fun-filled itineraries, all the while keeping money in your wallet, but the blog wasn't always lucrative. Subsequently, she'd been receiving a monthly stipend from her father to cover some of her expenses.

For most of her life, she'd felt invisible to the Barrington clan, which was why she'd acted out in her youth to get their action, but that attitude always managed to land her in hot water. Meanwhile, Corey was living up to their father's dreams. He was a workaholic, just like the elder Barrington. Then there was Francesca, Corey's pretentious wife. Wynter wasn't a fan, because Francesca looked down at Wynter when *she* came from a working-class family.

Life as a Barrington was an endless merry-go-round of staying on top and trying to stay relevant. It was why Wynter had left home the first opportunity she could.

She was heading to her room when Agnes, their long-time housekeeper, rushed toward her and enveloped Wynter in a warm hug. Now *this* she remembered, Wynter thought as the Spanish woman held her tight. Agnes had been with their family since she was a child. Agnes was the one who had told Wynter about the birds and bees. Her mother had been too busy to explain what was happening to Wynter's body as she had navigated puberty.

Agnes grabbed both sides of Wynter's face with her weathered palms. "I'm so sorry to hear about Miss Helaine. She was such a good woman."

Wynter nodded. "Thank you, Agnes. She was phenomenal."

"We need more like her." Agnes touched her cheek. "How are you doing?"

"I'm coping," Wynter responded honestly.

"That's all you can do, but if you want to talk…" Agnes left the statement open-ended. Wynter appreciated that Agnes didn't push. Instead, she asked, "How about you go wash up and get ready? Dinner will be here before you know it, and you know how your mother is."

Boy, did she, Wynter thought.

Her mother required everyone to dress for dinner as if it was a formal occasion. Wynter hated it. She had always felt less than, as though she never measured up, probably because she didn't. Her mother always found fault with what she was wearing, her hair or her makeup. Wynter just couldn't win.

"Sounds like a good idea," Wynter stated and went to

lift one of her bags, but Agnes shooed her away. "I'll take care of them."

They climbed the spiral staircase to the second floor and toward Wynter's room, located in the east wing of the house.

"How long are you staying this time?"

Wynter shrugged. "Not long. Once the funeral is over, I'll be leaving."

"That's a shame. I would love to have you home for a while."

"I'm sorry, it can't be helped. Where's my mother?" Wynter inquired, raising a brow.

"She's having a facial in the spa room downstairs."

"Spa room?"

Agnes chuckled. "Your mother's made some changes since you were last here. With you gone and Corey married, she said it was time for her."

"I see," Wynter said, but she really didn't. Her mother always made time to ensure she looked 100 percent perfect before she walked out the door. Heaven forbid anyone see her not looking her best. Wynter would have to accept that her family was never going to be the cast of *Black-ish,* and the sooner she got over that delusion, the better off she'd be.

"We are so glad to have you join the firm." Brock Jamison, one of the partners of the law firm Jamison and Charles, shook Riley's hand later that morning when the partners met him at their office in downtown San Antonio. "We need someone with your killer instinct on our team."

Riley had been dubbed "the Shark of the East" because he knew how to figure out an opponent's weakness, exploit it and flip the script to ensure his divorce cases went his way. Ever since he graduated from Harvard Law School, Riley had pursued excellence. He'd joined a top law firm in New York right out of Harvard and quickly gained a reputation as a shrewd negotiator.

He'd garnered several high-profile clients and minimized their exposure during their divorces. Once word got out that he intended to relocate, firms across the country had jockeyed for him to join them. All they saw were dollar signs, and that was fine with him. Riley knew what it was like to go without, because he and his sister, Shay, had had everything they could ever wish for—until their parents' divorce took it all away.

"I'm excited to be back home," Riley finally said. He'd met with Brock and his partner, Gina Charles, a couple of months ago when they'd flown to Manhattan, where he'd been based. They'd been eager to hire someone with Riley's talents. He was a closer and always got the job done. Although he had always intended to relocate home, he'd made it a condition that his becoming partner had to be on the table. Gina and Brock agreed, and now that he was accredited in Texas, the firm was Jamison, Charles and Davis.

"If you need anything while you're here—" Gina lightly touched his arm on her way out "—just let us know."

He saw the appreciative glint in her eye. Riley knew he was easy on the eyes, because ever since he was fifteen, women of all ages had tended to congregate around him. Today, he was dressed in a three-piece suit that he knew emphasized his six-foot-three frame. When he went to court, he towered over his opponents, which gave him an advantage. He portrayed power, and he usually got what he wanted, when he wanted and how he wanted it.

After Gina and Brock left, Riley placed his briefcase on the modern glass desk and stalked over to the window to look at the view of San Antonio. It was good to be home. He could check on his mother regularly and periodically give his little sister a little tough love. She was working as a yoga and Pilates instructor at a fitness studio in town. Although she had a loyal fan base, surely there was something else she could be doing?

As if she had ESP, his cell phone rang, and the display read Shay. Riley picked it up. "Hey, sis."

"Hello to you, too, big brother," Shay responded. "You got back in town yesterday and didn't come by and see me."

He sighed. What was it about little sisters that they loved to tease their older brothers? "I'm sorry. I got caught up on a case, and today I've been getting acclimated at the new firm."

"And? How is it?"

"Exactly what I expected," Riley said. He never made a move that wasn't well thought out. Shay was the exact opposite. She led with her heart and not her head, which explained her early divorce at twenty-four. Riley, on the other hand, looked at all the angles before diving in.

"That's good, I guess. Can we meet up for dinner? I would love to see you."

"Absolutely—I'd love that," Riley replied, and he meant it. He missed his sister. They'd grown close after their parents' divorce decimated their mother. It had been hard for Eliza Davis to get out of bed some mornings and take them to school or fix them a meal. Eventually, Riley had learned how to fend for himself and subsequently help his four-years-younger sister, who hadn't understood why Mommy couldn't shake off her depression.

"Great. I'll see you tonight at seven?" Shay asked. "I'll pick you up at your hotel."

"That's not necessary. I can meet you someplace."

"Riley, let me do this for you."

It was hard for Riley not to be in charge in their relationship. He was supposed to take care of her, but his Bentley, which he was having shipped from Manhattan, wasn't arriving until tomorrow. "All right. All right, but you'll have to pick me up from work."

Ending the call, Riley glanced around his new corner office. He'd finally arrived. Maybe it was time to take his foot off the gas and relax a little. He snorted. As if that were possible—he lived for the game.

Wynter awoke from her nap with a start. Glancing around the room, she had to remember where she was, but when she did, the grief she'd kept inside since Bali came hurtling back to the forefront of her mind. Her aunt Helaine was gone. At least she'd passed away in her sleep and hadn't felt any pain. Wynter wished she could have talked to her one more time. Told her how much she loved her. How much she respected her and how thankful she was to have her in her life—but she couldn't.

Instead, she recalled the special moments they'd shared. Like the first time they went for tea and scones when she was eight years old and they wore fancy dresses, hats and gloves. Or the time her aunt took Wynter to Paris and they rode to the top of the Eiffel Tower. Wynter supposed that was where she got her zest for traveling, because her aunt had included Wynter on her trips. And in her teens, her aunt had always included her group of friends, known as the Six Gems, whenever she could on their outings because, she said, they were the daughters she never had.

Slowly, Wynter moved into an upright position. It was dark out, which meant she'd slept longer than she thought. She normally didn't wear a watch, because she liked to enjoy life without being tethered to a schedule. Reaching for her iPhone, she read the time. It was six o'clock—cocktail hour at the Barrington residence. If she hurried, she could shower, dress and be downstairs in fifteen minutes. While traveling abroad, Wynter had learned not to sweat the small stuff. But here? Her mother expected everyone to be on time for dinner, and Wynter was no exception.

Fifteen minutes later, after throwing on a knee-length sweaterdress and her favorite fringed boots, Wynter rushed down the stairs to the great room. The dress wasn't as chic as her mother would expect, but it would have to do, because her wardrobe was limited with Wynter being on the road most of the year. She'd spritzed her naturally wavy shoulder-length hair with shea moisturizer, arched her eyebrows and added a swipe of lipstick.

When she arrived, her mother and father were bickering. Her brother and his wife were drinking wine, but all conversation ceased when they saw Wynter standing in the doorway. Wynter couldn't miss the disdain in their stare. They were all dressed to impress. Her father and Corey looked as if they'd come straight from work in their business suits. They were both of average height, with medium-brown complexions and the same close-cropped haircut. Her mother wore a fit-and-flare jacquard dress, and Francesca was in a slim-fitting black-and-white sheath.

"Wynter, good heavens, what are you wearing?" Francesca asked. Francesca was everything a woman of Wynter's standing was supposed to be: poised, elegant and refined—or so her mother liked to tell her. Tall, at five foot nine, with a slender figure and long ebony hair in a sophisticated cut, Francesca oozed sophistication and made Wynter look dowdy in comparison.

"I got this dress in Bali during my travels," Wynter replied as she walked in the room and headed to her parents. She mustn't let their negative opinion bring her down. "Mother," she said, giving her a kiss on each cheek. "Daddy." She leaned over to give him the briefest of hugs.

"Glad you could finally join us, darling," her mother replied. "Agnes told us you arrived earlier and went straight to sleep."

"It was a long flight from Bali."

"Perhaps you shouldn't travel so far," Corey replied with a smirk. "Then you would be a little closer to home."

Wynter ignored the dig, reminding herself this visit would be a short one. Once she buried her aunt and said her goodbyes, she would be on her way. "How are you doing, Mother? Losing Aunt Helaine so sudden…"

Her mother's expression softened. "It was a shock. My big sister was always so big and bold. I never thought anything could take her out."

Tears welled in Wynter's eyes. "I can't believe it, either."

"Well, dry your eyes," her mother said, handing Wynter a handkerchief. "We must carry on. It's what Helaine would want."

So much for commiserating over their shared grief. Wynter had hoped her aunt's death might bring her and her mother closer, but now she wasn't so sure.

"I wonder what her will says," Francesca said aloud.

It was one of the first times Wynter had ever heard Francesca say anything in poor taste. Wynter and her mother both scoffed. Even her brother had the decency to look uneasy at his wife's social faux pas.

Francesca lowered her head. "My apologies, Melinda. I don't know what came over me."

Wynter knew. Francesca hoped Aunt Helaine had left Corey a big inheritance, but their aunt had never warmed to her brother. They'd been like oil and water.

"I, for one, am going to miss the old battle-ax," her father stated.

"Gregory!" her mother admonished.

Her father shrugged and drank some of the dark-colored liquid in his crystal tumbler. "What? You know Helaine never thought I was good enough for you. I came from a working-class background, while the both of you were from the upper crust."

"That's all water under the bridge," her mother responded. "Look where you are now."

"I suppose," her father replied grudgingly.

"I'm going to check on dinner."

When her mother left, Corey wasted no time in going in on Wynter. "What have you been up to the last few months, squirt?"

He loved to tease her about her five-foot-two height. "You would know if you followed my blog," Wynter replied and went over to the bar nestled against the far side of the room. She poured herself a bourbon, something she'd gotten used to drinking after a stint in the Bluegrass State.

"Isn't that a rather strong aperitif?" Francesca asked, quirking her overly arched brow.

"I'm twenty-seven years old. I don't need you or anyone else policing what I drink."

Francesca puffed out a breath. "Well, excuse me."

"You are excused." There was no love lost between Wynter and her sister-in-law. She'd known Francesca since they were teenagers, and she'd been just as hoity-toity in high school as she was now. Back then, after Wynter wrecked her father's brand-new Porsche, her parents retaliated by taking Wynter out of the private high school and placing her in a public one. They thought they were punishing Wynter, but instead she ended up meeting five incredible women who would become her best friends. Meanwhile, Francesca had gotten worse, because she'd married into the family.

"Don't go getting your panties in a bunch," Corey responded. "Franny was probably worried you could have developed a drinking habit or something. Not many women drink bourbon."

Wynter turned her eyes to Corey. "Well, I do." Corey looked as if he was ready to say something back, but her mother announced that dinner was ready. She was thankful for the interruption, because Corey couldn't even manage cordiality. Wynter followed her mother down the hall to the exquisitely decorated dining room, boasting vintage French furniture, where they'd sit for an elaborate four-course meal.

"I'm glad you're back, Wynter," her father said, once the first course of gazpacho was served. "Because it's high time we talk about you coming back to Barrington Investments."

Here we go again, Wynter thought, suppressing an eye roll. She knew her father was not a fan of her leaving, but she'd hoped, in time, that he would accept her decision. Apparently, she was wrong. "I'm very happy doing my travel blog."

"A blog that makes you no money," he responded hotly.

"Yes, it does," Wynter replied. It might not be the amount she wanted, but with more followers, she would secure advertising dollars.

"Not enough," her father replied curtly. "And we will no longer subsidize this hobby."

Wynter's eyes darted up from her soup bowl. "Pardon?"

"You're not hard of hearing," her father responded, and she saw Corey smirk from across the table. "It's long past time for you to come back to the firm and work with me and your brother."

"I can't believe you're doing this now," Wynter said. "You couldn't even wait until after the funeral?"

"Delaying won't change my mind," her father stated.

"Mom?" She turned to her mother for help, but Melinda lowered her head as if she were unearthing jewels in her gazpacho.

"Either you come back to Barrington Investments and the marketing department, or you're cut off financially. This family is no longer going to support you gallivanting across the world."

Wynter supposed she shouldn't be shocked. Her parents had never understood her need for freedom and her passion for exploring new cultures. Wiping her mouth with her napkin, she quietly rose from the table and started for the door.

"Well, aren't you going to answer me?" her father asked.

Wynter swung around to face him. "My leaving should be answer enough. I will not be railroaded or blackmailed into doing things your way, Daddy. I have a vision for my future, and it doesn't include sitting behind a desk, shuffling papers."

Her father was outraged while Corey shot daggers at her. "Wynter, I'm warning you..." Her father thumped his fist on the table, causing it to reverberate.

"And I've received your message, loud and clear," Wynter responded. "Mother—" She glanced in her direction. "My apologies, but I won't be staying for dinner. Good night."

Wynter stalked out of the room. The monthly stipend she counted on to supplement her income was gone, and she was going to have to figure out her next move quickly, because her father had drawn a line in the sand. But then again, so had she. She hadn't used the entire allowance every month. Instead, she'd saved the majority of it so she would have breathing room. Wynter was glad she had, because she was going to need it. She only had one life to live, and no one was going to tell her how to go about it. Somehow, she would figure out a way to support herself without coming back home with her tail tucked between her legs.

She just had to come up with a plan.

Two

"It's so good to have you back, Riley," Shay said when he met her at their favorite restaurant, a cozy family-owned eatery specializing in Italian food on San Antonio's River Walk. They sat at a small table with a red-checkered tablecloth.

Riley took a good, long look at his baby sister, who wore her hair in long dark locks. She'd always been petite, at five foot four, which was why he'd always felt protective, but she was a grown woman now.

"It's good to be back." It had never been his intention to stay away this long. He was supposed to get a college education at Princeton and obtain his law degree somewhere in Texas. Riley had never imagined he'd get accepted into Harvard Law, but once he was, he'd figured out a way to make it work. The problem was, it left Shay alone to deal with their mother's depressive episodes.

"Mom will be thrilled, too. When I told her you were back, her face lit up like it was Christmas."

"I'm sorry I left you alone to deal with the fallout," Riley replied. When he'd been younger, he'd shielded Shay from the damaging effects of their mother's mental health issues, but once he went to school, she'd been left alone to carry the load. He'd been selfish, wanting to carve out a life for himself away from the manic depression that had consumed so much of his teenage years. When he came home, Riley never knew whether their mother would still be in her pajamas at 3:00 p.m. Or if he might get called away from lacrosse practice because she was having an episode.

"It's okay," Shay said, sipping her wine. "It was your time."

"And what about you?"

"What about me?"

"Dealing with Mom can be a full-time job some days," Riley responded. "It couldn't have been easy for you."

It certainly hadn't been for him. It's why he struggled to form lasting relationships—it's why he didn't believe in love. He'd seen firsthand what loving someone could do to you. His mother had never recovered from losing their father. So Riley refused to acknowledge the emotion.

Shay sighed and put down her glass. "It wasn't. It's one of the reasons why Kevin and I had so many troubles, not to mention we were way too young to get married. Kevin couldn't accept that he didn't come first and that Mama needed me."

"Kevin was a knucklehead anyway," Riley replied. "I never understood what you saw in him. He wasn't going anywhere or doing anything with his life. I'm glad you didn't have any kids with him."

"Not for lack of trying," Shay responded dejectedly.

Riley frowned. This was the first time he was hearing about this, and the strain on his sister's face told him it was real. "What are you talking about?"

"Kevin wanted a baby and I wanted to give him one,

but the more we tried, the farther apart we became. Add my devotion to taking care of Mama and you have a recipe for divorce." Shay's voice cracked on the last sentence, and Riley reached across the table and placed his hand over his sister's.

"I'm so sorry, Shay. I wish I had known."

Shay shrugged. "There's nothing you could have done."

"Did you see a doctor?"

Shay shook her head. "We were young and barely making ends meet. We couldn't afford a fertility specialist."

"Then there's still a chance you could be a mother someday if that's what you want," Riley replied. And if it was, he would do everything in his power to ensure his sister achieved her dream. It was the least he could do after leaving her with their mother all these years. Once he'd started making real money, he'd hired a caregiver to help, which finally allowed Shay to focus on herself and get her fitness credentials.

"Oh, my God!" Shay chuckled. "How did we get so far off topic? My fertility, or lack thereof, is beside the point. It's not like there's some man in my life."

"You mean my little sister doesn't have men beating down the door?" Riley teased. Shay was a beautiful woman, with smooth toffee skin and a killer figure most women would be envious of, because she was a health nut. He supposed it had a lot to do with her seeing their mother's downward spiral and wanting to be the antithesis of her.

Shay smiled at him. "Sadly, no, but I wouldn't have the time anyway. I've been focused on my work and helping others achieve their best self."

"You have to make time for you."

"Ha!" Shay laughed, and Riley realized he was the pot calling the kettle black. "You're one to talk. You're as driven as I am. No—" she shook her head "—you're definitely more."

Riley let out a hearty chuckle. "I won't to try to deny it. You're right."

Although their father had sent child support when they were young, he'd checked out on their family when he left, and his children had been left to pick up the pieces. Riley had been ill-equipped to handle the responsibility he'd been given, and the money their father sent hardly covered the household bills when their mother couldn't work. It was why he was so driven now. He never wanted their family to go without again.

"How about we order?" Shay said. "I'm starved. All I had for lunch was a cauliflower rice bowl with some avocado."

Riley frowned. "Sounds appetizing." He signaled the waiter over, and soon they'd ordered enough food to feed an army. Riley was happy he could be there for Shay and his mother again. He was at a point in his life where he'd achieved what he wanted to professionally. It didn't mean he didn't keep working hard, because that was what you had to do to stay on top.

"What's next for you?" Shay asked after they finished their meal and were enjoying dessert and cappuccinos. Thanks to her usually healthy eating preferences, Shay hadn't minded when he suggested a treat.

Riley shrugged. "Maybe buy a house?"

After they finished dessert, Riley escorted Shay back to her car and then decided to go for a stroll along the River Walk because it was close to the penthouse he had purchased.

As he went, he noticed he'd caught the eye of several women. He was used to drawing attention, but one woman in particular caught his eye, even though she stood a few feet away, staring off into the distance. She had tawny skin and tumbling waves of dark hair that fell to her shoulders, while her figure, in a snug, fitted sweaterdress, was petite yet curvy in all the right places. His heart throbbed when he looked at her. Hell, every part of him throbbed.

Riley didn't know how this beautiful creature had landed in his lap, but he wasn't going to look a gift horse in the mouth. He'd wanted to get his feet wet now that he was back in town, and his prayers had been answered. But as he moved closer, Riley realized he knew her. Had grown up with her.

He'd just lusted after his little sister's best friend— Wynter Barrington.

Wynter stood on the edge of the river and wondered what she was going to do. She was on her own in more ways than one. Her family had turned against her, but had they ever really been *with* her? She used to go to her aunt, and Helaine would talk her off the ledge. But now she didn't have her aunt to rely on. Wynter supposed that was why she'd come tonight—to feel closer to her in some way. The River Walk had always been one of her aunt's favorite places to talk.

Wynter thought about her girlfriends, the other members of the Six Gems: Lyric Taylor, Asia Reynolds, Teagan Williams, Shay Davis and Egypt Cox, whom she'd met in public high school. Wynter had seen the other five girls around school and wanted to talk to them, but they'd seemed like a close-knit circle, no outsiders allowed. Until one day, a bigger girl picked on Wynter in gym class. Suddenly, the five girls came to her defense because they didn't like bullies, and a friendship was born.

Boys were always trying to hit on them, and Teagan had decided the group needed a name. Egypt had said they were all priceless and any boy would be lucky to date them. Asia had said they were like the gemstones she used in the jewelry she made. Suddenly, the Six Gems came to be. The name stuck, and they'd been using it ever since.

Wynter's friends would be a godsend and offer their support and a crying shoulder if she needed one, but it was late. She didn't want to call them with her troubles. Could they honestly relate to her crisis? She would probably sound like a poor little rich girl, while the rest of them were working hard and saving to start their own businesses. Egypt was hoping to leave her popular Raleigh food truck and open her own restaurant. Former ballerina Lyric was tired of all the dance moms at the studio where she worked in Memphis and wanted her own place. Meanwhile, Shay was adamant she could become the next fitness guru if she had a retail spot. Up-and-coming Phoenix real estate agent Teagan was working toward launching her own brokerage. And Asia's jewelry was selling like hotcakes online and in Denver, but she wanted a brick-and-mortar store.

They all had a goal, and so did Wynter. Hers was to monetize her travel blog. She sat down on a bench to feel sorry for herself.

"Wynter?"

Hearing her name being called was jarring, considering it was nearly 10:00 p.m. Glancing up, Wynter did a double take as she looked into the gleaming depths of Riley Davis's ebony eyes. He wore a white silk shirt with a few buttons undone and dark trousers that hugged his narrow hips while emphasizing his muscular thighs. A suit jacket hung over his impressive shoulders. At thirty-one—she remembered their exact age difference because she'd crushed on him as a teen—he looked rich, powerful and utterly masculine.

"Riley?"

He smiled, revealing a perfect set of white teeth. "One and the same, but what are you doing out here?" he inquired as he moved closer toward her. "It's late."

Wynter soaked Riley in, from the classic haircut framing his chiseled face, to his broad nose, to his generous mouth, surrounded by a trim black beard. He was a fine specimen of male beauty *and* he smelled amazing.

"I needed some air," Wynter found herself saying.

"Is everything okay?" he asked, sitting beside her.

Wynter glanced down and noticed she was clutching the handkerchief her mother had given her earlier. She shook her head. "No, not really. I'm here in town because my aunt…" Her voice cracked on the last word, and she began crying. "She…she passed away a few days ago, and I'm… I'm here for her funeral."

"Wynter, I'm so sorry," Riley responded, and before she could say another word, he pulled her into his arms.

How did he know that a hug was exactly what she needed? What she craved from her own family but hadn't received? She clung to him probably longer than was appropriate, and Riley let her. It felt so good to be held. Wynter felt comforted and protected even though she hadn't seen Riley in years.

She'd once had a serious infatuation with this man, but he'd never treated her as anything other than Shay's friend. However, for a second, when he had approached her, she'd sensed male appreciation in his eyes. Surely she must have been deceiving herself? Wishing something didn't make it a reality.

Reluctantly, she pulled away and blotted her eyes with her sleeve. "Thank you."

"You're welcome. You must have needed that."

Wynter nodded, glancing at him. "I did. My aunt meant everything to me. She was the one person I could count on, and I guess I assumed that meant she would live forever. I know that must sound foolish."

"No, it's not. Her death must have been a shock."

She nodded. "I had planned to return in a few weeks and spend some time with her, but it's too late." She sniffed. "And now I'll never be able to tell her how much she meant to me."

"She knew you loved her. You have to hold on to that and the precious memories you have of her."

Wynter gave him a sideways glance. She didn't remember this kind and caring side of Riley. It went against the ruthless image Shay told her he'd garnered as a divorce attorney. Wynter was interested in this juxtaposition of traits.

"What?" Riley asked when she stared at him intently.

"You're not who I thought you were."

To her surprise, he stared right back, and they locked gazes. Wynter tried to ignore the fluttering of her pulse, but she couldn't. This was Riley, the boy she'd crushed on in her youth, but now he was *all* man. His scent teased her nostrils and tantalized every one of her senses.

"Neither are you, Wynter Barrington," Riley replied. One of his hands began to play with a tendril of her hair in an absent fashion. "You're all grown-up."

Wynter swallowed, unsure of what to do next. If she was reading his signals right, Riley was interested *in her*. She wished she could act on it, but she wasn't in the right headspace to start something she couldn't—or didn't dare—finish. Riley had a reputation as a ladies' man, and she didn't want to be just another notch on his bedpost, no matter how attractive she might find him.

Blinking, she pulled back, and Riley released the tendril. "When did you get back? I'd heard you were doing great things up north."

At her sudden change of topic, his eyes shuttered, and Wynter could no longer read what he was thinking. Was it that easy for him to turn his attraction for her on and off? Or had she imagined it because she was in distress and her emotions were all over the place?

"This week," Riley answered.

"Will you be staying long?" Wynter was curious how long she would have this enigmatic man in the same stratosphere as her.

"Indefinitely."

"Really?" Her heart lurched, and she let out a long breath she hadn't realized she'd been holding.

"Yeah, I want to be closer to Shay and my mother, so I've relocated back to San Antonio and joined a law practice."

"Congratulations!" Wynter couldn't resist the wide grin that spread across her features. "I know Shay will be very happy."

"I hope she's not the only one," he quipped.

Now he was definitely flirting with her.

"Well, I should go." Wynter rose to her feet, and when she did, so did Riley. She didn't want to get ahead of herself. Riley was a bright light in an otherwise unpleasant evening.

"Of course. Can I walk you to your car?"

"That would be lovely, thank you." They walked in companionable silence for a few blocks until she came to the street where her BMW was parked. "This is me."

"Nice ride."

"Thank you." But the more Wynter thought about it, the more she realized she would have to give it up. She couldn't afford the monthly payments or upkeep on this beast. If her family was divorcing her financially, she would have to be more frugal with her money, and keeping a Beamer was *not* within her means. The car had been her college graduation gift to herself. She'd thought she could afford it working for the family business, but that hadn't worked out too well. She would also have to move out of the family mansion. She could put her few meager belongings in storage. If and when she was home, she could always rent an Airbnb; it wasn't like she stayed home for long anyway.

"I'm sorry to hear about your aunt, but if you need anything—" Riley pulled a business card out of the suit jacket he'd been carrying and handed it to her "—this has my personal cell. Call me anytime."

Wynter looked down at the card embossed with his

name. He was giving her personal access to him. That meant something, right? Underneath her lashes, she glanced at Riley and found he was staring intently at her mouth. Wynter felt her body temperature rise, and she feared she might do something stupid, so she said, "I just might do that."

Then she spun around and, unlocking the door as fast as she could, jumped inside. The car roared to life as soon as she turned it on. She didn't dare look at Riley. She couldn't. She was too afraid of what she might see there. Lust. Attraction. Desire. Because she was certain he'd felt the heat between them as much as she had.

If she had given Riley the slightest hint that she was interested, what would have happened? Wynter guessed she would never know.

Damn.

Had he really been gone that long? When had Wynter become that fine? From the moment Riley saw her on the River Walk, he was attracted to her. She had an hourglass figure, with a round behind, shapely thighs and, Riley guessed, C-cup breasts. She was h-o-t!

He wanted her.

But, damn, if his timing wasn't off. Wynter had suffered a terrible loss and was grieving. It wasn't the right time to make a move, but that didn't mean he didn't want to. She was beautiful, her skin tawny and bright. Her lips full and juicy. And her eyes were light brown with a darker rim around them—they were eyes he could get lost in for hours. And if tonight had been another time and circumstance, he would have taken her back to his penthouse.

He had a high sex drive, and few women could match his intensity in the bedroom. Could Wynter hold her own? Of all of Shay's friends, she was the one he'd noticed because she'd been unable to hide her schoolgirl crush when he returned home during his infrequent visits. Back then, she'd been much too young for him. He'd been twenty years old and she'd been sixteen. He'd been flattered, but had given her a wide berth.

There had been plenty of college-age girls at his disposal who were down for casual sex. After having to care for his mother during high school, Riley had made up for lost time in college and law school. He knew ladies thought he was a playboy with commitment phobia, and it was true. Marriage wasn't on the menu, but good sex was, and Wynter Barrington fit the bill.

He was certain he'd see her again, and if he had his way, the next time, they'd end the night in his bed.

Three

Wynter stared out of the window of the Barrington estate several days after she'd returned home to San Antonio. Today was going to be tough—it was the day of her aunt's funeral, and she was giving the eulogy. At first, her mother had been against anyone in the family speaking, but Wynter couldn't bury her aunt without telling everyone what a great person she was.

Inhaling deeply, Wynter grabbed her peacoat and headed downstairs. Her family was waiting in the foyer when she arrived. Her father tsked as if she were late, but, checking her watch, Wynter confirmed that she was right on time. Her mother and Francesca wouldn't be able to find fault with her attire of a black cap-sleeved dress, because they were all wearing black, though Francesca had to be over-the-top with a fanciful hat and veil, as if it were *her* aunt she was mourning.

Without a word, Wynter followed her parents, Corey and Francesca to the limo. When they arrived at the church, the parking lot was overflowing with guests; Wynter could only imagine how many people were inside. People had loved and respected her aunt.

Tears welled in Wynter's eyes when she saw her best friends, Shay, Egypt, Lyric, Asia and Teagan, standing on the sidewalk, waiting for her. Shay lived here, but when had the other ladies flown in? After high school, they'd all gone their separate ways, with Egypt, Lyric, Asia and Teagan leaving San Antonio to chase their dreams, but they'd always kept in touch and tried to take annual trips together. She felt their love, and it was like a balm to her soul.

Wait—was that Riley at Shay's side? He'd come to her aunt's funeral? Wynter nearly stumbled as she exited the limo, but her father caught her and helped her straighten.

The funeral director came toward them. "I'm so sorry for your loss."

Her father shook his hand. "Thank you. Is everything in order?"

"Yes, Mr. Barrington. Exactly as your wife requested. We're still waiting on a few guests, but if you'd come with me, I can seat you in our family room until we're ready to start."

Her family headed inside, but Wynter remained where she stood. She needed her friends at a time like this. And, sure enough, once her parents were no longer in sight, the girls rushed toward Wynter and enveloped her in a group hug.

"We're so sorry, girlfriend." Asia spoke first.

"We loved Auntie Helaine," Lyric stated.

"She will be sorely missed," Shay added.

"Th-thank you," Wynter responded. She could barely speak. Glancing up, her eyes connected with Riley's. He was standing a discreet distance away, giving them their privacy, yet she couldn't ignore his presence. He'd comforted her several nights ago when she was trying to make sense of it all. And now, he was here again. Was he paying his respects? Or was there more?

"We're here for you," Egypt said, interrupting Wynter's inner musings. "We're all staying for a couple of days. Isn't that right?" She glanced in the direction of Teagan, whom they all knew was a notorious workaholic and constantly on the grind trying to build her real estate clientele.

Teagan's eyes narrowed, but she replied, "Of course."

"What can we do?" Shay asked. "Anything, anything at all."

Suddenly, Francesca loudly whispered behind her, "Wynter, it's time."

Wynter glanced at the double doors that led to the church, where she would be saying her goodbyes to her aunt for the last time, and then turned back to her friends. "Riley," she said, looking over her friends' shoulders, "would you mind sitting with me today?"

A warm smile spread across his attractive features, and he said, "It would be my pleasure." He walked toward Wynter and she saw her friends' collective mouths drop as he approached. He held out his hand, and Wynter took it as if he were her lifeline before she went underwater.

Together, they walked into the church.

Riley watched Wynter move sinuously around the living room at the Barrington estate. It was late afternoon, and only close family and friends had been invited to the Barringtons' for the repast. And the family had put on quite a display, which included a caterer, waiters passing appetizers and a food spread that rivaled that of a wedding.

However, he sensed Wynter was on edge after the heartwarming service for her aunt. He didn't know what had made him call Shay earlier that morning to find out the time of the funeral—he'd just known he *needed* to come. And he was glad he had. Wynter had needed him. Maybe not in the way he wanted her to need him someday, but, nonetheless, she had asked him to sit with her.

During the service, he'd held her cold hand in his, patting it when she tightened her hold after a particularly moving speech by one of her aunt's former suitors. When it had been Wynter's turn to give the eulogy, he whispered encouraging words in her ear before she rose to face the audience. She'd put on a brave front speaking about her late aunt and how she'd influenced not only her life, but her friends' lives. Riley had been touched. He hated that she was experiencing such a profound loss. So he'd determined right then and there to stay close to her side for the remainder of the day. Yes, he wanted a more intimate relationship with Wynter, but right now, she needed a friend.

"What's going on between you and Wynter?" Shay materialized at his side when he went to the buffet in the dining room. Rather than having to make himself a plate, the Barringtons had staff on hand to serve the food. After asking for a little bit of everything, Riley accepted his plate, along with a linen napkin set that he assumed held his utensils, and moved out of the line.

"Are you going to answer me?" Shay asked when, rather than speak, he set his plate on a nearby high-top table and began eating. He'd worked through breakfast, checking on cases and making sure everything was in order, so he was starved. As he ate, he watched his sister become annoyed at his silence. He loved giving her a hard time.

Once he'd taken a few bites, he wiped his mouth with the napkin and said, "There is nothing going on between me and Wynter."

Shay cocked her head and folded her arms across her chest. "Why don't I believe you?"

Riley shrugged and continued eating. "Can't I be there for a friend?"

"You and Wynter have never been friends."

"We've gotten better acquainted." Riley ate a few more bites of food.

"How better acquainted?"

"Get your mind out of the gutter, sis," Riley said, even though his mind had gone exactly there on more than one occasion in the past hour, seeing Wynter in her formfitting black dress.

"Like yours isn't there?" Shay whispered. "I know you, Riley, and you have a reputation for being a ladies' man."

"Don't believe the hype," Riley said, taking a sip of water. Though there was some truth to the statement; he had left a trail of more than a few broken hearts in Manhattan.

"I believe what I see, and you've been tagged with lots of women online."

"Doesn't mean I've slept with them all," Riley replied. "Besides, Wynter asked me to sit with her. What was I supposed to do, turn down a grieving woman in her time of need?"

Shay frowned. "Of course not. I just don't want to see her get hurt."

"I have no intention of hurting Wynter," Riley stated. He wanted to spend some time with her, learn what made her tick. And from everything he'd seen thus far, she was a woman worth knowing.

Wynter stood at the far side of the room, away from everyone. It had been a long day and just as difficult as she'd imagined it would be. Laying her aunt to rest had taken every ounce of strength she possessed. Although she felt mentally and emotionally exhausted, physically, she felt *alive*. It was as if all her senses were heightened.

Because Riley was here.

Not here literally, because while one of her aunt's friends had been giving their condolences she'd lost sight of him, but she knew he was on the premises. He wouldn't leave without saying goodbye. Wynter didn't know how she knew this. She just did. It was as if they were tethered together by some invisible cord.

Wynter feared the only way they'd break it was if they crossed the line of intimacy, but Riley had been a perfect gentleman and companion. She hadn't known what she was going to say outside the church, but when she said she wanted him by her side, intuitively, she had known it was the right thing. Riley had been a shoulder, a rock all day, and she would be forever grateful. And if given the chance, she might show him how much she appreciated him.

"Earth to Wynter." Egypt snapped her fingers in front of Wynter's face.

Wynter blinked. "What?"

"You were daydreaming," Egypt responded, "and if I had to guess who about, I would say that fine specimen of tall, dark and chocolate who's been by your side today."

Wynter chuckled nervously. "Who, Riley?" If anyone could ferret the truth out of her, it was Egypt. She was a natural lie detector and always seemed to know when Wynter was telling a fib. At five foot ten, Egypt was tall, beautiful and buxom in dark slacks and a black wraparound silk shirt that showed off her cleavage. Wynter loved her confidence and often wished she could imitate it.

"Don't act coy now," Egypt replied with a saucy grin. "I done peeped you two. Heck, we all did, because the man has been glued to your side."

"He's being a good friend."

"Who wants to get in your pants."

"Egypt!" Wynter pulled Egypt away from the crowd. "You can't talk like that. What if someone heard you?"

"So what?" Egypt shrugged with a smirk. "You've always cared much too much about what other people think."

Egypt was never afraid to speak her mind. It was one of the many traits of hers Wynter admired, but in this instance, she would rather Riley not find out she might still harbor the itty-bittiest of crushes on him.

"I do not."

"Yes, you do," Egypt said emphatically. "So, when are you going to stop worrying about them?"

"Starting now," Wynter stated. "My father cut me off."

"Really?"

"Yep. He wants me back at Barrington Investments. Since I refused, he told me I'll have to support myself if I choose to keep traveling and working on my blog."

"Good for them."

"Egypt!" Wynter couldn't believe her friend was being so unkind.

"Quite frankly, I think this is exactly the kick in the butt you need to get you out of your rut. Your writing is amazing. You have a gift for lifestyle and travel articles. You're truly talented, Wynter, but you've always hidden behind your family's wealth. Now you'll be forced to put a little more time and effort into your dream. That's not necessarily a bad thing. Look at it on the positive side. Without your dad's purse, you have the freedom to do things your way. You're not beholden to anyone."

"I guess I never thought about it like that." Wynter had thought about everything she wouldn't have, not what she stood to gain. That was why she needed her friends around; they gave her perspective.

"When I was working as a sous chef for other people, I hated it," Egypt said. "Now I have my food truck. I'm the owner, manager and chef. I make the final decisions. And now you will, too."

Egypt was right. She could do this. She was already on her way. Once she had more subscribers, the advertising dollars and sponsors would come.

"Now, don't think you've fooled me because we changed topics," Egypt said. "I want to know about you and Riley."

"So do I," Asia said, sliding closer to them. Wynter hadn't even seen the petite diva come up. At five foot two, with a blunt, straight bob and wearing an off-the-shoulder black dress and knee-high black boots, Asia had a fire-cracker personality and was always the life of the party. In Asia's case, big things came in small packages. "You two have been awfully cozy today."

"That's right." Before Wynter knew it, Lyric had joined their group of three and wrapped her arms around Wynter's shoulder. Lyric was more subtle and reserved than Egypt and Asia. Her café au lait complexion and almond-shaped eyes bore a subtle hint of makeup, as was appropriate for a service, while her lithe ballerina's figure was ensconced in a simple black V-neck sheath dress. Her long auburn hair was in a sleek ponytail.

"Listen, there is nothing going on between Riley and me," Wynter responded.

"Not yet," Egypt surmised, "but I see you." She pointed her index and middle fingers at herself and back at Wynter.

"My aunt just passed away and…"

"And you need someone to help ease the pain?" Asia chuckled coyly, placing her hand over her mouth.

Wynter laughed. "You guys are terrible, you know that?"

"We might be, but you love us," Egypt replied.

And Wynter did. Having her friends present made the day bearable. Now she just had to get through the reading of her aunt's will. And she suspected that was why her aunt's lawyer, Sidney Carter, a salt-and-pepper-haired gentleman wearing a bespoke suit, was coming toward her.

"Ms. Barrington, it's that time," Sidney said. "And are you ladies Egypt Cox, Lyric Taylor and Asia Reynolds?"

"We are," all three women said in unison.

"And where might Shay Davis and Teagan Williams be?" he asked.

"Right behind you," Teagan responded, lifting her hand.

Her friend was always professional and, today, she sported a black pantsuit and chic short haircut. Her caramel skin gleamed and her makeup was top-notch, but then again, that was Teagan. "And who wants to know?"

Sidney cleared his throat. "Pardon the interruption, but the five of you have been asked to attend the reading of Helaine Smith's will along with Ms. Barrington."

"So, you're Mr. Carter," Teagan responded. "You left a message with my assistant confirming that I was attending the funeral."

Sidney nodded. "Yes, ma'am. I called each of you." He looked around at each of the five women.

Wynter was surprised as each of the women shrugged. It was the first time she was hearing of the request. "They've been invited? Why?"

"More will follow during the reading of the will," Sidney replied and motioned ahead of him. "Would you all mind coming with me? The rest of your family is headed to the study."

"I honestly have no idea," Egypt said. "I assumed when he called maybe it had something to do with the head count for food."

Several of the ladies laughed, but they followed Wynter in a single file out of the living room and down the hall to the study. Her parents were already seated on the sofa, while Corey and Francesca sat in adjacent chairs.

"What is your posse doing here?" Corey inquired, folding his arms across his chest. "This is for family only."

"Posse?" Egypt asked. "If it wasn't your aunt's funeral, I'd take off my hoops and show you a posse, Corey."

Her brother rolled his eyes and his wife scoffed as if her friends were being uncouth. *Whatever*, Wynter thought. She wanted to get this over with so she could move on to the next phase in her life.

"I've asked Ms. Barrington's friends to attend," Sidney

responded. He shuffled behind her father's desk and took a seat. Opening his briefcase, he pulled out a blue document.

"I don't understand why," her mother replied. "They aren't family."

"Bear with me, Mrs. Barrington. You'll understand in a moment. Shall we begin?"

Sidney began reading. "'I, Helaine Smith, being of sound mind and memory'—"

"Excuse me, Mr. Carter, but if you don't mind, there's no need to read all the fluff," her father interjected. "Can you get to the heart of the matter?"

"Why is everyone in such a rush? Aunt Helaine has only been buried a few hours. Can't you show some respect?" Wynter cried. She didn't realize she had verbalized her statement until her family looked at her in shock. They weren't used to her speaking up, let alone speaking out. Properly chastened, the room quieted and Sidney continued.

He read the special requests and donations her aunt was giving to her favorite charities, but when it came to her personal belongings, everyone sat a little straighter in their chairs. "I leave my jewelry and all the artwork to my sister, Melinda Barrington,'" Sidney stated.

"That's it?" her mother asked. "What about the house?"

Sidney sighed in exasperation, but he continued. "'I leave my home and all its remaining possessions to my niece, Wynter Barrington. You were like the daughter I never had, and now you will always have a home no matter where you are.'"

"Wynter!" Corey said, jumping up out of his chair. "But what about me? I'm her nephew." He looked at the lawyer. "Is there nothing for me?"

"If you will allow me to finish," Sidney huffed impertinently.

"Carry on." Her mother fluttered her hand in the air.

"'As to the personal wealth that I've garnered, I leave

two hundred fifty thousand to my longtime housekeeper, Hope, and her husband, Mark Nelson. To Egypt Cox, Lyric Taylor, Asia Reynolds, Shay Davis and Teagan Williams— you girls have always been kind to an old woman and were like daughters to me. You treated my Wynter like the queen she is. I leave each of you two hundred thousand dollars to help you pursue your dreams of starting your own business."'

"What?" Her brother looked absolutely poleaxed. "She's giving it to them!" He pointed at Wynter's friends. "That's a million dollars! She must have been out of her mind. I mean, really, loony tunes."

"I will not have you speak that way about Aunt Helaine," Wynter stated.

Corey snorted. "What do you care? You got the house."

Sidney cleared his throat. "I'm afraid that's not all. Miss Smith acquired a substantial fortune worth several million after she and Melinda sold their family business."

"Although I don't agree with my sister giving these ladies that kind of money," her mother said, leaning back, "surely I'll be inheriting the rest. Isn't that right, Mr. Carter?" Her dark brown eyes landed on the attorney.

"I'm afraid not, ma'am," he replied and picked up the document. "'I leave the remainder of my estate to my niece, Wynter Barrington.'"

Shocked gasps echoed throughout the room, including from Wynter.

"What did you say?" her mother asked, tilting her head to regard him. "Are you telling me my own sister cut me out of her will and left everything to my daughter?"

"Not exactly, Mrs. Barrington. As you're aware, your sister named you as beneficiary on her life insurance policy to help pay for the funeral expenses and any debts and taxes Helaine may have owed. Further, Ms. Smith has made you the executor of her will. I trust you can fulfill these duties?"

"Oh, my God!" Her mother clutched her chest. "I can't believe this. My sister and I are the only Smiths left. She wouldn't exclude me and leave me trinkets, art and a small life insurance policy. Not when her personal wealth came from the sale of our family business."

Sidney huffed. "A quarter of a million dollars is not small, Mrs. Barrington."

"What did you do, Wynter?" Corey asked, rushing toward Wynter. Fury blazed across his light brown features. "You cozy up to the old lady so she'd leave you everything?"

"Back off, Corey!" Egypt stepped in front of Wynter, because she was too shell-shocked to move. Aunt Helaine had essentially left her everything she owned. It seemed unreal. One minute she was thinking about how she was going to survive, and the next she was a multimillionaire.

"Or what?" Corey inquired, puffing out his chest. "What are you going to do, Egypt? Matter of fact, why don't you and your girl group leave? I think you've done enough for one day."

"Not only were they asked to be here by the attorney, but they are here for me," Wynter responded hotly, finding her voice.

"When was this drafted?" her mother inquired, peering at Mr. Carter. "My sister wasn't well the last couple of years."

"Ma'am, Ms. Smith was of sound mind and body when she wrote this will a few years ago," Sidney replied.

"We'll see about that." Melinda rose to her feet. "I'm challenging this will."

"Mother!" Wynter quickly moved to her side. "Why would you do that? You would be going against Aunt Helaine's wishes. Is that really what you want to do? If the money is that important to you, surely we can figure this out as a family?"

Her mother grasped Wynter by the shoulders. "Wynter, I know you mean well, but do you have any idea of the magnitude of your aunt's wealth? You're ill-equipped to handle it."

"And you aren't?" Wynter snapped.

"Your mother is right," her father said, coming to his wife's aid and wrapping an arm around her shoulder. "You're always gallivanting across the world, and there will be matters to attend to. *We*—" he looked down at her mother "—can address them."

"Clearly, Aunt Helaine felt otherwise," Wynter replied. "And I will fight for what's mine." She turned to Sidney. "Mr. Carter, legally, the house is mine until the court states otherwise, is that correct?"

"Yes, Ms. Barrington."

"Because that's where me—" Wynter turned to her best friends, who had remained silent during the exchange "—and my *girl group* will be staying, since it's obvious I'm not welcome here." She already had keys to her aunt's home yet hadn't been able to bring herself to go alone, but she wasn't alone now. "C'mon." She looked at Egypt, Lyric, Asia, Shay and Teagan. "Let's go."

Her mother wrenched out of her father's arms. "Wynter, stop this!" She blocked Wynter's path. "I don't want to fight you, but I will. I will not let you squander my family's legacy."

Wynter faced her mother. She was tired of being pushed around. "Bring it on." Then she stepped from around her mother and exited the study with her friends behind her.

She heard her mother yell, "I will bury you in paperwork. Neither you nor your friends will see a dime of that money!"

Wynter didn't turn back around. Instead, she kept walking. She focused on putting one foot in front of the other before the tears stinging her eyes fell. She had to get to her room, get her belongings and get the hell out of this house. She refused to take abuse from her family a moment longer. She'd buried the most important person in her life, and when she was feeling at her lowest, adrift without any support, she'd learned her aunt hadn't left her at all. She'd given her a home and the financial wherewithal to fulfill her wildest dreams. But Wynter would give it all away in a heartbeat if she could have her aunt back.

Now she would have to fight her entire family for the privilege of keeping what was rightfully hers. But they'd underestimated Wynter. They had no idea what she was capable of when push came to shove—but they were about to find out.

Four

It was time for Riley to go home. He'd done a good deed by standing by Wynter, but the funeral was over and the family had moved on to the reading of the will. He was about to throw in the towel when he saw the Six Gems striding down the hall. The heartbroken look on Wynter's faced brooked no discussion. He went to Shay instead and pulled her aside while the other women rushed up the stairs behind Wynter.

His eyes pierced Shay's. "What happened?"

"The Barrington family," Shay hissed, pulling him into a corner. "They're terrible. If you could have seen how they treated Wynter. It was horrible, Riley."

His brow furrowed. "On a day like today? Why? They should be sticking together as a family."

Shay rolled her shoulders upward and then glanced around to be sure no one was listening. "Because Wynter's aunt—she left Wynter nearly everything, the house and most of her money. Plus, get this, Riley—" she paused several beats as she sucked in a deep breath "—her aunt left each of us Six Gems two hundred thousand to pursue our dreams of opening up our own businesses."

"What?" he asked, his voice rising.

"Wynter's mother is furious. Claimed Wynter must have done something to sway her aunt to leave her everything and leave her mother nothing."

"Her own mother said that?" Riley couldn't believe what he was hearing. How could Wynter's mother turn on her like that?

"She vowed to contest the will. Sounds like she's prepared to fight Wynter to the death for that money."

"Unfortunately, death doesn't bring out the best in people," Riley stated. He'd done a stint in inheritance law when he'd been an intern in law school. He'd been surprised by how families turned on one another for the sake of the almighty dollar. "Well, I hope Wynter knows she's not alone and that we'll do all we can to help her."

"We?" Shay asked, cocking her head to regard him. "Why are you so buddy-buddy with my girl?"

"I'm not. I told you, we're old friends who caught up." He hated lying to his sister, but he wasn't ready to define whatever was going on between him and Wynter. He wanted it to evolve naturally and without artifice.

Shay didn't look like she believed him one bit, but she let it go when Wynter came down the stairs moments later, carrying a suitcase. Egypt was behind her, carrying an oversize duffel bag over her shoulder and a laptop bag.

Wynter walked out into the cool January night air. Once outside, she turned to them as they gathered around her. "That was very difficult. You have no idea how much. Just know that I appreciate you all."

"And we love you," Egypt responded, which brought a smile to Wynter's somber expression.

"But, if you don't mind, I'm going to need some company at my aunt's place."

"Give me a second to check out of my hotel," Teagan replied, "and I'll be there in a flash."

"Same here," Asia said. "We've got you."

"So do I," Riley replied, surprising himself when he said the words out loud. He hadn't meant to, but he felt compelled, and not because Wynter was a woman he was attracted to, but because it was the right thing to do. Wynter glanced up as if she were coming out of a fog and had just noticed him standing there. "I'll do everything I can to help you with your legal case."

He watched her swallow, and then she said, "Thank you. Shay, do you mind taking me to Aunt Helaine's?"

"Of course not," Shay replied and gave Riley a suspecting look before rushing off.

With this newest development, Riley didn't know what might happen between him and Wynter, but he knew they were intrinsically joined, and he wasn't ready to separate until their relationship reached its natural conclusion. All he had to do was wait.

Wynter felt like she was in self-preservation mode. She'd had to get out of the Barrington house before she went nuclear. Did her family honestly think she was some evil mastermind who had convinced her aunt to leave her everything? The only thing she ever did was love Helaine. Love her like a daughter, and, in the end, that was exactly how her aunt felt. Wynter was the daughter she'd never had, and hearing those words meant everything.

But more surprising than the announcement of her inheritance were her interactions with Riley. From the moment she ran into him at the River Walk, she could feel a palpable energy between them. It was an awareness between a man and a woman and not the friendship vibes she'd felt in the past.

Wynter didn't know what to make of it, and apparently, neither did Shay, because she questioned Wynter on the drive to Helaine's. "What's going on between you and my brother?" Shay asked point-blank.

Wynter turned to her. "I don't understand."

"C'mon. Don't act coy. There is definitely a vibe between the two of you."

"I'm not saying there isn't," Wynter replied honestly, "but if there were, would that bother you?"

"You betcha!" Shay responded quickly. "Riley likes playing the field and isn't interested in settling down with one woman. And you? Wynter, you wear your heart on your sleeve, and I would hate to see you get hurt by getting involved with my brother. Will you stay away from him?"

Wynter received Shay's message loud and clear: *hands off!*

And she wanted to heed her best friend's advice because she understood everything Shay said. After their walk the other day, she'd read up about Riley's reputation online, but that didn't stop her wayward heart from wanting to know if Riley felt the same pulse, the same kinetic energy she felt when he was near.

"Well?" Shay asked. "Are you going to answer me?"

"Riley has been a great friend to me today and the other day, when he happened to find me crying in public. I hardly think that's making a play for me. I don't think I should have to keep my distance."

Shay gave her a rueful smile as she drove. "My brother is great in the clutch, always has been, but he doesn't stick around. When we were growing up, he always took care of me and Mama. Until I was older, I had no idea my mother had any sort of mental health issues. It wasn't until Riley went to college and his calls and visits became less frequent that I realized how much he'd been holding inside. So, trust me when I say this—don't pin all your hopes and dreams on Riley. He will let you down."

"Sounds like you speak from experience," Wynter replied, giving her friend a sideways glance.

"I don't blame him for pursuing his passion," Shay said, and at Wynter's disbelieving look, she continued, "I don't. I wish I would have known a little sooner and been prepared for what awaited me once he left."

Wynter nodded. She would have to remember Shay's advice. Otherwise, she could be in a world of hurt if she allowed herself to go down the rabbit hole with Riley.

Hours later, Wynter, Egypt, Shay, Teagan, Asia and Lyric were in their pajamas and nightshirts, cuddled in blankets on the floor of her aunt Helaine's seven-bedroom, seven-and-a-half-bath house in Elm Creek.

Once they had arrived, they'd been greeted by Hope, Aunt Helaine's live-in housekeeper, who'd returned to the house after the service and hadn't heard of Wynter's aunt's bequest. Hope had been shocked to hear she'd received an inheritance, and even though she didn't have to, Hope had ensured the bedrooms for Wynter and her friends were set up and scrounged up some light snacks.

The housekeeper's version of "light" included a charcuterie board of thick-cut salami, prosciutto, Gouda, brie and herb-flavored cream cheeses, fig jam, pepper jelly, cornichons, water crackers, nuts, and an assortment of fruit. It had been difficult to eat after the service, so the snacks were welcomed by all.

"It's so nice to have all you guys here," Wynter said. Wearing her favorite cotton pajamas, she settled her back against the sofa in her aunt's living room. "I remember having our pajama parties here."

"So do I," Egypt quipped after having changed into a

tank maxi sleep shirt. "Your aunt would make it an event, with popcorn and pizza and hot baked cookies. I'd forgotten how much I missed this place."

"How are you feeling?" Lyric asked. Her long auburn hair was in a messy updo, and she was dressed in jogger pants and a cropped top. Wynter would kill for her sleek dancer's body.

"Still in disbelief," Wynter replied honestly. "It felt like I was having an out-of-body experience. It was as if I was watching the reading of the will, but I wasn't present."

"I felt your mother's displeasure that your aunt deigned to give us anything," Teagan replied with a frown. Teagan had opted for long satin pajamas. "She's always been tightly strung, but this was a whole new low."

"How *low* can you go?" Egypt said with a laugh. "You mind passing me more of that wine, Teagan?" She held up her empty wineglass.

Teagan and Asia had brought several bottles of wine with them, because they'd known Wynter was going to need something strong to help take the sting out of her family's harsh treatment of her.

While Teagan filled Egypt's glass, Egypt asked, "So, what do we do now? Should we all—" she glanced at the other women in the room "—move forward with opening our own businesses, or should we prepare for battle?"

"That's a good question," Wynter said. "I need to talk to Riley, since it appears my mother is serious about contesting the will."

"She believes you conspired to steal her family legacy," Asia stated bluntly.

Wynter jumped to her feet. "And that's utterly ridiculous." She looked down at the other women. "When would I have had the time? I've been traveling and writing. This has me shook."

Shay rose from the floor and came over to wrap her arms around Wynter. "You're not in this alone."

"I know that here," Wynter said, pointing to her temple, "but tell that to my heart." She patted her chest. "My entire family is against me." Tears slid down her cheeks. She leaned her head on Shay's shoulder and let them fall. "It's so unfair."

"Yes, it is." Teagan placed her wineglass on the cocktail table and stood up. "But we will fight with you."

"Against my family?" Wynter asked, lifting her head.

"If necessary," Asia replied. "Your aunt wanted you to have this house—" she motioned her arms around the room "—and to have that money. They've no right to circumvent her wishes."

Egypt walked toward Wynter and softly grabbed her chin, forcing Wynter to look up at her. "And we won't let them. First thing tomorrow, we fight. Ain't that right?"

Wynter nodded.

"I can't hear you!" Egypt cried.

"That's right," Wynter replied, this time a little louder and a whole lot stronger. "I will fight for what's mine." She would get what was due her, even if she had to fight the entire Barrington family.

Five

On Sunday, Riley woke early and hit the hotel's gym for nearly two hours of cardio and weights. He even did a few hours of work, going over case files. Now he was ready to face the task he'd been avoiding since arriving in San Antonio nearly a week ago—it was time to see his mother. Although work and the funeral had kept him busy, the real reason he'd shied away was because he'd needed to prepare himself.

He had to be in the right head space when he visited his mom. He never knew which Eliza Davis he was going to find. Was it happy Eliza, who was thrilled to see her successful lawyer son? Or was it depressed Eliza, who couldn't get out of bed, much less comb her hair or shower? He had to be prepared for whichever version he encountered.

He'd had a lot of practice dealing with her mood swings. Back then, she hadn't been officially diagnosed as a manic depressive. However, once he had been making good money at his first law firm, Riley had been determined to ensure his mother received the best care. But despite that, she didn't always take her medication as prescribed, which meant her moods fluctuated.

After showering, he changed into jeans, a pullover sweater and a leather jacket, and he drove the Bentley, which had arrived a few days ago, to the Heights at Stone Oak, a gated subdivision that had tennis and basketball courts, as well as a swimming pool and jogging trails. He'd moved his mother and Shay there once he became one of the top lawyers on the East Coast. It had been difficult uprooting his mother from the familiar house she'd known for nearly twenty years, but once she saw the big backyard with room for a garden and tranquil koi pond, she'd been thrilled.

He pulled the car into the driveway and looked around. He'd done good by his family, though he was sure they might say different because his trips home were infrequent. Riley ensured they had everything they could need: a nurse, a lawn service and a housekeeper who came once a week to keep the place tidy. It was the least he could do, but now that he was back in San Antonio permanently, he intended to pitch in.

Turning off the engine, he sauntered to the front of the house and used his key. "Hello!" he called out.

Several seconds later, his mother came bounding down the stairs in jeans and a pullover sweater. Her dark brown hair was brushed back into a ponytail, and her dark eyes were bright and clear. It was going to be a good day. "Riley!" She rushed into his arms. Having his mother hug him back was a good feeling.

Riley hadn't realized how much he needed today to be a good day until he saw her smiling face beaming up at him. At five foot six, she was a few heads shorter than he was. "Hey, Mom, how are you?"

"Fabulous, now that you're here." A warm glow suffused

her medium-brown cheeks. "Would you like something to drink? I was about to head back to the garden."

"A drink sounds great." Riley followed her inside toward the back of the house, which had a large eat-in kitchen and butcher-block island. He watched as she opened the double-sided refrigerator and pulled out a beer for him.

He raised a brow because he couldn't remember his mother keeping alcohol on hand, but he accepted the drink. He screwed off the top and took a swig.

"Don't give me that look, Riley," his mother said. "I don't drink, and you know Shay is a health nut."

"Then whose is this?" He held up the beer bottle.

A blush crossed his mother's symmetrical features. "A friend."

"Friend?" he asked, sitting down on one of the wicker bar stools. "As in, the male variety?"

She shrugged. "Is that so wrong? I am entitled."

"Of course you are." Riley was happy to hear she had emerged from the cocoon she'd been in to embrace life once again.

"Darryl is a wonderful man and occasionally while watching a football game, he wants a beer. I keep a six-pack just for him."

Why hadn't Shay told him his mother had a man in her life? It would certainly have eased his anxiety. He would have to have a word with his sister about it. "Good for you, Ma. I'm glad to see you're doing well."

She sighed and walked over to sit beside him at the island. "I know growing up with a mother like me was challenging for you, Riley. I'm sorry I wasn't there for you. I didn't understand my condition or know how to take care of myself."

"It's okay, Ma. I don't blame you. You have a medical condition."

"All the same, it was a terrible burden to put on you. You

didn't get to have a chance to be a teenager because you were always keeping me upright. It wasn't fair."

Riley reached for her hand across the short distance and took it in his own. "I'm glad you're better. That's all I need right now."

"And Shay?" Her mother shook her head. "Caring for me took a toll on her, too, and was the cause of her divorce. And now she doesn't date much. She needs to get out more and make time for herself."

"Now that I'm back, I'll ensure she does."

"And you?" His mother searched his eyes. "What's going on with you on that front?"

He shrugged.

"Riley?" She touched his cheek with her palm. "There's no one special?"

His mind immediately went to Wynter. She was in a vulnerable state, and he wanted to do anything he could to help her. He didn't know why he felt protective over her, but he did. The battle with her parents over her aunt's estate could be long. He doubted she had any idea what was in store. He'd already reached out to the head of the local probate department at his firm.

Then there was the lady herself. She was absolutely not his type. He was used to women who understood the score and could accept an affair. She deserved a man who could give her more, and Riley wasn't it, but that didn't stop him from desiring her. Her beautiful caramel skin and those waves of delicious curls, her figure with the right amount of curves to fit in his palms— He imagined peeling off her clothes, stripping her bare and splaying her beneath him. Would her kissable, full lips part in surrender? Would her eyes flicker with desire as they had that night on the River Walk?

"So, there is someone?" His mother picked up on what he wasn't saying.

He thought about Shay and how she wasn't keen on him spending any time with Wynter. It was best he kept any interaction with Wynter to himself. "There's no one," Riley stated. "I'm too busy with work and getting reacclimated to life in Texas."

"I imagine it's very different from the East Coast."

"Very." Riley laughed. "Why don't you show me this garden? I want to see what you've done with the place."

It would be a good distraction to keep him from picking up the phone and calling Wynter, but he couldn't anyway. Shay had spent the night at Wynter's aunt Helaine's house, and if he were to call, she would surely snoop into his affairs. Because that was certainly what was going to happen between him and Wynter. They would have an affair. It was just a matter of when.

"I'm going to miss you," Wynter said as Egypt, Lyric, Asia and Teagan stood outside her aunt's home after their suitcases had been loaded into the hired Escalade idling nearby, ready to take them to the airport. Having her best friends for the weekend had been just what the doctor ordered, but now they were going back to their lives and careers. Careers Wynter hoped would blossom once she could assure them they would receive the gifts her aunt left them in the will.

"We're going to miss you, too." Asia leaned in for a tight squeeze of Wynter's shoulders before moving away so Lyric could hug her.

"I know we might be far, but we're only a phone call away anytime you need us," Lyric stated, grasping both sides of Wynter's face. "Remember that, okay?"

Tears welled in Wynter's eyes, and she nodded.

"Okay, let's not get all sentimental," Egypt fussed, breaking the trio apart. "Y'all acting like we're not going to see each other. We have our annual girls' trip in Barbados this year!"

Teagan snapped her fingers. "That's right, and it's going to be the bomb, just like Vegas was last year! Wynter, we can't thank you enough for always finding affordable deals and giving us a payment schedule. You're our personal travel agent." She did have a knack for planning getaways, something she enjoyed incorporating into *Wynter's Corner*.

Wynter chuckled. "You're welcome. Once you see the villa I've got, it's going to blow your minds."

The women chuckled, and after a few more hugs and kisses, they slid into the vehicle and drove away. Wynter sighed audibly.

"It's going to be okay," Shay said, patting her hand.

"I know it will," Wynter replied. Before the fiasco at the will reading on Saturday, she'd come to the realization she was going to have to put on her big-girl panties and figure out her next move. Over the weekend, she'd discussed with her friends that it was best they didn't count on the money until the will was settled. In the interim, the ladies would work on their business plans and getting everything in order in preparation for when the matter was resolved.

Wynter would work on building her blog and garnering the followers she needed to ensure its success. It would be difficult, but she was going to do it. The first thing she needed to do was find an estate lawyer.

But one name dominated her thoughts.

Riley Davis.

He was gorgeous, sexy and superbly male. Heat spilled over Wynter's skin just thinking about how he'd held her during her aunt's service. Riley had been the steadying influence she needed and *wanted*.

Shay had warned Wynter to avoid any dealings with Riley, and he should be taboo, but that only made Wynter want him more. She was in a quandary. Should she pursue her heart's desire? Or always wonder if she imagined the need she'd seen reflected in his dark eyes as he'd supported her the day of the funeral?

"Wynter?"

Wynter blinked several times and realized Shay was speaking to her. "Hmm…?"

"I was asking if you wanted me to stay with you tonight?"

Wynter glanced up at the two-story stone house. This had been her second home, a place of shelter and comfort. She couldn't get into her own head. Her aunt had wanted this place to be hers. She shook her head. "No, I've got this."

A frown creased Shay's forehead. "Are you sure?"

"Yes," Wynter said. And she was. It was time for her to stand on her own two feet. Starting now.

As he poured himself some brandy in his penthouse, Riley thought back to how the day with his mother had gone. He was pleasantly surprised by the progress she'd made. She was taking her meds and getting the help she needed. Mental illness was something that could be managed with the right care, but his father had turned a blind eye when they'd been married.

He'd been so busy screwing other women behind his mother's back, he hadn't seen the signs. And when he chose to leave, he hadn't looked back to the children he was leaving in her care. Instead, he married again and started a new life, devastating Eliza. She'd already been fragile, so losing her husband had been the straw that broke the camel's back. And now, over two decades later, she was finally the mother he'd always wanted.

Riley sipped his drink as he stared out at the San Antonio skyline. Seeing the demise of his parents' marriage had made Riley want the exact opposite. He didn't want love and commitment. They only brought heartache. Riley was happy with the here and now. His relationships with women were short-lived, and that was exactly the way he wanted it.

But he did want Wynter Barrington, his sister's best friend. He wanted a scorching-hot night with the sultry woman with the wavy hair and an ass that was made for squeezing. Shay was adamantly against him getting involved with Wynter in any way, shape or form, but Wynter was a grown woman. Surely she could make her own decisions? If Wynter gave him the slightest indication she was interested, Riley doubted he could resist the invitation.

His cell phone rang suddenly, and Riley swiped his thumb across to answer. "Hello."

"Riley, hi. It's Wynter."

"I know who it is," he responded. He recognized her voice. "How are you?"

"I could be better," Wynter said. "And that's where you come in."

"Oh, yeah?" He couldn't resist smiling. "How can I help?"

"I was hoping we could meet tomorrow at your office and discuss my aunt's will in further detail. Are you available?"

Damn. Riley had been hoping for dinner and maybe adjourning to his place. He mentally ticked off the appointments he had scheduled for tomorrow. "It would have to be later, around 3:00 p.m., if that works for you?"

"Oh, yes, that's wonderful. I really appreciate you fitting me in."

"I told you I would help you in any way I could," he responded.

She chuckled softly. "I know, but sometimes people say that when you're grieving, but they're only being kind. They don't actually expect you to call."

"*I* meant it."

"Thank you," Wynter said. "It's nice to have someone in my corner."

Riley was hoping that wasn't all she wanted, but all too quickly, after he gave her directions to his office, Wynter terminated the call. He would have preferred to talk to her longer, but he didn't want to push. He had to be sure Wynter was as interested as he was in pursuing a deeper connection, but he would have to wait to find out.

Riley groaned. It was going to be a long night, spent dreaming about having Wynter underneath him.

Six

Wynter gazed up at the imposing skyscraper, her heart pounding about her meeting with Riley. After all these years, her schoolgirl crush had turned into full-on attraction. However, she wasn't here to act on those feelings, especially because she didn't want to ruin her friendship with Shay.

Although she could have gone to Sidney Carter, the lawyer who'd read the will, Riley was someone she trusted, and Wynter was hoping he could lead her in the right direction when it came to her mother contesting her aunt's will. She hadn't heard from her family since the funeral on Saturday, and that was disheartening. They truly believed she had coerced her aunt into leaving her the lion's share of her estate.

Pushing aside her nerves, Wynter walked swiftly across the polished marble floor of the lobby toward the bank of stainless-steel elevators. Pushing the up button, she waited for the elevator to take her to Jamison, Charles and Davis, Riley's new law office.

Moments later, she was exiting the elevator and walking toward the U-shaped reception desk, where a beautiful brunette with an impeccable updo sat. Wynter glanced down at her outfit. Underneath her peacoat, she wore a pencil skirt and a long-sleeved button-down silk top that flared out with a waterfall of ruffles. She looked smart and sophisticated and worthy of being there.

"May I help you?" the brunette asked.

"Wynter Barrington. I have an appointment with Riley Davis."

"Of course—I'll get him right away. Please have a seat."

Nodding, Wynter made her way to an expensive-looking group of armchairs and sat down. Wynter removed her coat. She was nervous, and not about the matter of fighting her family for her inheritance, but because she was meeting with Riley. During their past two encounters, he'd been kind to her, but there had been something—a gossamer-fine thread—connecting them that was about more than comfort.

Wynter felt the hairs on the back of her neck rise and looked up to see Riley in front of her. How long had he been standing there, watching? She didn't know. She just knew that with the sunlight streaming in from the floor-to-ceiling windows, he looked extraordinarily delicious. He was clean-shaven and wore a dark blue pinstriped suit with a silver tie. He looked every bit the high-powered divorce attorney.

His dark eyes locked on hers, and Wynter felt something unravel inside her.

"Wynter, it's good to see you." Riley offered her his hand.

She curved hers around it, and a jolt of electricity rushed through her fingertips. His grip was firm as he helped her up, and her heart skipped a beat. She suspected Riley's hands knew how to stir and torment a woman's body to the point of release. "Thank you for seeing me."

"Of course." He smiled and released her hand, but Wynter's heart was thumping so hard in her chest, she could feel it in her ribs. "Let's go to my office."

Mutely, Wynter followed him, and in doing so, got a view of his broad shoulders and tapered waist as he walked ahead of her. Riley was fit, and it showed in the way he wore his clothes. Before she knew it, they were stopping in front of a glass corner office. Riley allowed her to precede him before joining her.

"Please have a seat." He motioned to the sofa as opposed to the chair in front of his large desk. She was hoping Riley would sit behind it and give her some breathing room, but instead, he was going for a more casual approach. When he pushed a button on his desk and the glass in his office went from clear to opaque, her heart began to pound against her rib cage. No one would see them. They would have complete privacy.

Wynter tried not think about what that meant. Instead, she sat on one end of the soft, plush beige sofa, while Riley, after unbuttoning his jacket, sat on the other side.

"So," he began, crossing a muscular leg over his knee, "I assume you're here about the will?"

Wynter struggled to think, because all she saw were his thick, toned thighs. She wondered what it would feel like if she straddled him. She blinked. She had to stop this. *Focus.* She glanced up and found he was looking at her expectantly.

She swallowed thickly. "As you know, my family was very unhappy after the reading of my aunt's will, and they've vowed to contest it. I can only assume they have engaged counsel—or *will*—and I have to do the same. I need to know how to fight them and what my options are."

He nodded. "Contesting your aunt's will is going to be time-consuming and expensive for your parents. The burden of proof is on them to show you coerced your aunt, had some undue influence or that the will was improperly prepared or executed, and they'll need to find witnesses who can support that claim."

"That's crazy, Riley. There's no one who will say I unduly influenced her. Everyone knows how close we were."

Riley sat upright. "That's great, because your main priority will be showing your aunt was of sound mind and body when the will was executed."

Wynter nodded. "My aunt wasn't mentally incapacitated."

"Good. We have a great estate division here that handles these sorts of cases, and I can refer you to one of them."

"Refer me?" Wynter's voice rose slightly. "You can't handle my case yourself?"

Riley shook his head. "Wynter, I'm a divorce lawyer, and I'm damn good one because I stay in my lane. I don't know the nuances of estate law, and you need someone who does. I would be remiss if I didn't refer you to someone else. Given that we're friends as well, that would make you being a client problematic."

Her mouth formed an O. She hadn't realized that, but then again, she didn't know anything about the law. "All right, I would appreciate that, thank you." She rose to her feet and lowered her lashes. She'd been so eager to spend some time with Riley that she hadn't done her research. She felt foolish. "I'm sorry. I won't take up any more of your time."

"You're not. I wanted to see you again."

Wynter glanced furtively up at the man who stood opposite her. His words were provocative. Had he meant them to be? Once again, she felt that strange, unsettling wave of attraction. Suddenly, her mouth became dry and her cheeks felt warm. "You did?"

"Yes." He walked toward her, not in her personal space, but close enough that she could feel his heat, see the black of his irises and have his scent tease her nostrils. He smelled of spice, wood and amber. It was a heady fragrance, and Wynter wanted to taste him. Her eyes immediately went to his lips, and her heart began to race.

And when she glanced up, she was lost.

Riley didn't know why he said it. He could have let Wynter leave his office and she would have been none the wiser to how he felt, but he couldn't. He'd seen the disappointment in her eyes when he told her he couldn't be her attorney. But was there more? He sensed there might be, so he was honest and told her he wanted to see her again.

And now, he caught the look of heat in her brown eyes, because she was looking at his mouth like she wanted what he wanted, which was to taste her.

Getting involved with Wynter could be a mistake, he told himself. His sister was dead set against this, but Riley didn't care. Wynter's scent was filling his head, and she was leaning closer to him. Unable to stop himself, he fused his mouth with hers.

The kiss was soft and tender at first as he acquainted himself with her mouth. Her lips were soft and pillowy, and she tasted sweet, like warm honey. The encounter took a turn when she pressed her full, round breasts against his chest. When he felt Wynter's hand slide up over the muscles of his back, he framed her face with his hands and deepened the kiss, wanting more.

And she gave it to him, parting her lips to let his tongue slide between them. His hand curved around her waist, pulling her closer. His body erupted. He felt hot and hard, as if he were forged from fire—all because of *this* woman.

A woman he shouldn't want but couldn't deny he did. She moved against him so that the hard ridge of his erection was pressing against her lower half.

She felt so good. He ran his hands down the contours of her body, and his fingers itched to explore the rest of her.

"Riley..." she whispered, and it was enough to drag his mind back to the present situation.

Had he lost his mind? He was at work!

He stepped away from her so fast, he felt light-headed with desire. His body was protesting at the speed with which he moved, but all he could do was stare back into her wide and desire-glazed eyes. She touched her swollen lips. "I—I don't know how that happened."

It happened because they were both attracted to each other, and now Riley knew it wasn't one-sided. Wynter wanted him, too. "And yet it did."

Wynter smoothed down the hem of her skirt, which somehow had risen to her thighs during their encounter. Had he done that? He saw a hint of caramel skin as she quickly righted it. "I should go. You'll send me the name of that attorney?"

He nodded, and she was nearly at the door when Riley rushed over. "We should meet again."

She glanced behind her. "Do you really think that's wise?"

Hell yeah, he did. There was no way they could refute the sexual attraction between them, so why try and suppress it? "I do. Meet me for dinner. *Tonight.*"

Wynter whirled around at the demanding tone of his words.

He added, "*Please.* I want to see you again. Please— say yes."

Wynter looked down, and Riley thought she was going to deny him, but then she said, "Yes."

"I'll pick you up around seven. That sound good?"

She nodded and then quickly slipped around him and out the door. Riley took a breath and leaned against the glass door. He wouldn't be able to keep his promise to Shay to stay away from Wynter, even though she was forbidden fruit. When he tasted her, he'd lost control to the point where he'd forgotten common sense. They were in his place of work, yet he'd wanted to take Wynter up against the desk and bury himself deep inside her.

Riley scrubbed his face with his hands. He had to get a grip. Once they consummated their relationship, he would be able to ease the ache he felt. Only then could life go back to normal.

Wynter sat in her car in the parking garage, stunned by what had happened upstairs. She'd gone to Riley for help on fighting her parents for her inheritance. She'd never imagined they would end up kissing.

And what a kiss!

Riley kissed like a man who knew what to do with his mouth and tongue. Lord, Wynter could only imagine what he would be like in bed. She wasn't a novice and had enjoyed her sexual encounters with the handful of lovers she'd had, but she suspected being with Riley would be different.

Just kissing him felt different. If they hadn't been in his office, how far would they have gone? All the way? Wynter bit her lip. She should feel shame and regret at her behavior, but she felt elated and aroused because Riley desired her. When he'd run his hands over the curves of her body, she'd wanted him to go underneath her skirt and touch her where she wanted him most. She was still aching.

Would she let him ease the ache tonight?

Wynter closed her eyes. Shay's image popped in her mind, cooling her ardor. Her best friend thought it was a mistake for Wynter to get involved with Riley. Was Shay right? Should she give Riley a wide berth because of his playboy reputation?

The thought of canceling their dinner filled Wynter with dread. This was her opportunity to take charge of what she wanted. She refused to be a passive participant in her life any longer. She wanted Riley, and if he wanted her, too, she had to see where this led. She would have to deal with the consequences of her actions on another day.

Seven

Wynter excitedly dressed for dinner with Riley later that night. She'd already determined she would take the evening as it came. She wasn't going to put any pressure on herself for the night to end one way or the other. However, she also wasn't going to play it safe.

After she left Riley's office, she stopped by her favorite lingerie store and splurged on a sexy bra and panty set so her confidence would be in full bloom for their date. The scalloped edges and floral lace of the panty fit snugly over her bottom, while the deep-V plunging bra was perfect for the cocktail dress she'd chosen, with rhinestone details adorning the low-cut neckline. Wynter sprayed perfume at her touch points, and after pinning up one side of her hair with a rhinestone hair clip, she was ready.

She knew Shay wouldn't approve of this date, but Wynter couldn't ignore her feelings for Riley any longer. And she didn't want to. She understood the risk inherent in dating a playboy like Riley, but this was her chance to see if the spark between them was real. Would it extinguish quickly or light a fire? Wynter had to know. Tonight would be a moment she would always remember.

A gentle knock sounded on the guest room door. Wynter couldn't bear to sleep in her aunt's quarters. It was going to be some time before she would be able to clean out her aunt's things. For now, she needed to focus on her blog and social media content as well as meeting with a lawyer.

Wynter opened the door to find Hope on the other side. "Your guest is here."

"Thank you, Hope. I'm coming down now," Wynter said, grabbing her clutch. Walking down the stairs, she found Riley in the foyer looking resplendent in a dark suit, with a few buttons casually undone on his crisp white shirt. He watched her as she descended. When she reached the last step, Riley strode toward her and offered his hand to assist her.

"Thank you."

Riley's eyes devoured her. "You look incredible."

Wynter smiled. It wasn't often the man you'd admired from the sidelines said you looked beautiful. "So do you."

He gave her a wide grin. "Ready for dinner?"

"Yes."

After helping her into her coat, they exited the house and she slid into his Bentley. When he joined her, Wynter caught another whiff of the spicy scent that was uniquely Riley's. She told herself she wasn't giving up the goodies, but deep down, she knew it was a lie. It was entirely possible that she and Riley would become lovers tonight.

The restaurant was crowded with the usual mix of suave businessmen and glamorous women. Riley's table was set slightly apart from other diners, because he not only wanted the best view, he wanted Wynter all to himself.

All day, when he should have been focusing on his clients' cases, his thoughts had wandered to that mind-blowing kiss they'd shared in his office. He hoped that, after dinner, he would get another taste of this beautiful woman.

Once their dinner choices were made and the wine, poured, he picked up his glass. *"Salut."*

"Salut."

The wine was superb, and after she drank a bit, Wynter put down her glass. "Are we going to address the elephant in the room?" she inquired.

His brow quirked. "Are you talking about this afternoon?"

She nodded.

"I equate it to lust. Pure and simple."

Her cheeks flushed at his bold statement.

"Do you always speak so plainly?"

"If you mean, am I always this direct? Then, yes," Riley responded. "I see no reason to beat around the bush. Do you? We find each other attractive."

Wynter chuckled. "That doesn't surprise you? We grew up together and you never looked at me before. Why now?"

"You're all grown-up," Riley stated, looking at her over the rim of his glass. "We both are free to act on our desires." He took a sip of his wine before placing it on the table. "But to answer your question, you were always a surprise to me, Wynter. Of all of Shay's friends, you weren't afraid to have a conversation with me."

"You don't scare me, Riley Davis."

When she picked up a piece of bread and popped it into her beautiful, delectable mouth, Riley nearly groaned. "Perhaps you should be afraid. I bite."

"I don't mind love bites." A blush crept across her décolletage, and Riley was certain she hadn't meant to say that out loud. But in doing so, she directed his attention to her bosom, which was on lush display in her deep-V-neck rhinestone dress. It might seem demure, with its long sleeves and length that hit at the knee, but it didn't feel that way to Riley. He wanted to rip it off. "I didn't mean to say that."

"You don't mean to do a lot of things around me," Riley stated. "Do I bring out the best or worst in you, I wonder?" He leaned back and regarded her.

"That remains to be seen," Wynter replied cheekily. Their eyes met, hers rebellious and his dark and glinting. Riley realized it was going to be a fun night.

Their meals arrived, and the food was delicious and beautifully presented, though Riley would expect nothing less. His assistant had told him it took months to get a reservation at the restaurant, and the menu prices reflected it.

"How's your mother?" Wynter asked as she worked on her plate of pan-seared mahi-mahi with cauliflower-broccoli whip and lump crab in white-wine butter.

"She's doing much better than I expected," Riley said, cutting into his Angus steak with butternut squash and truffle puree and a peppery red-wine sauce.

Wynter smiled. "That's wonderful news."

"Yes, it is. I was worried what her condition might be, but she's taking her meds and even seeing someone. I'm glad, because it takes some of the load off Shay. I know it was difficult for Shay when I left home."

"It was." Wynter didn't even try to deny it. "Shay went through a lot with your mother, especially when she was married to Kevin."

"I was against her committing so young."

"Because you yourself refuse to commit?" Wynter asked. "Why is that? Were you hurt in a previous relationship?"

"Whoa!" Riley didn't like being in the hot seat. He didn't like talking about his past, though he doubted he could really call those casual encounters relationships. "Since when did this become the Quiz Riley Show?"

Wynter shrugged. "I'm just trying to get to know you. You're welcome to ask me anything you want."

"Oh, really?" He rubbed his hands together with glee. "Are you ready for the shoe to be on the other foot?"

"I guess that's a no on telling me your reason for remaining single?" Wynter inquired.

The saucy minx was giving it back to him, and Riley found it oddly refreshing. Most women caved to his every whim because they were eager to be with the great Riley Davis. Wynter didn't seem to care at all, and he liked that, but he also wasn't about to talk about other women. It was bad enough she knew about his mother's mental illness.

"You assume right," Riley replied. "And you, why do you travel the world instead of staying at home?"

Wynter chucked wryly. "You've seen my family, haven't you? We're a hot mess, and this weekend showed we couldn't be farther apart. So, I'm not too keen to stay on the home front. Traveling, aside from providing fodder for my blog, gives me the freedom I love."

"What are you running from?"

"Do I have to be running from something?" she asked sharply and picked up her wineglass and sipped. After setting down her glass, she continued, "Can't I be running *to* something, towards my future? My blog means everything to me. One day, I was so bored with the status quo and doing what others expected of me, I decided to explore and start living my life doing things that were important to me. Traveling is one of those things, and it made me feel like I was a kindred spirit with my aunt. Plus, I found something that I'm really good at, and that speaks to me."

"You're very passionate about it."

"I'm passionate about a lot of things," Wynter responded hotly.

Riley was surprised by Wynter's boldness but didn't mistake her tone. Wynter was up for how he intended the night to end. In fact, if he were a guessing man, he would say she was as eager as he was to move their evening to a different location.

Meeting her again, he'd thought she might be fragile from losing her aunt and enduring her family's squabbles. How wrong he'd been. He should have remembered the Wynter from his youth, who was impetuous and feisty. When he'd picked her up tonight, his mouth had salivated because the rhinestone dress showcased her mouthwatering body. A body he couldn't wait to see in all its glory, and he would. Tonight.

He called her bluff and gave her a slow, sexy grin. "Care for dessert?"

"Not at all," Wynter said. "I have something else in mind."

He lounged back in the chair, his gaze never leaving hers. "You amaze me, Wynter."

"I hope in a good way?"

"Oh, definitely that," Riley returned. He'd thought she might be skittish about tonight, but Wynter wasn't afraid to let him know exactly what she wanted. What Shay might think about this whole interaction gave him a moment's pause. She would be furious, of course, but Riley would have to take that on the chin, because there was no way he was turning down what Wynter was offering.

He motioned the waiter over. "Check, please."

Wynter stared at her reflection in the mirror of the women's restroom. She couldn't believe how direct she'd been with Riley. There was no way he could mistake that she wanted to spend the night with him. It was a fantasy come true, but she wouldn't play the role of being naive ingenue.

Instead, she was being the aggressor and taking over. Riley was a man she'd wanted for years, and she might not ever get another chance with him. She wasn't about to take a back seat and let him take charge. No, if she was going to do this, it would be on *her* terms.

Losing her aunt had made Wynter see that life was short. She couldn't waste time, because tomorrow wasn't promised. She had to live for today. And who knew if she would ever get another opportunity to be with Riley? Even though she knew this would be one night only and he wasn't offering her a commitment, she had to take her chance, because he hadn't been able to take his eyes off her. She felt the same way—there was something about him that sparked something deep within her.

After powdering her nose and adding another swipe of lipstick, she glanced at herself. Her eyes glittered, and her skin looked flushed with desire. There was no turning back now; she'd laid down the gauntlet, and Wynter couldn't wait to see what happened next.

When she returned to the table, the plates had been cleared. "I'm ready."

Riley's eyes searched hers. For regret? Or a change of heart? He wouldn't find it. She knew what she wanted.

Him.

Riley led Wynter out of the restaurant and to the passenger side of his Bentley, waiting at the curb, and then came round to the driver's side. Before turning on the car, he turned to her. "Are you sure about this, Wynter? Because if we do this, you need to understand that it's only for one night. I don't do commitments or relationships. Besides which, I just became partner at my law firm. I have no room in my life for personal entanglements."

She understood, because she wasn't looking for more than tonight. Her world was already topsy-turvy. Spending the night with Riley would be her choice, something she could control. She was owning her feminine power and taking what she wanted. "Yes, I'm sure. I want you, Riley, but if the feeling isn't mutual…"

He snorted. And before she knew it, Riley's mouth came down hard and demanding on hers. Desire rushed through Wynter as her arms slid around his neck. She returned the kiss and gave him everything. Riley growled against her mouth as he plundered its depths. His tongue mated with hers in an erotic dance that made her belly swoop and dive like a flight of doves taking off. Wynter's mind became frenzied with a blur of sensations. If they didn't stop, she was afraid of what she might let him do right there in the car. Slowly, she pulled away.

He frowned. "Did I come on too strong?"

She shook her head. "Not at all. You were just right, but unless you want to get cited for indecent exposure, I think it might be a good idea for us to take this back to your place."

Riley grinned. "I think you're right." After giving her a heated stare, he turned on the ignition and eased the car out of the parking lot.

The ride to Riley's penthouse at the Alteza, above the Grand Hyatt, was thankfully short, and Wynter was happy for that. Not that she intended to change her mind. She just wondered if he would live up to her expectations after all these years.

The bellhop greeted them upon arrival and immediately opened Wynter's door.

"Thank you," she responded, alighting from the vehicle. Riley was quickly by her side, wrapping his arm around her waist and leading her toward the entrance. Wynter didn't notice much about the lobby, only saw polished marble floors and a teakwood front desk as she allowed Riley to lead her to the private elevator for the residences. He had one of the penthouses on the top floor. Wynter wasn't surprised he would pick a place with all the bells and whistles, such as a twenty-four-hour concierge. He had done quite well for himself since leaving San Antonio.

Once inside the elevator, where they were the only occupants, Wynter stared at Riley. She didn't move, let alone breathe, as he stepped closer, never taking his eyes off her. He reached out and lightly stroked her cheek. "You're not exactly who I thought you were, Wynter."

"I suppose you thought I'd become a shrinking flower? Well, that's not me—it's just been a trying week."

"I can only imagine, but we're going to put that behind us." He tilted her head back with his hand, exposing her throat. Then he leaned down and kissed her neck.

"Yes, let's," Wynter managed to eke out. A gasp of surrender escaped her lips when he trailed hot kisses down her neck. His caresses were smooth and silky, and when he nipped at a particularly sensitive spot, her breathing became labored and her body shivered with delight.

"You've handled it very well," he whispered, his lips brushing her ear.

Wynter sucked in a deep breath. "Th-thank you." She refused to swoon in his arms, but damn it if her legs didn't feel weak. "But let's not talk about that anymore. In fact, let's not talk at all."

She grasped Riley by his suit lapel and pulled his mouth down on hers. He felt like heaven, and a sigh escaped her lips. Riley took over and kissed her deeply. His tongue slipped inside her mouth and teased and tangoed with hers in an intimate dance she couldn't wait to finish. Instead, the doors of the elevator pinged. They separated, and Wynter stepped out into a stunning penthouse with floor-to-ceiling panoramic views of downtown San Antonio.

"Riley, this is amazing." Wynter walked over to take in the sights.

"Nothing is more amazing than you." His eyes were dark and flared with heated desire. "But I should remind you that I don't do commitment, Wynter."

She spun around to face him. "Well, that's good, because I'm not looking for one."

If Riley thought she was looking for a ring on her finger, she wasn't. Wynter had seen what marriage and commitment looked like with her parents and Corey. None of whom had a union she was looking to imitate. Wynter considered herself much like her aunt, a free spirit with a zeal for life and new adventures. She wasn't looking to settle down with a man, not even her dream guy, Riley Davis.

"Can I tell you that's hella sexy?" Riley responded and started removing his suit jacket and toeing off his shoes. "You're a woman after my own heart."

Wynter smiled. Riley, apparently, was done waiting and didn't want any further delays for the main event, and neither did she. She suspected they weren't going to make it to the bedroom. She'd never been an exhibitionist, but she kind of liked that all of San Antonio was laid out in front of them. Reaching behind her, Wynter pulled the zipper down on the rhinestone dress and let it pool around her feet.

She watched as Riley began stripping with speed rather than any sort of finesse. Wynter couldn't wait to see his sculpted body. And when he took off his shirt, revealing his broad and chiseled chest, she wasn't disappointed. She was transfixed as he removed his trousers. Her eyes moved to the hair that arrowed lower beneath the waistband of his boxer shorts, which revealed the jutting proof of his arousal. She let out a pent-up breath when his shorts hit the floor. "You are beautiful."

"I should be saying that to you."

She smiled and went to shove her panties down her legs, but Riley had covered the space between them quickly. He placed his hands over hers. "Please, let me."

He removed her panties and undid the clasp of her bra, releasing her full breasts. Immediately, her nipples turned turgid when they were exposed to air and his heated gaze. He cupped them in his palms, swiping his thumb back and forth across the hard peaks. When he leaned forward to take one of her nipples between his teeth and tongue, she let out a satisfied moan of pleasure.

Riley grinned. "You like that?"

"I do."

"Good. Because I'm about to give you a whole lot more." Then his mouth was closing around the nipple. He sucked it deep into his mouth, and Wynter threw back her head as shock waves of need coursed through her body. He feasted on the one breast and then transferred his attention to its twin, drawing it into the hot cavern of his mouth.

When he was finished with that torment, he began working his way down her body until he came to her abdomen. He dropped to his knees so he could run a probing finger between the tight curls at the apex of her thighs. A sob escaped Wynter's lips at being touched where she wanted him most. And Riley didn't stop there; he pressed his finger inside, pushing upward until he hit that spot full of nerve endings.

"Ah…!" Wynter cried out.

He slipped another finger inside, sliding them both in and out in an erotic dance. Wynter sobbed his name when the first exquisite spasms of pleasure overtook her body. "Riley!"

She flew apart and her legs gave out, but Riley held her tight, pushing her toward the floor-to-ceiling windows to keep her upright. Sensations were still coursing through her and Wynter didn't think she could withstand any more, but Riley wasn't done. He changed course and began to minister to her with his mouth, slowly licking her damp folds.

When he flicked his tongue against her tight bud, Wynter could once again feel herself teetering on the edge of that magical place. When he began to suckle, her eyelids fluttered closed and uncontrollable shudders began to rack her body as a second climax struck. This man understood a woman's body and knew how to give intense pleasure.

He reached beside them on the floor and pulled protection out his wallet and dealt with it. Then he surged to his feet. Her entire body was trembling with the need to feel him inside her. She tilted her head and they were back to kissing again, the hunger between them passionate and unabated. When she felt the solid ridge of his penis against her moist opening, she instinctively knew to part her legs as he thrust deep.

"Yes!" Wynter cried out because the sensation of having Riley inside her was so perfect. He pushed her thighs apart and set a hard and fast rhythm as he took her against the window. He pistoned into her body with unfettered passion, and their bodies grew slick with sweat as their breaths commingled in pleasure of the acutest kind.

"Oh!" Nothing had prepared her for this moment. All Wynter could do was circle one leg around Riley's waist and hold on for the ride as he drove deeper into her. Anyone with binoculars could see them against the window, and it gave her an illicit thrill until a spasm ripped through her. She dug her nails into his shoulders, and Riley clamped his hands on her buttocks.

He thrust hard and deep one final time before groaning out, "Wynter…!"

They stood together with their bodies pressed tight for several minutes in silence as the enormity of what just happened hit them. Wynter thought Riley might immediately retreat, but instead, he lifted her into his arms and carried her into his bedroom.

Eight

Riley brought Wynter to his bed. He wanted to make love to her properly. That first time in his living room had been a feverish coupling because of the intense attraction they felt. But now, he wanted to take his time. If tonight was all he had, he wanted to show Wynter how much pleasure they could have together.

Wynter wasn't some naive virgin. She returned his touches and kisses and showed him she knew exactly how to make him moan. And when she wanted to be on top, Riley let her without hesitation. She was skilled and brought them both to a culmination that had Riley seeing stars.

Eventually, they took a shower together, but even that turned into a sensuous glide of naked bodies that kept them up until the wee hours of the morning. Afterward, Riley fell into a deep sleep, which was unusual for him. For years, he'd never been able to get more than four or five hours of sleep because, when he was a teenager, he'd been on high alert. He had to make sure his mother was okay and wouldn't harm herself. The pattern stuck when he went to college and then, later, law school. The long nights of studying to stay on top and be the best took their toll until Riley didn't need much sleep to operate.

But last night, he'd slept like a baby because he'd had Wynter's lush body wrapped around him. However, awakening this morning, something was very clear.

He was in bed *alone.*

Sometime in the early morning, after they'd just had the best sex of his life, Wynter had slipped away from his bed. Riley sat upright. *That* had never happened before. He was used to being the one who left, not the other way around.

Riley didn't know whether he should be offended or not. Or perhaps Wynter hadn't been as satisfied as he thought last night? No, he shook his head. Women could fake it, but Wynter hadn't faked a moment of their intimacy. He could tell. She was responsive and very vocal about what she wanted. She hadn't been afraid to take charge of her pleasure or his.

Riley groaned when he thought about the way she'd wriggled down the bed last night to position her head close to his groin. The way she'd run her fingertips over his erect shaft. Her touch had been featherlight, as if she'd reveled in the sensation of having him at her mercy. He'd been enthralled, and rather than fight it, he'd given in. She'd bent her head, taken him in her mouth and sucked him.

Afterward, she'd raised her head and given him a triumphant smile, all the while licking her lips as she caught a drop she must have missed.

It was one of the most erotic experiences of his life. Wynter had moved to the top of the list as the best lover he'd ever had. Although he wished they could have a repeat of the night before, Riley appreciated that Wynter understood the parameters. As a result, she'd left of her own ac-

cord, without him having to show her the door like some
of his ex-lovers.

At least he would always have the memory of their one
hot night. But, in the back of his mind, Riley would always
wonder what might have happened if she had stayed.

Wynter stood under the shower taps and let the water
pour down on her. The last few days had been crazy. The
funeral, the reading of the will, her date with Riley—which
had culminated in the most amazing sex of her life! Sweet
Jesus! She'd had no idea how in over her head she truly
could be until she tangled with a man like Riley Davis. But
she gave as good as she got, Wynter thought with a smile.

She'd brought the man to his knees when she pleasured
him with her mouth, but that was only after he damn near
had her speaking in tongues after the way he'd taken her up
against the glass, later, in his bed and, again, in the shower.
Riley had an insatiable appetite, which matched hers. Wynter never knew her sex drive was so high until Riley had
brought it out in her. She guessed it took a special person
to tap into that side, and Riley was that person.

Wynter didn't have any more illusions about how good
they would be together, because Riley had shattered them.
It was why she had exited before Riley could wake. She
wasn't interested in the awkward morning-after talk. Riley
had been up-front about his feelings on commitment. He
wasn't looking to settle down. And neither was she. Her
family life was abysmal, and it had only gotten worse since
her return to San Antonio.

She was hoping things might improve today. Her mother
had invited her over to the house to talk. Turning off the
taps, Wynter dried off and dressed. She didn't know what
to expect, given how they'd left things after the reading of
the will, but Wynter was willing to listen. If her mother
knew her in the slightest, she had to know Wynter would

share her aunt's wealth. She certainly wouldn't spend all the money in one lifetime. Wynter just wanted to live comfortably and be able to travel and write.

Looking through her suitcase, Wynter found what she was looking for in a pair of slacks and a belted snake-print tunic top. An hour later, she was pulling her BMW into the driveway of the Barrington estate. Agnes had been kind enough to drive her car over and Wynter had driven her home. She hadn't gotten around to turning it in yet. She had barely exited the vehicle when her mother opened the front door. That was unusual. Her mother didn't deign to answer her own door. Wynter's Spidey sense went on alert.

"Wynter." Her mother kissed her cheek when she approached as if they hadn't not spoken in the three days since the funeral.

"Mother," Wynter said, "is everything all right?"

"Yes," her mother responded, closing the door. "I'm so glad you came. I'm hoping we can put all this unpleasantness behind us."

"I would like that." Wynter didn't know what was going on, but followed her mother to the great room, where sunlight peeked out from the two-story windows. But then, after glancing around the room, Wynter noticed they weren't alone. A strange man was with them. "I'm sorry, did I come at a bad time? If you're finishing up business, I can come back later."

"No, no," her mother said, motioning her forward. "I wanted you to meet Reginald Price, my lawyer."

"Lawyer?"

"Yes, he thought it best we sit down and hash things out like family before we get the courts involved."

Wynter's eyes narrowed. "And you thought bringing your *lawyer* to a family meeting was prudent?"

"Don't take that tone with me, Wynter Barrington."

"Then don't blindside me," Wynter responded. "I came

here in good faith, thinking you wanted to repair the rift in our family, but instead, you brought your attorney? Why? To browbeat me into signing over my inheritance?"

"Of course not," her mother huffed. "But surely you see this is too much for you to take on. My sister's estate is vast, and you don't even stay in one place longer than a week. How are you going to handle her business affairs?"

Wynter sighed, inhaling deeply. "I'm capable of handling the household, Mother. I'm not inept, and as for the inheritance, that's what financial advisers are for. I thought you wanted to talk."

"I do."

"And what is your definition of working this out, Mother?" Wynter inquired. "Me giving up everything so you can have your way?"

Melinda jumped up from her seat and began pacing the room. "I'm only doing what's best, Wynter. You have no idea how devastated I was to learn my own sister cut me out of her will. I thought we were close. I feel slighted."

"So, this is about revenge?" Wynter asked. "I can see I was misled about this meeting. I think it's best I go."

"Please don't leave, Wynter. I don't want to this to turn into a battle between us. Think of the scandal this could cause if the press got wind of our family squabble."

"Scandal? I'm not the one causing it. You've ambushed me with your attorney when I have no counsel present." Wynter moved toward the doorway.

"Where are you going?"

"I have some pressing business obligations I need to attend to. When I get back, we can discuss it further—when my attorney can be present."

"Wynter, don't you dare walk out that door! We need to resolve this. Just because you're heading out to gallivant all over the world doesn't mean business stays at a standstill."

Wynter shrugged. "You're the executor of the will—it's

up to you to keep the estate running. I did speak with Hope and her husband, however, and they've graciously agreed to stay on and take care of the place until I return."

"You're acting like a spoiled and willful child. You can't run away when you don't like the outcome of a situation."

"I'm a grown woman, Mother, and I don't answer to you," Wynter replied. "Now that you and Daddy have cut me off, I will be looking after myself from now on. Here's my first act of independence." She dropped the keys to the BMW on the table.

"That's your car," her mother stated.

"I know, but until the will is settled, I can't afford it." Wynter was already calling an Uber. When she returned, she'd utilize her aunt's Rolls-Royce until she found a used vehicle she could afford.

"Your behavior shows me more than ever that you're not equipped to handle this responsibility. And you've made my decision clear. I must protect my sister's legacy." Her mother turned to her attorney. "Start the paperwork to contest Helaine's will."

Wynter stared across the room at her mother. How foolish she'd been to think that something had changed—that her mother would finally see how capable she was. For the first time, she was standing on her own two feet and taking care of herself. She had drawn a line in the sand. A line they couldn't come back from.

"Is that really what you want to do?" Wynter asked.

"You give me no choice."

Wynter turned on her heel and walked out. There was nothing more to be said. She had to ready herself for battle.

"Thank you for meeting with me, Ms. Gilbert," Wynter said the following day when she met with the estate attorney Riley had referred her to at her aunt's home. There had been too great a risk she'd run into Riley if she'd gone to their office.

"Of course. Mr. Davis told me to take good care of you." LaTanya was a beautiful woman with deep chocolate skin. She wore her hair in a ponytail but had on an expensive suit.

Hearing Riley's name made a swarm of butterflies take flight in Wynter's belly. She tried her darnedest not to think about the sexy divorce lawyer, but she was having a hard time forgetting the incredible night they'd shared, and it wasn't like she could talk to Shay about it. She had expressly forbidden Wynter from getting involved with her brother.

And yes, she could tell Egypt or one of the other girls, but she didn't want to share the experience with anyone just yet. It was private. Her secret was hers and hers alone. Plus, it wasn't as if it was going to happen again. It was a one-time thing. Or, at least, that was what Wynter told herself. Besides, she had too much on her plate as it was. Growing her business and staying afloat, all the while fighting off her family for control of an inheritance that should be hers.

"What can I do, Ms. Gilbert? My family seems intent on contesting this will."

"They've already taken a big step by filing an injunction against the estate," LaTanya responded.

"When did they do that?"

"Yesterday."

After her meeting with her mother. The attorney must have prepared the documents and had them ready to go. The meeting yesterday was merely a stopgap measure before they went full speed ahead with their plans.

"The injunction prevents you from spending any of your aunt's money or selling the estate."

"Can they do that?"

"Temporarily, yes," she replied. "But the burden of proof is on them to show your aunt wasn't of sound mind and body when the will was executed or that you coerced her in some way."

"That was my aunt's home and now mine. I'm not selling. I understand my mother blocking me and my friends from getting the money, but she's preventing the charities and Helaine's staff from getting the money due them." Wynter covered her face with her hands. "This is a nightmare."

"Can you come to an agreement with your family? A settlement, if you will."

"I'd planned on it," Wynter replied, "but then my mother acted as if it was foolish of my aunt to leave me her estate. My aunt thought of me as the daughter she never had."

"Wynter, I'm sorry to distress you. That wasn't my intent. Your family is playing hardball. It's a tactic."

"Which could take months or years, even," Wynter added. "Isn't that right?" She'd done some research online and read the horror stories.

"Possibly. We can try to resolve the issue through mediation. If you're open to it."

Wynter needed time. Time to figure out what she wanted to do. Right now, she was too upset and angry to make any decisions. She rose to her feet. "I appreciate you being frank with me, Ms. Gilbert. Let me digest all of this and get back to you."

Wynter watched the woman leave. The last week had sucked the life out of her. The only bright spot had been the amazing night she'd spent with Riley, but her life was spiraling out of control. All she wanted to do was run. Run far away. And that was exactly what she would do. When she returned, *Wynter's Corner* would be in the black. She would prove to the Barrington family she was a lot stronger and more resourceful than they gave her credit for.

Nine

Two months later

"Ms. Barrington, we're so excited to have you here at the Aspen Summit ski resort," the resort's general manager, Karen Holt, stated when Wynter arrived in Aspen late that afternoon. It was a brisk thirty degrees out, but the snow made the entire city look like a winter wonderland. "We've loved the stories you've done for other hotel brands and thought you could do the same for us."

"I'm excited to be here," Wynter replied as the manager showed her around the resort.

She'd arrived in Colorado Springs after spending the past couple of months in Europe, with a stint in Thailand. When she'd left San Antonio, she'd needed to get away, not just from the contentious relationship with her family, but from her mixed emotions after the incredible night she'd shared with Riley.

She had never felt the kind of raw passion she felt when

they'd been together. She hadn't recognized the woman she'd become in Riley's arms. She'd been so shattered by the experience, she'd left before dawn. For him, it might have just been sex, but for her, it had been a transformative experience. A few days later, she was on a flight, one of many over the past couple of months. And now she was at this beautiful ski chalet where she would find loads of inspiration and material for *Wynter's Corner*.

"We have lots of amenities," Karen stated. "Our spa is world-renowned, plus we have a salon, a fitness center and heated indoor and outdoor pools with a water slide. We are all about offering a holistic approach to restore and rebalance your health and well-being through a combination of nutrition and natural therapies."

"Sounds wonderful," Wynter replied. The resort was hosting her in exchange for a lifestyle story on her blog and their website.

"Allow me to show you to your room."

A bellboy followed behind them with Wynter's meager luggage, consisting of her usual suitcase and a duffel bag. The resort was known for catering to the rich and famous. She wouldn't be surprised if she saw a well-known actor or singer walking the luxuriously appointed corridors.

Wynter was awestruck when they arrived at the king-size guest room that would be her retreat for the next week. It had a contemporary mountain design and offered stunning views of Aspen Mountain. More impressive was the black stacked-stone fireplace and the limestone en suite bathroom with soaking tub and shower. The walk-in closet easily fit her belongings, and Wynter looked forward to trying out the minibar.

"The terrace is out here." Karen opened French doors to reveal a small table and chairs for two.

"You've thought of everything."

"It's our pleasure. I've already scheduled dinner for you

this evening at La Toc, but if you need anything at all, please don't hesitate to ask."

"Thank you so much," Wynter replied.

After she'd tipped the bellboy and closed the door, Wynter flung herself across the massive bed. It was soft and plush, and she sank right in.

She needed this.

She'd been going nonstop for months, because she was determined to do everything in her power to make sure *Wynter's Corner* was a success. And she was well on her way. Within weeks of leaving San Antonio, Wynter's efforts at connecting with famous female basketball star Jasmine Butler who loved to travel paid off. They had partnered and shown how to live like rockstars at a St. Bart's resort and consequently, *Wynter's Corner* had blown up. Jasmine had an enormous following, all of whom wanted to know everything about Wynter. Consequently, her subscribers list on her social media skyrocketed. Suddenly, advertisers and sponsors were calling her to show off their travel destinations including the Aspen Summit resort. Now her blog was in the black.

It came right on time, because she had a lot on her plate. Her mother had doubled down on her efforts to contest the will by having Mr. Price depose all her aunt's staff, as if Wynter had bamboozled her right under their noses. Although her mother had mentioned a scandal, she seemed uncaring of the attention challenging the will could bring their family. Her mother was clearly so upset by Aunt Helaine's actions that she didn't care about negative publicity.

Wynter was thinking about checking in with Hope on her aunt's estate when her cell phone rang. It was Egypt.

"Hey, diva," Egypt said from the other end. "Do you have a time for a Zoom call? You've been pretty remote the last couple of months, and the Gems want to catch up."

"Absolutely. Give me five minutes and I'll send a link."

Soon, Wynter's five friends were staring back at her from her laptop screen and firing away questions like old times. It felt good to be Stateside. After she'd filled them in on the resort, it was Egypt who asked the tough questions.

"Wynter, are you sure you want to keep fighting your family over this inheritance?" Egypt had the phone propped up, and Wynter could see she was shucking corn in her food truck. "It's honestly not worth it. If your family doesn't want us to have the money, it's fine. We'll figure out how to make our businesses work, but we—" she pointed to Asia, Teagan, Shay and Lyric on the call "—don't want the charities or your aunt's estate employees to suffer. Settle."

Wynter snorted. "I'm surprised to hear you, of all people, say that." Months ago, she'd been Wynter's staunchest supporter. "Because settling is the furthest thing from my mind. My parents are doing this to punish me, like I'm some errant child. They are trying to rule me and, consequently, rule you." She pointed toward the laptop camera for emphasis. "I won't allow it. I will agree to my aunt's wishes and nothing more. If *I* choose to give my family a portion of the inheritance, it will be my choice. I will not be bullied or pushed around—not anymore."

"Good for you," Egypt said. "How's the blog?"

"*Wynter's Corner* is gaining followers," Wynter responded. "All because Jasmine Butler and I hung out and the pictures and video went viral."

"The power of social media is amazing, isn't it?" Egypt wondered aloud.

Wynter laughed. "Yes, it is." Being seen with Jasmine had really raised her profile. There had even been a few offers for clothing and makeup.

Wynter's Corner was not only out of the red, but last month it made a profit. If this continued, she could keep fighting her parents until the courts decided in her favor. But Wynter knew her friends were eager to start their own businesses. She knew she should call a ceasefire with her parents, but *she* wasn't willing to bend, not this time.

"Will Jasmine be visiting us in Barbados?" Asia asked, folding her arms across her chest.

"No, Asia," Wynter quipped. "It was just a publicity stunt."

Egypt wagged her finger. "Doesn't matter because it worked. And now, you don't need your parents' support. You've got this!"

All the women cheered. "Listen, ladies, I have to go. I arrived at the ski chalet after hours of traveling and I'm ready for a long, hot shower," Wynter said. "I'll talk to you soon." She waved and closed the laptop.

Wynter wished she could tell her friends about Riley, but she knew Shay wouldn't approve of their involvement, though Wynter couldn't call the night they'd shared a relationship. It was a one-night stand, and that was all it could ever be, because Wynter refused to allow herself to get hung up on a commitment-phobe like Riley. She'd rather remain single.

An hour later, after showering and changing into jeans and a thick sweater, Wynter took her laptop with her to the resort's café, where she'd order a drink to warm her up. Weather in Aspen was in the low thirties, and after coming from balmy Thailand, she was chilled to the bone. The café was decorated in a farmhouse style with a modern twist. An exposed ceiling showed the beams and piping overhead, while the floors were vinyl "wood" plank and the countertops were made of stone with wood siding. Wooden tables and chairs were scattered throughout, as were cozy bar nooks, if you were alone and needed to power your device.

Wynter chose one of the empty spots at the bar to park herself and enjoy the authentic coffeehouse vibe. She pulled out her laptop and plugged into the power source. She had to catch up on her wrap-up post about Thailand and her experience there, but first, she needed a drink.

Sliding off the bar, she made her way to the line and ordered a medium chai latte. While she waited, she caught up on replying to some of her Instagram comments. Now that *Wynter's Corner* was doing well and she had more followers, keeping up with her social media took more of her time.

"Large chai latte!"

Wynter heard her drink called and walked to the counter. She was reaching for her drink when her phone pinged with an alert. Wynter was reading the notification when she ran into a wall of solid male. Her instincts went on high alert and her skin prickled with awareness. She recognized that smell, because she had luxuriated in it when they'd gone to bed together.

Riley.

Her mouth became dry, and she swallowed. Of all the places she'd expect to run into him, Aspen, Colorado, wasn't one of them.

Slowly, she raised her gaze and met his dark one. He wore the same look of surprise, and he was holding her cup. "Wynter? What are you doing here?"

Wynter's mouth crooked into a small smile. Well, this was incredibly awkward. She had to face the man she'd gone to bed with, then ghosted. "I'm here to do a piece on the resort for my blog. And you're holding my latte."

"Good to know," he replied, "but this is my drink."

Her brow furrowed. "You like chai lattes?"

He grinned, and Wynter couldn't help it—her stomach flipped. "Yes, I do. And I was here first. I ordered a large."

Wynter immediately let go of the beverage, because she'd asked for a medium. She watched Riley's mouth close around the lid and had to close her eyes. Memories about what exactly Riley could do with his mouth assaulted her. Sweet Jesus, she was in trouble.

Suddenly, the barista was calling out, "Medium chai latte!"
Thank the Lord.

Once she took her drink, Wynter stepped away from the counter and walked back to the bar, but Riley was hot on her heels. When she was seated, he took the empty stool beside her. She wasn't sure how to behave in a situation like this. She'd never had a one-night stand before. Usually, if she went to bed with someone, she expected to see them again. Although he was Shay's brother, Wynter hadn't anticipated she would see Riley again so soon.

He seemed equally as flummoxed and stared at her over the lid of his latte.

She had to break the silence. "And you? What are you doing here?"

"I already had a vacation planned before I was hired, so I'm combining relaxation with work. I'm here to woo a potential client," Riley responded. "A reclusive tech billionaire is in the market for a divorce attorney. I'm hoping to convince him I'm the right fit."

"I'm surprised you would need to *try*," Wynter replied.

Riley's reputation was stellar on the East Coast, as well as in San Antonio. Although she'd told herself not to, since she left, she'd kept up with Riley, who'd made a big splash since his arrival.

Riley laughed. "I've had wealthy clients before, but this one is going to be tricky."

"How so?" Wynter asked, taking a sip of her drink.

"Because custody is involved," Riley explained. "And although I have an excellent track record for my clients, I typically try to avoid cases where children are involved, but it's not always possible."

"Why?"

Riley hungrily ate up the sight of Wynter, with her wavy hair and gorgeous light brown eyes. To say he was thrown

was an understatement. And not just by her question, but by
Wynter herself. When they ran into each other, his breath
had jammed into his lungs and his heart had hammered in
his chest. He'd felt winded, as if he'd been punched in the
gut, because all he could think about was the softness beneath the snug sweater and denim jeans she wore. She was
a burst of heat on a cold winter's day.

Two months ago, they'd shared the most memorable
night of his life. Although he tried to bury himself in work,
he'd been unable to forget. He felt a tug of lust deep in
his belly that told him the attraction toward his sister's
best friend hadn't ended after one night. It was still there.
Brighter and hotter than ever.

"Are you going to answer me?" Wynter asked. Her question forced Riley to blink several times and reset—before
he hauled her over his shoulder and took her back to his
room, where he could reacquaint himself with all her lush
curves.

"Of course," he replied. He put his latte on the bar. "The
kids are put in the middle during a divorce. Sometimes having to choose between one parent and another. When I do
cases with children, I make damn sure kids are left with a
parent who can love and support them."

"Because you know from personal experience?" Wynter asked.

He nodded. He didn't usually talk about his parents' divorce, but it was different with Wynter because she was
Shay's friend. "Yes. It wasn't easy. My father wanted to
split our time between him and Mom fifty-fifty, but she
was adamant we stay with her full-time. Shay and I felt like
we were in a tug-of-war. And seeing how hard the separa-
tion was on my mom, we chose to stay with her. My father
was disappointed, and I think it's why he chose to push us
away when he remarried."

"He punished you for choosing your mother?" Wynter inquired.

Riley nodded. "But we had to stay with her. Mom was fragile. If we had gone, I'm not sure if she would be with us today." He'd never told anyone that, but with Wynter, he felt he could be open about the hardships he and Shay had endured as teenagers.

"But your mother is doing better now."

Riley nodded. "It wasn't an easy road to get here, Wynter. She needed the right treatment and care, but yes, now that we've found the right combination, she's well."

"I'm so happy for you and Shay." Wynter touched his arm, and Riley's nostrils flared as he caught a hint of her sweet perfume. It dragged him back to that night at his penthouse when Wynter had aroused him like no other woman.

Everything stilled as he looked deep into her eyes. The world narrowed to nothing but the two of them, and Riley battled to control the craving he had to tunnel his hands through her hair and bring her closer to him right there in the middle of the café. So he talked about work.

"It's not easy for me to take on clients with children, but this case is different. The wife doesn't really want the kid. She's using the child as a poker chip in a power game with her husband. She's holding custody over his head so she can get what she wants."

Wynter's hand flew to her chest. "That's horrible."

"Exactly. It's why I want to help. When my partners told me about it, I knew I needed to put aside my qualms and step in, but the client has refused to meet."

"Then you'll have to change his mind," Wynter said. "And if anyone can, you can."

Riley cocked his head to one side. "I never knew you had such faith in me." When he locked his gaze on her, Wynter licked her lips. He wished he could taste her one more time.

Wynter broke their gaze and looked over at her laptop. "Well, I need to get back to work."

"Of course—I'm sorry to have kept you."

"You didn't."

"How long are you staying?" Riley inquired. "Perhaps we can have dinner? That's if your boyfriend doesn't mind."

Her brows knitted together. "Boyfriend?"

"I can't assume a woman as beautiful as you is still single, especially considering how popular you've been lately."

Wynter laughed. "Sounds like someone has been following me."

Riley chuckled. She wasn't wrong. After they'd connected in San Antonio, he'd subscribed to *Wynter's Corner* and followed her on her social media accounts. "Not closely, but if you were putting it out there for public consumption, can't blame a guy for looking." Yes, that sounded better. He didn't sound like he'd been stalking her or was some lovesick puppy.

"If you must know, there's no one."

"That's good. Because that means there's no reason we can't have dinner."

"Do you really think that's wise after...?" Her voice drifted off. It was the first time during their conversation they were acknowledging what had occurred between them months ago.

"C'mon. We're friends, right?" Riley asked. "Surely we can enjoy a meal together without ripping each other's clothes off?"

"Speak for yourself," Wynter murmured under her breath, but Riley heard her.

"Well, I'm going to be down at the bar around seven," Riley said, getting up from the bar stool. "If you're there, great. If not, the message has been received loud and clear." Grabbing his latte, he tipped his head to her and left the café. Riley didn't look behind him, even though he wanted to. She wanted to pretend they were immune to each other, but he knew otherwise.

Tonight he would find out if Wynter was willing to take a risk and acknowledge that what they shared was far from over. In fact, it had only just begun.

Ten

As he drove to Derek Webster's twenty-thousand-square-foot ski chalet on Aspen Mountain, Riley's mind should have been focused on his upcoming meeting. The tech giant had finally consented to giving him an audience so Riley could pitch himself as the best attorney to help fend off Derek's soon-to-be ex-wife from walking away with half his assets. Texas being a community-property state, his spouse wouldn't get half his company, because he had owned the business prior to their marriage, but the ski chalet, among several other properties, had been acquired during the marriage and thus was jointly owned.

Instead, he was thinking about his run-in with Wynter. He hadn't thought he'd seen her again, at least not for a while, and certainly not in Colorado on a business trip. The relationship between them had changed; she wasn't just a friend of his sister—she was the woman he wanted. And he wanted her in the worst way. One night hadn't been enough to satiate his needs. If Wynter chose to come to the bar tonight, he would ask for the whole week, the entirety of his stay. He didn't know how long she was going to be here; all Riley knew was that he wanted her in his bed. And he suspected she wanted the same thing.

When he arrived at the stunning chalet, even Riley had to admit he was impressed with the four-story single-family home. He'd read the reports and knew it was worth upwards of seventy-five million and was one of the bones of contention in the Webster divorce. His wife wanted it, and Derek openly refused to give up the oasis that came with a full spa, indoor and outdoor pool and Jacuzzi, a movie theater, and a bowling alley.

Closing the door on the Jeep he had rented for his stay, Riley walked up the path to the front door. He hadn't bothered getting dressed in his finest suit, because Derek wasn't likely to care about that. He was informal, preferring jeans and a T-shirt to a designer suit. More importantly, Derek could afford thousands of Riley's suits several times over; he would instead impress the man with his knowledge and legal acumen.

He rang the doorbell and, to his surprise, Derek answered himself. The man had a mop of dark hair, piercing blue eyes and wore a hoodie and jeans.

"Riley, c'mon in." Derek motioned him inside. "I was watching March Madness. Are you into basketball?"

"Yes, I am," Riley said, closing the door. "Though I'm more into the NBA, I'm happy to watch a college game."

"Good, then you can join me for a beer," Derek said and turned on his heel. Riley had no choice but to follow him. He walked across the custom Italian-porcelain tile floor, past the Lalique crystal chandelier, to the elevator. They took it to the top floor, which housed the kitchen and an open-concept living and dining room, as well as a recreation room. The game was playing on a large television. Riley recognized the other gentleman in the room as Derek's right-hand man, Craig Abbott.

Riley walked toward him. "Craig," he said, shaking the slender blond man's hand. "Good to see you again. I appreciate you setting this meeting up."

"You're welcome," Craig responded. "We heard what you were able to do for David Goldman, and I suggested to Derek that he should at least meet with you."

"What are you drinking?" Derek asked from the hidden refrigerator that was seamlessly integrated into the kitchen's white walls.

"I'll have a Miller Lite if you have it."

Derek handed Riley a bottle and joined him and Craig on the couch to watch the game. Riley didn't know when they would talk business, and he wouldn't push it. When Derek was ready, Riley would pitch exactly how he intended to save the tech giant billions.

That time didn't come for nearly two hours. Instead, the three men enjoyed beers and trash-talked until the game finally ended and Derek wanted to talk shop.

"Tell me why I should hire you," Derek asked, using the remote to turn off the television. "You don't usually take cases where custody is involved."

Derek had done his research. Riley was not surprised. "No, I don't, but I'm very familiar with your case. I'm sure you've seen my stats. I've won my last ten cases."

"None involving children," Derek replied.

"True, but I'm one of the best divorce attorneys out there. Losing is not in my DNA. I will go to battle for you, Derek, and make sure your wife abides by the prenuptial agreement she signed."

Derek snorted. "That woman is a lying, cheating barracuda. She will do anything, say anything, to get her way. I want custody of my son, and my wife knows this. Knows there's nothing I won't do, including give her more than the prenup says is required."

"What does she want?"

"This house. Shares in my business, which, as you know, is not community property."

"Yes, I'm aware. Mrs. Webster is devious, but I've beaten her lawyer in court many times and I will again if you give me the chance to represent you."

"And you'll win me custody of my son?"

"I will do my very best to ensure your son is with a loving parent, and that's you."

"You intrigue me, Riley," Derek replied, "but I'm meeting with several attorneys while I'm here. I'll have to get back to you."

"Of course." Riley rose to his feet. He didn't want to overstay his welcome. "I appreciate the beers and the game. Would you be interested in joining me tomorrow to go snowmobiling? Fresh snow is expected later this evening— it would make for a great ride. You could get to know me from an old family friend who knows my character."

"Not a bad idea. Tell Craig and he'll arrange everything."

"Sure thing," Riley said. On his way to the car, he wondered what else he could do to show Derek he was the man for the job. It was true, he didn't usually take cases with children, because he hated seeing families split apart and the effects it had on the children. He knew this firsthand. His parents' divorce had torn him and Shay asunder. Riley wasn't sure he could handle dealing with the fallout day in and day out. But based on a private investigator's report, Riley suspected emotional abuse by Nina Webster, and now he felt compelled to intervene. He couldn't let her go unchecked. He just hoped this case wouldn't unearth his own demons, which had been dead and buried for years.

"Wynter, so glad I was finally able to catch up with you," LaTanya stated later that evening. Wynter had been working on her blog all afternoon and had just returned to her room. "You've been a hard woman to find."

"I'm sorry, Ms. Gilbert. I've been traveling and am now Stateside. Do you have an update for me?"

"I do, but I'm afraid it's not what you wanted to hear."

Wynter sighed. Although the answer wasn't unexpected, she'd been hoping her mother would let the matter go. She supposed that was wishful thinking.

"They've asked the judge to have an independent audit of your aunt's financials completed."

"Why?"

"My guess is they want to see if there any anomalies or irregularities, such as large outlays of cash to you or anyone else. This is all to support their case that your aunt was not of sound mind and body when she executed the will."

"That's ludicrous!"

"Are you sure you don't want to settle? Or do you want to stay the course?"

Wynter was silent on the other end. Over the past couple of months, she'd given the situation a lot of thought. Every time she thought about giving in, she remembered that her aunt had wanted her to have her home and the means to enjoy whatever lifestyle she wanted, nomadic or otherwise.

"Are you there?" LaTanya asked.

"Stay the course."

After the call, Wynter looked at the time. It was 6:00 p.m. and getting close to when Riley said he would be at the bar. Wynter's mind told her to stay in the room, but another voice told her to go downstairs and meet Riley for that drink.

Months ago, she'd justified the one-night stand by telling herself they were just scratching an itch and she would be able to move on afterward. She'd been wrong. She hadn't been able to so much as look at another man, much less be intimate with anyone, since Riley. He'd left an inedible mark on her. It was as if he'd branded her *his*. Her self-preservation instinct told Wynter to run, but that was what she always did when life got too difficult. Staying and seeing if the spark she'd still felt in the coffee shop was real or imagined would be a test for her.

She could either leave what they shared that one night as a fulfillment of her teenage crush, or she could take a risk, as Riley had suggested, and face the music on what was going on between them. Wynter was scared. She feared she could fall for Riley, a self-professed serial dater. He wasn't interested in the long-term, just the right now.

Even if Wynter wasn't looking for a ring and a white picket fence at the moment, she did want a family *someday*. If she got too close to Riley, it was quite possible he could penetrate the shell she'd erected around her to protect herself and she'd want more. The only way she'd dealt with not belonging in her family was not letting anyone in, except maybe her girls. Her best friends were like her sisters. They were the closest thing she had to a family, but they weren't a lover. Riley had the power to undo her defenses with one look or caress of his lips.

She should definitely run.

But instead, somehow her feet led her to the bar. The lounge offered a wood-burning fireplace, a 165-inch television and lots of comfy and plush sofas and chairs paired with small cocktail tables. Then there was the bar itself, with high-backed chairs that easily sat twenty. Four chandeliers that looked like art installations hung over the bar. There was even an outdoor patio that gave an uninterrupted view of the mountain. It was exactly the type of place Wynter's parents would frequent, but usually not her. She preferred a more casual setting. However, she was determined to show Riley she could handle whatever he dished out.

She found him standing near the only empty bar stool in the place. He smiled as she approached. "I'm glad you came."

"Did you think I wouldn't?" she challenged.

"No. You don't strike me as a coward," Riley said and pulled out the empty stool.

"Thank you," she said when he slid it underneath her.

"What can I get you to drink?"

Wynter glanced around. "I feel like in a place like this, I need an old-fashioned."

He chuckled while signaling the bartender over. After ordering her drink, he turned his full attention to Wynter, and she sucked a deep breath as his clean yet spicy scent reached her nose.

"What have you been up to the last couple of months?" Riley asked. "Were you able to come to an agreement with your family?"

Wynter shook her head. "Afraid not. They seem determined to paint me as the bad guy, but I refuse to accept the role. They're contesting the will, and I get that they're upset with me and don't want my friends to inherit anything, but they are preventing good charities from getting funding and allowing my aunt's employees the compensation due them."

"I'm sorry to hear that," Riley said. "I hoped things would be different by now."

"You mean, you didn't ask Shay about me?" Wynter lifted a brow.

Riley reached for the bottle of Miller Lite he was drinking and took a swig. "And risk her wanting to know why I was asking?" He shook his head. "No, thank you. My sister wasn't happy during your aunt's funeral when she thought we were spending too much time together."

"Why is she so dead set against it?"

Riley regarded her. "She thinks I'll hurt you."

"Will you?"

"Not intentionally," Riley responded, looking her in the eye. "Listen. I like you, Wynter, and I thought one night together would be enough to quench the hunger I have for you. After we were together, I realized it wasn't, but you were already gone."

His words, like a silken caress, wrapped around Wynter's fast-beating heart. She shouldn't still feel like this. They had only been together one night, yet it seemed as if that invisible cord she'd felt before kept bringing him back into her orbit.

"I thought it was better than having an awkward morning after," Wynter replied. Picking up the old-fashioned the bartender had set down, she took a sip.

Riley's dark eyes were lit like two flames, and she could feel her nipples puckering underneath her shirt in response.

"I haven't stopped wanting you since that night."

The atmosphere suddenly became charged, and Wynter had to remind herself to breathe. Hazarding a glance at him, she said, "Weren't you the one who said you didn't do commitments?"

Riley nodded. "That's true, and I'm not looking for marriage and happily-ever-after. I see the dark side of marriage every day, Wynter, after the vows and the recriminations. I don't know if I can believe in the institution. I've seen too much. I know how devastating it can be for both parties."

"It's a jaded view of the world, Riley. Not every marriage fails."

"The divorce rate in the US is steadily increasing. It's 2.7 to every thousand. The major cause is infidelity, because we're not meant to be with one person."

"Are you saying if you made that commitment, you would be unfaithful?"

"Hell, no!" Riley's emphatic response was rather shocking, considering his view on marriage. "I'm never marrying, so that wouldn't happen, but if I did, I would take my vows seriously. People give up too easily. Marriage is about a choice. You have to choose that person every day, even when the going gets tough."

"That's very powerful."

"I guess. I never thought I'd have a heated discussion about marriage with a woman I can't wait to get alone."

"Well, you're going to have wait a little longer, because I'm starved," Wynter responded. After the topic of conversation and the heated stares Riley had given her earlier, she needed to cool things off between them until she could figure out her next move. Though she feared she was a lost cause.

She wanted Riley.

Could she resist his advances?

And did she really want to?

Riley was doing his best not to let his mind drift and think about how good it could be with Wynter, but it was difficult when she smiled at him across the dinner table. It made him think of her soft moans when he'd been buried deep inside her.

Wynter was doing a good job of distracting him with other topics. He learned she was a basketball fan like him and had loved the San Antonio Spurs in their heyday. She didn't like food that was too mushy in texture. He couldn't believe it when she said she didn't like soft-serve ice cream and preferred hand-scooped ice cream because it was hard. The suggestive comment made her blush and made Riley want to lean over and give her the openmouthed kiss he was longing to, but instead, they continued talking well into the evening.

Riley discovered Wynter wasn't a fan of classical music and instead liked old-school rhythm and blues groups. They had a heated discussion on Boyz II Men versus Jodeci. He was a Jodeci and Silk fan himself and doggedly defended that "Forever My Lady" and "Feenin" were some of the best songs of the '90s, while Wynter preferred sweet love songs such as "End of the Road" and "I'll Make Love to You."

"You say I'm a romantic," Riley said, "but those are baby-making songs."

Wynter laughed, and the sound was rich, firing his body on all cylinders. Flames licked over his skin, and Riley had to shift in his seat. To change the subject, he asked Wynter if she wanted to accompany him on the snowmobiling excursion. Having Wynter and Derek together might lighten the mood so the billionaire didn't think him too pushy.

"I would love to come," Wynter said.

"Great!" Riley responded.

When the waiter came and asked if they wanted dessert, they simultaneously responded with an emphatic "No."

"I really enjoyed dinner and the conversation," Wynter said after Riley took care of the bill and they rose from their seats.

"So did I." But he also wanted to enjoy *her*.

Anticipation zinged in his veins when he placed his hand on the small of her back and led her out of the restaurant.

They made it to the bank of elevators, and Riley sensed Wynter's uncertainty. He pressed the up indicator, and they waited in silence. Riley would never push her into doing something she wasn't ready for. If tonight wasn't right, he'd wait. He was going to be here a week, or however long it took to win Derek's business.

When the elevator pinged and the doors opened, they entered the cab. Wynter pressed the fifth-floor button. It took all Riley's willpower not to take Wynter in his arms, but he stayed on his side of the cab. Several moments later, they arrived on Wynter's floor. She didn't say anything as Riley walked beside her until they arrived at her door.

Suddenly, she turned to face him. "I…"

Riley looked down at Wynter with her sexy, wavy hair and bee-stung lips. A hungry possessiveness came over him, but it would have to wait for another time. He placed his thumb on her lips. "Nothing has to happen tonight,

Wynter. I'll see you tomorrow." He turned to leave, but Wynter clutched his arm. Her pupils were dilated and her lips parted.

Riley felt his soul sing, and as he tilted his head, he told himself, *Just one kiss.*

And then he took her mouth.

One touch of Riley's lips on hers was like a flame to dry kindling, because Wynter swore her entire body ignited. Hot and firm, his mouth teased hers, brushing softly at first and drawing out the pleasure. She restlessly moved against him, urging him on. He deepened the kiss, and a moan broke through the heated silence of the corridor as his tongue boldly caressed hers.

Wynter was drowning in sensation, so when he angled his head for better access, she gave it to him. She wrapped her arms around his neck, and his fingers surged into her hair as the kiss took on a frenzied feel. Their bodies were plastered together, hip to hip, chest to chest, and their mouths were fused, their tongues gliding together as one. It was every bit as glorious as she remembered.

When his hips sought the cradle of her thighs and Wynter felt the evidence of his erection against her, liquid heat began to form between her legs as her body readied itself for his possession. That was when it hit Wynter—they were in the hall, where anyone could see them.

With a hoarse cry, she pushed against the solid muscle of his chest until he released her.

He frowned, a dazed look in his eyes. "Wynter?"

"I'm sorry. That shouldn't have happened." She tucked her hair behind her ear.

"As kisses went, it was pretty damn incredible," he responded, but he backed up to give her some space.

"I need to think about this," Wynter said, even though her body ached for more. "Before we start something."

"I understand, and I won't push. When you're ready, you'll have to make the first move. Good night." Riley pressed his palm to her cheek, and then he was striding down the hall and making Wynter wish she'd called him back to finish what they'd started.

But she was right to stop. She needed to be sure she could take having a full-blown affair with Riley. Because, although he made her feel wanted, it was only sex to him. She couldn't make the mistake of thinking the attraction between them was anything more than physical. The moment she did, she would be opening herself up to heartbreak.

Eleven

Riley didn't know how he'd walked away from Wynter last night. He only knew he'd had to. He was trying to be a decent guy, but it wasn't easy. The way she responded to him told him she wasn't unaffected by him, but he understood her reluctance. He didn't believe in love and marriage and the whole bit. He'd discovered how much love cost. Had lived in the shadow and pain of that love. It was why he enjoyed the company of women *casually*.

Although she hadn't said it, Riley wondered if Wynter wanted marriage and babies. Maybe not right this second, but at some point. And he would never be able to give her that. He was too jaded. But he could give her this amazing week. They would enjoy each other's company, and when it was over, they would move on with their lives.

Those were his thoughts as he walked down to the ski resort. For the day's activities, he wore a puffer jacket, a turtleneck and ski pants, and underneath were wicking long johns and a long-sleeved top to ensure he was warm yet comfortable. He was stopping for a coffee when he heard his name called.

He smiled when Wynter approached, wearing a similar ensemble of ski jacket and pants and a crew top. "Good morning," she said brightly.

"Good morning. How did you sleep?" he replied. Was her sleep as miserable as his? She'd occupied his thoughts for much of the night. Thinking about having Wynter in his bed had made him hard, and he'd finally gotten up in the middle of the night and taken a cold shower.

"I slept wonderfully."

Liar.

"Great, then you'll be ready for a day of snowmobiling. I hope you don't mind, but I invited the client I'm wooing along."

She shook her head. "Of course not. And although I've never been snowmobiling, it's going to make a great article for my blog."

"Good. C'mon, let's get that coffee."

After they ordered their coffees, they made their way to the lobby, where Derek and Craig were already waiting for them. Derek was in appropriate ski clothing and ski boots, but Craig wasn't.

"Great day for a ride, Riley!" Derek stated.

"Indeed," Riley responded. "Derek Webster, I'd like you to meet Wynter Barrington."

"Nice to meet you," Wynter replied.

"Likewise," Derek said, nodding.

"Craig, are you not coming with us?" Riley asked.

"Oh, no. While you guys zip through the forest, I'm having a spa day. You guys enjoy." Craig waved them off and walked away.

Derek scoffed. "Why did I give him the day off? I should have made him join us."

"And what fun would that be, having a Debbie Downer

along?" Wynter asked. "That just means there will be more fun for the three of us."

Derek glanced at Riley. "I like her. She's a keeper."

"I think so." Riley looked at Wynter, and he loved that she still blushed. "C'mon, follow me."

Riley had a private limo waiting outside that would take them to a ranch that specialized in snowmobiling. "Nice touch, Riley," Derek said when they climbed into the warm vehicle. "What else do you have in store for us?"

"I would love to know the answer to that, too," Wynter said.

"We're going to tour Maroon Creek Valley and have lunch at a private cabin," Riley replied.

"You thought of everything," Wynter said, winking. "I'm impressed."

Riley wasn't just wooing Derek; he was using all the tricks up his sleeve in the hopes that, by the end of the day, Wynter would be willing to move from a one-night stand to a full-blown affair.

Wynter was glad Derek was in the limo. It made it easier to keep her distance from Riley. After that kiss outside her hotel room door, Wynter's resolve was crumbling. She had wanted him to come inside, but was glad her sanity returned before she dived headfirst into a physical relationship with Riley.

Shay hadn't been wrong when she said Riley had the power to hurt her, but the other side of the coin was that Wynter enjoyed being with him, laughing with him, talking with him. And, yes, making love with him. Riley was an amazing lover, and Wynter wanted to experience the pleasure she'd found in his arms again. But was it worth the risk?

It didn't help that Riley was looking across the limo at her as if she were a double scoop of double-fudge ice cream.

His heated gaze made Wynter squirm in her seat, until she eventually looked out the window to avoid his stare.

When they made it to the ranch, Wynter was the first out of the limo and eager for their lesson, but first they had to sign a release waiver and listen to the safety briefing. Once the lesson was over and they were outfitted with helmets, it was time to ride.

"Are you sure you can drive one of these on your own?" Riley inquired, glancing down at her.

"Of course," Wynter snapped. "And in case you didn't notice, the minimum age is eighteen."

"Don't give the lady a hard time, Davis," Derek said. "She's got this." He gave Wynter a fist bump.

"Thank you," Wynter responded.

They followed their tour guide, Matt, down to the snowmobiles. Derek would follow the instructor, then Wynter and Riley would bring up the rear.

"Are you guys ready?" Riley asked once they'd all hopped on their snowmobiles.

Wynter gave a thumbs-up. "Let's rumble!"

Soon, their snowmobiles were barreling through exquisite mountain scenery. Wynter couldn't believe this was her life. It was so far removed from how she lived in San Antonio and what her parents wanted for her. She felt completely free.

The two-hour tour was brisk and concluded with them stopping at a beautiful rustic cabin, tucked in the mountains, for a late lunch. As soon as they arrived, the chef on-site poured hot cocoa to warm them up. Derek was busy chatting up the tour guide, which left Wynter and Riley alone with their mugs to look at the view from the large bay windows.

"It's beautiful here," Wynter said, sipping the hot drink. The cabin had a spectacular view of the Maroon Bells.

She felt Riley behind her as he came closer. "Yes, it is,

but I honestly only have eyes for you," he whispered in her ear.

"Riley," she said, glancing behind her. "Don't."

"Don't what?"

"Put on the charm," Wynter muttered. "You already sampled the goods."

He laughed heartily behind her. "True, but I would like a repeat performance." He circled his arm around her waist and brought her closer into his body. It felt good having him hold her, and it made Wynter want to set aside her misgivings. They were supposed to have only had one night. If they changed course and became lovers again, it was a risk—mostly to her heart.

She spun around until they were facing each other. Wynter looked up into Riley's scorching gaze and knew she already had her answer.

Yes, yes, yes.

She would throw caution to the wind for a chance to be in his arms again.

"Here's the lovebirds." Derek approached, and Wynter stepped backward. "Oh, don't separate now because of me. I appreciate you letting me join you. Today was a lot of fun. I think my son would love something like this."

"I hope you don't mind me saying so, but that's why you should hire Riley. He thinks outside the box," Wynter said, putting down her empty mug.

"Let's talk over lunch," Riley interjected. "The food is ready."

The chef was motioning them over to a circular wooden table, where he'd laid out a delicious three-course meal. The appetizer was charred squash with Asian pear soup, and the main attraction was a braised veal loin with cipollini onions and fingerling potatoes, accompanied by crispy brussels sprouts. They all dug in, but soon Derek got a call and stepped away from the table.

"Can I give you some advice on how to convince Derek to hire you?" Wynter asked.

"I'm all ears."

"Over the appetizer, you were reiterating your stats and why Jamison, Charles and Davis is one of the best firms in the country, but you haven't made this personal to you."

"What do you mean?"

"I think if you share your past and tell Derek how your parents' divorce affected you, it might give him some perspective on why this case is important to you."

"I don't talk about my personal life with clients."

"I get that," Wynter replied, "and you don't have to share everything, but help him understand…" Her voice trailed off when Derek returned.

"Help me understand what?" Derek inquired.

"Why he's the right man for the job," Wynter stated. She inclined her head toward Riley. His hesitant look told her he wasn't sure of her plan, but Wynter knew it was the right thing to do. Every attorney was telling Derek what they thought he wanted to hear, but showing a touch of vulnerability and humility could go a long way to helping him see why Riley was different.

Riley leaned back in his chair and regarded Wynter. Being with her today had been fun. He liked her carefree spirit and willingness to try new things. She was kind and honest and had hit it off with Derek instantly. When they stopped for photos earlier, he'd seen the other man's spark of interest in Wynter. Riley supposed that was why he'd made his presence known once they got to the cabin, so Derek would know she was taken.

Derek was being good-natured about it, but he also hadn't given Riley a decision yet. Maybe Wynter was right—if he opened up about himself, Derek might find him more relatable. Not that he was in a rush to seal the deal, because the longer he was here, the more time he got to spend with Wynter.

"I've talked about my stats," Riley began, "told you why I'm one of the best divorce attorneys out there, but what I haven't told you is that I've been in your son's shoes."

"Pardon?" Hearing his son mentioned made Derek sit up straight.

"My sister and I were pawns in my parents' divorce," Riley stated. "I know firsthand what it's like to be shuttled back and forth between parents. To have them pit us against the other. To feel powerless because you didn't get a say in who you want to be with. If you hire me, Derek, I will fight for your son and his best interests. I'll ensure custody is given to the caring and stable parent who loves him. And that's you."

"You're very impassioned, Riley," Derek replied. "I appreciate you sharing your story with me. Unfortunately, I have to head back to my chalet. I have an important business meeting to attend."

"Completely understand," Riley said.

Derek turned to Wynter. "You, my dear, are enchanting." He kissed Wynter's hand.

Suddenly, the roar of a helicopter could be heard overhead.

"That's my ride!" Derek smirked. "I called my pilot. Enjoy dessert. And you—" he pointed at Riley "—I'll be talking to soon."

Several moments later, he was rushing out the door.

"Oh, my God! Do all billionaires have a helicopter at the ready?" Wynter inquired.

"Apparently, yes," Riley replied as they watched the helicopter take off. "And where did the chef and the tour guide head off to?" he asked and walked into the kitchen. He found a note on the counter.

The cabin has been rented for you both to share for the remainder of the day, courtesy of Mr. Webster. The chef has left the dessert on the counter, and there's meals in the fridge. I will be back for you in the morning.
Matt

"What does it say?" Wynter asked, leaning over Riley's arm.

Riley couldn't help but chuckle. That sly devil Webster had just ensured he would have uninterrupted time with Wynter. If they were alone, there was no way she could deny the attraction between them.

"Did Derek really strand us here without our guide?" Wynter asked, folding her arms across her chest.

Riley turned around and leaned against the counter. "It appears that way."

Her eyes narrowed. "Did you arrange all this? Was this your way of convincing me to reignite our affair?"

Riley's brows furrowed. "Wynter, I don't have to resort to these sorts of games to get a woman in my bed."

"Is that so?"

"Yes, because they usually don't need convincing."

Wynter scoffed. "Maybe I do."

Riley shook his head. "You know what you want. Don't be scared. Take what you want."

He hoped she would. Their eyes locked from across the room. He dared her to forget logic and go with her instincts. He wanted to splay his hands all over her body and remind her how good it was between them, but she had to want it, too. The lust Riley felt for Wynter overpowered him. It had since the moment he laid eyes on her at the River Walk.

Would she give them what they both wanted?

Wynter huffed out a breath.

No man had ever gotten under her skin like Riley. Everything within Wynter urged her to let go, because the need she saw in Riley's eyes mirrored the primal pull she felt inside her own body. But he didn't make a move to meet her halfway. He'd told her last night that *she* would have to come to him.

No time for second thoughts. Wynter stepped toward him and planted her palm on his chest. She felt the solid muscle underneath, and his drumming heart.

Riley's dark eyes were hooded as they looked down on her, hard. "Are you sure? Because if you're not, I'll call someone to come get us."

Her response was to lean her body into his and circle her arms around his neck. Then she brushed her lips gently over his as if she were relearning the taste and texture of his mouth. Her body craved this man, and Wynter felt she might fly apart just from kissing. He tasted so damn good, and his lips fit hers perfectly.

Wynter tossed out logic and went with the moment.

With need.

With longing.

They stripped off each other's clothes along the way to what she presumed was the bedroom. Once there, their mouths and hands feverishly explored each other's bodies until she moaned for him. When he joined them as one, she felt full, complete.

For a moment, they both stopped breathing, and Wynter wanted to stay like this forever, but the need was inevitable. Their bodies rocked together as one, and Wynter reveled in the ecstasy she could only find with Riley. A tidal wave crashed over them both. Riley collapsed on top of her, and Wynter held him to her as if she never wanted to let him go.

Twelve

Riley brushed Wynter's damp curls away from her face as she lay snuggled against his chest. The incredible sexual intimacy they'd shared blew his mind. He'd never felt it with another woman. In his casual relationships with others, it had been about physical gratification, but with Wynter it felt different. He didn't recognize the emotion; he knew it was special. He loved Wynter's uninhibited responses and that she freely gave of herself during lovemaking.

He was thoroughly bewitched.

He would, however, have to make it clear that the affair would last only while they were here in Aspen. Once they returned to their separate lives, they would resume their friendship. Riley hoped that was possible. The women in his life usually understood the rules of engagement when it came to dating him, but Wynter was different. They had grown up together. He *knew* her, and not just in the biblical sense. He would have to tread carefully, because he didn't want her to get confused or hurt. He cared about her. He wanted her to be okay afterward.

He must have voiced his concern aloud, because her eyes fluttered open and she looked him square in the eye. "Do I not seem okay?"

"I want to be sure you have no regrets," Riley replied. "This was rather...*spontaneous*. And I want you to know that I in no way planned for this to happen, but I'm not sorry it did, either."

"Neither am I." Wynter caressed his chest with her warm palm. When she touched him, his heart rate sped up, and his erection swelled to life.

"Then what do you say to a round two?"

Rather than answer, she curled an arm around his neck and brought his mouth down to hers. Riley sank into her arms and into the unfettered passion between them.

Much later, after having made love for much of the evening, they surfaced for food. It was dark outside, and Riley found a few candles to make the setting feel romantic and special. Wynter wore Riley's long-sleeved shirt, while he'd slipped on his boxer briefs. They found the makings of dinner in the fridge: Wagyu burgers, a container labeled Truffle Mac 'n' Cheese, and a platter of petit fours.

Riley fired up the stovetop grill and cooked the beef to perfection while Wynter heated up the pasta and sourced plates and cutlery. Once they had plates in hand, Riley opened up a bottle of pinot noir from the wine cellar they'd found next to the walk-in pantry and poured them each a glass. The chef hadn't lied; they definitely wouldn't go hungry.

"This mac 'n' cheese is to die for." Wynter closed her eyes and sighed after she'd indulged in a couple of bites. When she opened them, she found Riley's scorching gaze on her. "What?"

"If you keep making those little moans," Riley said, picking up his burger, "I'll have you back in the bedroom and flat on your back before you can finish your meal. I'm already having a hard enough time concentrating with you wearing next to nothing."

Wynter blushed and glanced down at the shirt, which stopped above her knee. She wasn't wearing anything underneath. They'd been so eager for one another when they'd made love, their clothes had gone flying, so she couldn't find her panties. It wasn't as if Riley was clothed, either. His chest was bare, and all Wynter wanted to do was press her mouth to his pecs and run her tongue down the hard planes of his stomach. She wanted to taste his skin. And those thighs? The man must hit the gym pretty hard, because they were like granite.

She had to remind herself that, although she was living in the moment, life was short and her time with Riley was fleeting. It wouldn't be long before they were back to their normal lives and this would all be a memory.

"You're frowning," Riley stated.

Wynter blinked. "Am I?"

"Yes. And I think I know why, which is why I propose we spend the rest of the week together," Riley responded. "I don't know how long you're staying in Aspen, but I have to be here until the end of the week. I was hoping…" His eyes grew dark with desire.

Wynter picked up where he left off. "We continue sleeping together while you're here?" she offered. She didn't know if she should be excited or offended. Excited, because the sex between them was off the charts and she couldn't wait to wash, rinse and repeat. Or offended that he thought she was so *easy*.

He looked a bit stunned at her directness, but answered, "Yes. Do you have a problem with that? You could even move into my suite."

She didn't. After Aspen, she had a month before the girls' trip to Barbados. She would go home to San Antonio and see if she could finally make peace with her family.

"If you have other plans…" Riley started, but Wynter shook her head.

"It's not that." Wynter sighed. "It's just difficult being estranged from my family." Yet somehow, looking across the candlelit table at Riley, a man she'd known and crushed on since she was a teenager, Wynter felt she could share her truth. "I've never felt like I belonged."

"I can't understand what it's like to feel that way in your own family, but when I went to Princeton, most of the kids there were legacy. Their parents and their grandparents attended, and here I was, this Black kid from San Antonio on scholarship. I didn't feel like I was a good enough, like I belonged."

"What did you do?"

"I pushed myself to be the best. When I began to rise to the top of my class, my confidence grew. Suddenly, everyone wanted to talk to me and be my friend, especially the ladies."

"Is that when you decided to only pursue casual relationships?"

Riley shook his head. "I've always known I'd never marry. I saw the destruction it caused when you loved someone and they left you. I never wanted to feel that way."

"So you don't stay," Wynter surmised. "You leave them first."

Riley chuckled wryly. "I think this conversation has gotten way too deep."

Wynter didn't think their talk had gone deep enough. Riley was the first man she'd felt comfortable sharing the bad stuff in her life with, but he was hesitant to reveal more about himself.

"You haven't told me about any of your relationships," Riley said, changing the subject.

Wynter shrugged. "I've dated."

"Has there ever been anyone special?" Riley inquired. "A long-term, committed relationship?"

No, because they weren't you, Wynter thought. She supposed she had built him up in her mind as her ideal man so much that no other man ever came close. She shook her head. "Not really."

"Then we're alike," Riley responded. "We keep people at a distance."

"You may prefer an arm's-length relationship, but not me," Wynter replied.

"No? Then why haven't you found the one? Are you too picky? Are you one of those women with a laundry list that has to be checked off before you'll deign to get serious?"

"Not at all. I'm just selective. *When* I settle down with that someone special, it'll be because they're the one person I can't live without."

"You're living in a fantasy if you think one person can ever measure up or be all that you need. It's foolish to love. I've seen how it can hurt, especially when someone lies or leaves."

"It doesn't always have to end up like that. If you both grow together and want the same things out of life, then no one gets hurt. Love is the reward."

"You're an optimist, Wynter. I'm a divorce attorney, remember. I've seen just how bad it can get."

"You're saying that because you're hurt," she murmured under her breath. Wynter wasn't sure if Riley heard her, but if he did, he chose to ignore it.

Instead, he said, "You never answered my question."

"You mean about whether I'd like continue our affair while in Aspen?"

"I do believe that's the question on the table."

"Well, Counselor," Wynter said, turning toward him at the bar, "I think I need some convincing."

The intense look Riley gave Wynter sent shivers through her, and she could scarcely breathe. His gaze raked over her in his shirt until her nipples tightened into hard points. Riley noticed, because his eyes became laser focused on her breasts. Her breathing became rapid, and her breasts began to rise and fall as she thought about what Riley could do to them.

When he rose to his feet, anticipation prickled her skin and lust slammed into her. She never suspected Riley would throw her over his shoulder and stride to the bedroom, where he promptly tossed her on the bed before joining her.

Soon, they were creating their own rhythm, until sensations began to build inside her and all Wynter could see was this one pleasurable moment. And when it arrived, breaking free from its constraints, she let out a keening cry, while Riley roared out his climax.

White-hot pleasure licked through her veins, and Wynter felt completely satiated, because she was with Riley—the man she was falling in love with.

As promised, the next morning, Matt, their tour guide, arrived to take them back to the ranch by snowmobile.

Riley and Wynter were ready, having already donned their ski outfits after a sublime morning session in the shower that started with Riley washing every inch of Wynter's body and ended with her plastered against the tile wall as he plunged deep inside her body. Riley was thankful he'd kept a pack of condoms in his wallet. If he and Wynter were going to spend the rest of the week together, he would need an entire box.

No one made him feel the way Wynter did.

Making love with her, he discovered things about his body and hers. He was totally attuned to her, and his response, as a result, was heightened. This week was going to be one helluva week to remember, especially because he'd have Wynter in his bed every night.

They arrived back at the resort and parted ways, vowing to get together later that evening once Wynter had a chance to pack. She indicated she would be trying one of the resort's yoga classes and the spa, so she could write about the experience while Riley caught up on work. Although this was technically a vacation, Riley didn't know how to press the off switch. He was getting ready for opening arguments on one of his cases that couldn't be settled while working on Derek's contract. He was certain the tech giant was going to hire him. He was the best, after all.

Once he was back in his suite, Riley immediately turned on his phone and found he had missed several messages. He'd turned off his phone while he was at the cabin and forgotten to turn it back on. There were a couple from his assistant, Ronda, about an urgent matter on one of his cases, and then there was Shay. He thought about calling his sister back and then thought better of it. What if Wynter told Shay she was staying at the same resort? His sister could have a million questions, and he wasn't in the mood to answer them.

He went for work instead, contacting his assistant and working straight through lunch until his stomach growled and demanded satisfaction. Grabbing a quick sandwich gave him time for his mind to drift to the silkiness of Wynter's skin and the waviness of her hair. Or her amazing scent, which drove him wild.

Since they'd agreed to dinner, Riley had his assistant arrange for them to eat at the chef's table. Chef Francois Du Bois had a six-course tasting menu that was divine. Afterward, Riley planned on taking Wynter to bed and ravishing her until they were spent. He didn't understand the hold Wynter had on him and why he couldn't get enough of her, but by the end of the week, the chemistry would burn itself out. It always did.

Wynter was impressed by the resort. After yoga, the staff had arranged for her to get a facial, manicure and pedicure at the spa, and when she mentioned she was having dinner later, Karen, the resort manager, treated her to getting her hair and makeup done at the salon. By the time she left, Wynter felt hydrated, plucked and made into the best version of herself. She would need it for her evening tonight.

Yesterday's rendezvous with Riley had certainly not been something she had planned. Wynter had assumed their one night a couple of months ago was all she would ever have to remember Riley by, but instead, he'd shown up at the resort where she was working and somehow still found her desirable. It seemed too good to be true.

But it was real, because she had the soreness between her thighs to prove it. They were very active in the bedroom. Riley was an exciting and inventive lover, the best she'd ever had. Deep down, though, Wynter knew her feelings for him ran deeper than lust alone. She genuinely liked him, possibly loved him. Had she ever stopped?

They could talk for hours, as they had last night by candlelight. The topic didn't matter, because Riley was knowledgeable on politics, art, music and films. It made Wynter want to delve deeper to the man underneath.

Riley, however, wanted to keep her at arm's length and restrict their relationship to this week in Aspen. In her head, Wynter understood. He and Shay had endured a lot during their childhood, but he was throwing the baby out with the bathwater. He wasn't allowing himself to feel anything because he was afraid of the effect it might have on him—that he might turn into his mother and never recover if he lost that love.

Instead, he was willing to go through life never experiencing the emotion. Wynter wanted him to see that sometimes it was worth taking the risk. Being on her own the past couple of months felt like teetering on the edge of the abyss with no idea of what lay below, but she'd done it. She'd had to. Her parents had given her no choice. Why didn't they believe in her? Why were they so willing to think the worst? Wynter couldn't understand it.

On an impulse, after returning to her room, Wynter dialed her mother's number. It rang several times before her mother's curt voice came on the line. "Wynter, I'm surprised to hear from you. I thought all our conversations had to be handled through our lawyers."

"They don't have to be," Wynter responded.

"I'm glad to hear that," her mother said. "When we hadn't heard from you, I was beginning to think you wanted all of my sister's wealth for yourself."

"That's not true." Wynter was hurt by her mother even thinking that, making her feel the need to lash out. "I didn't ask for any of this. You're the one contesting the will and making me the villain in this scenario."

Her mother sighed wearily. "What was I supposed to think, Wynter? You refused to even consider a settlement."

"Because that isn't what Aunt Helaine wanted," Wynter replied hotly. "I'm honoring her wishes. Why can't you see that? Or are you blinded by the money? Heaven forbid, Wynter, the screwup in the family, should have what's rightfully hers by law."

"It's not fair!" her mother yelled into the phone.

Wynter was taken aback. Melinda Barrington rarely raised her voice, but Wynter also wasn't about to be her whipping girl. All her life, she'd wanted to be seen by her parents, but she had always fallen short. This time, she wasn't backing down. "I'm sorry you feel that way, Mother. I'm sorry to have bothered you."

"Wynter, wait!" her mother whispered. "I'm sorry I yelled, okay? I'm just out of sorts about all of this."

"You think I'm any better? I hate this." Although they'd never been close, at least they'd always been civil and sociable.

"Come home, Wynter," her mother said. "You haven't been home in months."

"I haven't been home because I've been working on my business. *Wynter's Corner* is finally making a profit."

"Oh, my God, Wynter, I had no idea. I'm very proud of you."

"You are?" That was a surprise. Wynter wasn't used to receiving any praise from her parents. Usually they were telling her what she did wrong or what she needed to improve on.

"Yes, I am. Please come home so we can talk in person," her mother said.

"I'll give it some thought."

"All right. Take care of yourself, Wynter." And then the line went dead. There were never any *I love you*s with her parents. They didn't do warm and fuzzy. That was for other people.

Wynter expected it. When she'd fallen down and bruised her knee or someone at private school pushed her down and ripped her uniform, there hadn't been anyone to wipe away the tears and kiss the boo-boos. Eventually, Wynter had hardened her heart and acted like she didn't need love and affection, but there was another part of her that had always yearned to be loved.

Embarking on a casual affair with Riley ensured she would never get that love from him, but Wynter couldn't walk away. He did it for her in every way imaginable. Could she navigate the murky waters of this affair and come out unscathed? Or was she making the biggest mistake of her life, getting involved with a man who would never give her the love she so desperately craved?

Thirteen

"This is way too much," Wynter said several days later when Riley ordered nearly everything on the room service menu, from ahi tuna, calamari and goat cheese croquettes to a wild mushroom flatbread, so they could have a picnic on the floor of the suite.

Since she'd moved into his suite, they'd established an easy rhythm. While Riley attended to his cases, she worked on her assignment for the resort. During their free time, they'd gone skiing, snow tubing and dogsledding, which was exhilarating. Tonight, however, they weren't in the mood to dress up in bulky gear. Instead, she was in her flannel pajamas, while Riley wore a T-shirt and sweats.

She loved how comfortable they were, hanging out together and just talking. Tonight, their conversation had segued into their college experiences.

"Leaving home was a breath of fresh air," Riley said. "It was the first time I was free to have fun without fear of getting a call about my mother. When I was in high school,

I would be called away from lacrosse practice or a party because my mom was freaking out."

"I'm so sorry. I know how hard that was," Wynter said. She'd seen how hard it was on Shay.

"When I arrived at Princeton, all I did was keep my head in the books, but then my roommate reminded me that I was young. There would be plenty of time to figure out who I was going to be, and I should be a little bit naughty. I frequented the frat parties on campus, and soon I was a hit with the ladies."

"Is that when you became a ladies' man?"

"Not initially. I didn't have as much experience going into college, but I more than made up for lost time," Riley said, grinning.

"I just bet you did. Tell me your craziest college story," Wynter said. "I know you have to have one."

Riley's eyes were alight with mischief. "If I tell mine, you'll tell yours?"

Wynter grinned and nodded.

"One night, we were all sitting around the dorm with not much else to do and started playing a drinking game. I got dared to streak across the dorm."

"Did you do it?"

Riley laughed. "I did and narrowly escaped the RA. Needless to say, I never did that again. How about you? What's your story?"

"Well, I'm not proud of it," Wynter began, "but I was jealous of a friend of mine going out with a guy she knew I wanted to date. When they arrived at a friend's birthday party, words were exchanged, and, well, I sort of threw the birthday cake in her face."

"Oh, my God!" Riley roared with laughter. "No, you didn't."

Wynter nodded. "Oh, yes, I did. It was hilarious in the moment, but then she proceeded to chase me across the campus in the dead of winter. When she caught up to me, she pushed me into the snow, and an epic snowball fight ensued."

Riley held his stomach as he laughed. "Your story is way funnier."

"Needless to say, neither one of us ended up with the guy. He thought we were too immature."

"Thanks for sharing."

"Oh, I made plenty of boneheaded decisions in my youth, more so to get my parents' attention than anything else."

"Have you always had an acrimonious relationship with them?" Riley inquired, nibbling on a piece of the flatbread.

Wynter shook her head. "Quite the opposite. They've never seemed to care what I did so long as I wasn't embarrassing them. Now, the shoe is on the other foot, because they're choosing to air our dirty laundry in public. I don't understand why. It's not like my mother isn't wealthy in her own right. Why is she so insistent on fighting for Aunt Helaine's estate? The only thing I can think of is she doesn't want *me* to have it."

"You really believe that?"

"There's no way else to think, Riley," Wynter responded. "If this were Corey, she wouldn't be putting up a fuss. I know every parent has a favorite, and I'm clearly not it."

"Well, you're my favorite person right now," Riley said and, to her surprise and utter delight, pulled her into his arms. But instead of giving her an earth-shattering kiss like he always did, he held her tight like he had that first night on the River Walk. It was exactly what she needed.

She'd been right in her decision to live in the moment and take advantage of being with Riley, because it might never come again. After the compliment, he had added "right now," meaning their time would soon come to an end. Wynter refused to be one of those clingy women who hung on. When the time came, she would be the first to walk away.

"Riley, thank you for coming back up the mountain," Derek stated when Riley arrived at his home the next morning. Derek brought him to the dining room table on the upper floor of his villa. "Please have a seat."

Riley sat down and waited. He had done everything in his power to win Derek's business, including talk about his past, but the billionaire had been a hard nut to crack.

"Of course." Riley took off his overcoat and slung it over the back of his chair. He was done pursuing Derek. It had been nearly a week, and Riley had to get back to San Antonio. If Derek didn't know Riley was the best man for the job by now, Riley would have to accept it.

"I was hoping we could finally settle some business," Derek said. "I appreciate your patience in allowing me to conclude all my interviews with the other attorneys."

"Have you made a decision?"

"Yes," Derek responded. His blue eyes were trained on Riley. "I'd like you to represent me."

Riley clapped his hands. "Excellent news. Derek, you won't be disappointed. I've already taken the liberty of drafting the contract." He pulled the document from his briefcase and slid it across the table.

"I'll have my attorneys look this over. Honestly, I knew the day you told me about your parents' divorce that you were the right man, but the businessman in me had to be sure and check all the boxes," Derek responded. "Seeing you this week with the lovely Wynter made it clear that you have a good head on your shoulders."

"I do," Riley said. "And I've already prepared a draft of a temporary order to get you visitation rights, since your wife has taken custody of your son."

"You're not wasting any time," Derek said.

"No, I'm not. I want to win, but I also want to see you with your son," Riley replied. Hearing Wynter's story last night was tough. She had wanted her parents' affection so desperately. Even now, at twenty-seven, she still wanted it. He would do everything in his power to prevent Derek's son from experiencing that sort of heartbreak.

Wynter was falling hard for Riley. Since she had discovered him in the café, they'd spent every day together, in and out of bed. And now, on their last day, Riley had told Wynter he had something special planned after he met with Derek. There were times throughout the week she had found Riley watching her with such an intensity, her blood had sizzled. Wynter hoped the affair they were having might morph into something more, but he'd been mum so far.

Yesterday, when they'd walked to the shops in town hand in hand, Riley had picked up gifts for his mother and Shay, which was to be expected. However, he'd surprised Wynter when he chose a beautiful necklace in the shape of a butterfly for *her*. It was a simple piece, and Wynter didn't wear much jewelry because she traveled, but when he'd seen her admiring it, he'd insisted on purchasing it. Told her it matched her perfectly, just like she matched him.

Wynter had felt dazzled. She'd never received gifts like that from other men. Maybe because none of them had been the right one, the one for her, like Riley was. She wanted to believe they could *be* more, *have* more someday, but Riley was so adamant he didn't believe in love or marriage. With each passing day, her hopes had begun to crumble. Was she a fool for staying with him?

All these musings kept replaying through her brain, so when Egypt called, Wynter spilled her guts. She'd kept their affair to herself the entire time because it had been their secret, but now she *had* to confide in someone or she'd burst. Thankfully, Riley was out of the suite for a meeting with Derek, so she had it all to herself.

"Hey, girlfriend," Egypt said cheerfully on the other end of the line. "What's it like hanging out with the rich and famous in Aspen?"

"Wonderful, crazy and romantic."

"I don't understand. I get the wonderful and crazy part if the hotel is pampering you and giving you anything and everything to ensure you write a great puff piece, but where does the romance come in?"

"It's Riley," Wynter blurted out. "We've been having a clandestine affair the entire time I've been here, and now I think I might be in love with him, but he doesn't want love and marriage and I don't know what to do."

"Whoa! Wait a minute," Egypt said, interrupting her tirade. "You and Shay's brother have been getting busy? Say it ain't so."

"It's so. Very so," Wynter replied. "Riley is an amazing lover. Hell, he's the best I've ever had, and I knew I shouldn't have gotten involved with him. I should have let San Antonio be a onetime thing, but then we ran into each other again and—"

"Wait just a minute," Egypt interjected. "Are you telling me you and Riley slept together in San Antonio? Like, a few months ago, after your aunt's funeral, and I'm just now hearing about this?"

"Oh, Lord!" Wynter covered her eyes and hung her head low as if Egypt could see her. "Don't be mad."

"Mad? Girl, I'm not mad if you want to get your swerve on, but at least spill the tea to your best friend!"

Wynter chuckled. "I'm sorry. It was supposed to be a onetime thing, but then I saw him here in Aspen. And, well…"

"The panties dropped."

"Honey, yes!" Wynter laughed, which released some of her tension. "I can't resist the man. When I'm with him, I feel complete, like I've found my person."

"But he doesn't feel the same way?"

"That's the thing, Egypt. I think he does. I don't think he could make love to me the way he does otherwise."

"Sometimes sex is just sex to men, sweetheart," Egypt responded. "They don't get emotionally attached like we do."

Wynter sighed. "That's what I'm afraid of. What if I'm all in and he's got one foot out the door?"

"I'm worried. I don't want you to get hurt."

"It's a little late for that. I guess that's why Shay warned me away from him," Wynter replied. "But I didn't listen."

"She doesn't know?"

"No."

"I wouldn't tell her," Egypt said. "No sense in causing a rift between siblings if you guys don't last beyond this week. If the connection turns into a relationship, then you'll have to let Shay know."

"Egypt…what do I do next?"

"Wynter, you know I have always kept it real with you. I don't know how to do anything else. Talk to Riley. Tell him how you really feel."

"And if he doesn't feel the same?"

"Then you'll know one way or the other, but at least you won't be guessing and tying yourself in knots."

Wynter knew Egypt was right, but it didn't make it any easier to listen to her advice. "Thank you, girlfriend." She stared down at the phone. Was she prepared for the end of their love affair?

No.

But she needed to know how Riley felt. Or was she deluding herself into thinking he could feel anything more for her other than affection, caring and lust? Wynter sighed.

She would never know unless she went out on a limb and revealed her true feelings, but she was afraid of his response.

She was used to her family's indifference, used to being invisible, but with Riley she felt seen, heard and *wanted*. But if he verbalized that he didn't feel the same way, it would be a crushing blow to her self-esteem, and it might take Wynter years to recover. She would weigh her options, and only if the situation presented itself would she tell Riley she loved him.

"Is everything all right?" Shay inquired later when Riley returned to the suite for his special day with Wynter. She was in the other room putting a bag together, so Riley had FaceTimed Shay to do a well-being check on their mother. That was when she told him Eliza was not only happy but thriving with her new male companion. They were at brunch and going to the movies later.

Riley could hardly believe the change in his mother. It was so profound, he struggled to understand how she could go from the despondent creature ravaged by heartbreak to the smiling and alluring woman he'd seen over the past months. It was as if the last two decades hadn't happened, and she was the mother he remembered from his youth. It was unsettling, but he'd felt hopeful about his mom's situation for the first time in years.

"Everything is fine," Riley said to Shay, who peered back at him from the screen. "Why you do you ask?"

"I dunno, there's something different about you." Shay tilted her head this way and that, as if she were trying to figure out a puzzle. "You seem lighter, less weighed down. If I'm honest, you seem relaxed."

"Do I normally not seem that relaxed?"

Shay shook her head. "Absolutely not. I'm afraid you always have a stiff upper lip, brother, as if you've perpetually tasted something sour."

Riley couldn't resist laughing at her comment. "Thanks a lot, Shay."

"Hey." She shrugged. "What can I say? I know your career can be stressful, dealing with the demise of marriages and families."

"It can be," Riley admitted, but he tried his best not to show it. Apparently, though, he wasn't doing a very good job of hiding it. This week, however, he did feel lighter, freer, as if anything was possible. And he knew why.

Wynter.

She had been a ray of sunshine in his life. They held engaging conversations, and when she wasn't around, he wanted to be with her. Yesterday, when an adorable necklace caught her eye in a store, he'd had to buy it just to see her face light up. Riley would have bought Wynter a more expensive trinket, as he usually did for his women when the end of their affair was near. This time, however, he'd bought the gift because he wanted to. Even though she'd been born into wealth, Wynter didn't care that the necklace wasn't expensive or extravagant, because she was a down-to-earth, kind woman.

"Riley!" Shay was calling his name.

"Yes?"

"Did you hear a word I've said?"

He blinked and racked his brain, but the past couple of minutes had been a blur. He'd been fantasizing about Wynter.

"I'm sorry, no," Riley replied. "I missed what you said."

"It's not like you to daydream." Shay's eyes narrowed on his iPad screen. "Now I'm definitely on alert. Are you seeing someone?"

"Why would you ask that?" Riley said, his voice rising.

"Well, are you?"

"Wherever would I find the time?" Riley responded. "I'm here in Aspen for vacation and partly for work, to catch that big client I told you about. I don't have time to date."

"If you say so."

"I do."

"Well, then you should be dating," Shay responded. "I don't want you to end up alone. Although I may have made a mistake with Kevin, I still believe in love and want to find the one."

"You're an optimist, Shay, you always have been. I'm just not wired that way." Although spending time with Wynter had given him pause. If there was ever a woman who might make him want to change his mind, it was Wynter, but Riley didn't believe in all the love mumbo jumbo. So he shook it off. "I'm glad Mom is doing well, and I'll call you when I'm back in town." He hung up before his sister could wax poetic about the joys of matrimony. His feelings on the subject hadn't changed, but he was beginning to see the merits of having a permanent lover.

Wynter was incredible, and they shared a connection. Riley had enjoyed himself more in the past week than he had in years. It didn't have to end here in Aspen. Rather, they could see each other whenever Wynter was in San Antonio. Once the will was validated and Wynter gained her inheritance, she would need to check in on the estate often. Perhaps she would consider extending their rendezvous indefinitely?

There was only one way to find out.

He was going to have to ask her.

Fourteen

"You've really outdone yourself," Wynter said, sinking down in the hot springs after a refreshing cold-plunge dip. He had brought her to this resort outside Aspen that had over twenty-five steamy geothermal pools. The therapeutic waters were known for their healing benefits due to the minerals found inside.

"I'm glad you like it," Riley responded. "We're both leaving tomorrow, and I wanted to do something special for an exceptional woman."

"It's very thoughtful," Wynter replied. Even though Riley tried to act cold and distant, he cared about those closest to him and did thoughtful things for them. It's one of the reasons she admired him, aside from the fact that he was gorgeous, smart and funny.

She and Riley had already tested out each pool, because each one had a different temperature and feel. Some were for socializing, while others were quiet and spacious. They opted for a quiet one so they could have privacy.

When they'd arrived, they'd changed in the locker rooms, and after they'd emerged, Riley had been naked from the waist up, with a smattering of black hair on his powerfully broad chest, which tapered into a path below to his swim shorts. Wynter had wanted to eat him up as if he were chocolate ganache.

Riley had caught her tongue wagging, and his eyes, which sometimes were darker and deeper than the night, had connected with hers. Even though she'd seen him naked tons of times, he still had an effect on her. He was gorgeous, with a masculine assurance all his own, and Wynter was absolutely head over heels for him—but he had no idea.

She resolved to keep her feelings tucked away until the right moment. It didn't happen that afternoon, when they enjoyed the pools, or when they had a relaxing aromatherapy couple's massage, or at dinner when they returned to the ski resort. Only later, in Riley's room, when she found champagne and strawberries waiting for them, had Wynter thought about having the talk Egypt had suggested.

Riley had set the stage for a romantic day, and Wynter loved it, but she was also on pins and needles. Should she tell him her feelings? Should she broach the subject of a relationship or commitment? She knew Riley was against it, but she also couldn't help feeling as if the past week might have changed his perspective.

"How would you feel about continuing to see each other after this trip?" Riley inquired after he poured the champagne and handed her a glass.

Wynter paused midsip. "I hadn't thought about it." She placed the glass on the nightstand and tried, unsuccessfully, to locate the zipper at the back of her strapless dress. She caught her reflection in the mirror and reminded herself to keep away the tears that were threatening to leak out of her eyelids. She didn't want to read too much into his words, but it was hard not to. This man made her weak, and she would have to be strong to tell him how she truly felt.

"Well, give it some thought," Riley said, coming behind her. He swept her hair aside and unfastened the clasp that kept the zipper from moving. Then he slid it down until the dress fell into a pool at her feet. "I don't want this to end." His voice was a gruff rumble as his hands skimmed over her waist and pulled her back against him. She felt him grow large behind her. "We could see each other whenever you're in town."

His other hand went to her breasts. She hadn't needed a bra for the dress, so they were left bare for Riley to knead and caress with his palm.

"So, we would be casual, like your other relationships?" Wynter asked. Desire weakened her, especially when Riley deftly teased her nipple between her fingers and thumb. Heat emanated from his body, and Wynter's breathing became rapid, as if she were running a marathon. When she looked in the mirror and their eyes met, Riley's were glazed with hunger.

Riley tensed behind her, but he didn't stop looking at her. "Don't make it sound like that. We've had a good thing this last week, haven't we?"

Wynter kept her eyes locked on Riley, but she didn't say a word.

"Then say yes."

She watched, transfixed, as he stripped his clothes off behind her and slid on a condom. Even though she was speeding headlong toward disaster, need was ignited inside her.

She uttered the only word she could. "Yes." Then he reached for her panties and pushed them down her legs. She leaned her backside against him and felt the swell of his erection. Reaching around, she grasped him, sliding her fingers up and down his hard length.

Riley's jaw clenched and he groaned, but that didn't stop him from sliding his hands forward, past her stomach, to her nest of dark curls. She sighed when he parted her folds and his fingers stroked that sensitive spot. "Ah-h-h…" she cried out.

Every part of Wynter felt aflame with hunger, because Riley knew exactly how to please her. Her wet inner muscles clenched around his fingers, but then he suddenly moved away.

She moaned. "I need you."

Riley understood and sat on the bed. "Come here," he ordered.

Wynter walked over to him and prepared to ride him, but Riley turned her back around to face the mirror. "Spread your legs."

Wynter wasn't used to him ordering her around in the bedroom, but she didn't mind. She wanted him too much. His large hands splayed around her hips so she could sit astride him with her back to him, her legs on either side of his thighs. She shivered, and her eyes fluttered closed.

"Open your eyes and look at us in the mirror."

Wynter glanced up and was shocked by the wanton woman staring back at her. She was spread wide-open and completely vulnerable. With dazed eyes, she watched Riley's fingers delve inside her slick core. The sensation was so incredible that Wynter rocked against his fingers.

Riley's eyes gleamed with fiery desire, and Wynter could feel molten heat licking along her flesh…her orgasm was coming lightning fast. He must have sensed her need, because he lifted her up so she could sink down onto the thick head of his erection. She shuddered, and he shifted so she could take all of him. When Riley grabbed her thighs and urged her up and down his shaft, blood began pounding through her veins and intense sensations hit Wynter at the friction.

"I'm so close…so damn close," she cried.

"Don't fight it," Riley whispered.

She watched in the mirror as he grazed her neck, pinched her nipples and then slipped a hand between their bodies to the swollen heart of her. The action sent Wynter over the edge into a cataclysmic orgasm that surpassed anything she had enjoyed with Riley so far. Starlight burst behind her eyes, and fireworks exploded inside her head.

"Oh, God. Oh, God!" She panted as Riley pushed hard and insistently into her one final time. She heard his agonized groan as his entire body tightened and he gave himself over to his release.

Wynter's head fell back against his shoulder, her entire body slick from their efforts. Riley bent his head and gave her a deep, searing kiss. Afterward, he eased her away and visited the bathroom, but Wynter's senses were swimming and she was too spent to speak. Instead, she slid underneath the covers in a heap of satiated completion.

Riley sat beside Wynter on the flight back to San Antonio. He'd convinced her to continue their affair past Aspen, and one would think he felt in control, but he didn't. He felt as if he'd lost all perspective.

Last night, the sex with Wynter had seemed even better than before, but it hadn't felt like just sex. He felt as if he'd been reborn after a long winter.

How was that possible?

This was supposed to have been an affair for a week, but he hadn't been able to end it, because the electric chemistry between them was unmatched by anyone else.

Each time Wynter surrendered to him, it was genuine, fresh and sweet, and Riley was becoming worried. Fear was creeping in. Fear that this woman could mean more to him than any woman ever had. His instinct for self-preservation was asserting its presence. There was going to be a price to pay for this affair with Wynter. He was addicted to her. Perhaps it was her big brown eyes that seemed to understand so much. Or her warmth and compassion for others.

He never allowed a woman in because the act of doing so was fraught with danger, but Wynter Barrington, damn her, was a puzzle he couldn't solve. He didn't understand her hold on him, when he never allowed women to cross the threshold of making him feel anything. But Wynter was getting perilously close to doing just that. He was starting to forget that this was supposed to be just sex. He'd forgotten that their affair would *end*.

He should let her go now before she got hurt, because she deserved so much more. However, as soon they arrived back in San Antonio, with a limo waiting to take them home, he'd smashed his mouth over hers, demanding more, and Wynter, God help him, gave it right back to him as if she, too, had been stripped down to her raw sexuality.

And so, with a wildness filling his mind and heart, he made love to her for hours.

Wynter returned to her aunt's mansion the next morning. When she stepped inside, she received a warm welcome from Hope, her husband and the rest of the staff. She knew she shouldn't have stayed away so long, but at the time, losing her aunt and facing a battle with her family over the estate had felt like too much. She'd also had to get *Wynter's Corner* into the black, which she'd done. She was super proud of what she'd accomplished in such a short span of time.

If only her love life were such an easy fix. When Riley had suggested they continue their affair in San Antonio, she'd immediately wanted to say no, but then he'd made her come apart so completely in his arms, she hadn't been able to. By avoiding Riley, she would only be hurting herself and going back to self-imposed celibacy. For what? The man she had fallen for wanted to be with her, and despite her qualms, she wasn't prepared to let him go. Maybe Riley was right, that love made you foolish, because Wynter certainly felt he could come to love her. He was halfway there. Or at least she thought so. The way they'd been together last night. So in sync. So in harmony.

It wasn't mindless sex. They'd made love. Afterward, he'd reached for her, hauling her closer to him and snuggling her into his heat. It was as if he'd needed her energy and her strength, and she'd given it. When he'd taken her again, later in the night, savagely driving into her, she hadn't flinched. Instead, she'd wrapped her legs tightly around him and accepted whatever conflict was raging inside him. And when need had morphed into a storm and overtaken them both, they'd looked straight into each other's eyes as if they were the other's safe harbor.

Last night had been a monumental one Wynter doubted she would ever forget.

Wynter did, however, need to speak with her mother and finally settle her aunt's will once and for all. Although she'd traveled the globe for a little over two months to build her business, she'd also needed to get away to heal. But it was time for this feud to come to an end. Rather than wait for an invitation to the Barrington residence, Wynter decided to make a surprise appearance later that week. She and Riley had agreed that both had some pressing matters to attend to and would get together soon. After unpacking her things in the guest room, Wynter took her aunt's car to the Barrington estate.

Agnes was there to greet her as always and led her into the drawing room, where her mother was having tea.

"Wynter." Her mother looked effortless in a sleeveless floral tunic and white pants. The weather in San Antonio was blazing hot, in the nineties, and Wynter had opted for a simple romper and sandals. "Oh, my God! I can't believe you're here."

"You suggested we talk," Wynter said, taking a seat on the sofa across from her mother, "and I agreed. It's time."

"Would you like some tea?" Her mother sat down across from her and gestured to the teakettle and cups sitting on the settee in front of her.

"I'm not here for tea and crumpets," Wynter said. "What do you want, Mother? What do you want to end this battle?"

"You're so blunt," her mother said. "What crowd are you keeping?"

"Don't sidestep. What will it take to end this so everyone gets the bequests Aunt Helaine wanted them to have?"

Her mother sighed. "You make it sound as if I'm money hungry."

If the shoe fits, Wynter thought, but she remained mum. She couldn't stoke the flames. Instead, she stared at her mother expectantly, waiting for a response.

"Well, the Smith family business was sold a number of years ago, so I think it's only fitting the profit should come to me."

"I know you've done an audit of the financials," Wynter said, "so if there's enough to pay all the bequests, I will split half the remainder with you, but I keep the house as gifted to me. Does that sound fair?"

Her mother cocked her head to one side and stared at Wynter. "Yes, it does. I can live with that. We can put all this unpleasantness behind us. I will contact my attorney and stop the challenge of the will immediately."

"Good." Wynter rose to her feet. They'd come to an agreement, and she could finally move on with her life. She didn't know why it had taken so long, but maybe she could see things more clearly now that she was finally out from under her parents' thumbs. Fighting was not the answer.

"Wynter, wait!" Her mother touched her arm. "Why are you in such a rush to leave? I've missed you."

Wynter snorted. "Well, that's a first."

Her mother's crestfallen expression caused Wynter to regret her harsh tone. "Listen, Mother, what do you want from me? I don't belong. For years, I have tried to fit my round peg in the square hole of this family and come out wanting. I'm tired of trying. I'm tired of trying to please you. It's not good for me. It has made me miserable for too many years, and I refuse to give you or anyone else that sort of power over me. It stops today."

"Wynter, I never knew you felt this way."

"C'mon, Mom. I've always done things your way, and you're always critical of everything I do. Growing up, I could never do anything right. All you ever did was praise Corey and his genius while I was the screwup."

"I'm sorry," her mother said. "I'm sorry I made you feel that way."

"It wasn't just you. It was Dad and Corey," Wynter responded. "I've never felt good enough. Or wanted, for that matter. I've felt invisible in this family."

"Why have you never spoken up before now?"

"I couldn't!" Wynter yelled. "Why do you think I left? I left to escape the negativity and to find my own voice, without my family in my ear. I needed to find out who I was, and I did. But you don't know her. I don't think you ever did."

"I would like to know her now. Do you think it's possible to start over?" her mother asked. "Or try and find a middle ground? I know I'm not the perfect parent. Look how I've behaved about this will—once I started on this path, it just gained steam and took on a life of its own. I don't need the money, Wynter. I never have. I guess it just stung not being acknowledged by my sister, and I was angry and jealous and bitter. But I had no right to take it out on you. And I'm sorry."

Tears slid down Wynter's cheeks at her mother's confession. It was the most honest they'd ever been with each other. "I'm not the same Wynter that I was a few months ago. I've changed. I'm stronger, and I won't accept your indifference and Corey's animosity. I just wanted to be loved. It's all I have ever wanted."

"I do love you, Wynter. I may suck at showing it, but I do. Please forgive me." And to Wynter's utter surprise, her mother held open her arms and she rushed into them. It was a shock to the system, and at first, Wynter thought she was dreaming, but when her mother laid her head down on hers, she knew it wasn't a dream.

They were finally on the road to reconciliation.

Fifteen

"Riley, I'm so glad you could come so quickly," Derek said when Riley arrived at the billionaire's home in an exclusive part of San Antonio later that day. As usual, the dark-haired man was dressed in jeans and graphic T-shirt and a pair of Nike Air Yeezy sneakers.

"Of course," Riley stated. "Your voice mail sounded urgent. What can I do to help? Has something happened with your ex-wife?"

"Yeah, it has," Derek said, lowering his voice. "If you don't mind, I'd like to talk to you in my study."

Riley followed him into a bright room decorated in muted blues and grays. The furniture was minimalistic and included a large desk and a laptop, along with a single lamp.

Derek glanced around him. "I'm renting this place temporarily while we sort out the divorce. If I bought another place, it would be considered community property."

"No worries. Your interior design skills are not why I'm here. I take it your wife has made a move?"

"Damn right, she has," Derek said. "She's all but moved her trainer into the house where she lives with my son—while spending my money! Max tells me they are up all hours of the day and night, partying, drinking and Lord knows what else. They've already run off half the staff, so sometimes Max has to scrounge up dinner for himself. This is ridiculous! We need to go to court now to get temporary custody."

"I couldn't agree with you more." Riley hated hearing about a child with an incompetent parent. Parents were supposed to love and care for their children, not leave them to fend for themselves. He remembered what it was like when Eliza couldn't get out of bed and he'd had to cook and clean for himself and Shay. He didn't want that for Max or any child. "We'll file for an emergency hearing immediately."

Derek released a huge sigh. "Thank you, Riley. I appreciate it."

"Of course. That's what I'm here for."

After getting more information from Derek, Riley headed straight back to the office, where he stayed for the remainder of the afternoon until the paperwork was ready. Then his assistant rushed off before the court closed to file the documents. When it was over, Riley leaned back in his chair. This case brought up a lot of memories. Bad memories of growing up. He'd thought he'd handled them, but maybe Wynter was right. He needed to let it out, talk about it.

He hated emotions. They were messy. After the childhood he'd had, he liked tidy, with everything in its proper place. This case was certainly not ordered. Nearly half of his cases settled before they made it out of court, but he suspected this case was going to get ugly.

He was excited that he would be able to let it all go and find comfort in Wynter's arms tonight. They'd spent the entire week in Aspen and their first night back together and both agreed to a bit of a breather. Riley wasn't ashamed to admit that the space helped him gain control again.

Just one week with Wynter had been a game changer. He missed seeing her smile, hearing her laughter, smelling that sweet, heady scent that was uniquely hers. However, he knew if they hadn't taken some time apart, the feelings he'd started to feel in Aspen but usually kept at bay might have taken over, and that scared him most of all. He would have to reinforce the gates and pray Wynter didn't breach them with her warm and caring nature—because he wasn't ready to let her go.

"I'm so happy you and your mother had a good talk," Riley said when he stopped by Helaine's estate later that evening. He'd gotten tied up at work but had finally made it over there. And when he had, he'd given her a hot, passionate kiss that caused her toes to curl. She hadn't realized how much she'd missed him this past week.

"Yeah, it was," Wynter said. "It was so surprising. And not just about the inheritance. I think both of us allowed pride to get in the way and we both refused to budge. Instead, we let months go by and allowed the resentment to fester."

"What made you decide to give up half the money?" Riley asked. "You were entitled to the whole sum."

"Money doesn't mean everything to me," Wynter said. "It never has. My parents, my brother—they were always trying to fill their world up with things. I care about people. I want the Six Gems and all of my aunt's staff to get what they deserve. So what if I get a little bit less? I have this beautiful home—" she spread her arms out "—I'm not poor."

"That's what I admire about you, Wynter. How warm and giving you are," Riley said, pulling her into his lap and softly brushing his lips across hers. "I don't think I've ever met a woman like you."

"That's because I'm an original," Wynter said with a smile.

"That you are," Riley said, cradling her face in his hands.

Wynter was reminded once again why her life was so much sweeter with Riley in it. Maybe he was coming around yet; maybe forever wasn't out of the question.

The next few weeks floated by, and Wynter began to enjoy life in San Antonio again. She loved staying at Aunt Helaine's estate. Hope made her life so easy. She didn't have to cook or make her own bed. All she had to do was work on *Wynter's Corner*. With the blog's success, advertising offers were pouring in. If this continued, she would need to hire someone. She was giving a lot of thought to expanding her blog into a full online travel magazine. Though she did like to occasionally join Hope in the garden Hope started nearly three months ago, in her aunt's memory. Wynter loved the idea and often tried to help, though she did not have a green thumb.

That wasn't the only bright spot in Wynter's life; she and her mother met for coffee occasionally, and they were slowly starting to get reacquainted. Then, of course, there was Shay; she had a lot of ideas about the new studio she wanted to build. Would it be cycling only? Did she want yoga and Pilates? Wynter was glad she could be there to listen and dispense advice.

And then there was Riley. He was easy to be with and to say yes to. Desire between them continued to be strong. She'd thought maybe she was being fanciful about their relationship, but as weeks passed, they were still connected. Her body just wanted his. All the time. She wanted his kiss, his touch and everything in between.

In only one week, she would head off to meet the girls

in Barbados. She'd come over to Riley's this time so Hope could have the night off. If she was in residence, Hope felt compelled to cook. Tonight, though, Wynter had tried her hand at cooking. She couldn't make much, but spaghetti and pasta sauce were pretty hard to mess up. She'd even asked Hope for a few pointers, and voilà, the meal wasn't a disaster.

The pasta was perfectly al dente, and the sauce tasted great thanks to the extra spices and fresh herbs she'd added. Riley ate every bit of it, all the while talking to her about how happy Derek was now that Riley had garnered him temporary custody of Max. Apparently, the first hearing had been pretty vicious, but the Shark of the East was victorious. Now, they were lounging on the sofa, eating chocolate ice cream.

"That was very good for a neophyte," Riley said, patting his belly.

She slapped his chest. "Don't sound so surprised."

"Hey," he said, laughing, "no fair. You were the one who told me you don't cook."

"I'm not great," Wynter said, "but I can scramble an egg."

"Good to know, but I'm not with you for your cooking," Riley said, taking both their bowls and placing them on the cocktail table nearby.

"Oh, no?" she inquired, raising a brow.

He shook his head and then rubbed his thumb against her bottom lip. Wynter sucked in a deep breath when he lifted it long enough for her to see a smear of chocolate on his finger. He licked it off, never taking his eyes off her.

"Riley…"

An arc of electricity went through her, and Riley instinctively knew what she needed, pulling her into his arms. She felt the fierce passion of his kiss as he plundered her with untamed desire. It didn't take long for them to retire to his bedroom, where their clothes melted away as Riley took her from the edge all the way to oblivion.

Sometime during the night or the next morning— Wynter didn't know which—Riley reached for her, and he was already protected. They didn't speak. There were just gasps and groans of pleasure and encouragement, and then he was settling between her thighs. His gaze held hers, and when their bodies merged, Wynter swore it felt as if she was coming home. They held each other's gaze for infinitesimal seconds, but then the need to move became overwhelming and Riley began to thrust rhythmically inside her.

When he held her hip and tilted her to meet him, Wynter arched her back as the pressure began to build to a powerful crescendo. She clung to his wide shoulders, taking him deeper, as if it were possible to take him to the very heart of her. Her brain scrambled and a maelstrom of emotions, from the glorious to the sublime, hit her. Riley must have felt the same, because his control shattered and they both cried out simultaneously. She gasped, shuddered and quaked as wave after wave, ripple after ripple, of pleasure engulfed her.

It was always this way with them. The bond, not just their physical connection, was so strong that Wynter knew without a shadow of a doubt that she'd fallen for this incredible, smart, funny, sexy man. And he seemed to be falling for her, too. He was everything she'd ever wanted. A high school crush had morphed into so much more because she'd gotten to know the real man underneath the facade.

With their hearts beating in unison, Wynter finally felt like she could say it, could reveal her true feelings. Their mouths were fused together and their bodies were still clinging to one another. Their bodies, minds and souls were in sync, so she said the words aloud. "I love you, Riley."

Riley tensed above her, as if Wynter had tossed a bucket

of cold water on him, and then, to her surprise, he tossed off the covers and moved away from her.

Wynter knew then she had made a grave mistake. She was about to lose the man she loved.

Riley should have known this was going to happen given how intimate they'd been the past month. Was it any wonder Wynter thought it equated to love? But Riley was incapable of loving another human being who wasn't a member of his family. He wouldn't allow it. He'd always made sure his casual sex partners understood they couldn't expect anything in return, because he wasn't willing to risk his heart.

"Look… Wynter." He lowered his eyes. "You're confusing passion with feelings."

"Don't tell me how I feel!" Wynter replied.

"Then what do you expect me to say? That I love you, too? I've been honest with you from the beginning about what I can give." He heard her sharp intake of breath at his words and glanced up to see her eyes fill with tears.

"I want more," she said and slid from the bed with a sheet wrapped around herself as she began looking around the room for her clothes.

"You don't have to leave, Wynter. It's the middle of the night. Stay, we can talk."

"Why? I already feel like a fool," Wynter replied, picking up her dress and shoes. "I don't need you to bury the knife in my heart any further."

"I'm sorry, Wynter. I thought you understood this for what it was, a casual relationship—an incredible one," Riley responded with a wry smile. "I told you early on—"

Wynter held up her hand. "Please spare me. I remember, okay, but I thought that was before we…" She stopped speaking, and he could only assume she meant *fell in love*.

She brushed past him toward the bathroom, and he stopped her. "Wynter, please. Try to understand. I can't do the love and marriage thing. I've seen the devastating effects it can have, and I refuse to put myself through that."

"That's because you're scared, Riley. Why are you afraid of putting yourself out there and loving another person? Surely, after the last few weeks we've spent together in and out of bed, you feel something for me?"

"Of course, I do. I care for you a great deal, Wynter. Haven't I been there for you with everything that went down with your family? This isn't easy for me, either. I don't want to hurt you."

"Then why are you doing this? I know that loving someone comes with great risk because you're not sure if the other person reciprocates, but even so, at least I'm willing to try. Why aren't you willing to give us a chance?"

"Because I don't believe in happily ever after, Wynter. I can't give you what you're looking for—what you need."

Wynter shook her head because she couldn't understand the words coming out of his mouth. "You may not have told me you loved me, but your actions made me think otherwise. I can see I was a fool."

Wynter wrenched her arm free of his grasp and rushed to the en suite. Riley went to the closed door and placed his hand over it. He sensed Wynter on the other side. Sensed her agony and heard her crying, but he couldn't open the door to go to her. She was looking for a man who could give her a happily-ever-after, and he wasn't the man for her.

She deserved someone who wasn't damaged. Someone who could love her the way she deserved to be loved. And that man wasn't him. Or, at least, he didn't want it to be. Even though a part of him wished he were. She was right. He was dead inside. He'd walled himself off from any feeling or emotion after seeing his mother sob for his father night after night. After seeing her unable to shower and get dressed, let alone brush her teeth.

Love hurt, and Riley refused to be another victim.

He heard the shower run, and then, ten minutes later, Wynter emerged from the bathroom. Her cheeks were tearstained and her eyes red and puffy, but she didn't look at him. Instead, he watched as she found her purse.

He couldn't let her walk out. Not like this.

He followed her to the door, and when she went to open it, he closed it. "Wynter, if you leave here with nothing else, please know that I care for you."

When she finally glanced up at him, her light brown eyes were filled with hurt, and Riley hated that he was the cause of her pain. "Care for me? You couldn't. Because if you did, you wouldn't do this to me."

"I'm so sorry."

"You shouldn't be," Wynter said. "Because of you, I've realized I am special. I deserve to be recognized, loved and wanted by someone, and if that person isn't you, so be it. But I am going to tell you something."

"What's that?" Riley asked quietly.

"I'm the best thing that ever happened to you, Riley Davis, and you will regret letting me go."

Wynter swatted away his hand, walked out of the room and slammed the door, leaving Riley staring after her, feeling desolate. He had to wonder—*was she right?* Had he made the biggest mistake of his life?

Sixteen

"Egypt," Wynter cried and flung herself in her best friend's arms later that evening. Even though she was due to meet her friends in Barbados in a week, after Riley's rejection, Wynter hadn't known where else to go. No one else but Egypt knew about their Aspen affair. She would understand and, sure enough, Egypt had welcomed her to her home in Raleigh, North Carolina.

"Come in," Egypt said, leading Wynter to the sofa in her one-bedroom apartment, which reflected Egypt's personality: bold colors, a zebra-print rug and comfy micro-suede couch, a kitchen with pots and pans hanging down from the ceiling.

Egypt came beside Wynter and pulled her into her embrace. "Tell me what's happened. I couldn't make heads or tails of what you said at the airport."

"I'm sorry." Wynter sniffed into a Kleenex. She'd been in full meltdown mode on the plane, so much so that one of the flight attendants had asked if she was okay. Wynter had informed her that she'd broken up with her boyfriend and was dealing with a broken heart. The attendant had understood and comped her a drink. Wynter had guzzled the beverage in one gulp. It had taken off the edge and calmed her enough to get through the rest of the flight until she could make it to Raleigh.

"It's okay. I'm just surprised, I thought you guys were happy together," Egypt inquired, tucking her legs underneath her.

Wynter shook his head. "Oh, he was happy with the sex, but love? No. He doesn't love me." And she wanted it all. It wasn't just about spectacular sex anymore. She'd been prepared to give him everything, all of herself, but he didn't want her.

"Just because he doesn't realize what a gem he has doesn't mean you're not worthy of love."

"I know that," Wynter responded even though Egypt wore a disbelieving expression. "I do. If being with Riley taught me anything, it showed me I'm worthy of love."

"Yes, you are."

"I will no longer tolerate being ignored or accepting less than I deserve, whether it's from Riley or my parents. For too long, I accepted the crumbs they offered, content to be in the background, to be invisible. Not anymore."

Egypt smiled broadly. "I'm glad to hear you say this, Wynter. You've allowed your family and other people to treat you less than kindly."

Her friend was right. After having been starved of her parents' affection, attention and love, for once, she wanted to be the center of someone's universe. And for a short time, she'd felt that way with Riley. When they made love, it hadn't just been the sensual power of his body, though his body did rival that of any Greek god. Instead, it had been a physical expression of her love.

"Well, that stops now. I am stronger," Wynter replied.

"But it still hurts, ya know? I thought, after all the time we spent together, in and out of bed, that he was developing feelings for me. That last day, the sex was so intense—the way he looked at me." Fresh tears sprang to her eyes, and Egypt reached for more Kleenex and handed it to her. Wynter took several tissues, blotted her eyes and blew her nose. "I—I misinterpreted it—thought I meant more to him."

"It happens," Egypt said. "We get so caught up in a man when we're falling in love and they're just having good sex. But that doesn't mean you were wrong to open your heart. One day, your true love will come."

"I never knew you were such a romantic, Egypt. I thought you were a realist."

"I'm both. I take what men say at face value and try not to read between the lines, but it doesn't mean I don't wish for a Prince Charming to sweep me off my feet."

"It will happen for you, my friend." Wynter reached across the sofa and squeezed her hand. "You are so deserving."

"And so are you," Egypt replied, patting her thigh. "What do you say we drown ourselves in some stiff drinks? I have some brandy in the kitchen I keep for recipes."

"I do need a libation." Wynter laughed and followed Egypt into the kitchen, but in the back of her mind, she couldn't forget the look in Riley's eyes as she'd left. It was as if he'd been hurt, too, that she was leaving, when *he* was the reason she'd walked away. It didn't make any sense.

Wynter sighed. She had to stop thinking about Riley and how he might be feeling. He'd hurt her with his refusal to take a chance on love. They could have had a good thing, but now they would never know, because he'd been too afraid to take a risk.

"How's Wynter?" Derek asked Riley when he stopped by Derek's rental several days later to check on him now that he had custody of his son. It was important to Riley that the child had time to adjust after what he'd been through with his mother.

However, hearing Wynter's name caused Riley's heart to race. She was gone because he'd sent her away, because he'd not allowed emotion to overrule him. He refused to be like his mother. He'd seen the effect of her tumultuous emotions on him and Shay and how it had toppled her.

He thought about lying to Derek, but he and the billionaire had formed a good relationship, so he decided to be honest. "We broke up."

"Broke up?" Derek's shocked expression said it all. "Why? She's an amazing woman."

"I agree," Riley said, "but…" He couldn't bring himself to say the words.

"She's in love with you," Derek surmised. "You don't share her feelings?"

Riley nodded. He couldn't make her promises or declarations of love. His father had done that, and he'd still walked out on their family and left him with his mentally unstable mother.

Derek regarded him and folded his arms across his chest. "Are you sure about that? Because the man I saw in Aspen was absolutely smitten with Ms. Barrington."

Riley shook his head. "You must be mistaken—I don't believe in love or marriage."

"So you say," Derek replied, peering at him intently. "But I suspect you're going to find out otherwise."

Later that evening, back at his penthouse, Riley wondered what Derek had meant. Although he missed Wynter's charm and wit and, of course, the passion they shared in bed, Riley told himself he'd made the right decision. He had freed her from the notion she could change him. Someday she would find a man who could love her and give her a ring. He wasn't that man. Romantic love wasn't part of his life. Period.

But he had wanted Wynter like he had never wanted anyone. She intrigued and excited him in equal measure. He missed her terribly, and that was the most surprising part. He couldn't stop thinking about her. Why had she asked for *more?* Why had she wanted him to express his feelings? For years, he'd cut himself off from feeling anything. When his casual relationships ended, it was on to the next case or the next woman to warm his bed. And yet, he couldn't deny he felt different now, changed somehow, and it was all because of Wynter.

"Wynter, you outdid yourself," Asia gushed when they arrived at the two-story home situated in Holetown, Saint James, on the coast of Barbados.

"Thanks," Wynter said as she gave the Gems a tour of their whitewashed vacation rental, which had direct beachfront access and included four bedrooms, four baths and a splash pool.

"It has all the amenities," Teagan said, whipping off the wide-brimmed hat she'd worn on the ride over in the large Escalade they'd rented for the week.

The top floor of the home had colonial-style furniture and a large, modern and well-equipped kitchen, and it boasted wood flooring throughout, including all the bedrooms. The downstairs had another bedroom, which overlooked the garden, as well as the living area, which offered a pool table, day beds and even a hammock.

"This is paradise." Lyric kicked off her shoes and plopped down on one of the sofas in the living room.

"How about we get this party started?" Egypt asked. "We need to do a store run and get all the essentials."

"Already done." Wynter went to the cabinets. She opened

each one up to reveal an array of wines, spirits and mixers. Then she went to the fridge, which was fully stocked.

"Oh, my God! I love you," Egypt said, pulling Wynter into a one-armed hug. Once she released her, she reached for the blender on the countertop and took out the ingredients needed to make a margarita.

"You're welcome." Wynter smiled and moved away to walk outside onto the covered deck overlooking the ocean. The owners had thought of everything; comfy white sofas covered by pillows decorated with green leaves greeted her there.

The terrace had a stunning view of the garden, with its lush palm trees and colorful plants. Below her, Wynter saw six loungers for sunbathing and a pool set off to the side. A rejuvenating stay was exactly what she needed after the horrible week she'd endured. She'd been sleeping on Egypt's sofa and crying on her shoulder every night as she recalled every waking minute of her short-lived affair with Riley. She intended to tell the rest of her friends this week, but she wasn't looking forward to Shay's response in particular.

Wynter knew Shay wouldn't be happy with her for not heeding her advice, but it was Riley. The man she'd crushed on since she was a teen. Meeting him as an adult changed *everything*, and she'd allowed herself to fall harder and deeper than she had with other men.

As if sensing her distress, Shay came toward her. "What's on your mind, Wynter?" she inquired. "You don't seem yourself."

"How can I not be, in a place like this?" Wynter asked, motioning with her arms.

"You don't fool me, Wynter Barrington." Shay leaned her back against the balustrade. "You've never been good at disguising your emotions. Something is bothering you. You can talk to me—to any of us." She inclined her head toward the kitchen, where the rest of the women were gathered around Egypt as she made their adult beverages.

Wynter offered Shay a small smile. "There is, but if it's all the same, I'm not ready to talk about it."

Shay nodded. "All right, but I'm here if you need me."

Wynter nodded. "Thank you." She was thankful when Shay quietly moved away and left her alone with her thoughts. She knew she would have to pull herself out of her slump and carry on. She was struggling to write, because, every time she did, memories of her and Riley filled her mind.

Was he feeling the pain as acutely as she was?

Wynter doubted it. He probably didn't feel anything at all.

Riley had had a devil of a time over the past week. He'd arrived late to an appointment and stumbled in court on a case that should have been a walk in the park. Opposing counsel came at him hard, and Riley had barely been able to string two sentences together. He felt discombobulated.

The nights were worse. He was restless and couldn't sleep. Every night, he stared at the ceiling and prayed for sleep, but it wouldn't come. Why? Because every time he closed his eyes, he saw Wynter. Wynter on the snowmobile. Wynter laughing on the thrilling dogsled ride. Wynter licking ganache off a spoon. Wynter in the mirror when he fingered her and made her come as she rode his stiff length.

This was ridiculous!

He had always been able to compartmentalize his feelings with other women and keep them in check. He had never been in emotional danger with any of them, because it had never been more than a physical connection. But now, looking out over the San Antonio skyline from his penthouse, his jaw shadowed with today's growth, Riley felt different.

Because *he* was different. Somehow Wynter, with her beautiful brown eyes, warm smile and giving nature, had breached the walls he'd erected around his heart and found her way in. She made him come alive in a way he'd never imagined. Joy and light had burst into his life the moment he'd seen her sitting on the River Walk, and it hadn't left. In their short time together, something invisible yet strong had melded to his central framework and become inseparable from his soul. It was Wynter. She was lodged here. Riley put his hand on his heart. She was a part of him.

The thought of what that something invisible was, that rare element that threaded them together, scared Riley. He was afraid to name it, didn't want to say it aloud, but he knew. Deep down, he knew.

It was love.

Despite him fighting it and pushing Wynter away, somehow love had found its way in and now resided in his heart. Riley rubbed his hand over his closely cropped hair.

What was he supposed to do now? He'd ruined any chance he had with Wynter when he shot her down after she'd professed her love for him. He'd said hurtful things to her in an effort to push her away and negate the emotions he'd seen shining back at him through her tearful eyes. Riley wasn't sure if he could live with this feeling and not say anything. He had to tell her, but would she ever listen to him? And why would she? She owed him nothing. He'd made sure of that.

But maybe, just maybe, deep down in the recesses of her heart, was there a place that still loved him? Riley had to find out. He wouldn't quit until she forgave him, because he always won. But this was different. He wasn't helping someone give up on love. This time, he would be fighting for it.

Seventeen

With blue skies overhead, fresh air and her friends by her side, Wynter felt good. Losing Riley had nearly flattened her, but then her mother dropped the challenge to the will officially with the courts and the article she'd written for the Aspen resort was a success. So much so, the luxury chain had asked her to write other pieces for them. This would do great things for *Wynter's Corner* and would allow Wynter the freedom and independence she craved.

Wynter spent the remaining time enjoying her friends' company. They swam in the pool, sunbathed on the loungers, went horseback riding on the beach and ate delicious food from the private chef she'd arranged to stop by several times during their stay. Their favorite meal had consisted of authentic Bahamian dishes, including cou-cou and flying fish, pepperpot and brown stew chicken with rice and peas. Egypt couldn't stop raving about the food and vowed to attempt to cook it herself when they returned to the States.

Now they found themselves at the Barbados straw market on Broad Street, where Egypt walked up and down the aisles picking up spices from this vendor and the next. Wynter was content to peruse the usual tourist fare of T-shirts, shot glasses, magnets and the like. She was holding up T-shirts and deciding which one to pick when Shay came up beside her.

"I like that one," Shay said, motioning to a black T-shirt printed with the blue-and-yellow Barbados flag.

Wynter nodded. She was leaning toward that one, too. "So do I. You know me so well." She pulled out her wallet and handed the vendor ten dollars.

Afterward, she and Shay continued walking down the aisle. Shay linked her arm with one of Wynter's. "And because I know you, I can say that you appear to be doing better than when we first arrived."

Wynter gave Shay a sideward glance. "I am."

"Are you finally ready to confide in me?"

Wynter sighed. She was. But Wynter was going to need some liquid courage, because she was certain Shay would be upset by the news. Asia, Lyric and Teagan wouldn't be happy, either, that she hadn't told them.

"Soon." Wynter patted Shay's arm that was linked with hers.

Later that evening, Egypt found Wynter in the kitchen. "What was up with you and Shay earlier?"

Wynter glanced around to see if they were alone. "She wanted to know why I've been in such a funk."

"Did you tell her about Riley?" Egypt inquired.

The moment Egypt said his name, Shay walked into the kitchen. "What about Riley?" Shay looked from one woman to the other.

Egypt hung her head low. "Oh, Lord, the shit is about to hit the fan."

"Shay..." Wynter started toward Shay, but her friend was backing up.

"Riley? You and Riley have been seeing each other?" Shay inquired. "For how long? Since the funeral?"

Wynter followed her and stood in the middle of the living room, ready to tell her truth to the remaining Six Gems. "No. Well…" She realized they had had the one-night stand. If she was going to be honest, she had to tell them everything.

"Well, what?" Shay asked.

"After the funeral, we had a one-night stand," Wynter replied, wringing her hands.

"Oh, my!" Asia clutched the junky necklace she'd purchased at the straw market as if she were clutching her pearls.

Wynter glared at Asia. "We both said it was going to be the one night, but then…" She lowered her head, and when she glanced up at Egypt, she gave her a nod to continue.

Shay caught the action and looked at Egypt with a sharp stare. "Did you know about this?"

Egypt shrugged. "I did. But if it wasn't going to amount to anything, I saw no reason for Wynter to tell you about it."

"She should have told me because we're friends!" Shay countered. Then she turned to Wynter. "Go on."

"When I arrived in Aspen, Riley was there, and the chemistry between us was still there. We spent the week together, and then afterwards, when we came back to San Antonio, we continued seeing each other. And I—I fell in love with your brother, but he didn't feel the same way. He told me he would never love me and wasn't capable or willing to try."

Shay sighed. "Oh, Wynter." To Wynter's surprise, she came forward and gave her a hug. "I'm so sorry. I warned you about him." She released her long enough to grasp both of Wynter's cheeks with her palms. "Riley was traumatized by our parents' divorce and swore off love and marriage."

Tears slid down Wynter's cheeks. "I know… I guess I thought, after our time together…"

"He would change?" Shay offered. "I hope he does one day, because you deserve love, Wynter. You always have."

Wynter offered a half smile. "Thank you. And I'm sorry I didn't tell you about us."

"It's okay," Shay said and wiped one of her tears with her thumb. "No man, my brother included, will tear us Gems apart. We vowed years ago that our sisterhood was unbreakable. That hasn't changed."

"Aw!" Asia cried, and before Wynter knew it, all the ladies were in a group hug, holding each other tight.

After they released one another, Egypt said, "Now all this lovey-dovey stuff is over, don't you think it's time we celebrate? Your mom dropped the case! We're getting our inheritance from Auntie Helaine!"

"Woo-hoo!" Asia began popping her bottom up and down in a little dance.

It was Teagan who went to the kitchen. When she returned, she was holding a bottle of champagne and six plastic champagne flutes. Teagan handed each of the women a flute and popped the cork, pouring each of them a glass. Once they were filled, she said, "Here's to Auntie Helaine and opening our own businesses."

"To Aunt Helaine." They toasted and drank the delicious champagne.

The celebration continued well into the night, when they all retired to the terrace to listen to the waves and discuss their upcoming ventures. In the months they'd been waiting for the will to be resolved, Teagan had obtained her brokerage license and was prepared to start her new real estate firm. Egypt, having already secured a location for her new restaurant, was retiring her food truck. Based on the private dance lessons she was currently giving, Lyric had compiled a list of students for her new dance studio. Shay's built-in clientele from the yoga and Pilates classes vowed to follow her to her own studio. Meanwhile, Asia's jewelry had been selling out at farmers markets and online, and she couldn't wait to have her own store.

"This is great and exactly what my aunt wanted for each of you," Wynter responded after hearing their updates. "I'm so proud of all of you." And thankful to her aunt for giving them the opportunity to follow their dreams.

"What about you, Wynter?" Lyric asked. "What's next for you?"

That was the million-dollar question. Wynter had done a lot of soul-searching during her travels, so she knew what she wanted to do next. "I'm going to start my own online travel magazine."

"That sounds fantastic!" Teagan said brightly. "But what about *Wynter's Corner*?"

"I'm not giving it up entirely, because I'll still give my insights on various destinations, but I plan on incorporating them into the magazine," Wynter replied. "And I'll hire a staff to help me write the articles. For now, I'd like to sit in one place and smell the roses. I have a home now." Her aunt's home was now officially hers. "I want to plant some roots."

Egypt nodded and gave her a wide smile. "Sounds like a mighty fine idea to me."

"Thank you, love." Wynter thought so, too. And when she got back to San Antonio, things were going to change. First, she would continue to try to heal the rift between her and her parents; she'd already made progress with her mother.

As for Riley, she would always treasure the moments they'd shared—the way he'd laughed with her, kissed her, made love to her—but she would have to store them in a vacuum-sealed part of heart until time passed and it no longer hurt so much.

She should thank him, though. He'd freed her from the shroud of being hidden and staying safe in the shadows. Spending time with him had made her want more. Want love. He might not love her, and she couldn't force him to. Instead of pining for something that couldn't be, she was moving on with her life.

One day, she would find love again. She just didn't know when.

Eighteen

Riley pulled into the parking lot of a strip mall in a popular part of town to meet Shay. From what he heard, all the yuppies and new families were flocking here, but he had no idea why Shay would be here. Did she have news to tell him?

Turning off the ignition, he exited the vehicle and headed to the suite number Shay had given him. When he tried the door, it opened freely to a wide-open retail space with a bare concrete floor.

"Shay?"

His sister emerged several moments later from the rear of the suite. "What do you think?" Her eyes were gleaming with excitement.

"About what?"

"About this place for my yoga and Pilates studio?" Shay asked as if he were a mind reader.

"So, Wynter's family officially dropped the case with the courts and the estate will be dispersing funds?" Just saying her name again made his newly recognized feelings rise to the surface. Feelings he hadn't been able to share because Wynter had been in Barbados with his sister.

Plus, he hadn't figured out the best approach to win her back.

"That's right," Shay replied with a wide smile.

"Really? That's fantastic!" Riley reached for Shay and swung her around. He was happy for Wynter. She would finally get her inheritance and her aunt's employees and charities would finally get the bequests they were entitled to.

When he released her, Shay looked at him. "You sound awfully happy for Wynter."

Riley gave a small smile. "Well, um, I saw how devastated she was after the funeral and…"

"Stop!" Shay held up her hand.

His brows knitted into a frown. "Stop what?"

"Stop with the lies," Shay said, poking her finger at his chest. "I know the truth, Riley. I know about you and Wynter in Aspen." And when Riley tried to interrupt her, she added, "And I know about the one-night stand, too. And your time together in San Antonio."

Riley lowered his head. He supposed he shouldn't be surprised. Wynter and Shay were best friends. How long would she have been able to keep something like that from her best friend, especially when she was hurting? And Riley knew she was. He'd seen the devastation in her eyes when she'd left his penthouse.

"Shay, I'm sorry."

"For which part? For sleeping with Wynter or for breaking her heart?" Shay glared at him. He hated seeing the disappointment in her eyes.

"For breaking her heart, of course," Riley responded. "I never wanted to hurt Wynter, but I did anyway. I regret that."

"That's good to hear. I would hate to think my brother is one of those men who only want one thing."

"Our relationship was more than just sex, Shay. We joked and teased each other. We could talk about anything. We had fun together in the snow in Aspen. We had more fun together here."

Shay shook her head. "Then why—why did you let her go?" she asked, her pitch rising several octaves.

"Because I'm a fool," Riley yelled back. "I didn't realize what I had until she was gone."

Shay's expression softened, and she walked toward him and touched his arm. "I suspected you'd met someone, because your entire demeanor was different when we spoke while you were in Aspen, and then later back home."

"You could tell?"

She nodded.

"I was afraid, then, of the feelings Wynter was evoking inside me. I don't want to end up like our mother, Shay. She was devastated by losing Dad. We lost her for so long."

"I know, Riley," Shay said, cupping his cheek, "but you're not Mom. Marriage is what *you* make it. Don't you see? Love is not a weakness, it's your greatest strength, but you have to allow it to happen."

"How can you still believe in love after your divorce?"

Shay shrugged. "Kevin may not have been my person, but that doesn't mean the institution of marriage is flawed. It means I made a mistake, but I'm not giving up on love."

"What do I do now, Shay? I want her back."

Shay chuckled. "Of course you do. Wynter is an amazing woman, but you've got an uphill battle. She's angry and hurt. I'm not sure how you're going to repair the damage you caused."

"I don't know, either, but I have to try. Will you help me?"

Shay looked upward and rubbed her chin.

"Hmm…let me think about it."

"Shay, please."

"Of course I'll help you," Shay replied. "Listen, Wynter is going to her parents' anniversary party on Saturday. You should go."

She wouldn't be expecting him, which gave Riley the advantage. He just prayed it wasn't too late to win his woman back.

As soon as she'd landed in San Antonio and returned to her aunt's after Barbados, Wynter had found an embossed invitation to attend her parents' thirtieth wedding anniversary celebration that week. Although her relationship with her mother had thawed, Wynter hadn't been up to forging a path of forgiveness with her father, brother and Francesca in the weeks before Barbados, but she knew she had to if she wanted peace in the family. She'd checked yes on the reply card.

The day of the event, however, she thought about chickening out, but it was Egypt who gave her a good pep talk over the phone.

"Do you recall telling the Gems you were going to demand what you're worth and no longer accept what your parents, Riley or anyone else dished out?"

"I didn't realize I was on the witness stand," Wynter replied.

Egypt laughed. "You're not, but I want you to remember the new, improved Wynter you've become. If I could, I'd go with you."

"It's okay," Wynter said. "You're in the middle of construction on your restaurant. You can't afford to take your eye off the ball. I'm fine. I don't need a babysitter or a bodyguard. I'm going to put on my big-girl panties and handle my business."

"All right—are you sure?" Egypt asked. "I could call Shay for reinforcements."

"I told you. I've got this."

When evening arrived and the limo drove her toward her parents' house, Wynter's resolve to not let anyone get into her head tonight was starting to vanish. She reminded herself she wasn't a child in need of their love and acceptance anymore. She was a grown woman who was independently wealthy and didn't need anything from them.

Wynter was no longer dependent on her family for handouts. Even if she never received the money from her aunt's estate, Wynter had learned she could make a living and support herself with her blog. That had been the biggest revelation throughout the past few harrowing months. She'd found a strength she hadn't known she had.

Digging deep, Wynter called upon that reserve so when the limo pulled up outside her familial home, she was calm, cool and collected. Tonight, she wore a strapless red silk chiffon gown with a sweetheart neckline and a slim, draped skirt, accompanied by red peep-toe shoes and a sparkling gold clutch. She'd finished the look with a dazzling pair of gold earrings, kohl-rimmed eyes and a nude, shimmering lip. Wynter knew she looked her best and no one could find fault, though she wouldn't be surprised if someone in her family did.

Agnes wasn't there to greet the guests. Instead, there was a uniformed butler. Once inside, Wynter stood inside the foyer. The mansion looked familiar because she'd lived here for years, but it didn't feel like home anymore. She'd come to think of her aunt's place as *her* home, because it was where she had *always* belonged.

Wynter walked into the living room, and her parents immediately approached her. Her father looked debonair in a black tuxedo, while she could tell her mother had gone to great effort, because her hair was in a sophisticated updo and she wore a one-shouldered black dress with an enormous bow and a long train.

"Wynter!" Her mother's arms were outstretched, and she grasped both of her hands while her father lagged behind. "I'm so happy you came. It means a lot."

"Yes, it does," her father said, smiling at her. "A lot has happened."

"I agree, but I wouldn't miss your special day. Happy anniversary," Wynter replied, feigning a smile. "Thank you for inviting me."

"It would be bad etiquette if they didn't." Corey and Francesca joined their small circle. Her brother gave her a sardonic smile.

Wynter didn't bother to feign happiness at seeing him. "I see you haven't changed."

"But you have," Francesca replied. "You look amazing in that dress, Wynter, and your skin looks radiant, but, then again, you do have money at your disposal now."

"Thank you, Francesca. If you'll excuse me." Wynter didn't waste further time on her brother and his uppity wife. The time for her being the family's whipping post was over. She moved farther into the room to mingle.

She went to the bar and ordered a bourbon. She would need one to make it through this evening. The only reason she was here was to speak with her family. Once that was done, she was headed home to watch Netflix.

She was sipping her bourbon when her neck prickled. Only one person gave her that feeling—the feeling that she couldn't breathe. Wynter's eyes scanned the great room and connected with a pair of dark eyes. She tensed, and her heart beat painfully fast.

Riley.

He was wearing an all-black tuxedo and shirt and looked like a dark knight, but he was no longer her knight in shining armor. Why was he here, at her familial home? What did he want? Another romp in bed? And why now? It had been weeks and she was finally starting to be able to sleep without wishing his arms were wrapped around her.

She couldn't deal with this right now. She had mustered just enough energy to get through meeting with her family and nothing more. She threw back the rest of her drink and felt the burn in the back of her throat. Then she rushed out of the great room. She was down the hall when she heard loud voices from a nearby room. She recognized them.

It was her parents and her brother.

"Why can't you be nice to your sister?" her mother asked. "Is that too much to ask?"

"Why?" Corey asked. "You've never cared before. In fact, I think you both have always liked pitting both of us against each other. But now that Wynter has agreed to share Auntie's inheritance, you're going to kiss her ass? Is that why you invited her?"

Wynter flung open the door of the room. "I'd like to know the answer to that question." Startled, they all turned around to look at her. Her mother's expression was one of guilt. Was Corey right? Were they using her?

Wynter felt sick to her stomach and slowly began to step backward.

"Wynter, wait!"

"Why, Mother? So I can hear more lies?" Wynter asked. "Corey's right, isn't he? You brought me here so we could play happy family, but you don't really mean it, do you?"

"Of course we do," her father responded. "We wanted you to come tonight to heal this family and mend the rift between us."

"I never should have contested the will," her mother said. "I should have honored my sister's wishes, but I was so upset and angry with Helaine for choosing you instead of me that I took it out on you. It wasn't fair."

"No, it wasn't," Wynter responded. "But you've never treated me fairly." Wynter looked at her father. "And you've always looked down on me and treated me as if I wasn't good enough. As if I didn't belong."

"I know. I've been a terrible father, Wynter," he admitted. "Can you ever forgive me? I didn't know how to love you because my father was cold and distant, too, so I pushed you away, but I want to try now."

"I don't know," Wynter responded.

"It may be too soon, sweetheart, and we get that," her mother said. "We just hope, in time, you'll give us a chance to make things right. To be the parents you deserve."

Wynter stared at her parents and then at her brother, who was leaning against the wall as if he'd been hit by a Mack truck.

"And the money?" she asked.

"If you think I love money over you, you're wrong. You can take it all. The money is yours," her mother responded hotly. "Your aunt wanted you to have it, but it's not like you need it. I told your father how *Wynter's Corner* is a big hit."

"I'm proud of you, baby girl," her father said. "You did it all on your own, without any help. I wanted you to stand on your own two feet, and you did. Not that you should have had to, but you showed me and any other naysayers that you're a strong, independent woman."

That brought a smile to Wynter's face, but all wasn't forgiven yet. It would be a long time before she could say they were a happy family, but she supposed tonight was a start.

"So, now we've all kissed and made up," Corey said, "what's next? Singing 'Kumbaya'?"

Wynter spun around to face her brother. "Why do you hate me so much?"

"I don't hate you, Wynter," Corey said. "I never have. I'm jealous of you, and I supposed that's why I've always been so angry with you because you have been free to live your life without our parents'—" he flung his arms at their parents, who were watching the encounter in stunned silence "—expectations. You weren't the firstborn with all their hopes and dreams weighing down your shoulders. You've been free to figure out your own life, make mistakes and learn from them, while I've always had to walk the straight line."

"No offense, Mom and Dad—" she glanced in her parents' direction "—but who cares what they want? It's your life, Corey, and you have to live it on your own terms. And the first thing you can do is stop being an ass to your sister."

He stuck his chest out. "Is that right?"

"It is indeed. I'm stepping off my soapbox." She walked over to her parents and, to their surprise, gave them each a brief hug. "Happy anniversary." And then she swept out of the room.

She was so involved in her feelings that she didn't look in front of her and collided with a hard chest. Glancing up, she found Riley looking down at her.

"Wynter, can we talk?"

She shook her head. "I can't!" First her parents, then Corey, and now Riley—it was all too much for her to deal with in one night. "I just can't!"

"When, then?" Riley asked. "You pick the time and day."

This was new; Riley wasn't trying to control the situation. He was letting her take the lead. "All right, I'll call you."

She'd accepted his offer to talk for no other reason than for her own curiosity. She thought they'd said everything they had to say before she left for Barbados. What had changed? She still felt the same way. She still wanted love and commitment. Was that why he'd come? Was he no longer afraid? Was he finally ready to love?

Nineteen

Riley felt terrible. He felt so bad he did something he'd never done in his entire career—he called out sick from work. How had he thought showing up to the Barrington estate on Saturday night was a good idea? It wasn't. He'd ambushed Wynter after telling her he didn't love her and never would.

Was it any surprise that she ran away from him?

He'd thought about chasing after her and pleading with her to listen, but he didn't. She needed her space. From the look on her face as she'd left that room, something had gone down between her and her parents. Something she hadn't been able to handle or verbalize. Damn them.

He'd assumed her family wanted to heal their relationship. If that was their version of healing, he would hate to see what happened when they ripped each other to shreds.

Yesterday, he'd stayed in bed and stared at the ceiling, wondering what he should do. How could he make things right? He was the fixer, after all. People paid him hundreds of thousands of dollars to fix their lives after their marriages fell apart. But now, when it was time for him to fix his own life, Riley felt ill-equipped to do so. Wynter had been right when she'd said he'd regret letting her go. He regretted being a coward and not opening himself fully to receive her love, which was a precious gift.

And now he was sitting outside a café alone on the River Walk, where he'd run into Wynter all those months ago. For what? In the hopes he might see her? And say what? *I'm sorry for being a jerk and turning my back on the best thing that ever happened to me.* Check. *Sorry for hurting you.* Check.

He was stunned when, several minutes later, Wynter did indeed come to the café, but rather than walk inside and place an order, she headed to his table. She looked sexy as hell in a maxi dress. It showed her cleavage, and Riley swallowed hard.

"Would you care for a walk?" she asked.

Riley's heart hammered loudly in his chest when her brown eyes pierced his. "I would love one." He tossed several bills on the table and joined her on the sidewalk.

They walked side by side for several minutes before Wynter stopped and turned to face him. "I'm sorry for running away the other night."

"You have nothing to apologize for," Riley responded. "*I* ambushed you."

She shook her head. "It's not that. It's just that I promised myself I was done running and I would face my problems head-on, but when put to the test, I ran. So, here I am. What did you want to talk to me about?"

Riley was proud of Wynter. She'd grown in the past several months and wasn't afraid to deal with her problems. He had to do the same thing. Inhaling deeply, he thought about the speech he had prepared on Saturday. An opening statement, if you will, but when he glanced down and saw Wynter's wary expression, he knew he had to speak straight from the heart. "Wynter, I'm sorry for the things I said to you at the penthouse."

"You don't have to apologize for being honest, Riley. It was my fault for thinking I could change you."

"Your love changed me."

At that bold statement, Wynter glanced up questioningly, so he continued, "For so long, I've been angry with my father for walking out on our family and my mother for falling apart after the divorce. Watching her pain, day after day, hurt. So, I began to see love as a sickness that needed to be cured. I never wanted the emotion and adamantly refused to have anything to do with love, but then I saw you sitting here on the River Walk and my heart expanded in a way it never had."

"I appreciated your kindness to me that night."

"It wasn't just kindness. I wanted you then as I want you now."

She shook her head. "Riley…"

"Please let me finish, Wynter." His heart was tight in his chest, as if iron bands were squeezing it. He had to tell her his feelings or he would burst. "I opened up to you and shared things about myself about being a workaholic and my history of choosing short-term relationships."

"Yes, you did, because you wanted me to know that I could never be more than just a fling. Well, guess what? These casual flings will never fill the hole deep inside you, Riley."

"No, they can't, because you have."

"Pardon?"

Riley reached for Wynter's hand, but she stepped away. He didn't blame her. He would have to earn her love. "I've been imprisoned by my past and carefully guarding my heart because I was afraid to fall in love, but my wise sister told me that love isn't a weakness, it's a strength. It made me realize I can't be a coward anymore, afraid of getting hurt because, like you said, I could be letting go of the best thing that ever happened to me. And no one ever said I'm not a smart man."

"What are you saying, Riley?"

"I'm saying that I love you." He waited for her reaction to the words because he rarely said them, but she was staring back at him with disbelief, so he repeated them again. "I love you, Wynter."

Wynter shook her head and clenched her hands into tight fists at her side. "Why are you saying these things? You told me you didn't believe in love."

"Because it's true, sweetheart," Riley replied softly. "I'm half a man without you. I can't sleep. I can't think. I can't work without you by my side. I won Derek's business because of *you*. Because you told me to speak from the heart about why I was the best attorney for him."

"I'm glad you won Derek over, but you don't have to say you love me when you don't mean it."

"Why don't you believe me?" Riley asked. "Because you don't think you're worthy? Because your parents haven't given you the love and affection you deserve? Well, I'm here to tell you, Wynter Barrington, you deserve all the love and happiness your heart and hands can hold."

Tears slipped down her cheeks, and that was when Riley knew she was finally hearing his words. He was starting to get through to her.

Wynter wanted to believe Riley and that all her dreams were coming true, but so many times she'd given her love to her family, and then to Riley, only to have tossed it aside. She was afraid to put her heart on the line again.

Riley grabbed both of Wynter's hands and brought her to an empty bench nearby. "You know as well as I do that we found something special on that first walk. You knew you could trust me. It's why, even though we hadn't seen each other in years, you asked me to sit with you at your aunt's funeral—because, intuitively, you knew could lean on me."

He was right about that. Her friends had thought she was crazy with grief when she asked Riley to sit beside her, but his presence had been a comfort when she needed it most.

"And later, when we made love, I didn't know it yet, but you ruined me. Ruined the old me," Riley said, "because I couldn't stop thinking about you. When we were apart, I was never with anyone else, because *you* were all I wanted."

"I was?"

"And when we came back together, I was made whole again," Riley replied. "Only to mess things up because I ran scared. You were right. I was a coward because I was afraid to feel. I told you I didn't believe in love, but it wasn't true. I do love you, Wynter. Please tell me it's not too late and I can have a do-over to make things right between us?"

Wynter nodded, her eyes filling with tears.

"I need to hear you say it, sweetheart."

"It's not too late, Riley," Wynter responded softly. "I've been enthralled with you since I was a teenager, and when I saw you after all these years, I was attracted to you and my feelings grew after our one night together, then grew again in Aspen and during our time together here. I tried pushing them aside, but, like you, I couldn't be intimate with anyone else because you already had my heart."

"Oh, thank God!" Riley leaned his forehead against hers, and Wynter stroked his cheek.

"I love you, Riley Davis."

Riley reached for her, pulling her close and kissing her with the fiery intensity he always did. Wynter answered the thrust of his tongue by mating it with hers in a playful duel that reminded Wynter she would never tire of kissing him.

When they finally parted, Riley lifted his head long enough to ask, "Will you marry me, Wynter?"

Wynter didn't hesitate, because her heart overflowed with love for this man. "Yes!" She threw her arms around Riley's neck and pulled him closer. They kissed until they shared the same air—shared the same breath. Because, in that moment, they were of the same heartbeat.

And later, when they were alone and Riley moved over Wynter, joining them as one, it wasn't just their bodies fused together—it was their souls, in a love that would last a lifetime.

Epilogue

Six months later

"Congratulations, Egypt!" Wynter said when she and Riley arrived at the opening of her best friend's restaurant, Flame, in Raleigh. They'd just flown in from San Antonio because court had ended late for Riley due to the final hearing for Derek's case. The Shark of the East had won. He'd not only been able to show how unfit Derek's ex-wife was, but they'd also found she'd been having an affair with her trainer for months. The prenup had expressly stated that she would forgo her settlement if infidelity occurred. Derek had not only been able to retain his company but had garnered full custody of his son, Max.

Riley was over the moon and had wanted to stay and celebrate with Derek, but knowing how important this night was and how much Wynter needed to be there, he'd chartered a private jet to ensure they made it on time.

Wynter handed her friend a large bouquet of flowers. "I'm so proud of you."

"Thank you so much." Egypt beamed with pride while accepting the arrangement. She looked like a professional restaurateur in her black chef's coat and simple updo.

"This is for you, too," Riley said, holding up an expensive bottle of bubbly. "Where should I put it?"

"Over there with the other gifts," Egypt said, indicating a small table with cards and wrapped gifts.

While he went to handle the gifts, Wynter grabbed Egypt's arm and linked it with hers. "Well, how do you feel?"

"Amazing. Scared. Overwhelmed," Egypt said. "What if I fail? Half of new restaurants fail in their first year."

"Shh." Wynter shook her head. "We are not going to claim that. Flame is going to be a success, and I'm not going to hear another negative word."

"That's right!" Shay said from behind them. She'd hitched a ride with them on the jet.

All the Six Gems were on hand to support Egypt as they always did. Egypt had been saving for the restaurant for a couple of years, but it would have taken much longer to open it without Aunt Helaine's endowment. Meanwhile, the rest of the Six Gems were still working through the particulars of starting their own businesses.

"I say we toast to Egypt," Teagan said, taking charge like she always did.

"Hear, hear!" the ladies cheered.

Soon, champagne and well-wishes were flowing. Wynter was thrilled to see everyone so happy.

She didn't even mind when Riley swept her into a secluded, dark corner and planted a searing kiss on her lips, because in a few short months, she was walking down the aisle to this incredible man and her happily-ever-after.

The past few months, their relationship had grown by

leaps and bounds, because Riley had opened himself to feeling his emotions. Nowadays, it wasn't uncommon for him to express how much he loved her, because he knew that she would always be there. He might be her best friend's brother, but he'd stolen her heart years ago, and she'd never come close to loving another man the way she loved him.

"You're incredible," he whispered, and when he looked at her, she could see the love shining from his eyes.

She felt the same. Before him, she hadn't known where she fit in, but she did now. She belonged with Riley. He was her universe, and together, their love would have no bounds.

* * * * *

COMING SOON!

We really hope you enjoyed reading this book.
If you're looking for more romance, be sure to
head to the shops when new books are
available on

Thursday 5th January

To see which titles are coming soon, please visit

millsandboon.co.uk/nextmonth

MILLS & BOON

THE HEART OF ROMANCE

A ROMANCE FOR EVERY READER

MODERN

Prepare to be swept off your feet by sophisticated, sexy and seductive heroes, in some of the world's most glamourous and romantic locations, where power and passion collide.

HISTORICAL

Escape with historical heroes from time gone by. Whether your passion is for wicked Regency Rakes, muscled Vikings or rugged Highlanders, awaken the romance of the past.

MEDICAL

Set your pulse racing with dedicated, delectable doctors in the high-pressure world of medicine, where emotions run high and passion, comfort and love are the best medicine.

True Love

Celebrate true love with tender stories of heartfelt romance, from the rush of falling in love to the joy a new baby can bring, and a focus on the emotional heart of a relationship.

Desire

Indulge in secrets and scandal, intense drama and plenty of sizzling hot action with powerful and passionate heroes who have it all: wealth, status, good looks...everything but the right woman.

HEROES

Experience all the excitement of a gripping thriller, with an intense romance at its heart. Resourceful, true-to-life women and strong, fearless men face danger and desire - a killer combination!

To see which titles are coming soon, please visit

millsandboon.co.uk/nextmonth

LET'S TALK

Romance

For exclusive extracts, competitions
and special offers, find us online:

[f] facebook.com/millsandboon

[y] @MillsandBoon

[◎] @MillsandBoonUK

Get in touch on 01413 063232

For all the latest titles coming soon, visit

millsandboon.co.uk/nextmonth

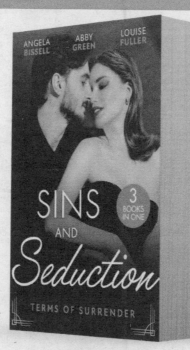